W9-BHA-332

LARGE
PRINT
EDITION

RANDOM
HOUSE

The Chimney Sweeper's Boy

A NOVEL

BARBARA VINE

Published by Random House Large Print
in association with Harmony Books
New York   1998

Library of Congress Cataloging-in-Publication Data
Vine, Barbara.
The chimney sweeper's boy :
a novel / Barbara Vine.
p. (large print) cm.
ISBN 0-375-70293-8
1. Large type books. I. Title.
[PR6068.E63C47 1998] 823'.914—dc21
97-51824 CIP

Random House Web Address: http://www.randomhouse.com/
Printed in the United States of America
FIRST LARGE PRINT EDITION

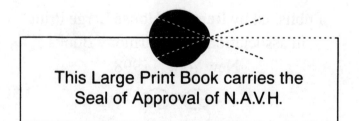

**This Large Print Book carries the
Seal of Approval of N.A.V.H.**

To Patrick Maher

The
Chimney
Sweeper's
Boy

He wanted a family of his own. He was very young when he understood this, fifteen or sixteen. Because he was accustomed, even then, to examining his thoughts and searching his soul, he corrected himself, deciding that what he wanted was a family to add to his existing one. Children of his own. He imagined giving his brothers and sisters children to love and giving his children uncles and aunts. His dream encompassed them all living together somewhere, in a big house, the kind they had never known. He was old enough to know how unlikely this was.

A little later on, he understood that it is not acceptable for men to feel like this. Few men do. Women want children and men agree. Or if men want children, it is to carry on a name or inherit a business. He wanted them because he loved being one of many and wanted to add to that number. Friends were not very important in their lives. Why have friends when you have family?

Many things he felt and thought were not acceptable among men. Not right for a man. For instance, if he were to found that family, a woman would be a prerequisite. He knew the pattern, how it should be. He must meet a girl and fall in love, court her, become engaged to her, marry her. It seemed insurmountably difficult. He liked girls, but not in that way. Without knowing much, he knew what he meant by "that way," kissing, touching, all the things they talked about endlessly, monotonously, at school. Those others longed to do such things to girls, and some said they had, but he clearly understood that for him to do it, even to get to the point of doing it, would be an endurance test, a labor comparable to taking an exam in French, his worst subject, or taking part in a hated cross-country run.

How did he also know that it would not be the real thing?

—Gerald Candless, LESS IS MORE

1

---

*It is an error to say the eyes have expression.
Eyebrows and eyelids, lips, the planes of the face,
all these are indicators of emotion. The eyes are
merely colored liquid in a glass.*
— A MESSENGER OF THE GODS

"NOT A WORD TO MY GIRLS," he had said on the way home from the hospital. *My* girls, as if they weren't also hers. She was used to it, he always said that, and in a way they were more his. "I'm not hearing this," she said.

"You're going to have major surgery and your grown-up children aren't to be told."

" 'Major surgery,' " he said. "You sound like Staff Nurse Samantha in a hospital sitcom. I won't have Sarah and Hope worried. I won't give them a day of hell while they await the result."

You flatter yourself, she thought, but that was just spite. He didn't. They would have a day of hell; they would have anguish, while she had a little mild trepidation.

He made her promise. It wasn't difficult. She wouldn't have cared for the task of telling them.

* * *

The girls came down as usual. In the summer they came down every weekend, and in the winter, too, unless the roads were impassable. They had forgotten the Romneys were coming to lunch, and Hope made a face, what her father called "a square mouth," a snarl, pushing her head forward and curling back her lips.

"Be thankful it's only lunch," said Gerald. "When I first met the guy, I asked him for the weekend."

"He *refused*?" Sarah said it as if she were talking of someone turning down a free round-the-world cruise.

"No, he didn't refuse. I wrote to him, asked him for lunch, and said he could stay at the hotel."

Everyone laughed except Ursula.

"He's got a wife he's bringing."

"Oh God, Daddy, is there more? He hasn't got kids, has he?"

"If he has, they're not invited." Gerald smiled sweetly at his daughters. He said thoughtfully, "We might play the Game."

"With *them*? Oh, do let's," said Hope. "We haven't played the Game for ages."

Titus and Julia Romney were much honored by an invitation from Gerald Candless, and if they had expected to be put up in the house and not have to pay for a room at the Dunes, they hadn't said so, not even to each other. Julia had anticipated eccentricity from someone so distinguished, even rudeness, and she was pleasantly surprised to encounter a genial host, a gracious, if rather silent, hostess, and two good-looking young women who turned out to be the daughters.

Titus, who had his naive side, as she well knew,

was hoping for a look at the room where the work was done. And perhaps a present. Not a first edition, that would be expecting too much, but any book signed by the author. Conversation on literary matters, how he wrote, when he wrote, and even, now the daughters had appeared, what it was like to be *his* child.

It was a hot, sunny day in July, a few days before the start of the high season at the hotel, or they wouldn't have gotten a room. Lunch was in a darkish, cool dining room with no view of the sea. Far from discussing books, the Candlesses talked about the weather, summer visitors, the beach, and Miss Batty, who was coming to clear the table and wash up. Gerald said Miss Batty wasn't much of a cleaner but that they kept her because her name made him laugh. There was another Miss Batty and a Mrs. Batty, and they all lived together in a cottage in Croyde. "Sounds like a new card game, Unhappy Families," he said, and then he laughed and the daughters laughed.

In the drawing room—so he called it—the French windows were open onto the garden, the pink and blue hydrangea, the cliff edge, the long bow-shaped beach and the sea. Julia asked what the island was and Sarah said Lundy, but she said it in such a way as to imply only a total ignoramus would ask. Coffee was brought by someone who must have been Miss Batty and drinks were poured by Hope. Gerald and Titus drank port, Julia had a refill of the Meursault, and Sarah and Hope both had brandy. Sarah's brandy was neat, but Hope's had ice in it.

Then Gerald made the sort of announcement

Julia hated, really hated. She didn't think people actually did this anymore, not in this day and age, not grown-ups. Not intellectuals.

"And now we'll play the Game," Gerald had said. "Let's see how clever you are."

"Would it be wonderful to find someone who caught on at once, Daddy?" said Hope. "Or would we hate it?"

"We'd hate it," said Sarah, and she planted on Gerald's cheek one of those kisses that the Romneys found mildly embarrassing to witness.

He caught at her hand briefly. "It never happens, though, does it?"

Julia met Ursula's eye and must have put inquiry into her glance. Or simple fear.

"Oh, I shan't play," Ursula said. "I shall go out for my walk."

"In this heat?"

"I like it. I always walk along the beach in the afternoons."

Titus, who also disliked parlor games, asked what this one was called. "Not this Unhappy Families you were talking about?"

"It's called I Pass the Scissors," said Sarah.

"What do we have to do?"

"You have to do it right. That's all."

"You mean we all have to do something and there's a right way and a wrong way of doing it?"

She nodded.

"How will we know?"

"We'll tell you."

The scissors were produced by Hope from a drawer in the tallboy. Once kitchen scissors had been used for the Game, or Ursula's sewing scissors or nail scissors, whatever came to hand. But the Game and the ascendancy it gave them afforded so much pleasure that, while his daughters still lived at home, Gerald had bought a pair of Victorian scissors with handles like a silver bird in flight and sharp pointed blades. It was these that Hope now handed to her father for him to begin.

Leaning forward in his armchair, his feet planted far apart, his back to the light, Gerald opened the scissors so that they formed a cross. He smiled. He was a big man, with a head journalists called "leonine," though the lion was old now, with a grizzled, curly mane the color of iron filings. His hands were big and his fingers very long. He handed the scissors to Julia Romney and said, "I pass the scissors uncrossed."

Julia passed the scissors to Hope as she had received them. "I pass the scissors uncrossed."

"No, you don't." Hope closed the scissors, turned them over, and put them into the outstretched fingers of Titus Romney. "I pass the scissors crossed."

Titus did the same and handed them to Sarah, saying with a glance at Gerald that he passed the scissors crossed.

"Wrong." Sarah opened the scissors, held them by one blade, and passed them to her father. "I pass the scissors crossed, Dad."

He closed them, turned them over twice clockwise,

and passed them to Julia. "I pass the scissors un-crossed."

Dawning comprehension, or what she thought was dawning comprehension, broke on Julia's face. She sat upright and turned the scissors over twice counterclockwise, handed them to Hope, and said she passed the scissors crossed.

"Well, well," said Hope. "But do you know why?"

Julia didn't. She had guessed. "But they're crossed when they're closed, aren't they?"

"Are they? You have to pass them crossed and know why, and everyone has to see. Look, when you know, it's as clear as glass. I promise you." Hope opened the scissors. "I pass the scissors crossed."

So they continued for half an hour. Titus Romney asked if anyone ever got it, and Gerald said yes, of course, it was just that no one ever got it at once. Jonathan Arthur had gotten it the second time. Impressed by the name of the winner of both the John Llewellyn Rhys and the Somerset Maugham prizes, Titus said he was really going to concentrate from now on. Sarah said she wanted another brandy and what about everyone else.

"Another port, Dad?"

"I don't think so, darling. It gives me a headache. But you can give Titus one."

Sarah replenished the drinks, then sat down again, this time on the arm of her father's chair. "I pass the scissors uncrossed."

"But why?" Julia Romney was beginning to sound irritated. She had gone rather red. Signs of participants beginning to lose their tempers always amused the Candlesses, who now looked gleeful and expectant. "I mean, how can it be? The scissors are just the same as when you passed them crossed just now."

"I told you it was unlikely you'd get it the first time," said Hope, and she yawned. "I pass the scissors crossed."

"You always pass them crossed!"

"Do I? Right, I'll pass them uncrossed next time."

As Titus was receiving the scissors, opening them and turning them clockwise, Ursula came in through the French windows. Her hair, which was fair but graying, and very long and wispy, had begun flopping down out of its pins and she was holding it up with one hand. She smiled, and Titus thought she was going to say, "Still at it?" or "Have you found the secret yet?" but she said nothing, only passing on across the room and through the door that led into the hall.

Gerald looked around and said, "Shall we call it a day?"

The way the girls laughed, Sarah leaning over to look into her father's eyes, told Titus this must be the phrase, rather dramatically delivered, he always used to terminate a session of the Game. Probably the injunction that followed was also requisite at this point.

"Better luck next time."

Gerald rose to his feet. Titus had the impression, founded on nothing that he was truly aware of, that the old man (the "Grand Old Man," he almost was) had been disturbed by the return of his wife, deflected from his pleasure in the Game, and was displeased. His face, though not as gray as his hair, had lost its color and grown dull. The daughter, Sarah, the one who looked like her mother, saw it, too. She glanced at her sister, the one who looked like her father, and said, "Are you all right, Dad?"

"Of course I am." He made a face at his glass but smiled at her. "I don't like port, never have. I should have had brandy."

"I'll get you a brandy," said Hope.

"Better not." He did something Titus had never before seen a grown man do to a grown woman: He put out his hand and stroked her hair. "We stumped them again, my sweethearts. We boggled them."

"We always do."

"And now"—he turned to Titus—"before you go"—a bright gleam in his dark eye—"you said you wanted to see where I work."

The study. Did he call it that? The room, anyway, where the books had been written, or most of them. It was stuffy in there and warm. You could see the sea from here, too, and more of the long, flat half-mile-wide beach, the water's edge almost invisible in the distance. Sky and sea met in a blurred dazzle. The closed window was large, stark, with black blinds rolled up, and the sun poured in. It flooded the desk and his chair and the books behind him and the book in front. Gerald Candless used a typewriter, not a word processor, quite an old-fashioned one, and had a bunch of pens and pencils in an onyx jar.

Proofs of a new novel lay to the left of the typewriter. A stack of manuscript about an inch deep sat to its right. Several thousand books filled the shelves ceiling to floor, dictionaries and thesauruses and encyclopedias and other reference works, and poetry and biography and novels, hundreds of novels, including Gerald Candless's own works. The sun bathed their leather and cloth and colored-paper spines in brilliant light.

"Do you feel all right?"

Titus had echoed Sarah's words, because the grayness was back in Gerald's face and his big gnarled right hand was gripping the upper part of his left arm. He made no answer to the question. Titus thought he was probably the sort of man who never said anything unless he had something to say, made no small talk, answered no polite questions as to his health.

"Are you really called Titus?"

The abrupt inquiry disconcerted him. "What?"

"I didn't know you were deaf. I said, Are you really called Titus?"

"Of course I am."

"I thought it must be a pseudonym. Don't look so peevish. Not all of us are really called what we're called, you know, not by a long chalk. Now take a look around. Look your fill. Have a book. Help yourself, and I'll sign it. Not a first edition—I draw the line at that."

One of the things Titus looked for was a copy of his own book. It wasn't there, or if it was, he couldn't see it. He stood in front of the row of Gerald

Candlesses, wondering which one to pick, then finally chose *Hamadryad*.

"Read Finnish, do you?"

Titus saw that he had chosen from the section of translations, so he made a second attempt, but was forestalled by being handed a book club edition of the same novel. Gerald signed it. Just his name, no good wishes or kind regards. Sunlight fell on his hands, which, if they didn't tremble, weren't quite steady.

"And now that you've had your lunch, seen my room, and gotten a book, you can do something for me. One good turn—or rather, three good turns—deserves another, wouldn't you agree?"

Assent was expected. Titus nodded. "Anything, of course, if it's in my power."

"Oh, it's in your power. It would be in anybody's who happened to be here. You see that stuff?"

"The page proofs?"

"No, not the page proofs. The manuscript. I want you to take it with you. Just take it away. Will you do that for me?"

"What is it?"

Gerald Candless didn't answer. "I'm going away for a few days. I don't want it left here in the house while I'm away. But I don't want to destroy it, either. I may publish it one day—I mean, I may finish it and publish it. If I have the nerve."

"What is it, your autobiography?"

The sarcastic reply came: "Of course. I haven't even changed the names." Then he said, "It's a novel, the start of a novel, or the end—I don't know which. But he is not he and she is not she and they are not they. Right? I don't want it left here. You were coming, I'd met you in wherever it was . . ."

"Hay-on-Wye."

"Right. You were coming, and it came to me that you'd do. Who else is there down here?"

"I wonder you didn't put it in a safe-deposit box somewhere."

"Oh, you wonder that, do you? If you don't want to take it and look after it for me, just say. I'll give it to Miss Batty, or I'll burn it. Come to think of it, burning might be best."

"For God's sake, don't burn it," said Titus. "I'll take it. How do I get it back to you? And when do I?"

Gerald picked up the pages and held them in his hands. Underneath them, on the desk, was a padded bag already addressed to Gerald Candless, Lundy View House, Gaunton, North Devon, and stamped with £1.50 postage.

"Do you . . . Do you want me to . . . Do you mind if I read it?"

A gale of laughter greeted that, a strong, vigorous bellow, incompatible with those tremulous hands. "You'll have a job. I'm the world's lousiest typist. Here, you can put it in this."

"This" was a cheap-looking plastic briefcase, the kind of thing that, containing the requisite brochures and agenda, is given to delegates at a conference. Titus Romney wouldn't have been seen dead with it normally. But he had only a short distance to carry it to

15

the hotel. They found Julia in the drawing room, carrying on a stilted conversation with Gerald's wife. Titus had already forgotten her name, but he didn't have to remember it, because they were going. It was 3:30 and they were leaving. The daughters had disappeared.

"I'll walk with you to the hotel," Gerald said. "I'm supposed to walk a bit every day. A few yards."

Julia gushed, the way she did when she had had a horrid time. "Good-bye. Thank you so much. It's been lovely. A lovely lunch."

"Enjoy the rest of your stay," Gerald's wife said.

They set off across the garden, Titus carrying the briefcase, at which Julia cast curious glances. The garden extended to about ten yards from the cliff edge, where there was a gate to the cliff path. From this path, all the beach could be seen, and the car park, full of cars and trailers. The beach was crowded and there were a lot of people in the sea. Somewhere Julia had read this described as the finest beach on the English coast, the longest, seven miles of it, with the best sand. The safest beach, for the tide went out half a mile and flowed in gently over the flat, scarcely sloping sand, a shallow, limpid sea. It was blue as a jewel, calm, waveless.

"You must love living here," Julia said politely.

He didn't answer. Titus asked him if he didn't like walking. The way he talked about it implied he didn't like it.

"I don't like any physical exercise. Only cranks like walking. That's why a sensible man invented the car."

A gate in the path bore a sign: THE DUNES HOTEL. STRICTLY PRIVATE. HOTEL GUESTS ONLY. Gerald opened it, then stood aside to let Julia pass through. The hotel, Edwardian red brick with white facings, multi-gabled, stood up above them, its striped awnings unfurled across the terrace. People sat at tables having tea. Children splashed about in a swimming pool that was barely concealed by privet hedges.

"Your children enjoying themselves?"

"We haven't any children," said Julia.

"Really? Why not?"

"I don't know." She was very taken aback. That should be a question people didn't ask. "I . . . I don't necessarily want any."

Another gate to pass through and they were on the turf of the big lawn.

"You don't want any children?" Gerald said. "How unnatural. You must change your mind. Not afraid to have a baby, are you? Some women are. Children are the crown of existence. Children are the source of all happiness. The great reward. Believe me. I know. Here we are, then, back among the throng."

Julia was so angry, she was nearly rude to him. She looked at her husband, but he refused to meet her eyes. She turned to Gerald Candless, resolved on silently shaking hands with him, turning her back on him, and marching quickly up to her room. Her hand went out reluctantly. He failed to take it, though this omission wasn't rudeness. He was staring up at the hotel, at the terrace, with an expression of astonishment and, more than that, amazement. His

17

eyes were fixed and so unblinking that she followed his gaze.

Nothing to see, no one to look at, nothing to cause this rigid, fixed stare. It was the elderly people who congregated there on the terrace, she had noticed from the previous afternoon, those who didn't swim or walk far or venture down the cliff, knowing they would have to climb up again. The old ones sat there under the umbrellas and the blue-and-white-striped awning, golden-wedding couples, grandparents, the sedate, the inactive.

"Have you seen someone you know?" Titus asked.

It was as if he were in a dream, as if he were a sleepwalker arrested in his blind progress and lost, his orientation gone. Titus's question broke the spell or the dream and he passed a hand across his high wrinkled forehead, pushing the fingers through that bush of hair.

"I was mistaken," he said; then the hand came down, and farewells were made. He was smiling the way he did, with his red wolfish mouth and not his eyes. His eyes not at all.

They didn't watch him go back. They didn't look back or wave. As she crossed the terrace to enter the hotel by way of the open glass doors into the lounge and bar, Julia paused briefly to take in the people who sat at the terrace tables, those grandparents. Old people smoked so much. They all sat with cigarettes, overflowing ashtrays, pots of tea and cups of tea, pastries on cake stands, packs of cards, but no sun lotion or sunglasses. They never went into the sun. A woman

18

was making up her face in the mirror of a powder compact, drawing crimson lips onto an old pursed mouth.

There was no one to interest him, no one who could so have caught his rapt gaze. More affectation, she thought, more games to impress us, and she followed Titus into the cool shadowy interior.

Sarah and Hope were going out. Hope had already made her plans, a barbecue on some beach farther up the coast. Almost before the guests were out of earshot, Sarah was on the phone, arranging to meet the usual crowd in a Barnstaple pub. Not even the prospect of their father's company would keep them in on a Saturday night. To go out with those old companions, school friends and friends' friends, was an obligation, almost a duty.

" 'Make my bed and light the light,' " said Miss Batty in the kitchen. " 'I'll arrive late tonight, blackbird, bye-bye.' There's a lot of truth in those old songs."

She picked up Titus Romney's glass off the tray and drank the port he had left. It was something she usually did when they entertained. Once she had gotten into such a state drinking the dregs from fifteen champagne glasses that Ursula had had to drive her home. But what on earth had they had champagne for? Ursula couldn't remember. Miss Batty—whom Ursula long ago had begun calling Daphne, just as Miss Batty called her Ursula—drained a drop of brandy and began emptying the dishwasher of its first load.

" 'Bye-bye, blackbird,' " she said.

Ursula never ceased to be amazed by the scope of Daphne Batty's knowledge of sixty years of popular music. If Gerald liked her for her name, Ursula's appreciation derived from this unceasing flow of esoterica. She went back into the living room. Gerald was standing by the open windows but facing the inside of the room. Since he had come back from the hotel, he had spoken not a word, and that look he sometimes had of being far away had taken control of his face. Only this time, he was even more distant, almost as if he had stepped across some dividing stream into different territory. He looked at her blankly. She could have sworn that for a moment he didn't know who she was.

Saturday nights when the girls were out, he worried himself sick. He thought she wasn't aware of his anxiety, but of course she was. While his daughters were in London, as they mostly were, they were no doubt out night after night till all hours, and it never occurred to him to worry. Ursula was sure he scarcely thought about it, still less woke up in the small hours to wonder if Hope was back safe in her bed in Crouch End or Sarah in hers in Kentish Town. But here, when they were out, he no longer even bothered to go to bed. He sat up in the dark in the study, waiting for the sound of a car, then one key in the door, then the second car, the other key.

She hadn't shared a bedroom with him for nearly thirty years, never in this house, but she knew. She was still fascinated by him. As one could be, she sometimes thought, by a deformity or a mutilation. He compelled her horrified gaze, her continual speculation. There was no actual way she could know if he was in his bedroom or not, no indication by gleam of light or hint of sound. The floorboards were all carpeted and the doors fitted trimly into their architraves. His bedroom was at the other end of the house from hers. But she knew when he wasn't in bed during the night, just as she knew when the girls weren't. One of the cars coming usually woke her. She was a light sleeper. And she, too, would be relieved that first Sarah was home, then Hope. Or the other way around, as the case might be. It wouldn't be before midnight, and probably long after.

His daughters mustn't know he sat up for them. He sat in his study in the dark so that they couldn't find out. They mustn't know he worried about them; they mustn't know he had a bad heart or that on Wednesday that bad heart was to undergo repairs. He wanted them as carefree as they had been when children, believing their father immortal. She thought for a moment of how it might be for them if he were to die on the operating table, of the abyss that would open before them, and then she put the light out and went to sleep.

She didn't hear the first car come in, but she heard the faint squeak Hope's door made when it was opened more than forty-five degrees. Sarah's car came in noisily and too fast, which probably meant she had drunk too much. Ursula wondered if the newspapers would know whose daughter she was and make something of it when the police caught her one of these nights for driving over the speed limit. The car door banged and the front door shut with almost a slam. Sarah made up for it by creeping up the stairs.

Gerald was almost as quiet. But he was big and heavy and he lumbered when he walked. If the girls heard him, they would think he had gotten up to go to the bathroom. She lay there listening but heard nothing more, and perhaps she slept. Afterward, she wasn't sure, certain only of the silence and peace and that when she put the light on, it had been just after 1:30. The tide was high at 1:50, she had noticed. Not that it made much difference these summer nights when the sea was calm and there was no wind. People said how lovely it must be to hear the sound of the sea at night, but she never heard it. The house might be on the clifftop, but it was still too far away from that creeping shallow sea.

He had had a shock in the afternoon. Realizing this woke her out of a doze. Or something woke her. Perhaps she had dreamed of him, as she sometimes did. She remembered his stillness, his stare. He had walked back to the hotel with those people and something had happened. He had seen something or someone, or something upsetting had been said to him. Shocks shouldn't happen to him, she thought vaguely, and she sat up and put on the lamp. Four. She must have slept. Dawn was coming, a thin gray light making a shimmer around the curtains.

It was then that she heard him. Or he had made that sound before and that was what had awakened her. Her nightdress was a thin thing with narrow shoulder straps. She put on a dressing gown, screwed her long hair up into a knot, and stabbed it with two hairpins.

She had never been in his bedroom. Not in this house. She didn't even know what it was like inside. Daphne Batty cleaned it and changed his sheets, humming pop or rock or country while she did so. Ursula said, "Gerald?"

A gasp for breath. That was what it sounded like. She opened the door. The curtains were drawn back and she could see a pale moon in a pale sky. It was quite light. He was sitting up in the single bed, crimson-faced, his skin sprinkled with sweat.

She spoke his name again. "Gerald?"

He struggled to speak. At once, she knew he was having a seizure, and she looked around for the remedy he had, the nitroglycerin. It might be anywhere. There was nothing on the bedside table. As she went toward the bed, he suddenly threw back his head and bellowed out a roar. It was an animal noise a goaded bull might make, and it seemed to come up through his chest and throat from the very center of his stricken heart. The echoes of it died away and he punched at his chest with his fists, then threw out his arms as his face swelled and grew deep purple.

She went to take his hands, to forget everything and hold him. As she had done once before, as she had done the night he dreamed his trapped-in-a-tunnel dream. But he fought against her. He punched again, this time at her, his eyes bulging as if his eyeballs would burst from their sockets, punching like a maddened child.

Aghast, she stepped back. He drew a long breath, a sound like water gurgling down a drain, liquid and rich and bubbling. The color seeped out of his face, red wine drained out of a smoky glass. She saw it grow pale and slacken, the muscles slip. As the death rattle burst out of him, a clattering salvo of final sound, he fell back into the bed and out of life.

She knew it was death. Nothing else was possible. It amazed her afterward that Sarah and Hope had slept through it all. Just as, when children, they had slept through his screaming when he dreamed of the tunnel. She phoned for an ambulance, although she knew he was dead, and then, unwillingly, fearfully, afraid of her own children, she went to wake them.

2

The meek may inherit the earth, but they won't keep it long.

—EYE IN THE ECLIPSE

SARAH AND HOPE COMPOSED the death announcement together. Sarah put in "beloved" because you couldn't just have "husband of," and both of them loved "adored." The lines from Cory's "Heraclitus" were Hope's choice, remembered from school and rediscovered in Palgrave's *Golden Treasury*. Sarah found them mildly embarrassing but gave in because Hope cried so much when she protested. The announcement appeared in several daily newspapers.

> *Candless, Gerald Francis, age 71, on July 6 at his home in Gaunton, Devon, beloved husband of Ursula and adored father of Sarah and Hope. Funeral, Ilfracombe, July 11. No flowers. Donations to the British Heart Foundation.*

> *I wept when I remembered how often thou and I, Had tired the sun with talking and sent him down the sky.*

The next day, his obituary was in the *Times*.

Gerald Francis Candless, OBE, novelist, died July 6, age 71. He was born on May 10, 1926.

Gerald Candless was the author of eighteen novels, their publication spanning a period from 1955 to the present. He will probably be best remembered for Hamadryad, *which was short-listed for the Booker Prize in 1979.*

His novels were unusual in that, though literary fiction, they were, in the middle years, at any rate, both popular with the public and highly regarded by critics. It was only from the mid-eighties onward, however, that his fiction regularly appeared on best-seller lists, a phenomenon that seemed to coincide with a cooling of enthusiasm on the part of reviewers. It was suggested that his books were "too plot-driven" and sometimes that they resembled the "sensation fiction" of a hundred years before. Nevertheless, in a list compiled by newspaper reviewers in 1995, he was named as one of the leading twenty-five novelists of the second half of the twentieth century.

Candless was born in Ipswich, Suffolk, the only child of a printer and a nurse, George and Kathleen Candless, and grew up in that town. He was educated privately and later at Trinity College, Dublin, where he obtained a degree in classics. After university, he worked as a journalist for various weekly and provincial daily newspapers, first the Walthamstow Herald *in East London and, more notably, the* Western Morning News *in Plymouth.*

It was while in Plymouth that he wrote his first

book, at the age of twenty-eight. Many years later, in an interview for the Daily Telegraph, *he said he had followed the example of Anthony Trollope, got up at five every morning and wrote for three hours before going to work. The novel,* The Centre of Attraction, *was accepted by the third publisher to whom Candless sent it and was published in the autumn of 1955.*

Three more books appeared, to increasing acclaim, before Candless was able to live by his writing. It was a long time, however, before he abandoned journalism altogether, as in the early sixties, about the time of his marriage, he became a fiction reviewer for the Daily Mail, *and later, for a while, its book-page editor, then deputy literary editor of the* Observer.

He was at this time living in London, in Hampstead, where his daughters were born. Later, he moved with his family to a part of the country that had been a favorite with him since Plymouth days, the north Devon coast between Bideford and Ilfracombe. There, on the outskirts of the village of Gaunton, he bought Lundy View House on the clifftop above Gaunton Dunes, where he lived and worked from 1970 until his death.

Candless became a Fellow of the Royal Society of Literature in 1976 and was awarded the OBE in the 1986 Birthday Honours. His death was from coronary thrombosis. He is survived by his widow, the former Ursula Wick, and by his daughters, Sarah and Hope.

There were not many at the funeral. Gerald Candless had no relatives, not even a cousin or two. The girls were there, and Fabian Lerner, who was Hope's boyfriend, as well as Ursula's widowed sister and her married niece, Pauline.

"When my mother was young, women never went to funerals," said Daphne Batty, washing sherry glasses. Old Mrs. Batty was ninety-three. "They called it 'following,' and women didn't follow."

"Why not?" said Ursula.

"They was the weaker sex, and it could have been too much for them."

"Aren't they the weaker sex any longer, then?"

"They've been getting stronger through the years, haven't they? You know that." Daphne looked over her shoulder, checking that she wasn't about to be over-heard. "That Fabian only came because he'd never been to a funeral before," she said. "He told me. He wanted to see what it was like."

"I hope it came up to expectations," said Ursula, thinking of Hope's display when the coffin was low-ered into the AstroTurf–lined pit. For a moment, she had thought her daughter was going to throw herself in on top of it like Laertes in Ophelia's grave.

Gerald's publisher had thought so, too. He took a step forward and she heard him mutter, "Oh no, no."

But Hope had only crouched down on the glitter-ing green plastic stuff and wailed while she watched the last of her father disappear into the earth. Wailed, and when Pauline—Why her? Who asked her to do it?—threw a handful of gravel in on top of the coffin, she sobbed and flung herself backward and forward, clutching handfuls of hair from under her black velvet pancake hat.

Sarah said, "She's taken it very hard. We all have. It's just as real for us, but we don't show our emotions the way she does."

Ursula didn't say anything.

"He was the most wonderful father anyone could have had. When I think of the fathers of other people my age . . . When we were little—but I can't talk about it. I can't yet. I just start crying. I'm as bad as Hope, really."

"You're not as ostentatious," said Ursula.

Sarah looked closely at her mother, who was sitting at the kitchen table with a mug of coffee in front of her. Ursula was a sturdy, straight-backed woman with rather pretty but not memorable features, a still-unlined, smooth face, calm blue-gray eyes, and untidy fairish gray-streaked hair that was always coming loose from its knot. Long hair done up in a bun from which strands constantly escape looks charming on a young girl, thought Sarah, but on an older woman, it's just a mess. But there were few people to see her mother, no one really now that Gerald was gone, except Daphne Batty.

That put her in mind of what she wanted to say. Not exactly what she wanted to say, but what she thought she should say. "You know I can't stay on here. And Hope can't. Not after tomorrow. So would you like to come back with me?" It didn't sound very gracious. She tried again. "I'll be happy to have you.

You can stay as long as you like. You could stay in and have a quiet time while I'm at work, or you could go shopping and . . . well, have your hair done." She thought of adding that Hope would come over in the evenings, but she couldn't be sure if this was true.

"You could go shopping at Camden Lock," said Sarah. "You're a great walker. It's a nice walk to St. John's Wood."

"It's a nice walk along the beach to Franaton Burrows," said Ursula. "It's very good of you, Sarah, but I shall be quite all right here. I think I should be alone. I should get used to it." She didn't say she had been alone in all important respects for three decades. Having someone else in the house, a large, clever, overbearing yet indifferent presence, mitigates loneliness not at all. But she didn't say it, because she had never said such things to her daughters or, indeed, to anyone. "In any case," she said, "Pauline is going to come and stay with me for a few days."

Although she cast up her eyes, Sarah made no adverse comment on this solution to what she saw as Ursula's problem. She and her mother were so unaccustomed to telling each other what they really felt, so habituated to the utterance of platitudes or casual remarks, that she didn't now say, "Rather you than me." Or "Why are you doing penance?" She said only, "I suppose she'll be company for you."

Pauline was company. She was more company than Gerald had been, because it didn't really matter much what you said to her, or if you said anything at all half the time. She was thirty-eight and had often come to stay when the girls were little. She was just sufficiently older to enjoy looking after them. And like all young girls who came to the house, the house in Hampstead and later this one, she had thought Gerald Candless the nicest, kindest, loveliest grown-up she had ever known. When she was fourteen, she had been in love with him. Then there had been that trouble. No one knew exactly what kind of trouble except Pauline and Gerald, but whatever it was, he had gotten over it and she had, and when she got married at the age of twenty-one, she asked him to give her away, her own father being dead by then.

Pauline's children were now adolescents and could be left at home with their father and their grandmother, who would come in to do the cooking. Pauline had worked for her living for just three years before she was married, and never afterward. This gave her a lot in common with Ursula, or she thought it did, for Ursula, too, had not worked, in the sense of being a wage earner, since some months before Gerald married her in Purley in 1963.

"You typed all Uncle Gerald's manuscripts, though, didn't you?" Pauline said one lunchtime after she had been at Lundy View House for nearly a week. "He wrote them and you made sense of his terrible handwriting and copied them on that old Olivetti you had."

"That's right," said Ursula. "Like Sonia Tolstoy."

"Who?" said Pauline.

"Tolstoy's wife. She made copies of all his books, seven copies of each one, and they were all very long, and she had to do it by hand because typewriters hadn't been invented. Or they didn't have one, anyway. So it wasn't as bad for me as it was for her."

"But you didn't get paid for it?" asked Pauline hopefully. If Ursula had been paid, even by her husband, this would partly have excluded her from the sisterhood of unemployed married women. "Uncle Gerald didn't pay you?"

"He kept me," said Ursula.

"Well, of course, that goes without saying. Brian keeps me, if you like to put it that way."

"I didn't always do it. *Hand to Mouth* was the last one I did, and that was 1984. After that, he typed them himself."

"But why did you stop?" said Pauline.

Ursula didn't answer. She was wondering how many minutes after they got up from the table she could go out for her walk. Twenty, probably. Pauline began to clear the table. She hadn't yet asked Ursula if Uncle Gerald had left her well-off or comfortably off or just able to manage. She hadn't asked if Ursula would have to sell the house or take in lodgers or do B and B, though Ursula knew she was dying to know the answers to all these questions. Everyone assumed that Gerald had left everything to Sarah and Hope, and Ursula, though she had gotten over the shock of his death, if shock it had been, hadn't yet adjusted to his surprising bequests.

"I shall go out for my walk in ten minutes," she said when they had loaded the dishwasher.

"In this fog?" said Pauline with an artificial shudder.

"It isn't fog; it's just sea mist."

"Oh, I know that's what you call it. You always did call it sea mist. It was the only thing I didn't like about coming to stay here, that white sea fog. And Uncle Gerald hated it, didn't he? I remember he would never go out in it; he used to shut himself up in his study. Why was that?"

"I don't know," said Ursula.

"Does it upset you when I talk about him, Auntie Ursula?"

"I think you could drop the 'Auntie,' don't you?" said Ursula, not for the first time.

"I'll try," said Pauline, "but it will be very hard to get out of the habit."

Hardly anyone came down to the beach when the mist rolled in from the sea. The car park emptied, the surfers retreated into their caravans, and the hotel guests went back to the indoor swimming pool. The beach, which was seven miles long and, when the tide was out, a half of a mile wide, was overhung by a white curtain, so that when you were on it, in the sand, the dunes and the sea became invisible. Ursula could see her own feet, and the beach stretching away in front of her and on either side of her for some yards, but she couldn't see the hummocky wrinkled green dunes to the left of her or the water, to the right of her, creeping silently across the sand.

The mist would wet her hair and settle on her clothes in fine droplets, but she didn't mind this. It wasn't cold. Sometimes she thought she preferred misty days to clear ones, when you could see the headland and the estuary and Westward Ho! and, looming on the clifftop, the hotel and its garden and all those flowers in primary colors. She walked southward halfway between the edge of the dunes and the edge of the incoming tide, sometimes looking up to see a distant dazzlement of sun through the thickness of white gauze, but more often down at the sand.

The sand was sometimes quite flat and packed hard, but on other days, by some strange action of the tide's passage, it was pulled into wrinkles like the skin that forms on boiled milk. Today, though, it was smooth, a dark ocher color, but streaked here and there in a chevron pattern with a fine glittery black dust. Visitors to Gaunton thought the black streaks, which looked as if a magnet had drawn them into that shape as it might draw iron filings across a sheet of paper, were from tar or some other pollutant, but Ursula knew that this powder was ground-up mussel shells, pulverized by the pounding and the kneading of the sea.

Shells were everywhere on the beach, white scallop shells and ivory-colored limpets, chalky whelks and blue-black mussel shells with a sheen of pearl or a crust of barnacles, razor shells that looked like a cutthroat razor in an agate case. When the girls first came here as small children, they collected shells every day, until they grew tired of it. Ursula found all the dull, dusty, smelly shells in a cupboard years later. She put them in a carrier bag and took them back to the beach, scattering them onto the sand as she walked along. The next day, when she walked the same way, the shells had been washed clean and shining by the sea and those she had restored to the beach were indistinguishable from those that had always been there.

Today, there was no one else on the beach. And the mist remained static, hanging, quite still. The solitude pleased her, the chance to think. No thinking could be done at Lundy View House while Pauline was there, and at night, when she was alone in her room, she took one of the sleeping pills the doctor had insisted she have. She asked herself why she liked the mist so much. Could it be because Gerald had disliked it? The possibility that this was true had to be admitted. She liked it because he didn't, and in a way, that made it hers, a secret, inviolable possession.

Perhaps, too, she liked it because it obscured so much. Lundy View House, the other houses on the cliff, people, Gerald. It hid everything but the clean flat sand and the pure white or blue-black glittering shells. Now, of course, she no longer needed this obfuscation. Savoring it, she repeated the word to herself. Obfuscation. Once, long ago, she had set herself the daily task of learning long, difficult words to impress and please him. What a fool, she thought, but she thought it calmly and in a measured, considered way.

As she turned back, or rather, wheeled round, to retrace her steps nearer to the incoming sea, she wondered not for the first time why she had reacted as she had to Gerald's death. At least she would have expected to feel shock. But there had been very little shock, only surprise and, very quickly, relief. No guilt, either. She had read somewhere—ah, what a lot of books and magazines and periodicals and journals and newspapers she had read over the years!—that bereavement brings with it a sad and bitter longing to have the dead back, if only for a few hours, to ask those questions that were always there but were never asked in life. And she thought, Yes, I would like to ask why. Why did you do this to me and take so much away from me? Why did you make me second-best— oh, much further down the scale than that—with my children? Why did you marry me? No, why did you *want* to marry me? It would have to be a different person, though, whom she brought back to life. The Gerald she knew wouldn't answer.

That brought Mrs. Eady into her head. She hadn't thought of Mrs. Eady for years. A big, sad old woman with a daughter in a nunnery and a murdered son, his photograph in a silver frame beside a small green-speckled vase. She could see it still as clearly as she could see the sand and shells. And less than a year later, they had moved away from Hampstead and come here to the clifftop and a house with a view of the Bristol Channel and Lundy Island.

The mist was lifting. Ursula knew the mist on this coast and the way it behaved and she understood from experience that it wouldn't lift fully all day, but come and go, rise and fall. The white curtain had rolled up a little ways and thinned a little to let in pale, steamy shafts of sunshine. She could see the hotel now, its angry red, the gables too shallow and the roof tiles matching the geraniums that hung all over it in innumerable hanging baskets. The fog curtain disclosed it almost coyly, as if there were an audience on the beach longing for a glimpse of its beauties.

Her own house was briefly revealed. It *was* her own now. Not held in trust for her to live in, not merely affording her a life interest, but hers. And his future royalties were hers, and, apart from generous legacies to Sarah and Hope, all he possessed. The will had been much more of a shock than his death. She had thought about it on these beach walks of hers and now she believed he had made this will to make up to her for what he had done. He wasn't showing her that he had loved her after all, but that he was in her debt. He owed her for taking her life and misusing it.

On the clifftop, Pauline had come out into the garden and was standing by the gate, waving. Ursula waved back, but less enthusiastically. Later on, she thought, she would do something seemingly out of character and take her niece to the hotel bar for a drink.

The mist descended again quite suddenly, as she had known it would, and hid the figure of Pauline, still waving.

3

---

*A man believes everything he reads in the
newspaper until he finds an item about himself that
is a web of lies. This makes him doubt, but not for
long, and he soons reverts to his old faith in the
printed word.*

      —THE CENTRE OF ATTRACTION

THREE NEWSPAPERS WERE DELIVERED to Lundy View
House every morning. Ursula had kept the paperboy
on for Pauline to have something to read at breakfast,
but once her niece was gone, she intended to cancel
the delivery. It was something to look forward to, not
seeing newspapers. She liked to look at the view of
the beach while she was eating her grapefruit and her
toast.

 The sea was calm this morning and a deep clear
blue, not streaked with emerald as it sometimes was,
and the sky was a pale, luminous, unclouded blue.
The tide was out, was still going out, and where the
sand was still wet, a boy of about twelve was building
an elaborate sand castle with a keep and turrets and a
moat. A man with his two small children was trying
to fly a large red-and-white kite, but there wasn't
enough wind to lift it off the beach. He reminded her

of Gerald, who had also flown kites, who had built innumerable sand castles.

"Have you noticed," said Pauline, looking up from the paper, "that no one ever points out a simple truth about unemployment. The fact is that half the unemployment is due to women working. If women didn't work, men wouldn't be out of work, but no one ever dares say this."

"It wouldn't be politically correct," said Ursula.

"Did you ever want to have a job? Apart from working for Uncle Gerald, of course."

"I once thought of taking on some baby-sitting at the hotel. They always want child-sitters."

Pauline looked at her to see if she was serious. Ursula's face was quite blank.

"But you didn't?"

"Gerald didn't care for the idea."

"I'm not surprised. The wife of a famous writer looking after other people's kids for a couple of pounds an hour!"

"It was three pounds," said Ursula. "If you've finished, I'll clear the table, because I like to do that before Daphne comes. No, sit there. I'll do it. Read your paper."

When she came back into the room to fetch the coffeepot, Pauline said, "There's a letter in here about Uncle Gerald. Would you like to see it?"

"Not particularly." Ursula had already suffered from her niece's propensity for reading aloud, so she sighed a little before saying, "You read it to me."

"It's rather peculiar, quite a mystery. It says: 'From the editor of *Modern Philately*.'"

"The *Times* always does that."

"Peculiar. Well, here goes. Listen. 'Sir, I refer to your obituary of Gerald Candless, the novelist (Obituaries, July 10). The writer states that the late Mr. Candless was employed as a journalist on the *Walthamstow Herald* in the postwar years. I was chief subeditor of that newspaper from 1946 until 1953 and can assure you that if that humble organ had been so fortunate as to number a graduate of Trinity and future world-famous novelist among its staff, this is not a distinction I would have forgotten. I am afraid you are in error when you name Gerald Candless as a *Walthamstow Herald* "alumnus." I am, sir, your obedient servant, James Droridge.' What's an alumnus?"

"Someone who is a former student at a university."

"Oh. Why did they say Uncle Gerald worked for that newspaper if he didn't?"

"I don't know, Pauline. It's just a mistake."

A burst of song from the kitchen heralded Daphne Batty's arrival. Ursula carried out the coffeepot to the strains of Merle Haggard's "Today I Started Loving You Again." Daphne had brought the *Daily Mail* with her, and while anxious for Ursula to read Mary Gunthorpe's interview with Hope, she had no aspirations to read it to her. It was titled "Oh, My Beloved Father! The Loss of Hope."

Ursula thought she might as well bow to the inevitable now. She remembered how Gerald had sometimes resolved not to read the reviews of his books in newspapers, but they had been impossible to avoid. Sooner or later, someone would ring up and tell him what was in them, or send them to him with passages underlined in red, or quote from them in letters. Daphne would leave the paper behind and Pauline would find it, and then she would be in for a worse ordeal. She began to read, with Daphne looking over her shoulder.

He was a tall, burly man with big features and a wide, ironic smile. She is slender and rose petal–skinned, her dark hair long and softly waved, her eyes almost too large for that heart-shaped face. Yet Hope Candless is the spitting image of her father, the celebrated novelist who died two weeks ago. There is the same intelligence in those same brown eyes, the same penetrating glance, and the same musical voice.

That voice has a catch in it now and those eyes are bright with tears. To her embarrassment, they spilled over as soon as she began to talk about him. Wearing a pink-and-white shirtwaister dress and white high-heeled sandals—impossible to imagine her in jeans and T-shirt—Hope, thirty, dabbed at her eyes with a lace-edged handkerchief. It was the first handkerchief I had seen since my grandmother died ten years ago. Hope's had a pink H embroidered on it.

"I miss him so much," she said. "He wasn't just my father; he was my best friend. I really think that if I could have chosen just one person in all the world that I'd spend my life with, it would have been him. I suppose you think that's totally mad?

"When my sister and I wrote that death notice that we put in the paper, we had to find an adjective that expressed what we felt. Beloved *wasn't strong enough, so we used* adored, *because we did adore him. And we had the lines from that Victorian poem because we really did tire the sun with talking.*

"Isn't it funny? Each one of us firmly believes she was his favorite. But I think he really loved us equally and he had so much love for us. I'm sorry, you must excuse me, the way I keep crying. He bought me this place, you know, and he bought a flat for my sister, too."

"This place" is the large, airy ground-floor flat of a house in Crouch End with a big patio and a garden full of fruit trees. The author of Hamadryad and Purple of Cassius *bought it for Hope when she qualified as a solicitor seven years ago. She had come second in her year in the Law Society's exams and before that had come down from Cambridge with a first-class honors degree. Her sister is Sarah, two years her senior, and a lecturer in women's studies at the University of London.*

"Sarah has a flat in Kentish Town. Do you know what he said? He said, 'I wish I was a rich man and could buy you homes in Mayfair or Belgravia.' He was always thinking of us. When we were children, he was with us all the time. If we cried in the night, it was he who got up to comfort us. He played with us and read to us and talked to us all the time. I've wondered since when he got time to write his books. When we were asleep, I suppose.

"He never punished us. I mean, it's laughable even to think of such a thing. And he used to get so angry when he heard of people who smacked their

43

*kids. I don't mean seriously abused them, I mean a
little smack. That was the only time we saw him
angry."*

*Talking to Hope Candless, you might be forgiven
for concluding she and her sister had no mother. Or
had a mother who left this paragon, ran off with the
milkman, and abandoned them when they were little.
But Ursula Candless is alive and well and living in
the north Devon house her husband left her.*

*"A lot of people would say she was lucky," says
Hope. "After all, women are always complaining
their husbands won't look after the kids or even
help. One hears about all these fathers who never
see their children from Sunday evening till Friday
evening, not to mention the ones the Child Support
Agency has to chase after. No, I think my mother was
a fortunate woman."*

Ursula threw the paper down in disgust. She would
have read no more if Pauline hadn't come into the
kitchen at this point. Pauline greeted Daphne with a
brisk "Good morning," seized the paper, and, as
Ursula had feared, read the rest of it aloud.

"Where did you get to, Auntie—I mean, Ursula?
'A fortunate woman,' right. It goes on: 'Has this happy
childhood and devoted father made Hope want children of her own? And does a life partner have to be
another Gerald Candless?

" ' "I'm very monogamous," she says. "I suppose
you could say I haven't had a problem forming a stable relationship, and that's said to be the result of my
sort of childhood and home life. As for children of

44

my own, we shall have to see." She laughs and then, remembering she shouldn't be laughing, brings out the handkerchief again. "My partner and I haven't actually discussed children."

" 'Her partner is fellow lawyer Fabian Lerner. They met at Cambridge and have been together ever since.'

" ' "Twelve years now," says Hope. Is her smile a shade rueful? She adds, surprisingly, "We spend most weekends together and go away on holiday together, but we've never actually lived under the same roof. I expect you think that's peculiar."

" 'Perhaps. Or is it only that Hope's significant other can't match up to her all-too-significant father?' Well, that's a bit snide, isn't it?"

"To say the least," said Ursula.

"I expect you're glad Hope and Fabian don't live together, aren't you? It wouldn't be very nice to have that in the papers."

Daphne Batty took the vacuum cleaner into the dining room, humming a song Ursula had never heard before called "Tiptoe Through the Tulips."

The day Pauline went home was bright and sunny and there were already a lot of people on the beach by nine in the morning. They came down the private cliff path from the hotel and out of the public car park behind the ice-cream kiosk and the beach-supplies shop. Some came from the village across the dunes and some from the caravan site at Franaton. The surfers, in their wet suits, had been out since before Ursula and Pauline got up. Pauline, looking up from her breakfast, wanted to know why Gerald had chosen to live here, since his roots weren't in Devon. She had never asked that before. Ursula shook her head and said she supposed he liked it. Most people did.

"I'm sorry, Auntie Ursula, I keep forgetting it upsets you to talk about him. I know I'm always putting my foot in it. I shouldn't have said that about women working, either, not with Sarah and Hope having such good jobs. You'll be glad to see the back of me, I'm so tactless."

"No, I won't, my dear," said Ursula untruthfully. "You've been very kind to me. I shall miss you."

She gave Pauline a signed first edition of Orisons as a parting gift. The jacket with the drawing on it of a young woman on the steps of a Palladian temple was pristine. The book was probably worth three hundred pounds, and she hoped Pauline would real-ize this and not lend it to people or give it away, as she couldn't exactly tell her its value.

"Will I understand it?" Pauline asked doubtfully. "Uncle Gerald was so clever."

There was nowhere to park the car at the station in Barnstaple, so she got out for only a moment and kissed Pauline, and Pauline said anxiously that she hoped Ursula would be all right on her own. Ursula drove off quickly.

After driving around and around for about fifteen minutes, looking for a parking space, she finally found one. She walked into the town center and into the first hairdresser's she saw. It was twenty years since she

46

had been to a hairdresser. In the late seventies, she had started to grow her hair, for what reason, she could scarcely remember. It had been a low point in her life, one of the lowest. They had been at Lundy View House for seven or eight years and the girls were thirteen and eleven, something like that. She had wanted to become a different person, so she had set about losing the weight she had put on after Hope was born and began to grow her hair. Those were two ways in which you could change yourself without it costing you anything.

She lost fifteen pounds and her hair grew to the middle of her back, but she was still the same person, just thinner and with a plait that she twisted up on the back of her head. If Gerald or the children noticed, they never remarked on it. Her hair was mostly gray now. Salt-and-pepper, they called it. Silver threads among the gold, according to Daphne, who sang the appropriate song. It was wispy, with split ends, and rather alarming amounts came out when she brushed it. She asked the hairdresser to cut it all off, to cut it short, with a fringe.

When it was done, she had to agree with the hairdresser that it looked nice and that she looked a lot younger. At last, she looked different, having succeeded at what she had been unable to attain twenty years before. The hairdresser wanted to give her an ash-blond tint, but Ursula wouldn't have that.

She did her shopping and drove home with the car windows wide-open. Now her hair was short, she wouldn't have to worry about wind and rain and the plait falling down and pins scattering. Two or three hundred people must have been on the beach by two o'clock. It was warm but not hot, the sun by now being covered by a thin wrack of cloud. Even when the tide was as high as it could go, there was always enough beach, more than enough, for sunbathers and castle makers and shell collectors and ballplayers.

Ursula, out for her walk, threaded her way among the recumbent bodies and the picnickers and the children and the dogs and headed south. For some reason, nearly all the people stayed up at the north end of the beach, and after walking for two hundred yards, she was alone. She repeated to herself, as she had often done, the last line of Shelley's best-known, even hackneyed, verse.

" 'The lone and level sands stretch far away.' "

She had learned it at school, along with the other poems children did learn then (though not later, and certainly not now): Masefield's "Dirty British coaster" and that "Heraclitus" thing Hope had put in Gerald's death announcement and "The Lady of Shalott" and Horatius saying, "Draw down the bridge, Sir Consul, with all the speed ye may." "My name is Ozymandias, king of kings" was something else to remind her of Gerald, especially "the wrinkled lip, and sneer of cold command."

" 'Round the decay,' " she said aloud in the empty silence, " 'Of that colossal wreck, boundless and bare/ The lone and level sands stretch far away.' "

This afternoon, she walked rather farther than usual. It was good weather for walking. Her mother had been a great walker in those pretty Surrey hills, though not her father, that stout, breathless man who used a car like the disabled use a wheelchair. Her mother said that if he could have gotten a car inside the house, he would have driven from room to room in it. They were both long dead, had been oldish when she was born, their youngest child, their after-thought. It would be easy to blame them now, but it hadn't been their fault; it had been hers, all her own work. Looking back, she could barely understand that youthful folly.

To have been so unadventurous, so idle and accepting of idleness as a way of life, accepting of ignorance, blinkered, an ostrich girl, with her head not in sand but in trash. Ripe for Gerald Candless. Flattered, honored, surprised at such amazing good fortune. A lamb to the abattoir. Waiting for him like prey waits for the lion, watching it come closer, circle, and approach, but not escaping, not knowing escape was possible, still less desirable.

Ursula wheeled around on the beach, but counterclockwise this time, so that her return journey would be made close up against the dunes, the sandy valleys and the green rounded hassocks, the deep shadowy wells and the grassy hillocks.

There were always couples in those dunes, making love, at all hours of the day. If not exactly making love, doing all but. Locked in each other's arms, kissing, rolling this way and that. Not for the first time, Ursula wondered what it would be like, to be in love with someone who was in love with you and go into the dunes with him and lie kissing him and holding him for hours and hours. Not get bored or tired of it, but want it more than anything in the world.

She began to climb the path that led up to the hotel. It was shallower and longer than the path that went up to her house and the other houses on the cliff. In place of the ragwort and the mesembryanthemum that grew alongside her path, there were fuchsia hedges here and morning glory climbing the low stone walls. Ursula was very hot when she reached the top and she expected her face must be pink and shiny, but at least her hair was tidy. It was very comforting to think that she never again had to worry about her hair.

She would call herself Ursula Wick today, she decided. "My name is Ursula Wick," she would say. And perhaps she would revert to this maiden name of hers for the future and drop the Candless, which immediately stamped her as the famous writer's widow. She opened the gate and entered the hotel garden. The borders around the lawns were filled with hydrangea, bright blue alternating with bright pink. Ugly, Ursula thought, even worse up here than they look from the beach. Hydrangea worked like litmus paper, she had read somewhere. You could put alkaline stuff on them and the pink ones turned blue, or else it was the other way around and the blue ones turned pink. In chemistry at school, they had used litmus paper, but she couldn't remember which color was alkaline and which acid. It probably wasn't true about the hydrangea, anyway.

She walked around to the front of the hotel and a man in a brown uniform opened the doors for her. It was rather dark inside and very cool. Arrows up on the walls pointed to the indoor swimming pool, the table tennis, the shop, the hairdresser's, the bar. She and Pauline had had a drink in that bar, but they hadn't stayed for dinner. She wasn't sure where the dining room was. There were glass cases on the walls full of jewelry and ceramics and beachwear.

A young woman with long red hair stood behind the reception desk, checking something in a ledger against a computer screen. She looked up as Ursula approached, and she said, "Good afternoon, Mrs. Candless."

So much for introducing herself as Ursula Wick.

"We were all so sorry to hear about Mr. Candless," said the redheaded girl, then added very convention-ally, "You have our deepest sympathy in your very sad loss. I believe Mr. Schofield did write to you to express the sympathy of the staff?"

Ursula nodded, though she couldn't remember. Hundreds of letters had come.

"Now, how may I help you, Mrs. Candless?" said the girl in a very caring, earnest way.

"I want to know if you still need baby-sitters."

The girl pursed her lips. They were juicy red lips, like the inside of a cut strawberry. "We always need them, Mrs. Candless, and especially at this time of the year. Did you wish to recommend someone?"

"Yes," said Ursula. "Me."

It took some sorting out, as Ursula had known it

would if they knew who she was. She had to explain that, yes, she was serious, that she really would like to baby-sit for the children of hotel guests, say twice a week. She was fond of children. It would be a change; it would—and here, somewhat to her shame, she found herself obliged to use an excuse, the widow's excuse of wanting to get out of the former marital home in the evenings. This the redheaded girl understood. The manager, Mr. Schofield, arriving opportunely, also understood.

"Anything we can do to help you in your bereavement, Mrs. Candless," he said, as if he was doing her a favor instead of she him.

"Thank you for your letter, by the way," she said.

"My pleasure," said the manager, going rather red as he perhaps realized this wasn't quite the thing to say.

"Start on Thursday, then," the redheaded girl said, evidently adhering to the principle that the sooner therapy begins, the better. She put something down in her ledger. Ursula thanked them and wondered, as she made her way out to the road, what exchanges about her strange behavior had taken place between them as soon as she was out of earshot. Once back at Lundy View House, she went straight into the little room they called the morning room, where she had piled all the letters of condolence on the small round table.

The stamps on the envelopes told her that they had come from all over the world. It was a pity she didn't know some boy or girl who collected stamps, but perhaps she would meet one when she started her baby-sitting. After all, it wouldn't be babies, but children up to ten. Ursula fetched a large black plastic bag from a roll in the cupboard under the sink and a pair of scissors from the workbox, which had been her mother's, in the living room.

She cut all the stamps off the envelopes, finding it a soothing and indeed enjoyable task. There were stamps from the United States and Australia, Sweden and Poland, Malaysia and Gambia. Some of them were very beautiful, with birds or butterflies on them. When she had finished, she had accumulated sixty-seven foreign stamps. She put them into a new envelope and then she dropped all the letters, all of them unopened, into the black plastic bag. It was a relief to have decided not to answer any of them.

4

*When the guests had gone, Peter said, quoting
Goethe or someone, "They are pleasant enough
people, but if they had been books, I wouldn't have
read them."*
— THE FORSAKEN MERMAN

HOPE GOT TO THE RESTAURANT much too early. She hid
herself inside the Laura Ashley shop on the opposite
side of the street. It was a principle of hers never to
be early or on time for an engagement with a man
(except Fabian, who didn't count), but to be between
two and five minutes late. This was difficult for her,
as she was naturally a punctual person, but she persevered.

That morning, in the interval between an interview with a client who wanted her to extract sub-
stantial maintenance from the wife he was divorcing
and a client who wanted to set up a charitable trust,
largely, as far as she could gather, for the benefit of
his personal friends, Hope had been making plans for
her father's memorial service. The trouble was that
each time she thought of some particular poem or
song or piece of prose that he had loved, she started

crying. The man wanting the charitable trust stared at her tear-stained face and asked her if she had a cold.

Hope wasn't a literary person, but her father's favorite pieces—at least their titles—were committed to her memory, or, as she put it, written on her heart, and would be there forever. Herbert's "Jordan" and Tennyson's "Ulysses" and a bit of Sartre, she thought as she wandered among the racks of floral dresses. "Is there in truth no beauty?" she asked herself. "Is all good structure in a winding stair?" But she had to stop that in case she began weeping again. Before leaving her office, she had made up her face with care and didn't want it washing off before she met Robert Postle.

He would very likely be there by now. It was three minutes past one, and as far as she could remember from his visits to Lundy View House that coincided with hers, he was as punctual as she would never allow herself to be. In the restaurant, they told her he was already there, and she soon saw him, standing up by his table and waving to her.

Robert Postle had been her father's editor at Carlyon-Brent since some time after *Hamadryad* was short-listed for the Booker Prize. The retirement of his former editor was the ostensible reason for this change, but the short-listing was the real reason. That had been a long time ago and Robert was getting on a bit. To the teenage Candless girls, he had been a striking, even sexy, figure, and his marriage soon thereafter had brought Sarah half mock, half real distress. He had developed a paunch since then and a lot of his dark silky hair had fallen out, leaving strange springy tufts occurring above his ears and patches on the bald crown like wooded islands on a pale brown sea.

He was a Roman Catholic, a devout man, who had apparently adhered to the letter of the law, for he by now had many children. In order to attend Gerald Candless's funeral, he had asked permission of his parish priest to enter an Anglican church, though this was no longer regarded by Rome as necessary, and the priest had privately thought him a bit of a stickler. Hope thought he looked even deeper into middle age than he had two weeks before.

Being kissed by him wasn't the pleasure it had once been. It wasn't a very graceful operation either, as she never went anywhere in London without a hat, and today she was wearing a cartwheel of coral-colored linen. She kept it on because she knew it brought a becoming rosy flush to her face.

"What did you think of that piece in the *Mail*?" asked Robert.

"Not a lot."

"I can't imagine you talking about your 'partner.'"

"No, well, my partners are three other people at Ruskin de Gruchy. What I said was my 'feller,' but they changed it. I really mind that stuff about my hand-kerchief. Of course I use handkerchiefs—tissues are so disgusting; they're so wet—but I haven't got an *H* on them. That was pure invention. Do you think I could have a drink? They do liter carafes of white wine here, and that's what I need after the dreadful morning I've had."

They also do half liters, Robert thought, which might be enough to be going on with, but he didn't say so. He had a proposition to put to Hope and he knew precisely the words he intended to use, but he delayed while she swilled down Orvieto, studied the menu, and whined about newspapers, journalists, and the media in general. She looked uncannily like her father, and that pink hat colored her normally white skin to the plum shade his had become in recent years. It was still hard for him to accept that Gerald was dead, as it is always hard to come to terms with the death of someone in whom the vital force has been particularly present.

"I expect you're aware," he said when Hope's risotto had arrived, "of the recent popularity of a certain kind of biography. I mean a child's memoir of a parent, usually, although not invariably, a father."

She looked up at him from under that hat brim. "A child?"

He didn't know how she had managed to get to Cambridge, still less achieve a first. Of course, a lot of it was affectation. She was the kind of woman who thought it amusing to have people put her down as a fool and to then surprise them, either with some profound remark or a passing comment on her achievements.

"A child in the sense of offspring, progeny, issue, heir, scion," he said.

"Oh, yeah, I see."

"But have you come across that sort of book?"

"I don't know," Hope said.

"Usually, it's the parent who's famous, not the child, though both may be. I can think of one or two where neither was famous, but the parent's life was so interesting and the writing style so absorbing that the memoir was still a success in spite of it."

"I don't have time to read," said Hope, wiping her plate with a piece of bread, as if she hadn't had a good meal for a week. Her eyes, bright now with repletion and alcohol, fixed on his face. They were Gerald's eyes, the rich dark brown of polished leather, the eyelashes thick as brushes. "I haven't read any books but Daddy's for years."

That might be no bad thing, he thought, a freshness of approach, a mind uncluttered by the magnificences of recent daddy biographies.

"All right, you don't read," he said as his fish and her veal came, "but would you write?"

She was staring at the carafe like a pet cat in front of an empty plate. He tapped it and said to the waiter that they'd better have another one of those.

˗ "Would you write a memoir of your father?"

"Me?" said Hope.

No, the wine waiter, he thought. That chap with the glasses at the next table. "Your relationship with him, how it was when you were a small child, what it was like being his daughter. Oh, and his origins, his background, his family, what he came out of. The stories he told you, the games he played with you."

To his horror, tears welled up in those eyes that were Gerald's eyes. She must be half-blinded, he thought. "Hope, my dear, I'm sorry, I didn't mean to upset you."

A couple of tears escaped and trickled down. She dabbed at them with a handkerchief. So it was true—she really did use handkerchiefs. She crumpled it up in her hand before he could see if there was an *H* on it or not. Facilitating her recovery with a big slice of veal, she said with her mouth full, "I couldn't write anything. I haven't any imagination."

This would be facts, not imagination. Well, *some* imagination, some emotion, surely. But he knew it was hopeless. The waiter refilled her glass. She swigged it as if parched, and Robert was incongruously reminded of that episode in *King Solomon's Mines* when Sir Henry Curtis and Captain Good crawl across the last lap of the desert sands to suck up muddy water out of an oasis pool.

She surprised him by asking, "Is this something Carlyon-Brent want to commission?" But after all, she was a lawyer.

He said cautiously, "I don't know about commission. If it was done the way we hope it would be, we'd want to publish it."

"Not if I did it, you wouldn't," she said. "I'll have the zabaglione—no, I won't. I'll have the tiramisù and some Strega, no coffee, and then I must fly; I've got a very full afternoon. Why don't you ask my sister?"

"It did occur to me, but she's always so busy."

"Thanks very much," said Hope. "I'm a lady of

leisure, I suppose. I'll ask her if you like; it'll probably appeal to her." He wondered how she kept so thin, how she did her work. Both Gerald's girls drank so much. Hope must have consumed over a liter of wine. "She doesn't get as upset about Daddy as I do," she said.

Robert watched her go, straight as a reed and as unsteady. He thought of bereaved children's memoirs and of titles. *Mommie Dearest* at one end of the quality scale and *When Did You Last See Your Father?* at the other. Classics like *A Voyage Round My Father.* Then there was that Germaine Greer book he had admired, with all the detective work in it. That brought him to the letter to the *Times* about Gerald never having worked for the *Walthamstow Herald.* Probably nonsense, but on the other hand, he, Robert, had never really believed Gerald had been at Trinity. Not that he would ever have said a word, to Gerald or anyone else, but he had had a feeling about it, a sense of something not being quite right.

He paid the bill and, a taxi-hater, he began to walk back to Bloomsbury.

5

Psycho may mean no more than pertaining to the
soul, but words that have it as their prefix are
frightening because of their associations with
violence and madness: psychopath, psychotic. *The
Psychopomp who takes the soul to the underworld
is easily imagined as gray and lumbering, but not
thin, not wraithlike. The Psychopomp is fat.*

—ORISONS

SARAH TOLD URSULA that she should have had her hair
cut years ago, but better late than never. Looking
over her shoulder into the mirror, she said that she
could see what people meant when they remarked on
her likeness to her mother, something she didn't
mind admitting now Ursula looked so much more
attractive. It was the first time she had been in the
house since the funeral, and she trod warily, casting
uneasy glances.

Hope cried, but not for long, and she had the
grace to say she knew she was stupid and that her
father would have hated it.

"That was the only thing about you Dad didn't
like," said Sarah, "the way you're always crying."

61

"I'm not always crying. I don't cry when I'm happy."

It would have been too much to expect them not to go out on Saturday evenings, and Ursula didn't expect it. Hope went to a party in Ilfracombe and another one in Westward Ho! and Sarah went drinking in Barnstaple. The Saturday they both came and both went out by six, Ursula was baby-sitting anyway. She had to be at the hotel and inside room 214 by seven sharp. It was a suite really, consisting of the parents' bedroom, the children's bedroom, and a bathroom in between. The windows had no sea view but gave on to the formal gardens at the front and the Ilfracombe to Franaton Road.

The parents were a Mr. Hester and a Ms. Thompson. Ursula didn't know if they were married or just living together. This was the third time she had sat for them since they had arrived ten days before, but they never said much to her, being anxious to escape downstairs to the bar and dinner and the postdinner country-and-western evening in the Lundy Lounge. The children were always in bed when she got there, with the television on in their room. There was a girl of six and a boy of four.

The first time she came, she offered to read to them, a suggestion greeted by Ms. Thompson with an incredulous stare. They had the telly. They had a stock of children's videos from the hotel's boundless store. And, of course, there was another telly in the main bedroom. Ursula sometimes wondered how many television sets there were in the Dunes. Hundreds. It was a daunting thought.

She had brought a book with her, but before settling down to read it, she went into the children's bedroom to say hello. The little girl smiled, but the boy gave her an indifferent stare. On the dazzling screen, Power Rangers struck attitudes and flashed swords. The little boy clutched a small yellow model of a Power Ranger in his left hand. The second time she came, tiptoeing in to check on the children, Ursula had eased the little figure out of the sleeping boy's grasp lest it dig into his soft cheek in the night. But he awoke screaming, fumbling and groping for it, so she was obliged to restore it to him.

For a while, she stood by the window in the main bedroom, watching the cars full of holidaymakers pass by. The evening was warm and sunny, but it had rained all afternoon and the hedgerows glittered with water drops. The grass was very green, the garden-center annuals in the flower beds bright as paint. She asked herself, not for the first time, why she was doing this, minding other people's children for a pittance, and she didn't really know the answer. It got her out of the house in the evenings—that was true. It removed her from those things that reminded her of him, so much of it everywhere, cluttering the place, his books, his manuscripts, his galley proofs and proof copies, his papers.

And to get out in the evenings, where else could she have gone? Perhaps to see the neighbors, all of whom had invited her, and who would have talked of him, questioned her, and required answers. There were cinemas still, a few, but she was wary of going to them alone. Obviously not to the pub or a bar. Baby-sitting gave her quiet evenings in neutral surroundings. She surveyed the room critically. There was nothing here to remind anyone of anything, unless some people's memories could be stirred by wall-to-wall beige carpet, chintz-covered armchairs, a pink-and-beige-checked bedspread, and two pictures, both abstracts in pink, blue, and gold.

No books, no papers, not even a magazine. She tried to read her own book. That was all right; that was her choice, Trollope's *Is He Popenjoy?* And she wanted to read it, but tonight, even the basic powers of concentration called for had deserted her. Would it be a melodramatic gesture to clear the house of everything that had been Gerald's? She had to think of the girls and their feelings. And then what was she to do with all that stuff? Only that morning, she had received a letter from an American university asking almost reverentially to be the guardian of his manuscripts.

"Not Daddy's manuscripts!" Hope had said, as if Ursula had proposed to desecrate his grave. "Oh, you can't. You mustn't."

"At least make them pay for them," said Sarah. "Though in my experience, that would be like trying to get blood out of a stone."

The university's keeper of collections boasted that

they had the world's finest accumulation of manuscripts by contemporary writers. Already they possessed three of Gerald Candless's, three treasured
manuscripts with the author's corrections, and it was
the keeper's dream to acquire more. Ursula realized
that she couldn't keep on cutting foreign stamps off
envelopes and throwing the contents away. Some
would have to be read and answered. So she had
crept—a Trollopian word for women's gait, but true
and appropriate here—into Gerald's study and opened
the cupboard where his manuscripts were kept.

But first, she had paused just inside the door and
looked almost fearfully about the room. It reeked of
him. He was powerfully and dreadfully present still, a
personality left behind when the body had been
removed, a fetch, an earthbound spirit. What was that
word he had once used in those scrawled, slowly to
be deciphered pages she had carefully typed? She
had had to look it up, first in *Chambers,* which didn't
have it, then in the *Shorter Oxford,* which did. Psychopomp. The messenger who escorts to the underworld the souls of the dead. Standing there in his
study, she felt that the psychopomp hadn't yet come
for him, had been deterred, perhaps, by his restless
energy, his hard, dark gaze, the ambience of him that
remained oppressively sexual even in age, even in
celibacy.

Ursula shivered. He used to say that novelists who
wrote that were writing rubbish, because no one had
ever shivered at some shock or unpleasant discovery.

But she had and would, she thought, all the time she was in here. It was a place from which to remove certain essential artifacts, those manuscripts, some notebooks, all the first editions, and then lock the door and throw away the key. She imagined locking the door and then having a builder in to take away the door frame and then plaster over the door and paper over the plaster so that the study behind became a secret room, sealed up and perhaps one day forgotten. She could also imagine what the girls would say to that.

In a sense, one's children never grow up. Their parents' home is always their home, to keep as a sentimental sanctuary in the heart, to return to at will, their first refuge, no matter what homes of their own they may have. Sarah and Hope would consider it their primary business to tell her how to manage and arrange and decide the future of Lundy View House. The study to them was a sanctum, a place Hope could easily turn into a shrine.

Eventually, she had opened that cupboard door and looked inside. But there were more manuscripts than she remembered, Gerald's own handwritten originals as well as copies of her copies, and there were attempts at novels that had never been finished, some of which contained only a chapter or two. He had tended to that—to start something and grow tired of it or be unable to make it work. And then he had been angry and bad-tempered until a better idea came. She hadn't reproached him, not then, but still he had said to her, "It is my life. Can't you understand that? All the life I have or ever will have. All the life I might have had has gone into it."

She didn't know what he meant. Hadn't he had success and adulation, money enough, herself and his daughters, this house?

"I pour out my life into it," he said. "I do it to save my life. And when it fails, it's death. I die. And then I have to be resurrected. But how many times can you die before the last time? Can you tell me that?"

"It" was always how he referred to his writing. The primal, the sole "it."

In there, in among the manuscripts that had become published books, would be a dozen of those "deaths." She had turned her gaze on his desk then and noticed something. The page proofs that he had been correcting the day he died still lay there to the left of the typewriter, but the pile of manuscript on the right-hand side was gone. Hope knew nothing about it—she said she couldn't bear to go in there—and Sarah didn't seem to know what Ursula was talking about. Daphne Batty, usually so reasonable, would nevertheless have taken any inquiry as an accusation of stealing, as if she could have found a use for a hundred sheets of indecipherable typescript.

Ursula, in the hotel bedroom, put the manuscript out of her mind and read the first chapter of her Trollope. She had read it before, but she didn't mind. At nine, she went softly into the children's room. They were fast asleep, the Power Ranger in the little boy's hand held up against his mouth. Ursula turned off the television set and went back into the main bedroom to pass the time in reading and pondering until Mr. Hester and Ms. Thompson returned at 10:30.

The idea was strangely unacceptable, one of those propositions that on the face of it cannot hurt or harm or even embarrass but yet are deeply unsettling.

"Robert Postle wants you to write a memoir of your father?"

"He asked Hope first," said Sarah. "I can't think why. It couldn't be you, because it has to be a child writing about a famous parent."

At least her daughters didn't ask her if it upset her to talk about Gerald. Ursula felt glad Robert Postle's invitation hadn't been put to her, because she might have been rude or said something she later would have regretted.

"Are you going to do it?"

"I've said I would. It might be just the thing for me."

Ursula thought she understood what that meant. Though almost thirty-two and teaching at the University of London for seven years, Sarah had published only one book, and that was her doctoral dissertation. A memoir of her father would hardly qualify as a learned work or enhance her academic reputation, but it might be better than that—it might bring her before the public; it might make her a name. It might, if well enough done, be a best-seller. Sarah began outlining the current fashion in biographies of parents and citing famous examples, but Ursula already knew what she meant. All she hoped was that it wouldn't much involve her.

"I'm going to make a start next week, so that I'll have nearly two months before term begins."

"Start the writing, do you mean?"

"There'll be some research to do first."

Ursula wished her daughters would sometimes call her Mother or Mum, or even by her Christian name—she wouldn't have minded that. Sarah occasionally did call her Ma, but Hope never called her anything and hadn't since she was about twelve, when Gerald said "Mummy" was babyish and some other style should be found. None, of course, ever had been, though Sarah had found a compromise, if not one that was much to Ursula's taste. Still, she was disproportionately and humiliatingly pleased to hear it, which she did perhaps once during each of Sarah's visits.

"There'll be research into Dad's background and family, and I'll have to see what ancestors I can trace. I don't know much about his parents, our grandparents, only that he was called George and she was called Kathleen and they lived in Ipswich. And he was a printer and she was a nurse. That was in the *Times* obituary."

"It's also on his birth certificate," said Ursula.

"Right. I'd better see that, then. They were dead long before we were born, of course."

"Before we were married," said Ursula.

"He used to talk about his childhood to us when

we were children. Did you know that? Fantastic stories of when he was a little boy, but a lot of them were literally fantasies; I think we always knew that. I mean, the boy could fly or swim for miles underwater, and in one, his mother was a mermaid."

"And the chimney sweep one," said Ursula.

"Yes, of course. That was our favorite." Sarah sighed. "He was an only child, so no nephews or nieces, but did he have any cousins? He must have done. George and Kathleen would have had brothers and sisters. Candless isn't a common name. If there are any in the Ipswich phone book, they're very likely to be relatives. But you'd know—did he talk about aunts or uncles?"

"Not that I remember."

Sarah said earnestly, "Will you try to remember? Will you think about it? I'll need all that, how you and Dad first met—didn't he come and speak to some association you belonged to? I'll have to talk to you, so will you think about it, Ma, before I come down next time?"

As if she didn't already think about it, dwell on it far more often than she really wanted to, recriminate, regret.

"Did you have a happy childhood?" she found herself asking Daphne Batty almost before she knew she was asking it.

"Of course I did. The best years of your life, they are." Daphne burst into song. " 'Back home in Tennessee, just try and picture me, upon my mammy's knee—' " She broke off, then sighed. "There's a lot of truth in those old songs. Not that it was Tennessee, wherever that may be. It was Weston-super-Mare."

"I expect Weston sounds pretty exotic if you were born in Memphis," said Ursula. "Or Purley, come to that."

Purley. A nice place, comfortable, pretty, safe, with a view of green hills. Why did people always knock suburbs? Why had Gerald? She had been born there, the youngest child of her parents, her brother, Ian, was twelve years her senior and her sister, Helen, ten. Though an afterthought or perhaps an accident, she was loved and cherished by her parents, spoiled by them and protected. Herbert Wick was a builder who had made money in the postwar building boom and who, though not rich, was very comfortably off by the time Ursula was fifteen. It was then that Herbert and his wife moved from their semidetached house at the Croydon end of Purley to a big ranch-style chalet bungalow at the Coulsdon end.

Ursula went to Purley County High School, where she secured eight O levels and two years later three A levels of B, B, and C. The head teacher wanted her to apply to various universities, but Ursula herself wasn't keen; she was apprehensive about going away from home, and, as her father pointed out, what good had two years at the polytechnic done Helen, who had married as soon as she finished her studies? A typing and shorthand course would be more valuable, and when she had completed it, she could go to work at H. P. Wick and Company, which operated from a pretty little custom-built cottage-type office in Purley High Street.

Ursula hadn't much enjoyed the typing course, but it was soon over, and working for her father was about as pleasant as she imagined any job could be. He drove her to Wick's in the mornings and back home for lunch, and twice a week she didn't have to go back in the afternoons because there wasn't enough to do to fill five full days. She and her mother went for long walks.

There was still plenty of beautiful open country around Purley, though Herbert Wick was doing his best to build on it, and sometimes they walked as far as Fairdean Downs or Kenley Common. Once a fortnight, Betty Wick liked to go shopping in "town"— that is, the West End of London—and in order that she might accompany her mother, Herbert would unfailingly give her the whole day off. They would take the train from Purley to London Bridge or Waterloo.

Both of them patronized the public library, and Betty was secretary of the Purley Library Users' Association. Ursula had always been a great reader, and by then she was reading five or six books a week—all fiction. Looking back now, across nearly forty years, she realized that she hadn't known there were any other kinds of books. Well, there were textbooks, of course, and scientific books, and the library had shelves marked BIOGRAPHY and POETRY and DRAMA, but she was blind to them; she walked past them without looking.

She read detective stories and romances and ripping yarns and a great many historical novels. That was how they came to invite Colin Wrightson to speak at the Library Users' Association's annual meeting, because she and her mother had such a passion for his books about Queen Victoria and Victorian London and the empress Eugénie and ladies and gentlemen falling in love in English country houses.

It was a very comfortable, very quiet, unadventurous life. Every other Saturday, Herbert and Betty Wick and Ursula drove over to Sydenham for tea with Ian and his new wife, Jean, in the little new house (built by Herbert, who also provided the deposit on it) that they were buying on a mortgage from the bank where Ian worked. After that, they often went to the cinema. Ursula and Betty went to the cinema without Herbert once a week as well, invariably to an afternoon performance so as to be home to cook Herbert's dinner. Sometimes Ursula went to Wimbledon to see Helen, and occasionally she stayed the night. Helen had a little boy named Jeremy and was pregnant again. So sheltered a life had Ursula led that this staying overnight at Helen's, traveling there on her own with her suitcase, walking up from the station and ringing Helen's doorbell at the appointed time, was a daring activity that made her feel quite sophisticated.

Once a year, the Wicks and Ursula went away on holiday together. Almost always the Isle of Wight, though not invariably the same place on the Isle of Wight. Once they went to the south of France, but they didn't much like it, and the following year they returned to Ventnor. At Christmas, Ian and Jean came and Helen and Peter with Jeremy and later on with the new baby, Pauline. Helen asked Ursula to be godmother to Pauline, and Ursula was very thrilled and flattered to say yes.

Few people, Ursula thought, could have changed as much in nearly four decades as she had. Their appearance, yes, that went without saying. Helen, for instance, though Ursula would never have said it aloud, looked so different at sixty-seven from what she had at thirty that the two versions of her, the young and the old, might be women quite unrelated to each other. They might almost be from different races—their weights, their heights, their coloring, the cast of their countenances, utterly disparate. No doubt—though not in respect to the weight and the height—the same was true of her. It wasn't the physical aspect of the matter that she meant.

She had been quiet, gentle, profoundly ignorant, deeply innocent, self-satisfied, complacent, affectionate, easily amused, quickly delighted, and possessing a kind of shy exuberance. And she had been an ostrich with a buried head. She had been ambitious for nothing. She had known nothing. In fact, it had been dangerous to let her out alone. Now all her ignorance was gone, her innocence brutalized, her complacency dead, her affections crushed, her ability to be delighted vanished, and her exuberance replaced by a defensive, faintly ironical self-control. Yes, she had changed beyond all knowing.

She had been a pretty girl. That was the word. No

one would have called her beautiful or handsome. She had a kitten face with small neat features, blue-gray eyes, fair hair, which she wore short and permed. Her figure was good and she had what her mother called a fine bust. Because her father paid her well— ridiculously well, she later discovered—and those shopping trips were so frequently made, she possessed a lot of clothes. Nothing fancy or daring or especially fashionable, but accordion-pleated skirts in pastel pink or lemon with matching sweaters, several tweed suits, a few tight-waisted full-skirted cocktail dresses for use at the Isle of Wight, and innumerable pairs of shoes. She had never had a boyfriend.

Once or twice, a man had taken her out. There was the one she had met at a dance in Ventnor. He took her to the cinema the next day, but they had no further contact after the Wicks went home. Someone who worked in Peter's office had been invited to dinner by Helen specifically to meet Helen's sister, and he had been keen enough. They, too, went to the cinema and for a drive in his car, but Ursula hadn't liked it when he kissed her, and the next time he phoned, she told her mother to say she had gone away. She met so few men, and the ones she did meet failed to match up to her secret romantic ideal.

At school, for O-level English, she had read Charlotte Brontë's *Shirley,* an experience that put her off Victorian fiction for years. She read *Jane Eyre* only because they had a copy in the house—she was in bed with a cold, and there was nothing else to read. Until she read it, her heroine, the woman she wanted to be like and whose husband she wanted to marry, had been the narrator in Daphne du Maurier's *Rebecca*. But *Jane Eyre* was to be preferred. She understood, as she finished the book, that she was on the lookout for a Mr. Rochester of her own.

Two evenings before the writer Colin Wrightson was due to come and give his talk at the library, his wife phoned Betty Wick and said he had broken his ankle. It was January and very cold and her husband had slipped on a patch of ice while walking down the garden path to replenish the nuts in a bird feeder. She went into considerable detail about how he never did this, because she always fed the birds, but for some reason, goodness knows what, he had gone out with his bag of nuts and slipped and broken his ankle in two places.

Over the years, when Ursula reflected on her life, she often thought about that icy patch on the garden path and the impulse to feed birds in a man who never fed birds. Suppose he had hesitated, then decided to wait till his wife came home, done something else, forgotten the bird feeder. Suppose the phone had rung just as he was going out there. Or suppose he had simply been a little more careful, avoided the ice, stepped onto the grass and walked around it. Her whole life would have been different. Her whole life had hung on whether or not a man walked down a garden path and slipped on ice. If he hadn't slipped, she would have married someone else, lived in different places, had different children, perhaps even been happy. It was a dreadful thought.

Mrs. Wrightson—her name was Sally, but Ursula didn't know that then—was deeply apologetic on the phone, contrite. Colin felt so guilty about the Purley Library Users' Association, the last thing he wanted was to let them down, so he had asked a writer he knew, a friend, to go in his place—Gerald Candless. No doubt Mrs. Wick was as closely acquainted with the work of Gerald Candless as with that of her husband. Mrs. Wick was not. But her daughter, whose eye she caught, was nodding, so she said, "Oh yes, that would be marvelous. Thank you so much," and she said she hoped Mr. Wrightson would soon be better.

"Have you ever read anything of his?" Betty Wick asked when she had put the phone down. "I'm sure I haven't. I've just about heard of him."

Ursula was already wondering why she had nodded, why she had urged her mother, by that nod, to accept the offer. "I've read *The Centre of Attraction*," she said.

It had shocked her, though she wasn't going to tell her mother that. It had made her feel uncomfortable and somehow dissatisfied. The sexual content was not so much responsible for this, though it was partly responsible, as were certain assumptions the writer seemed to be making—that people were free, for instance, to make love with whom they chose and to stay up all night if they liked, that they wanted to lead full and adventurous lives, that young soldiers had animal passions, and that families were hotbeds of anguish. She had had to tell herself once or twice that life wasn't like this; life was what she had. Real people didn't speak in sexual innuendo, use bad language, or have conversations about passion and death. But the novel made her uneasy, and when she had finished it, she had taken no more Gerald Candless novels out of the library.

Now, though, she thought she had better. She borrowed two more—there were only three more—and sat up late reading them. The effect on her was much the same as *The Centre of Attraction*'s had been. They left her uncomfortable, dissatisfied, and something else as well this time. Was it possible that she was passing her life foolishly, even wasting her life? Was it even possible that this fiction was *reality*? It felt like it. It convinced her of a kind of truth more than the thrillers and the romances did. His books made her feel that she was outside somewhere, looking in at real people doing real things. What kind of a man could make a reader feel like that?

She and her parents and one of the Purley branch librarians had intended to take Colin Wrightson out to dinner after the event. A small French restaurant had been chosen and Herbert and Betty Wick had been there the previous week to try it out. Now their guest at L'Ecu Rouge would be Gerald Candless. Ursula had given careful thought to what she should wear. Not one of the taffeta dresses—that would be overdoing it—and a suit would look as if she meant to travel somewhere. She finally settled for a powder blue pleated skirt with a powder blue sweater worn over a blue-and-white-striped silk blouse. Heavy makeup was fashionable, but she had seldom worn as much as some girls, largely because her father made jocular remarks if she did, asking her if she had been at the raspberry jam again or kissing a fire engine.

There was a photograph of Gerald Candless on the flap of the back jacket. The face was half-turned and in partial shadow, the curly dark hair low over his forehead, but from what she could see of him, she thought he looked arrogant, clever, opinionated, frightening, and as if he had to shave a lot. She wouldn't be able to talk to a man who looked like that, still less to a man who had written those things, because everything she said would sound silly. She would speak as little as possible and he would hardly notice she was there.

He was late. Not very late, no more than five minutes after the scheduled time for the start of his talk, but the librarian and the committee ladies were going mad. Ursula sat in the middle of the front row of seats, where they had told her she must sit, her hands folded in her lap, her legs crossed at the ankles. She was wearing navy blue suede pumps. Calm, resigned, unmoving as she waited, she had begun to hope— wickedly, for what about the librarian and her mother and the committee?—that he wouldn't come at all.

Then he came. He had come by car and gotten lost. She had expected him to be wearing a suit, but he sauntered up to the platform in an old pepper-colored sports jacket, a Fair Isle pullover, and ginger corduroy pants. His hair was long, and long hair for men hadn't yet come into style, but his was as long as a woman's, a thick bush of wiry dark curls.

She recognized her Mr. Rochester. Not Charlotte Brontë's hero, but Orson Welles in the film. His face wasn't as full as Welles's and his mouth wasn't bud-like—it was wide and curving—but he was her Mr. Rochester, and it terrified her. Another girl, another sort of girl, might have set out from that moment to get him, to attract him, fascinate him, tempt him. Ursula wouldn't have known how to begin. Besides, she was frightened. She would never dare speak a word to him.

He talked. About how he wrote and what impelled him to write and what he wanted to write one day. She didn't take much of it in. Because it was the theme of one of his novels, he talked about Freud's seduction theory and raised a gasp from his audience. But later on, she could remember hardly anything of what he had said. Afterward, at question time, the Purley librarian passed a note to her on which she had written that Ursula should ask a question. Ursula turned around and shook her head vehemently. She would rather die. One woman asked him if he wrote by hand or used a typewriter, and another woman—the audience was mostly women—asked him what advice he would give aspiring writers.

"Don't," he said.

More gasps and some laughter, but Ursula could tell they hadn't liked that laconic answer. She looked up at him, expecting him to say more, and found that he was looking at her. His eyes met hers and something very strange happened. He winked. It was a tiny wink, more of a tic really. She knew she must have been mistaken, but still she blushed, a deep fiery blush that made her want to bury her face in her cold hands, but she couldn't, not there. I will never dare say a word to him, she thought as the heat subsided from her cheeks. I wish I didn't have to go to dinner. I wish I could go home and go to bed with a nice book, *The Constant Nymph* or *Frenchman's Creek.*

In the restaurant, she was seated as far from him as it is possible to be when six people are sitting at a round table. But she was still opposite him. He drank a lot; he didn't eat much. The librarian looked dismayed when he asked if they could have another bottle of the red, but her father made reassuring faces, and Ursula knew that meant he would pay for it.

Her mother and the librarian persisted in talking to him about his work, though they should have been able to see, as she could, that he disliked discussing it. The less she said—and she uttered only essentials concerned with what she was going to eat and to pass the water, please—the more he began to pay attention to her. Mostly, at first, with smiles and requests as to what he could pass her, but then, when he had dismissed a particularly fatuous question (Ursula thought) about where he got his ideas, he asked her quite abruptly, turning his back on the librarian, where she came from and what she did.

Ursula would have been glad if the ceiling had

fallen in at that moment, engulfing them all, or if the proprietor had come in to say there was a bomb in the building and they must evacuate it in five minutes. Only there were no bombs in those days and nothing to make the ceiling fall. She had decided desperately that it didn't matter what he thought of her, because she would never see him again, so she said very quietly that she lived in Purley with her parents and worked in her father's office.

"And you're engaged to be married."

She shook her head, the blush returning.

"I'm sorry. I thought you must be."

She didn't ask why he thought that. Her father supplied an answer.

"Too pretty to be unattached, eh?"

Gerald Candless said coolly, "Something like that."

But then she thought he looked at her almost tenderly. It was hindsight that told her he was weighing her up, considering; she hadn't thought it back then. She doubted if she had ever seen that tender look on his face again. Because there was no need for it once he had decided not to spare her? The slaughterer strokes the calf only while he fattens it. There is no honey for the bear once captured.

Normally a good sleeper, she hardly slept that night. She kept thinking of her father saying she was pretty. It made her squirm. In her narrow bed with the rose-sprigged white curtains draped from a gold coronet, she wriggled with embarrassment. The room seemed silly now, the white carpet, the Cicely Mary Barker pictures, the looped net curtains. Perhaps he would put her in one of his books, a silly girl, a contrast to the intrepid heroine.

Next day, he phoned. He had phoned her mother first and asked if it would be all right to speak to Ursula, and her mother had passed on the number of Wick and Co.

"I told your mother I wanted to thank you for last night."

"It wasn't me," she whispered, almost voiceless. "It was them."

"Oh, no, it was you."

She had nothing to say. Her heart beat heavily.

"I'd like to . . . return the compliment. Isn't that what people say?"

She said truthfully, "I don't know." She knew nothing.

"I'd like you to have dinner with me."

Modern English is peculiar, though not unique, in that it has one form for both the singular and the plural of the second person. French or German would have been quite clear. The obsolete *thou* would have been clear. But this was 1962.

"Did you give my mother a date?" she asked. "I'm sure my parents would be free most evenings, and of course I am."

He laughed. "I meant you. You alone. You and me."

"Oh."

"Will you have dinner with me, Ursula?"

"I don't know," she said. She was almost stammering. "I mean, yes, of course. Of course I will. Thank you."

"Good. When would you like it to be? You say."

All her evenings were free or else occupied by events, by movable feasts, that could without trouble be changed. "Friday," she said. "Saturday. I don't mind."

"Your name means 'little bear'—did you know that?"

She hadn't then. She uttered a small, tremulous "No."

"I will call for you at your parents' house in my car at seven on Saturday evening, Ursula."

She didn't know what to say. Perhaps to thank him? Before she could say anything, he had rung off.

Honey for the Little Bear.

6

Our children when young are a part of ourselves,
but when they grow up, they are just other people.
—A PAPER LANDSCAPE

ONLY ONE CANDLESS was to be found. Sarah examined the Ipswich telephone directory in her local public library. J. G. Candless, in Christchurch Street. She noted down the address and the phone number. She was growing excited about her book, much more excited than she had expected to be. She had already written bits of it, although she had an idea that it ought not to be done this way, piecemeal, odd stories about her father and memories that she particularly liked jotted down, but methodically, research first, then time set aside for the serious writing. Now was the time to start the research. That was why she had been to the library and found a relative. A possible relative, she corrected herself. She was too much of an academic to make assumptions.

But she was excited. Enough to want to devote hours and hours to it. When a man named Adam Foley, whom she had met in the Barnstaple pub, phoned and asked her out, she said no, because she had to start on the research for the book. The sound of his voice excited her, but, perversely, she said no to him and said it absently. After that, his voice also turned cold and he was barely polite when he said good-bye. She had shrugged, had no regrets. She had to phone this man called J. G. Candless in Ipswich. On her way home, she bought a town map of Ipswich in a book-shop. She meant to be thorough about this. Anyway, she was bound to have to go there. She might even go this week.

Sarah's flat was on the top floor of a Victorian house, a big attic with skylights, and to get to it you had to climb forty-eight stairs. Sarah didn't mind this and usually ran up them, or ran up thirty of them. Her own front door was painted deep purple. The rooms were large, if few, a living room converted from three attics for the servants' use, a slightly smaller bed-room, a kitchen, purple like the door, and a bath-room. From the big new windows (put in and paid for by darling Dad), you could see all the way across to Primrose Hill, a green hill and green trees and rows of gray-and-brown houses and white-and-yellow tow-ers fingering the blue sky. At night, it was black and yellow and glittery.

Sarah had a look in the mirror, checking on whether she liked her new hair color, done in St. John's Wood that morning. Perhaps it was rather too red. On the other hand, it made her look less like her mother. Like most people—not like Hope, though— she was dissatisfied with the way she looked and would have preferred to resemble some dark beauty such as Stella Tennant or Demi Moore. Small neat features looked prissy. Her mouth was too rosebud-like, her nose too short and straight, her eyes too gray. She was seriously considering going in for brown contacts.

Because she thought her small neat features dull and prissy, a milkmaid's looks, Sarah sought to dress herself with contrasting wildness and drama. So she always wore high heels, sometimes thick high heels attached to clumping shoes or boots, and a lot of black, with fringes and red beads. Her hair was her crowning glory, so she never covered it with a hat as Hope did, though sometimes she wore a large tortoiseshell clip, whose teeth held up a spike of hair at right angles to the rest.

Sarah opened windows and kicked off her boots. She poured herself a big glass of chardonnay. The bottle had been standing in the sun and was at a temperature she liked. She hated ice. She opened the map and spread it out on the table. Districts of Ipswich had some very strange names. Gainsborough and Halifax and—could it be?—California. How could a grid of streets in an East Anglian town be called California? Perhaps her father had actually come from there.

She referred to his birth certificate. No. He had been born in Waterloo Road, which was in an area that didn't seem to have any specific name. Sarah had a large new loose-leaf notebook and this she opened and wrote on the first page, as if with the aim of making it part of a genealogical table: "George John

Candless, b. 1890; m. Kathleen Mitchell, b. 1893." She drew a vertical line underneath and at the tip of it wrote, "Gerald Francis Candless, b. 1926."

Christchurch Street, where the only Candless lived, was not far from the center of the town and near a large park. She looked again at his initials, J.G. John George? No assumptions, she reminded herself, and took a swig of her wine. Her father had had no siblings, so he couldn't be her first cousin. The son therefore (probably) of a brother of George John's. Would that make him a second cousin or a first cousin once removed? That was something she would have to check on.

When they were teenagers, she and Hope, their grandmother Wick had tried to interest them in their ancestry. On her visits to Lundy View House, she brought with her ancient albums of sepia photographs and rather less ancient ones of black-and-white photographs, and her granddaughters were supposed to look at them and ask who this was and that was. And absorb and remember names of great-grandparents and, to a lesser extent, great-aunts and great-uncles. But they had been inclined to regard this as a dreadful bore and—since they were already hardworking and ambitious—of no possible use to them in their future lives and careers.

They might have shown more interest if their father had encouraged them, but he at once took the same attitude as they did. Sarah could still clearly remember his words.

"It's not as if you came of some noble lineage.

Your father is first-generation working class and your mother second at best. Before that, your forebears, like most people's, were just a rabble of servants and farm laborers and factory hands. What possible point can there be in knowing who they were and putting names to their ugly faces?"

They had been ugly, Sarah thought, dimly remembering pudding-visaged women with hair like loaves and corseted bodies and glaring men whose mouths and cheeks were invisible under drooping mustaches and oddly cut beards. Now she couldn't even have named Ursula's grandparents, and she thought she regretted it. For if she had shown an interest in what Betty Wick called "the distaff side," wouldn't her father perhaps have instructed her in the helmet side? (Sarah's students in her women's studies course would have been horrified to know she used such sexist expressions even to herself.) He hadn't mentioned even an uncle or an aunt of his own, so far as she could remember. Relatives bored him, he said. You didn't choose them; they were thrust upon you, and the best thing to do was thrust them right back again.

Hope, clever and precocious, had said, "Surely the same thing must apply to your children, Daddy."

He had been ready for her. "Ah, but I chose my children. I married. I picked a good-looking, healthy young woman. I thought, I will have two children, two years apart, both girls, both beautiful, both intellectually brilliant. And I did. Therefore, you can't say I didn't choose them."

Of course they couldn't say it after that. Sarah poured herself some more wine and thought of her father. He had been so young to die. The death of anyone else at seventy-one she would have thought a quite reasonable and appropriate time for an old man to go. But her own father might have lived another fifteen years. She had expected that; she might have had him with her till she herself was middle-aged. She sighed, looked at her watch. It was nearly six. A good or a bad time to phone J. G. Candless?

He was probably the kind of man who worked in an office, an insurance office, she thought, or a building society, from nine till five. Possibly no more than walking distance from home, or a bus ride. He would be home by now but not eating yet surely? She dialed the number. It rang four times.

A man answered. He didn't say hello, just repeated the number, all eleven digits of it.

"Mr. Candless?"

"Yes?"

"Mr. Candless, you don't know me, but my name is also Candless. Sarah Candless. My late father was Gerald Candless, the novelist. I expect you have heard of him."

There was a hesitation. "No. I can't say I have."

She found it incredible. The man must be illiterate. A moron. She would have to be careful not to use long or difficult words. "I am researching—I mean, I am trying to find out something about my father's family. They came from Ipswich. You are the only

Candless in the phone book, so it seems likely that you are a relation and —"

"You'd better talk to my wife. My wife knows all about that side of things."

"But, Mr. Candless, wait a minute. It's *your* relatives I'm interested in—"

It was too late. He had gone. Sarah waited, feeling a mounting irritation. He reminded her of those men who, when asked if they had read her father's books, said no, but their wives had. Absurd. The woman who picked up the receiver sounded brisk and efficient, an altogether different prospect, in spite of the ugliest accent she had ever heard.

"This is Maureen Candless. What can I do for you?"

Sarah explained all over again.

"Yes, I see."

"I can't believe you haven't heard of my father. He was very famous."

"I've heard of him. I read about him dying in the papers." She didn't say she was sorry he was dead or express any sympathy for Sarah. "I noticed," she said, "because he had the same name as us."

"Mrs. Candless, did your husband have an uncle George and an aunt Kathleen? Or grandparents named George and Kathleen? They lived in Ipswich, in Waterloo Road."

"No, he didn't," said Maureen Candless. "My husband's Candless grandparents were named Albert and Mary." Here at least was someone who had paid attention to those albums and those names. "There was a cousin George, but he went to Australia, and I never heard of a Kathleen. You ought to talk to Auntie Joan."

"Auntie Joan?"

"She's not really an aunt, more a cousin of my husband's, his dad's cousin really, but we call her 'Auntie.' Her maiden name was Candless. She's Mrs. Thague, Mrs. Joan Thague, and she lives out at Rushmere St. Andrew, but she's a very old lady now and she doesn't go out much."

Sarah couldn't see the significance of this. She didn't want Mrs. Thague to go out, but to stay at home and talk to her. Did she have a phone?

"She has a phone," said Maureen Candless, "but she's a bit deaf and she says her hearing aid doesn't work with the phone. The best thing for you would be to go and see her."

Sarah thanked her and said she would like to. Maureen Candless said she would tell Auntie Joan to expect a visitor wanting to talk about the family, gave Sarah an address, and, when pressed, the phone number, adding that a call wouldn't be answered. Nevertheless, once Mrs. Candless had put the receiver back, Sarah dialed the number. As forecast, there was no reply.

By now Sarah was in a phoning mood, so she called her mother. Ursula repeated that Gerald had never talked to her about his relatives; she had no idea if he had a first or second cousin named J. G. Candless or a cousin or aunt named Mrs. Joan Thague.

"Didn't some of these people come to your wedding?"

"There were none of your father's relations there, only friends."

"Well, tell me about how you and Dad first met, will you?"

"I thought I was to do that when you came down for the weekend."

"I can't come down. I've got to go and see this Thague woman. So tell me now, will you, Ma?"

Some of it, only some of it. Ursula talked for ten minutes, censoring as she went. It was after Sarah rang off that she thought about it in detail, leaning her head back, closing her eyes, remembering.

The car was an MG, a two-seater. He called for her in it at precisely seven. She was ready; she had been ready for two hours—not a particularly good idea, as she had to keep running upstairs to comb her hair again and renew her lipstick (pale pink, so that Dad wouldn't say she'd been kissing fire engines). A run appeared in one of her stockings and she had to change them, too. Those were still the days, though they were passing, when women were supposed to look perpetually fresh and newly painted, not a hair out of place, like so many life-size Barbie dolls or Stepford Wives. *Bandbox* was the word. It had taken her days to decide what to wear before settling on the new pink shift with pink jacket.

The whole thing made her parents uneasy. Why did this man want to take their daughter out? He was old enough to be her father—well, not quite, but she knew what they meant. Why not take them all out if he wanted to make some return for the dinner at which they had entertained him and at which he had drunk far too much?

"He isn't courting you, is he?" said Herbert Wick.

"I'm just going to have dinner with him, Dad."

"I do think it's most peculiar," said Betty. "Don't you, Bert?"

"Writers are peculiar. Still, I suppose it's all right. He's a middle-aged man."

As if that made him safe. You could leave your daughter alone with a middle-aged man, whereas a young one would be dangerous. Was it a matter of greater physical strength or stronger physical urges? She didn't think of this at the time.

Her parents were pleasant enough to Gerald when he arrived. Her father offered him a drink. Gerald said, "Yes, please, how kind," and accepted a large gin and tonic. No one worried about drinking and driving in 1962. He was wearing a suit, not very clean and not pressed at all, but still a suit. His tie, he said, was in his pocket; he didn't like ties, but he would put it on when they got to the restaurant.

The restaurant was in Chelsea and quite a long way. Ursula dreaded to think how long it would take at this hour in a car. Well over an hour probably, toiling up through Streatham and Balham and Battersea, along one-way streets in heavy traffic—well, what they considered heavy then. It took Gerald about forty minutes. He talked to her all the way. He asked her questions. She had never been asked so many, never known anyone to take so much interest in her. Where had she lived as a child? Where had she been to school? Had she been good at school? Did she like working for her father? What were her interests? What did she read?

She plucked up her courage and said she had read three of his books.

"And did you like what you read?"

"I liked *The Centre of Attraction* best," she said. She had really read it; the others she had dipped into and skimmed through.

"That's not an entirely pleasing thing for a writer to hear, you know. That his first book is preferred. It implies he isn't getting better."

"Oh, I didn't mean . . ."

"I'll give you all my books and inscribe them to 'Little Bear.' 'To Little Bear from Gerald Candless, with admiration.'"

She blushed. "There isn't anything to admire about me," she managed to say. "I'm very ordinary."

"Perhaps it is your ordinariness I admire," he said.

Sixties food was not inspired, even in a good restaurant like that one. She ate prawn cocktail and roast chicken and peach melba and he ate smoked mackerel and roast chicken and apple pie à la mode. She asked him why ice cream made it à la mode and he said he didn't know, that it was American. Strange that she remembered the details of that meal but that she couldn't remember what they had eaten at any other until after they were married.

He had put on his tie before they got out of the car—imagine being able to park a car right outside a restaurant in the King's Road!—and it was a red tie, a bit greasy and frayed. When he smiled, she saw that one of his molars had been crowned with gold. It made her think Mr. Rochester must have had a gold tooth.

"Have you a boyfriend?" he asked her when their coffee came.

She was a little shocked, and she reddened again. He watched the color form and fade, his head a little on one side.

"I think that blush means yes, Little Bear."

"No," she said. "No, it doesn't mean that. I haven't got . . . anyone."

He said nothing. They left. In the car, driving back, she saw his large, long hands tighten on the wheel, the knuckles polished white, as he said without looking at her, of course without looking, "May I apply for the post?"

She had no idea what he meant. "The post?"

"The vacant position of boyfriend—or, since I am too old for such a term, suitor, swain, lover—in the life of Little Bear."

"You?" she said. She was horrified, aghast, amazed, delighted, incredulous.

He pulled the car to the side, then stopped it. "Do you doubt me?"

She found out later that this quotation from *Jane Eyre* was unintended. If he had ever read the novel, he had forgotten it. It was by the merest chance that he spoke Edward Rochester's phrase when Jane is incredulous of his proposal, using a common-enough expression. And therefore he had no idea that she herself was quoting when she replied in Jane's word, "Entirely."

But they had sorted it out. She had explained and he had laughed. They hadn't touched each other and it was to be a long time before he kissed her, but that evening they established that Gerald Candless was to be her accredited—well, boyfriend.

He took her out twice a week. He phoned her every day. Her parents thought it peculiar, but they came to accept him. He was comfortably off, if not rich, did fairly well from his books and very well from his journalism. He had a house in Hampstead, a small house, as he kept on saying. Everyone in the family, Herbert and Betty, Ian and Helen, expected him and Ursula to get engaged, but it was six months before he asked her to marry him.

She said yes at once because she was in love with him, though she could not have said, as Jane does, that no net ensnared her, that she was a free human being with an independent will. She could not have said that her spirit addressed his spirit, just as if both had passed through the grave, and they stood at God's feet, equal—though she would have liked to.

The truth was that he had ensnared her, hypnotized her almost, had her in thrall. And she still disbelieved. She still felt she might wake up and find herself back in January, on the day before Colin Wrightson was due to come and speak to the Purley

Library Users' Association. It was only a dream that he had slipped on the ice on his way to feed the birds, for two days later, he came to Purley and talked about Queen Victoria's daughters and she never met Gerald Candless at all.

Now that Sarah wasn't coming and Hope wasn't coming, Ursula told the Dunes that she could baby-sit on the Friday night if required, and the Saturday, too. They sounded pleased. A Mr. and Mrs. Fleming, who would be coming with two children, had attempted to book a baby-sitter in advance of their arrival, but they had been told it was unlikely anyone could be found.

As she walked down to the hotel, Ursula remembered that it was her wedding anniversary. Had Gerald lived, they would have been married thirty-four years. Not that any celebration would have marked the day. Only she herself would have remembered it, for the girls had never shown the slightest interest in that sort of thing, though indignant enough if their own birthdays weren't appropriately honored, and Gerald always appeared to have forgotten. Gerald, she thought, had forgotten he was married at all, had forgotten it for years, thirty years, and behaved—to put it bluntly but accurately—as if he were a widower with a housekeeper.

Still, she hadn't been very nice to him, either, in later years. She had tried, but it had been impossible. And then she had stopped trying. For the sake of peace, she had simply given in to some of his whims.

As in the matter of forbidding the baby-sitting. Well, she could do it now he was gone. She went into the foyer of the hotel, checked on the name and room number at reception, and went up in the lift to the third floor.

The couple in the room were further apart in age than even she and Gerald had been. There must have been nearly thirty years between them. He looked about her own age, a tall, very thin man with a lantern face and grayish fair hair, much the same color as her own. The mother of this boy of six and girl of three looked no more than Hope's age. She was very pretty, with long fair hair piled up above a high white forehead and eyes of a turquoise blue, which her sleeveless dress matched.

"Molly Fleming," she said, holding out her hand as he said, "Sam Fleming."

Ursula shook hands with them. The fair-haired children stood staring at her, the little girl with her thumb in her mouth.

"I am going to put them to bed, Mrs. Candless, but they won't sleep at once. Would it be too much to ask you to sit in there with them and maybe read or just chat to them?"

"Of course I will."

Ursula squatted down on their level, asked them what they were called, said that once they were in bed, she would come in and they must get to know one another. If they liked, she would tell them a story or read from the book she had brought, which was *The Tale of Samuel Whiskers*.

When they had been taken away, she crossed to the window and looked across the bay. This was one of the sea-facing suites, and this evening, Lundy was clearly visible, as a blue shape on paler blue glass-calm water. Though it was not yet dusk, the light on the point flashed and danced like a firefly.

She said to Sam Fleming, "Are you enjoying your view?"

"Not mine," he said. "My room's on the other side of the corridor."

She looked at him.

"You didn't think I was those children's father, did you?"

Naturally she had. "Of course," she said crisply.

"They are my son's children. My son is dead. He died last year."

"I'm sorry."

"Yes. It was very bad, very painful. Well, it is. It still is. Molly, of course, is his widow. I have tried to help her with the children all I can—Edith wasn't quite two when her father died—but I don't suppose I've been much use. More in the way, no doubt. But I like to be with the children."

Ursula said again, "I am truly sorry about your son. It's the worst thing in the world to lose a child, an unnatural thing."

Molly Fleming came back. "You won't be reading for long, Mrs. Candless. James is already crossing the frontier into the Land of Nod." She laughed. "If you're ready, Sam, we can go down." She said to Ursula, "I promise I will be back in here on the dot of ten."

Ursula went quietly into the children's bedroom. James was asleep. Edith said, "Story," or that was what Ursula thought she had said. It was hard to tell on account of the comfort blanket, one corner of which was stuffed into the little girl's mouth. Ursula said she would read to her and told her what she would read, and Edith said Samuel Whiskers was like her grandfather's name, which was Samuel Wiston Fleming. So Ursula read about Tom Kitten and his sisters and Tom going up the chimney, but by the time she got to Anna-Maria stealing the dough, Edith was asleep.

Leaving the door propped open, she went back into the main bedroom. Why had she used those particular words to Sam Fleming? "It's the worst thing in the world to lose a child, an unnatural thing." They were a direct quotation from Mrs. Eady and they had sprung into her mind and found their way to her tongue almost without her volition. Ursula felt a coldness along her shoulders and down her spine, what was called "a goose walking over one's grave." The worst thing in the world, the unnatural thing . . .

Presumably, Sam Fleming's son had not been murdered, as Mrs. Eady's had, nor was it likely he had a daughter who was a nun. No, James and Edith's father would have died in a road accident or of some young man's swiftly progressing cancer. He wouldn't have been beaten to death, his body discovered lying in his own blood. She didn't want to think of it, wished she hadn't summoned up those words, for they were like seeds that sprang up and grew and flowered, bearing poisonous fruits. They always were.

She sat down by the window, gazing outside to calm herself and drive away the image of the young man in Mrs. Eady's photograph, not smiling cockily and cheekily as he was in the photograph, but with his skull smashed in and blood on the walls. No, she told herself, no! Out there, the sea had turned to a dull, smooth pewter. The island had disappeared. The dark furry headlands lay as sleeping animals lie, relaxed, heavy, calm, but on the tip of Hartland, the firefly still winked.

The dark sea washed away the bloody image. Ursula thought of her daughters. What could she tell Sarah about her wedding? She would have to tell her something, and it must be something true, though edited, though expurgated. Much bowdlerization must be done. Sarah would take it for granted that she and Gerald had been lovers before they were married. Anything else was unthinkable these days. It had been very nearly unthinkable in 1963, but still, they hadn't been lovers. He hadn't asked and naturally she hadn't, because she'd thought that was for the man to do. She did wonder, but she thought it was something to do with his being fourteen years older than she.

None of that need be mentioned. Ursula had been married in white satin, low-cut, to show off some of the bosom she was proud of, and with a full skirt and detachable train. She carried white roses and white freesias. Her bridesmaids were her schoolfriend Pam and Helen's little Pauline, by that time three and a half. Ursula had a sapphire and diamond engagement ring and a gold wedding ring with a pattern of leaves chased around the band. She had stopped wearing the engagement ring in the mid-seventies and taken off her wedding ring for good in 1988. By that time, the leaf-pattern chasing had worn down and it had become a plain gold band like anyone else's.

In a gesture of defiance or anger or dislike (or something), Ursula had sold her engagement ring. She knew no one would know, just as no one had noticed when she ceased to wear it. She took the ring to a jeweler in Exeter and he gave her two thousand pounds for it. That meant it was worth much more, but she didn't care. She rather liked the idea of Gerald's expensive ring fetching much less than its true value. She didn't need the money; he had always given her what money she wanted, within reason, and all she did with it was put it into their joint bank account.

That engagement ring had made a nuisance of itself at her wedding. That was one way of putting it. She had forgotten to do as instructed by her mother and Helen and put the ring on her right hand so that the third finger of her left would be vacant, so to speak, and ready to receive Gerald's wedding ring. Helen noticed as Ursula was walking up the aisle on Herbert Wick's arm, and she made faces at her and pointed, but Ursula hadn't known what she was on about. She was observing, with a slight chill on this happy day, what huge crowds of her own relations there were on the bride's side and what a mere smattering of friends (including Colin Wrightson and his wife) and no relatives at all on the bridegroom's.

He was up there at the altar with his best man, whom Ursula had met once, which was how she knew this wasn't a cousin but just another friend. She wasn't nervous. She wanted to marry Gerald; she was in love with him, and she couldn't wait to be married to him and living with him and sleeping with him every night. She made all her responses in a firm, clear voice. Then the vicar said to repeat the words about "With this ring I thee wed and with my body I thee worship"—they hadn't gotten around to changing the prayer book by then—and Ursula held up her hand and saw the engagement ring on her finger.

Gerald had the wedding ring ready to slip on, so she quickly tugged at the engagement ring, and whatever she'd been before, she must have been nervous by then, because the ring fell out of her hand and onto the floor. It made quite a loud sound as it hit the floor of the nave, which was made of flagstones, with a bit of carpet runner up the aisle, but the ring hit the stones, not the carpet. Instinctively, she ducked down to retrieve it, and Pam ducked, too, and their heads collided, not painfully, but ridiculously. She felt about for the ring and Pam felt, but they couldn't find it, and she heard the vicar or someone whisper, and whisper crossly, not pleasantly, "Leave it. Leave it."

Gerald repeated those serious words, not at all crossly, but with an undercurrent of laughter in his voice, as if he was suppressing great amusement, and she loved him for that, as if she hadn't loved him already. When he came to endowing her with all his worldly goods (for she had already thrown one of his worldly goods onto the floor), she thought he would burst out into a crow of laughter, but he didn't; he controlled himself, and the vicar looked daggers.

Afterward, they had to go into the vestry while the congregation sang a hymn, and she was anxious all the time about her ring, but before they went back into the ceremony, little Pauline came up to her and gravely presented it to her. She had had it all the time. With great presence of mind in one so young, she had picked up the ring and slipped it on the stem of one of the flowers in her bridesmaid's bouquet, where it had remained until that moment.

Later on, frequently, Ursula had thought what a strange business that affair of the ring had been. Like an omen, but an omen of what? In another way, it was like a dream, for such things happen more in dreams than in reality: the dropping of the ring, the fruitless hunt for it, the shame of hunting for it, its retrieval with such precocity by a child, the image of it encircling the stem of a white rosebud.

She had never told her daughters. Perhaps she would tell Sarah now or perhaps not. Once, when the girls were little, she had asked Gerald if he remembered, but he had looked at her as if she had invented the whole thing, as if it were a product of her imagination. She had begun to notice at that time that he disliked being reminded he was married. He avoided using the words my wife whenever he could. Once, she saw him looking at the bare third finger of her left hand and his face bore a satisfied expression.

Ursula went to look at the sleeping children. When she came back into the room, Sam Fleming was there. He had come up to check that everything was all right.

"I hope you won't mind my asking, but have you any connection to Gerald Candless, the novelist who died this summer? I believe he lived near here."

"I was his wife," said Ursula.

"I'm sorry."

"So am I" was what she would have liked to say. Instead, she thanked him and said there was no need for him to stay, the children were fine, and there was something on the television she had been looking forward to watching. But instead of switching it on, she sat and thought and asked herself the questions she had asked so many times since his death. Had he been *sorry* for what he had done? And had he been trying to make amends by leaving her his house and his savings and his future royalties?

7

---

*They make a mockery of those Greek and Turkish
women they have seen on package holidays, but
most London girls dress entirely in black, as if in
mourning for the lost freedom of color.*
—THE MEZZANINE SMILE

THE DEPARTURE OF YOUR CHILDREN is not invariably a
cause of unhappiness. If they are happy, even though
distant, if they are prosperous and getting on with
their lives and have children of their own, that should
be enough for you. You didn't, after all, have them to
look after you in your old age. You never thought of
such a thing. Come to that, to be strictly honest, you
didn't have them intentionally at all; they just came.
But once there, you knew you had had them so that
they might grow up straight and strong, be successful, be happy, earn their livings doing what they
wanted to do, and take a fitting place in the world.

Thus the philosophy of Joan Thague. One of her
sons was in Australia, another in Scotland, while her
daughter lived in Berkshire. She saw them once a
year, sometimes more. Her grandson at the Anglia
Polytechnic University dropped in once a fortnight

and she knew the reason he came. He got a good meal. Maureen, her cousin John's son John George's wife, came and had a cup of tea and took her shopping in her car to the Martlesham Tesco, which was the best supermarket for miles around. Joan Thague still had her health and strength at seventy-eight and thought herself a fortunate woman.

If she had been able to cope with the phone, she could have talked to her children and her grandchildren once a week. But her deafness made things difficult. The doctors said she was deaf because the noise in the silk mill where she had worked as a girl had damaged her ears. Joan didn't argue. Doctors never listened if you did. She didn't say there was very little noise in the silk mill or that her uncle Ernest had been stone-deaf and her dad deaf in his declining years. It was obviously hereditary, but doctors didn't like it if you said an illness was obviously anything.

She had an attachment to put on the phone receiver and, of course, she had her deaf aid. With the deaf aid in place and with her sharp eyes on a person's lips, she could hear anything; she could hear words uttered in a normal voice, but the thing on the phone didn't really help her at all. She had described the noise that came out of the phone, the way it sounded to her, as like what a big dog's barking would be if it was in the bottom of a well. The audiologist had laughed and said, very well put, but she hadn't been able to do anything about improving the phone. Joan kept the phone in case she ever had to dial 999 for an ambulance, but she never used it. That was why the young lady whose dad had passed away was coming to the house and not phoning.

Saturday was the day, in the afternoon. Maureen had come around the day before and said this Miss Candless had phoned again and asked if Saturday afternoon at about three would be all right, and Maureen had said she was sure it would be, and she had come over to pass on the message. Then they had gone to Martlesham and Joan had bought chocolate-chip biscuits and Kunzle cakes (which had come back into the shops after an absence of forty years) for Miss Candless's tea. Luckily, Frank had left her comfortably off and she had always been thrifty, so she didn't have to worry about spending a little extra for special occasions.

While she busied herself dusting and vacuuming the already-immaculate bungalow, Joan speculated as to who the young lady could be. It was unthinkable that anyone called Candless and hailing from Ipswich shouldn't be one of their family. Miss Candless was trying to trace her father's roots, and Maureen had said this man's Christian name and something else about him but had turned her face away at that moment to catch sight of someone out of the window and Joan hadn't been able to read her lips. She put the vacuum cleaner away and laid on the newly dusted coffee table in the living room all the photograph albums she possessed, four of them.

There must have been a point, perhaps about the time of the Great War or perhaps a bit later, when photographs stopped being brown and fawn and became black and white. It would be precisely known, that date—people would know it, but Joan didn't. She rather liked the brown and thought it a shame it was gone forever. Then there was another point when black and white gave place to color. Of her albums, one held the brown photographs, two the black and white, and the latest one the colored. The young lady would want to see them and see if she could pick out her dad among the numerous cousins and cousins' sons.

Joan couldn't resist opening the first album of black-and-white photographs, the one that held her wedding pictures. She had been living in Sudbury and wanted to get married at the church of St. Gregory and St. Peter, so pretty down there by the Stour in May, with the water meadows all green and the white daisies blooming. But her mother wanted her home in Ipswich for the wedding, and she had thought she owed that to her mother. Frank had been so handsome then, the handsomest man she had ever seen. Joan felt very much like picking up the album and pressing her lips to Frank's photographed face, but she resisted; she didn't want to be silly.

Their first home had been in Sudbury, just two rooms in a white brick house on Melford Road, where Frank's uncle had his greengrocery business. She'd worked in the shop herself until Peter was born, and after that, it wasn't long before Frank was called up. They had been hard, those war years, with two babies at home and a husband in the western desert. But afterward, Frank had gone into business on his own in Ipswich, and if they had never been really prosperous, they'd done well enough and been happy. You could see that from the photo of Frank outside the shop, holding a giant marrow.

She closed the album once more and turned her mind to Miss Candless's tea. Would she prefer Darjeeling or Earl Grey? You couldn't have milk with Earl Grey and she hadn't a lemon in the house, so Indian it would have to be. Did "about three" mean before three or after? Joan was a stickler for punctuality herself and would never have made an appointment for "about" anything, but she understood about Miss Candless driving here from London and perhaps getting held up in traffic jams. "About three" could mean ten past. Nevertheless, she was at the window watching by two minutes to three.

It was twenty past before the car came. Joan was nearly distraught, pacing into the dining room and back to the window, putting on the kettle and taking it off again, wondering if she'd gotten the day wrong. She even looked at the newspaper to check that it really was Saturday, and she would have phoned the J.G.'s, in case Maureen hadn't actually said Saturday, only she had her deafness problem with the phone. Then the car came and Joan ducked in case the young lady saw her watching.

You never wanted to answer the door too quickly. People got the wrong idea about you if you did that. They thought you must be lonely or anxious. So when the bell rang, Joan counted to twenty and then slowly walked to the front door. She opened it in a casual manner.

The young lady stepped in, held out her hand, and said, "I'm Sarah Candless. How do you do? It's very good of you to see me."

She was a good-looking girl, with red hair and dark red painted lips. Her skin was thick and smooth like white suede. Joan had seldom seen anyone in such deep mourning, black suit, black blouse, black stockings and shoes, black macintosh draped around her shoulders. All for the dead father, of course. This made her view Sarah Candless with approval, and she ushered her into the living room, having first hung up the shiny black mac.

Getting down to business wasn't Joan's way. Small talk must come first, exchanges on the weather and the state of the road from London. Joan said it was cooler today than it had been; it was autumnal and one could soon expect the nights to draw in. Sarah Candless said that she supposed so. Yes, she had come on the M25 and the A12 and there were still roadworks on the approach to Colchester.

"I expect you'd like a cup of tea."

She never drank tea. She said that very firmly and it took Joan aback. Joan had never previously met anyone who didn't drink tea. At a loss, recalling a small jar of decaffeinated instant coffee brought by her grandson and deposited at the back of the kitchen cabinet, she asked what it was Miss Candless did drink.

"I don't want anything. Really."

"But you've come all the way from London," said Joan.

"It's quite all right. I don't want anything."

"After all those hours in a car?"

"Well, if you have any water . . ."

Joan couldn't imagine what she meant. Of course she had water. All her life, at her parents' home and after she was married, they had always been on the main water line. It did occur to her, while she was running the tap to get it really cold, that water was available from other sources; she had seen it in the supermarket at Martlesham, but she couldn't believe any sane person would actually pay good money for a bottle of water. No, Miss Candless must simply have been speaking politely.

She took the glass in on a tray, and the Kunzle cakes and biscuits, as well. She'd have her own tea later. Miss Candless refused the cakes. Joan had guessed she would as soon as she saw her. Girls like her all suffered from an epidemic called anorexia nervosa; she had read about it in the paper.

"Perhaps we can talk about my father."

Joan thought it a bit abrupt. The folder Miss Candless took out of her black briefcase looked very official, as did the briefcase itself, rather as if she had come from the gas company about going on the three-star contract, instead of paying a social call. But Joan nodded and sat very upright, looking expectant, her hands folded in her lap.

"I've brought a copy of his birth certificate." She held it up. "His name was Gerald Francis Candless."

Joan looked at her. She had taken her eyes off her for a moment, and perhaps she had misheard. A chill had run through her at the sound of what she had heard, or thought she had heard. Now she stared hard at Miss Candless's glossy, full dark red lips, which were parted a little, showing teeth as white and shiny as the china plate on which the biscuits lay.

"I am sorry," she said. "Would you say the name again, please?"

"Gerald Francis Candless."

The red mouth formed that name, the teeth just clipping the lower lip at the pronunciation of the two *r*'s. There could be no mistake. Sarah Candless said, "Have you never heard of him? He was a famous writer. A famous literary writer."

It meant nothing. It was nonsense. Joan said tonelessly, "There's no one in the family by that name."

"Mrs. Thague, let me tell you a bit more. My father was born in 1926. On May the tenth. His parents were George and Kathleen Candless. It's all here in the birth certificate. If you would just—"

Nothing like this had ever happened to Joan before. She was frightened, without knowing exactly what of. But she interrupted the girl with an explosive "No!"

"No?"

Joan clenched her hands. "No, no. I said, no!"

"What's the matter? What have I said?"

Anger came, an unfamiliar emotion. It was a long time since Joan had done what she called "standing up to" someone, but she was going to do it now. She was not going to be mocked. Somehow, for some unknown reason, this girl had come here, to her house, to get a rise out of her, to hurt her, too, and she wouldn't stand for it.

"You know what you've said. You know who George and Kathleen Candless were; they were my parents. And you know who was born on May the tenth, 1926." Joan was almost gasping with the effort of being rude to someone. Her hands had begun to shake. But she managed to stand up. "Now, I think you'd better go."

The girl stood up, too. "Mrs. Thague, I'm very sorry if I've upset you. I didn't mean to."

"Go away. Please go away."

"I don't know what I've done. Believe me. I don't know what I've done wrong. What have I said?"

"Let me see that."

Joan put out her hand for the certificate. It was passed to her without reluctance. The girl's face was puzzled, her lips parted. She didn't look cruel or spiteful. Joan's heart was beating hard. She had to sit down again, because it was Gerald's birth certificate; his name was on it, and her mother's and father's names, and the address of the house in Waterloo Road where she had been born and later Gerald had been born, and the date was the date of Gerald's birthday in 1926, when she was seven years old.

She said, "Where did you get this?"

"Mrs. Thague, please don't be angry with me. I don't mean to offend you. I don't know what I've done. This was my father's birth certificate. My mother had it; she kept it with all our birth certificates."

"It can't be your father's," said Joan.

"I'm sorry. I don't want to have to argue with you, but it is. It was. His name was Gerald Candless and that was his birthday, and he was seventy-one last May, which was two months before he died."

Joan knew what she had to do. She had to look in the tin. It was years since she had opened the tin and looked into it, not since she had lifted the lid and laid Frank's death certificate on the top of the papers. That would be the first thing she would see, but it couldn't be helped. Unless she proved to this white-faced, red-lipped girl with her false mourning and her dyed red hair—no one in their family had ever had naturally red hair—that Gerald was dead and had been dead for a lifetime, she knew she wouldn't rest, but would reproach herself throughout the night and next day and on and on. For not *defending* him against this girl, these people, these thieves of his life and his death.

"Wait here," she said.

The tin was in the dining room. Though a dining room was for eating in and also for keeping the cruet in and a bottle of sherry and a half a bottle of brandy for medicinal purposes, it was also suitable as the repository of documents. Bedrooms were not fitting places for the concealment of such things, and the sitting room too frivolous. But the absence of soft and comfortable chairs in the dining room, the austerity of the seldom-used mahogany table, the only partially carpeted floor, and the room's perpetual dimness due to a northern aspect all contributed to its appropriateness. The top drawer of the sideboard contained the best cutlery, the one below it Kathleen Candless's damask tablecloths and napkins, and the lowest the tin.

It was orange and black and had once contained biscuits, the products of Carr's of Carlisle. Joan kept her documents in a tin because her mother had done so, on the grounds that the metal would keep paper from yellowing. In this, at any rate, it had been ineffective, for Frank's death certificate had already become the same deep ocher color as those of George and Kathleen Candless, dead within a year of each other, which lay beneath it. What she sought would be at the very bottom.

First, her children's birth certificates, then her marriage certificate and Frank's father's death certificate. What had happened to his mother's, she didn't know. Perhaps one of her sisters-in-law had it. The two documents at the bottom of the tin were out of order, the record of birth above the record of death. Joan lifted out the top one, looked at the other lying there, and spoke his name involuntarily.

"Gerald."

She mustn't cry. Not in front of that girl. There was already the mark of a water splash on the faded brownish paper, where someone's tear had fallen years ago, decades ago. Her mother's? Joan heard his voice crying, "My head hurts; my head hurts." The tear had fallen onto the end of the long word written in the space under "Cause of death"—*meningitis*. She had never heard the word before, not until he died of it. It still sounded ugly and menacing to her, a crawling monster, crocodilelike, a thing to see in nightmares. She turned the paper over, blank side up, to hide the word. She read the birth certificate, identical to the one the girl had, and then she took both back into the living room.

Miss Candless had drunk all her water, the whole glassful. Joan no longer felt angry, only tired and very sad. She laid the papers on the table and said quietly, "He was my brother."

8

MOSTLY, IT WAS SHE who had answered the phone. A
daughter's voice at the other end would ask for Dad,
sometimes didn't even ask, but took it for granted
Ursula would expect nothing more than to say hello
and "I'll fetch your father." In the unlikely event of
Gerald's being out—taking manuscript pages to
Rosemary, walking for the prescribed hated twenty
minutes on the clifftop—Sarah's or Hope's disappointment sounded almost comically in a dying fall
of tone. They had to talk to her. Where was Dad?
There was nothing wrong with Dad, was there?
When was Dad coming back?

All was changed now. Inevitably. They had to talk
to her every time. The calls came less often. Hope
seldom phoned at all. Sarah phoned, Ursula thought,
because she was more inclined to guilt feelings, to a
sense of duty. And she phoned for information. But
Ursula quite liked it, to pick up the receiver and say

hello and hear a daughter who wanted to talk to her, *needed* to talk to her.

"How are you, Ma?"

After that came the requests. Would she like to write it down? Talk into a tape recorder? Just answer questions on the phone? Ursula thought about it and doctored her thoughts for daughterly consumption. Writing it down was all right if she was careful, a strict and controlled censor. She had talked about that first meeting with Gerald and subsequent meetings and Little Bear and even the Mr. Rochester exchange, and she had written some of it down and sent it to Sarah, the story about the engagement ring, among other anecdotes. But now dangerous ground was approached. Her words would find their way into Sarah's book. Women probably existed who were willing to talk to a daughter about their sex lives with that daughter's father, but she wasn't one of them. Would Sarah ask?

But Sarah didn't ask anything. Ursula had been expecting a call for three days. No call came, and Ursula began to worry. It was ridiculous, because a week might easily pass by without a call from either daughter, but Sarah had promised. Sarah had said, "I'll phone in a couple of days. I'll have gotten a lot of Dad's family background by then and I'll be ready to hear about when you were first married."

On the fourth day, in the evening, Ursula called her. It was because she was alone that she was prey to absurd fancies. It frightened her to think there might be no answer, or only Sarah's recorded voice. If that happened, she would be worse off than before. But Sarah picked up the phone after two rings.

She sounded cool and distant. "Is there something wrong?"

"With me, no," Ursula said. "I thought you'd want to talk about your father. For the book."

"I will, I suppose, but not now."

"I'm sorry. Have I interrupted something?"

"No."

"You said you were tracing Dad's family."

"Yes."

"Was that successful, Sarah?"

There was a pause, a silence; then Sarah's voice came in a rush, impulsive and strangely high-pitched. "I've been wondering, Ma, if you—I mean, if you've any idea why Dad . . ."

"Idea of what?"

"Nothing," said Sarah.

"Shall I write to you, then?" In the absence of any reply to this, Ursula said, "Is there anything you want to ask me?"

"No. No, nothing. I'll call you in a day or two."

She sounded just like Ursula's mother had when some forbidden subject had been raised—cagey, slightly embarrassed, almost dismissive. In Betty Wick's case, the subject had usually been sex, and for a moment Ursula wondered, as she replaced the receiver, if Sarah's awkwardness could have been from the same cause, shyness in anticipation of what her mother might have to say about her married life. But no, it must be something else, something she couldn't guess at, for both daughters seemed to her free from even mild inhibition. If Sarah wanted to know, she would come out with it, and if she was afraid of hearing, she would say that, too.

Her own mother had belonged to a time that must seem to Sarah and Hope a dark-age generation. The words she had used unconsciously on the phone came back to her. They were those her mother had spoken to her in a quite different context, words all mothers once perhaps used to their girls on the brink of marriage: "Is there anything you want to ask me?" One thing was for certain, she would never repeat them to Sarah or Hope in the sense they had been used to her.

The night before her wedding, her mother had said to her in a deceptively casual way, "Is there anything you want to ask me about, you know, tomorrow night?"

Ursula was terribly embarrassed and taken aback. "No, thanks," she muttered, not looking at Betty.

"There's not much in it, anyway," said Betty. "I mean, if you're expecting the sort of thing you read about in books, I can tell you you'll be disappointed. Just don't build your hopes up, that's all I'm saying."

Ursula had not built her hopes up. Indeed, having by then perused a number of sex books, which, by 1963, were becoming increasingly frank and explicit, she knew very well to expect no wonders the first time or even the second. Sexual fulfillment must be worked for, with mutual understanding and consideration.

For this reason, she rather wished Gerald had not been so circumspect and had taken her away for a couple of weekends in advance of their marriage so that their wedding night might be more perfect than could reasonably be anticipated. But, in the event, the books, not to mention Betty Wick, could hardly have been more wrong, and Ursula loved their lovemaking from the start. She found within herself a fount of sexual desire and free, eager response.

On their honeymoon, they went to the newly attractive holiday place, Yugoslavia, the Dalmatian coast. It was warm and sunny, and while the hotel was strange and rather primitive, with one bathroom to a floor and the key to it always missing, and the food consisted mainly of pork and green peppers, they had a large airy bedroom with lace curtains at the window and a tentlike mosquito net over the big wooden bed. Ursula could have spent all day as well as all night inside that all-enveloping white net, stroking Gerald's body, kissing Gerald, receiving him into herself with long sighs and delighted laughs of pleasure. It was he who laughingly resisted, made her get up, wrest that bathroom key out of the management, and, once they had showered in cold water, explore the town, walk the beach, swim.

She couldn't keep herself from touching him. When they walked, she hung on to his arm or put her arm around his waist. He said it was too hot for that, and it was, but still she needed to touch him, just to feel his skin on her skin, his brown skin under her fingertips, and when they sat on the rocks, she pressed herself against him, turning his face to hers to kiss him. Now, when she looked back, she was ashamed. She was so ashamed that even the memory could make her redden and her cheeks feel hot when she pressed her cold fingers against them.

One evening, he had said to her, "You are the sort of woman most men would dream of being married to."

She took it as a compliment and a warm tide of joy flowed through her body. She was especially delighted because that afternoon, when they had returned to their room for the siesta most people took, she had stripped off her clothes and pulled him down onto her, thrusting her full breasts into his hands, smiling and murmuring his name, parting her legs to receive him between them, shameless and wanton because she hadn't known there was any reason for reticence. And he, though also smiling, had shaken his head and made a little pushing away gesture with his hands, had murmured, "No, no, not now," and lain down under the net with his back to her.

So later, when he made that flattering remark, she was happy, and no less so at its corollary, though surprised. "I didn't know you; I just thought I did. I didn't expect ardor."

"What did you expect?"

She knew now. Indifference. Perhaps Betty's reaction. "I don't know, Little Bear," he said. "Ursa Minor, Constellation, I don't know what I expected."

Minor, yes. Acquiescence was what she got from

him. That was something she also knew now. Well, she had known it for years. Not on their honeymoon, though; she hadn't known it then. She had thought he was tired, reminded herself he was fourteen years older than she, when in those last days and nights there was no lovemaking and she was rejected, if with rueful smiles and amused protests. They went home, to Hampstead, to the house on Holly Mount, and she didn't know how sharply the image of that room in Cavtat would be imprinted on her mind, so that she would always associate in the future white net, draped, streaming, gathered, enveloping, with sexual pleasure.

But did he? Or rather, with sexual excess, profligacy, dismay? And was that the explanation for his recoiling from the mist, that it reminded him? Folds of white net, eddying billows of white mist. She thought this theory of hers far-fetched, but not to be entirely discounted. It was a long time since confronting the suspicion—no, the certain knowledge—that he disliked making love to her, that he *loathed* it, could cause her pain. So perhaps when he had seen the white mist hang from the white sky, he, too, had remembered that gauzy bedroom, the smell of sex, her wetness and softness and openness, her uninhibited passion.

He was writing a book and she understood that it exhausted him; sometimes he worked throughout the evenings. She even told herself that she was excessively desirous and, although she was enough of a child of her time not to think there might be something wrong with her, she did tell herself that she had gotten into an absurd habit. There was more to life than sex. Such as learning to be a wife. To cook, to entertain his friends. She found herself able to decipher his curious handwriting, and this surprised him. He was pleasantly surprised that she could read what he had written, when so many typists in the past had given up in despair. Without telling him what she was doing, she abstracted his first chapter from the bottom of the pile of manuscript, took it away, and typed it up, producing fifteen perfect pages.

Presenting it to him later, she half-expected a cold incredulity, even reproaches. By that time, the early signs of his rejection of her had begun to show themselves. She hadn't understood what they were, what she had done, but she was already wary; she was watchful for signs, on the verge of being afraid of him. The typing of the fifteen pages, she realized later, had been done to placate him, to make him pleased with her.

There was no indignation, no disbelief. He was clearly delighted. He looked at the pages in wonderment, told her she was clever. She thought he might jump up and put his arms around her, kiss her out of gratitude, and he did pick up her hand and bring it to his lips. She had to be content with that. It was a more affectionate gesture than she had received for weeks.

"Would you like me to type the whole book for you?" she asked him.

"What do you think?" he said, smiling.

The novel was *Eye in the Eclipse,* the story of Jacob Manley, a religious fanatic, who, in a gesture of self-sacrifice and for the sake of propriety, marries a widow with five children. He supports the family, encourages his stepchildren to work hard at school and better themselves, but he is unable to give them love. Ursula thought she had never enjoyed a book so much as this novel, set in East London in the forties and fifties. None of those books she had devoured before she was married had interested her half so much, and she understood that this was partly because he had written it and as she read she could hear his voice. She read each chapter before she began to type, relishing the characters and the dialogue, but looking for him in vain. Nothing in the book seemed to bear any relation to what he had told her of his early life.

The typescript she produced pleased him. Doing this for him would become her work, the job she had vaguely thought she ought to have. She was proud of herself.

That was something to tell Sarah. When she got over what was so evidently troubling her. When she phoned again with a spate of enthusiastic questions.

The mist had lifted, but its rising would be temporary. In half an hour, the pale blue sky and hazy white sun would once more be covered, the lone and level sands stretch bleakly under the dense canopy, the sky be gone as well as the view of the hotel and even the flat expanse of gently lapping sea. And the white cottony floss would press against Gerald's study windows. . . .

Meanwhile, it was almost bright down there, and with the lifting of the mist, the people had begun to return, as they always did, with the inevitability of birds appearing when dawn breaks. In the distance, she saw the Fleming family, up against the dunes, with a windbreak behind them, though there was no wind. James and Edith were digging in the sand, Sam Fleming and his daughter-in-law sitting in deck chairs. She had done her two baby-sitting stints and on the second occasion had handed over the stamps she had collected to be given to James. There had been no more demand for her services and she hadn't expected to see them again. She knew they were going home at the end of the week.

Now she thought there was no point in making them acknowledge her, and she would have passed fifty yards from them without turning her head, but she heard Sam's voice call, "Mrs. Candless!"

She turned and went up the beach. Something strange, unexpected, and unwelcome happened to her. Gerald had for a long time kept a photograph of Samuel Beckett in his study, pinned to the wall, as he occasionally did keep photographs of writers he admired. Ursula thought Sam Fleming, with his lantern jaw and piercing eyes and full, mobile mouth, looked a lot like Beckett. She didn't know if Beckett had also been tall and very thin, but she suspected so. The sudden powerful attraction he exerted over her, that she had been quite unaware of at their previous meetings, seemed to hit her between the eyes. It was enough to stop her in her tracks, cause her to take a deep breath. Then she went on.

They spoke to her, said things about the mist, the clearing of the mist. Molly said to her son, calling him from his sand-castle building, "What do you say to Mrs. Candless, James?"

"Thank you very much for the stamps," said the child.

"I'm glad you were pleased."

Sam Fleming was looking hard at her. Ursula thought there might be something in the idea that if you were very powerfully attracted to someone, that made you attractive to them, that there was some chemical or telepathic exchange. Then she told herself that should Sam Fleming be attracted to a woman, it wouldn't be to someone of his own age, a skinny woman of fifty-seven in jeans and a sweatshirt, with cropped graying hair, but a bright and nubile thirty-five-year-old. It wasn't the first time she'd been attracted to a man other than Gerald, nor would it be the first time that nothing had come of it.

She said, "I'm afraid the mist is coming back. It always does when the sky looks like that."

"Then we shall pack up and go in for our tea."

She said good-bye to them. It was unlikely she would see them again, so she wished them a good journey home. Her legs felt a little weak. Her body was given over to a yearning. It was exactly the same feeling she had had thirty-five years ago, when she had first known Gerald, and she marveled that such a sensation could repeat itself so faithfully after so long. When the woman who experienced it was utterly changed. When it had been so rudely mocked that first time and so roughly repudiated.

The mist rolled in and cloaked her. It hid them, so that even if she had looked back, they would have been concealed from her. And she was glad of it, glad of the isolation in which to recover. Then, as she approached the path and the steps, she heard someone running after her.

She turned around then and waited.

Sarah had gone early to St. Catherine's House. She expected to get it done with and to have the day to assemble her notes and draw her conclusions before going to Hope's for supper.

People were already queuing outside the Public Search Room. Even getting inside took time. And once the doors were opened and she had begun on her task, she found things more complicated than she had expected. Forms had to be filled in, as well as one ledger after another scrutinized.

These were heavy and there were a great many of them. Eventually, in the ledger for the summer of 1918, she found the marriage of George Candless to Kathleen Mary Mitchell. Now she had to move on to births. It was a tiring business. Luckily, she had a rough idea where to look, and she found the birth of Joan Kathleen Candless without trouble in June 1919. That of Gerald Candless was easy to find. May 10, 1926, and here it was.

The Candlesses had possibly had more children in between. Now Sarah wished she had asked Joan Thague. She hadn't been able to bring herself to do that, because Mrs. Thague had been so distraught. Bewildered and distressed and *deaf.* Tearful enough and upset enough for Sarah to have wondered about the facts, incoherently outlined, of a little brother dead in April 1932, a month before his sixth birthday. But within the next half hour, she came upon the registration of the child's death: "Gerald Francis Candless, age five. Cause of death: heart failure; contributory cause, meningitis."

So it was true. She hadn't really been in doubt, but reading it here in this official way was different from hearing it uttered by Joan Thague and different even from seeing the words on the little boy's aged yellow death certificate. She didn't relish telling Hope.

"You're not saying Daddy told lies!"

Hope stared at her sister like an enemy.

"All right, but what other explanation is there? It was really quite pathetic, this poor old woman, and the little brother dying. I don't think I'm easily embarrassed, but I was then."

"There must have been two Gerald Candlesses," said Hope.

"What, two boys named Gerald Francis Candless, both born in the same town on the tenth of May, 1926, and both with parents named Kathleen and George?"

Hope looked on the verge of tears. "But why

would Daddy do that? You mean he was someone else, don't you? Someone else entirely? But why would he do that? She was a lawyer, and she quickly saw why someone would do that. "Because he'd done something criminal? Because he was wanted for that? Oh, I won't believe it. Not Daddy. I can't believe that."

"That need not necessarily be the reason," said Sarah. "Something awful might have happened to him that he wanted to put behind him. The thing is, when did he do it? Obviously not when he was six. I mean, we don't even know if whoever he was was the same age as the little boy who died. Or came from the same place. Or was even English, come to that. He may have done it when he was eighteen, or five years later, but not ten years later, because that was when his first book was published, and he was Gerald Candless then."

"You've really thought about this, haven't you?" said Hope, not altogether pleasantly.

"Yes, of course I have. I haven't liked it, Hope. But if I'm going to write this book . . ."

"I wish to God you weren't going to write the bloody book! I wish we'd never had to know. I don't want to know this. I hate knowing this."

"Hopie," said Sarah, "if I hadn't found it, someone else would. Someone else writing his biography. There are bound to be biographers. Isn't it better it should be me than some stranger?"

Fabian, who had been cooking, stuck his head around the corner. "Ready in five minutes," he said, and then he said, *The Day of the Jackal.*

132

"The what?"

"In *The Day of the Jackal,* by Fr·derick Forsyth, there's a man who wants to change his identity to get a passport. So he goes to graveyards and searches till he finds a tombstone of a very young child of the same sex and who would now be approximately the same age as himself. And then when he's got the name and all the rest of it, he finds that child in the records and applies for a birth certificate in that name and thence for a passport."

"But the person would be dead," Hope objected.

"Nobody's going to know that, are they? The passport people aren't going to check. Maybe that's what your dad did. He couldn't have read the book, because it was published years afterward, but maybe he had the same idea."

"No, he didn't," Sarah said. "The Gerald Candless who died didn't have a tombstone. I asked. Oh, not because of what you're saying, but I suppose I just—well, I didn't actually believe her at first. It seemed so bizarre, so *awful*—it still does. I said to her, 'Where was he buried?' and she said—Oh, she was crying; it was dreadful—that they'd put a wooden cross on the grave, but when she went back to Ipswich and looked for it twenty years afterward, it was gone; there was no clue as to where it had been."

Sarah ate Fabian's pasta, but Hope didn't feel much like eating. She drank a lot of the wine Sarah had brought, gazing broodingly at her sister. Fabian, who had known him quite well, thought of the man

133

who was dead and tried to fit him into this role of a villain or fugitive but couldn't. Gerald Candless had been so decisive, so authoritative, so in control.

"What about Ursula?" he said.

"What about her?" Hope poured herself the last of the wine. "She won't know. I hope someone's going to open another bottle."

Fabian, because he had cooked and served the meal, sat tight, declining to make a move. "You can't assume that just because it happened before they were married she doesn't know anything."

"I nearly asked her," said Sarah. "I phoned her last night and I nearly asked her; it was on the tip of my tongue."

"What, like that, straight out?"

"No, not exactly. Of course not. I was going to say something about did she know if Dad had ever thought of changing his name."

"I like 'thought,' " said Fabian.

Hope rounded on him. "Well, I don't. I hate it. I hate all this."

She went outside, banging doors, looking for more wine. Sarah said, "That pasta was delicious. You're a good cook, Fabby."

"Someone has to do it," said Fabian, grinning.

"I don't know what to do now. I just don't know what on earth to do. I can't write a memoir about someone when I don't know who he was. D'you know, I feel quite sick when I have to say that. I feel sort of hollow. Because it's us, too, isn't it? If he was someone else, who are we? What's our real name?"

"Candless," said Fabian firmly. "Think of all the people there are whose fathers had foreign names. Polish names, for instance—they've almost always been changed to something pronounceable. They know who they are. They're the name their fathers changed to."

Hope came back with a bottle and a corkscrew. She dumped it on the table. "I haven't the strength to open it. I feel as weak as water."

"I'll do it," said Sarah.

"I think you ought to give up this memoir. I was thinking about it while I was out in the kitchen. Daddy wouldn't want you to find this stuff out; we know that. Otherwise, he wouldn't have changed his name in the first place. So you ought to stop. Ring up Postle and say it upsets you too much. Leave it where it is and maybe—well, maybe in time we could forget."

"Could you forget, Hope?"

Hope didn't answer. She snatched the glass of wine Sarah had poured for her.

"I've done something else," Sarah said almost shamefacedly. "Some checking up. Dad never went to Trinity. Or if he did, he went as whoever he was before he became Gerald Candless. And did you see that letter to the *Times*? The stamp-magazine man, Droridge? I didn't believe it when I first read it, but it's true. Dad never worked for the *Walthamstow Herald*."

"So what? It's just a backstreet rag. He worked for the *Western Morning News*."

Sarah nodded. "Maybe he did. Probably he did.

I've written to them, asking if they've a record of his employment there. It's a long time, forty-five years. As far as I can see now, Dad doesn't seem to have done anything or been anywhere before he was twenty-five."

Fabian said thoughtfully, "But doesn't that mean he'd done everything?"

"What?"

"It means he'd done too much."

9

Few people mind saying they have a bad memory,
but no one admits to having bad taste.

—PURPLE OF CASSIUS

IT WAS EXACTLY what Gerald had said to her all those
years ago, the precise words: "I'd like you to have
dinner with me."

If he had put it differently—"Will you have dinner with me?" or "Will you dine with me?"—she
might have responded differently. She might have
said an unqualified yes. But the words shocked her.
His voice wasn't unlike Gerald's, though his appearance was very unlike, but there in the mist, she
briefly experienced a dreadful and eerie carrying
back. In the intervening years, men had said many
things to her, but none had asked her to have a meal
with him in those words. She was sure her shock
must show on her face, even in the white gloom.

"I'll walk up the path with you if I may," he said.

She collected herself. She felt very cold. The sexual pull this man had exerted over her was for the
time quite gone. She walked mechanically ahead of

him. There was no room on the winding path, with its occasional steps, for two to walk side by side.

"I'm going home on Friday," he said, "and I'd very much like it if you'd have dinner with me tomorrow night or on Thursday."

She found herself nodding, though she didn't mean it as acceptance.

"It doesn't have to be at the hotel. You probably know good restaurants around here. You choose."

Afterward, she couldn't have accounted for her answer. She simply didn't know why she said what she said. "I won't have dinner with you, but I'll come up after dinner and have a drink."

They were almost at the top. At a place on the path where it was almost flat, just before the final steep ascent and the fork, she turned to look at him. They both stopped and looked at each other.

"If you are thinking that you would like Molly to be with us, I'm afraid she won't. She'll be upstairs with the children. She won't leave them alone, and she doesn't want any sitter but you. No, please don't say what you're going to and offer to sit instead of her."

Ursula nodded again. She said, "Your branch of the path goes that way. I'll come up on Thursday at about eight-thirty, if that's all right."

He smiled. "It will have to be."

When she got into the house, she went straight to her desk and to the three manuscripts she had put there before she went out. This was to avoid thinking about what had happened. If she did that, she would feel a fool and she might also feel other unwelcome emotions. Over the years, she had become very practiced in controlling the contents of her mind; she knew how to quell certain thoughts and allow others to rise to the surface. Now, quickly, she turned her attention to the manuscripts.

They were to go to the university that had asked for them. Two she had typed herself; the third was Rosemary's work. He had done the corrections and emendations himself, with a fountain pen, in black ink. Why was it that his handwriting was so nearly illegible but his corrections neat? She opened a drawer in her desk, looking for wrapping paper, padded bags, tape.

When the phone rang, she had begun thinking of Sam Fleming again. It was an altogether-welcome interruption. Or appeared so at first. She hardly recognized her daughter's voice. It was even more hesitant than the last time, almost tremulous. Fleetingly, she thought that if she were the kind of mother in whom her children confided, she would be about to receive a confidence of a disturbing kind. But she wasn't and they wouldn't, any more than their relationship allowed for her to confess to a daughter, suavely or delightedly, that a man had just invited her out to dinner.

"What's the matter, Sarah?"

The silence was so long and in a strange, indefinable way so profound that Ursula thought for a moment they had been cut off. She said, "Sarah?"

"I wanted to ask you something."

"Right. What?"

"I don't quite know how to put this." Ursula heard her daughter draw breath. Then, with a quaking of the heart, she heard her use a name she had never, so far as Ursula could remember, used before. "Mother," she said. "Mother, was Dad, was he always called Candless?"

Weakened by Sarah's form of address to her, Ursula said, "I don't understand."

"All right. Did he ever have another name? Did he change his name?"

"Not that I know of. No, he didn't. Where did you get that idea?"

Sarah didn't answer. "I thought of coming down for the weekend. I'd like to go through his study, go through all his papers. Would that be all right?"

Ursula was astonished even to be asked. She said too fulsomely, "Of course it would. Of course."

"And maybe I could be a bit of help. Sort things out for you. Would that be useful?"

"What did you mean about another name?" said Ursula.

Another silence. Then she said, "It's too difficult to explain on the phone. We'll talk about it when I come down."

Ursula sat in the living room, looking out to sea. The mist had gone and the sinking sun was a dark gold in the west. Lundy stood out against it, a dark rhombus. She reviewed what Sarah had said, making nothing of it. As the sun went and the shadows fell, she thought that if she turned around quickly, she

140

might see him there in "Daddy's chair." His name was as much a part of him as that big frame, that shaggy hair, that deep, authoritative, laconic voice. Gerald Candless. Not a name everyone would recognize, nowhere near a household word, but not to be passed over, not to be heard without a pause for thought, an "Ah, yes, of course."

She did turn then. If he were there, she'd be hallucinating. If he were there, she would be going mad. The chair, of course, was empty. The house was empty. She remembered then, weeks too late, that she had never told the hospital he wouldn't be having a bypass. No doubt they knew by now.

Her marriage might have been like other people's marriages. Perhaps this was what marriage was. How could you tell? She wasn't very interested in clothes or hairdressers or what her mother called "aids to beauty," but she went shopping in the mornings, window-shopping mostly, because there was nothing else to do. She went to St. John's churchyard and had a look at Constable's grave because Sally Wrightson told her she should. When it was fine, she walked on Hampstead Heath. A woman came in to clean the house. Gerald never ate lunch; he wouldn't stop for that. She took him coffee and a piece of bread with a hunk of cheese and he smiled at her and thanked her. In the afternoons, she deciphered his handwriting and typed another chapter of the book that would be called *The Forsaken Merman*.

The protagonist—he had taught her this word

when she called the leading character a "hero"—was a naval officer whose wife returned to live with her parents while he was away at sea and finally left him for the cousin she had been brought up with. There was very little in it about marriage and a lot about family relationships. If Ursula had hoped to find out his views on marriage from it, she was to be disappointed. She wondered how an only child, as he was, could know so much about what it meant to have brothers and sisters.

Gerald had thousands of books, so she no longer went to the library. It was at this time that she began reading something other than fiction. Not given to introspection then, she still saw them as Mr. Rochester and Jane Eyre, and if she thought about her marriage, though she didn't much, it was to conclude that life for Jane once she was a wife might have been similar to her own. Without the typewriter, of course. And without the memory of the madwoman in the distant wing. That Gerald might have had his own version of the madwoman never crossed her mind.

They had a drink together in the evening; they ate the dinner she cooked. Or they went out, or his friends came, or they went to them. The Wrightsons, the Arthurs, Adela Churchouse, Roger and Celia Pallinter. The conversation was of books, other people's books, book gossip, anecdotes about other authors, scandals. And about important things, their feelings, their beliefs, their principles.

Jonathan Arthur and his wife, Syria, were active in

the Campaign for Nuclear Disarmament. Syria's sister had actually refused to have children because of her dread of a nuclear disaster, of the world ending, and Syria said a day never went by without her worrying about a nuclear war coming. Ursula had never thought much about what her father still called "the atom bomb," or if she had, she had trusted in deterrence, but she joined CND and went to meetings.

For the sake of having something to do really and of becoming more like the people he knew and talked to. If she knew more and was more involved, he might not just ask her how she was and how the typing was going and what was she going to do that day; he might talk to her. He might treat her as an equal. Adela Churchouse tried to interest her in the anti-apartheid movement and in the Homosexual Law Reform Society, so she stopped buying South African apples and tried to be enlightened about homosexuals. This wasn't easy, because at home, her brother had made jokes about "poofters," while her father had thrown a book called *The Well of Loneliness* in the fire.

Much of *The Centre of Attraction* concerned a young sailor's guilt over Hiroshima and Nagasaki, but when she told Gerald about her new activities, he only seemed bored by CND. The anti-apartheid people he also seemed to find tedious, but he had put his foot down about HLRS. His reaction was almost as violent as her father's. What did she know about law reform? She was to have nothing to do with it. Change in the law would come in its own good time, nothing she could do would help it along, and what on earth was she thinking of listening to that old sapphist, Adela Churchouse?

At night, twice a week, they made love. Ursula had read in books of newly married people or new lovers—which was the same thing, wasn't it?—making love every night. Of course, she didn't believe everything she read in books, especially not now that she was married to a writer, but then Syria Arthur actually told her this was what she and Jonathan did. She mentioned it in passing almost, as if it was quite normal.

Perhaps all marriages were like that. Or perhaps they were like her own. How could she tell? One evening, an evening in on their own, when they had been married about eighteen months, Gerald asked her if she thought it was time she consulted a doctor about her failure to become pregnant.

That made her laugh. "I haven't failed, darling." She often called him darling then. It was what her parents called each other. "I've been taking care not to, haven't I?"

He hadn't known. Again, perhaps it was strange never to have discussed the subject. But she had no precedents. She didn't know she was supposed to ask him. A month before the wedding, she had gone to the doctor, been proud of herself for her courage and sophistication in doing this. The doctor had sent her to a clinic where she had been fitted up with a diaphragm. The sex books she read said it was unwise to leave this sort of thing to the man, so she hadn't. She

144

hadn't mentioned it to him, either. She supposed he must know, that he must have guessed.

He was angry on a level she had never seen before. Really, she had never seen him angry. The way he reacted to her proposal to join the Homosexual Law Reform Society was nothing compared to this. His face went a dark red and the veins stood out on his forehead. Anger made him look older than he was and as if given over to excesses, which he was not.

"You deceived me," he said. He shouted it.

"I didn't mean to, Gerald. I thought you knew."

"How could I know? What do I know about these things?"

"I thought you would," she said, almost stammering. "I thought men knew."

"Don't you want children? You're not like Syria's mad sister, are you, not wanting them in case they get blown up?"

"Of course I want children. One day. I'm only twenty-four. I want to wait a bit, a year or two."

"You have had your year or two," he said.

It was uttered in such a menacing tone that she was frightened. For the first time, she was really afraid of him. Not apprehensive, not wary, but frightened. She wasn't a small woman, but quite robust, above average height, and strongly built. But suddenly, he seemed enormous to her, a big, heavy, threatening man with a leonine head and angry black eyes.

She said quietly, almost timidly, "I'm sorry." She half saw that she had been wrong. It could look like deceit, what she had done. "I'm sorry. I didn't mean to do anything underhand."

"You aren't what I expected you'd be."

He had said that before, on their honeymoon. But then it had been a compliment. Now it sounded like a threat.

"Gerald, please," she said, and as he rose to his feet, she came up close to him, putting her hands on his shoulders. "Please forgive me. Please don't be angry with me."

That night in bed, he turned his back on her, but the following night—if she hadn't wanted him so much, it would have been rape. He made a violent onslaught that brought her a shuddering pleasure. She thought it a proof of his love and forgiveness.

Sarah was born the following December, nine months later.

At her age, to dress up for a man would be degrading. Ursula had seen plenty of that up at the hotel, old painted faces and teased, tinted hair, above-the-knee skirts on women whose daughters were past the age to wear them. She put on black velvet trousers, a black sweater, and a sand-colored jacket. Makeup had never been good on her; it either made no real difference or looked artificial and doll-like, so she had given up wearing it twenty years ago. Her face, she thought, looking at herself in the mirror, was like Sarah's would be in an out-of-focus photograph.

She expected to find her own way to the Dunes bar, but he was waiting for her in reception. She liked

that; it showed thoughtfulness. But she disliked, inso-
far as she could think about it at all, the lurch inside
her body and the racing of her heart when first she
saw him. It was unexpected. It was a sensation that
she thought past and gone.

He took her into the lounge, to a quiet corner that
was almost an alcove. The large picture window at
her elbow afforded a panorama of the sea and sky;
that was its purpose, what it had been built for, low to
the floor, a clear unbarred sheet of plate glass. The
sun had gone down, but the sky was still red, redder
than before sunset, with long black bars of cloud
ranged in parallel lines above the dark, gleaming sea.
She gazed at it to calm herself. He asked her what she
would like to drink, gave their order, and began, perhaps not unexpectedly, to talk about Gerald the
writer, Gerald and his books.

He had read many of them, knew them well, but
she didn't pay much attention to what he said. People
had been talking to her about Gerald's books for
more than thirty years; no doubt they thought it was
what she wanted to hear. She would very much have
liked to tell the truth to someone, someone she liked
and felt close to, tell that person she would gladly
never think about Gerald's books again, that they
interested her now only in that they were her source
of income, and the better they sold, the better pleased
she would be. She cut Sam Fleming short with a very
modified version of that and noted his startled look.

"Yes, his sales have gone up. I hope they won't
fall. Now he's dead, I mean."

He was very taken aback. "Is that likely?"

"There's no knowing. Sometimes when an author dies, his sales fall, and sometimes they rise."

"Was there," he began, "is there—is there a new book?"

"It's called *Less Is More*. He was reading the proofs when he died." She took a sip of her drink, then changed the subject abruptly. "What do you do? For a living, I mean."

"Thank you for not assuming I must be retired," he said.

"It never crossed my mind."

"You don't really want to know what I do, do you? It's just politeness."

She looked at him in a way she had tried to avoid doing. Into his face, his eyes. It was a mistake; it brought her close to trembling. She tried a light laugh. "Come on, what do you do?"

"All right. I'm a bookseller in Bloomsbury. Not antiquarian, and secondhand is an ugly way of putting it. Modern first editions."

Her face must have shown everything she felt. No, please, not quite everything, not that longing for him to touch her, to feel just the touch of his hand, which had been growing all the time they were talking. Not that, but the shock of learning what he did, which was like a shower of cold water hitting her. Then the blood came up into her face, burning after the cold shock.

She thought, I will say, "I see," and he will try to explain, and I will say it's all right and to forget it, and it will be impossible to have any sort of conversation after that. So she turned the subject yet again and talked innocuously about the children, his grandchildren, and, by extension, her daughters—never an easy topic for her—and that, of course, led to his son. His dead son.

But she heard very little of what he said, though she had encouraged him to talk, and she put on a show of interest. Her right hand lay on the table, beside her glass. She didn't think about it; it just rested there. But because of her shame and her growing indignation with him, she feigned an almost-effusive sympathy for him, uttering meaninglessly to herself, "I'm sorry, I'm so sorry."

He put out his hand and laid it over hers. Ten minutes before, this action would have been all she wanted. For the time, for a start. Now it had a deadening effect; it was hateful to her. She let her hand lie there, felt his above it, not as welcomed skin against receptive skin, but as an embarrassment, heavy, hot. The waiter came, called by him, and his arrival was an excuse for withdrawing her hand.

It was a relief to him as much as to her, she thought, when she rose to go at barely 9:30. He would walk her back to her house, he said. She argued a little, then gave in. The thought that he might want to come into the house on the chance of getting a look at Gerald's first editions was bitter. But in the event, he didn't even come to the front door, only to the garden gate. She realized that on leaving by that gate less than two hours before, she had imagined that on her return he might kiss her. Imagined it as fantasy, but still saw in her mind's eye the scenario.

"Good night," she said.

He had been going to say something—she had no idea what—but he didn't. He checked himself and echoed her own good night.

It isn't possible by looking at a woman to tell whether she will bear children easily. Ursula knew that even when she accused Gerald of choosing her for that reason. Anyway, it could be true that he *thought* he could tell, that he had *thought* that when he first saw her and noticed her generous hips, full breasts, youth, innocence, and ignorance. And he was right. She was in labor for only two hours before Sarah was delivered. In a later age, the hospital would have sent her home in the afternoon. As it was, they kept her in for three days.

Few women then were commenting on the injustice of a preference for baby boys over baby girls. Boys were best, and not only among Muslims. Because Ursula had begun to be frightened of Gerald, had been apprehensive and wary of him throughout her pregnancy, she thought he would mind having a girl. He would blame her, as men did blame women, for having a girl. But for once, he surprised her with a delight and an enthusiasm she had never suspected him capable of.

"I'd been worried," she said into Sarah's tape recorder, "that although he seemed to want a child very much, he wouldn't be so overjoyed when that child was a reality. I didn't think he knew what it meant to have a baby in the house. Well, I didn't know myself. But I thought I knew better than he did."

"And you were wrong," said Sarah. She said it in a satisfied way Ursula chose to ignore.

"As you say," Ursula said levelly, "I was wrong." She reflected on how wrong she had been. "He adored you from the first. He called you his treasure. He used to complain, you know, that no one took a writer's writing seriously. I mean that they think what a writer does is really a hobby, that it's not a job, and that it can be dropped for something else at any time, can be interrupted at any time. So a writer, being at home, can undertake any home tasks, is always there to answer the door, or take phone calls, or talk to people who come. And I thought he'd make a point of that not in fact being the case with the baby, with you. I thought he'd insist on never being disturbed by your crying and absolutely never, never being expected to look after you. But he forgot all that with you, with his treasure."

Sarah was smiling, so she smiled, too. She forced it, but she managed.

"He took you out for walks in your pram. Men didn't do that then, but he did. He changed your diapers. He would have fed you—only in the nature of things, I had to do that. The doctor was always in the house. GPs would still make home visits in 1966. Every time you weren't in the peak of perfect health, that poor GP was sent for."

"You must have felt yourself very lucky," Sarah said.

"To have that sort of man, you mean? That rare sort of man?" Ursula managed not to answer. "My mother didn't think it was right. Your aunt Helen didn't. They thought it must be some failure on my part. My father wanted to know why we didn't have a nanny or at least an au pair. We could easily have afforded it. Your father wouldn't. He said there was nothing she could do that he couldn't, and he did it with a love no mere nanny could feel. Of course, we had a nanny for Hope; we had to." Ursula paused. "Is this the sort of thing you want?"

"I'd like an anecdote. Something a bit more . . . well, individual?"

"I can't think of anything."

"Okay, then, that'll do for now."

Sarah switched off the machine. Just as well, Ursula thought, because I don't know how long I could go on with this. Anecdotes, indeed. She didn't know what she was asking. Of course she didn't. They were approaching dangerous ground, and if they hadn't stopped, she would have had to start lying.

"Dad changed his name when he was twenty-five," Sarah said. "I don't know why. Do you?"

Ursula didn't believe it. "Are you sure?"

"I'm sure he did, but I'm not sure of anything more. You never had the slightest suspicion?"

"Not about his name, no. Why should I?"

"Not about anything? About his not having any

aunts or uncles or cousins? You said there was no one belonging to him at your wedding."

"I suppose I did sometimes think it was rather strange his having no relations at all. No, I thought it strange he could write so much and so well about families when he hadn't got one."

"But you didn't ask him?"

"No."

"Shall we have a look at Dad's room?"

Ursula was touched by that "we," as she always was by anything either of her daughters said that might be construed as implying a bond or link between her and Sarah or Hope. She followed Sarah to the door of the room, and it was only then, when Sarah hesitated and turned her head, that she was aware of her daughter's stricken face. How self-centered I am, she thought, how absorbed in my own troubles, how *unnoticing*. It would be an effort for Sarah to go in there—she saw that—it would cause her real pain. Neither she nor Hope had entered the room since Gerald had died.

"Would you like to leave it for another time?"

Sarah shook her head. "I'll be fine."

Never had Ursula done her daughters the injustice of believing their affection for their father was less than utterly genuine. There had been no pretense, no affectation. They adored him. As I might have, she thought, if he had been to me as he was to them, if I had been his treasure. There came into her mind, unexpectedly, unbidden, the twelve-year-old

Hope saying to her with resentful abruptness, "Why can't you be nicer to Daddy?"

She opened the door of Gerald's study and stood back to let Sarah precede her. There was no mist today and the window revealed a bright sky, cold, with racing clouds, a choppy sea, Lundy standing out clear and dark. Sarah looked nervously about the room. She went to the desk, hesitated, and then sat down in her father's chair. His handwriting was nowhere visible; Ursula had seen to that. She had taken away those selected manuscripts and sent them to Boston, to Bond Street, to the anthologist in Cumbria. Sarah touched the cover on his typewriter, opened a drawer and then closed it again.

"Are there any more certificates?" she said.

"You mean birth, marriage, death? All we have are upstairs. Do you want me to fetch them?"

"Tell me where they are and I'll fetch them."

You will only have to come back in here, thought Ursula. You had better stay and get accustomed to it. She went upstairs and found the file that contained all the family documents, her parents' death certificates, her marriage certificate, those for her birth, the girls' births, and now the one for Gerald's death. Sarah was no longer at the desk, but standing in front of the cupboard with the door open, contemplating those stacked manuscripts. She had grown very pale.

"I'll give you back his birth certificate," she said tonelessly, then, vaguely indicating the manuscripts, added, "All these will have to be read, won't they?"

"Will they? I don't know."

She seemed interested only in the marriage certificate and not very interested in that. "Did Dad keep a diary?"

"Not so far as I know. Well, no, I know he didn't."

"He put all his life into his books, didn't he? Everything that happened to him, everything people said, the things he saw and heard."

He had been famous for it. In lectures, interviews, on radio and television, he had vaunted his tendency to constant autobiography. "Did he tell you that?"

"Not all that long ago, as a matter of fact. Three or four years? Hope and I were both at home and he was reading over something he'd written and he started talking to us about how he had written down everything that had ever happened to him. Well, not everything, not by then, but he intended finally to have written everything." Sarah paused, her voice not quite steady. "I don't know if he did. I wonder if he did."

Ursula said nothing.

"Of course, when it was made into fiction, it was sort of filtered through the author's creative process, so it changed; he explained that. Anyway, I knew it; it's something I explain to my students, who want everything Charlotte Brontë wrote, for instance, to be directly autobiographical. But he did use everything; his life was his material, to a degree that I think is unusual. So I suppose we can't expect a diary, as well."

Talking had helped Sarah. The academic in her was coming to her aid. Ursula saw the color beginning to return to her face.

"Are you interested in letters?" she asked.

"Not particularly." An old sharpness was also returning. "This is going to be *my* memoir—in other words, my memories. I may want Dad's background, but I don't want what he said to other people, and still less what they said to him. I may take a look at his notebooks and the latest proofs."

"Photographs?"

"We've got a boxful somewhere, haven't we? For some reason, we never had albums."

"No, we never had albums," said Ursula. "I'll leave you to it."

He put all his life into his books. . . . For a long time, she hadn't seen it. *A Paper Landscape,* published a year after Hope was born, had been another story of a family, poor Irish in Liverpool this time, and the eldest daughter's struggles to become a painter. In the next one, *A Messenger of the Gods,* a father dies young and his widow is left with two small children and his old mother to support. The change came with *Orisons,* written after the move to Lundy View House. This was the first novel of his she hadn't enjoyed, experiencing instead a sense of foreboding when she began to decipher a new chapter.

Yet for a long time, she had made herself resist. It was her imagination, she told herself. These characters couldn't be based on her sister, Helen, and her husband. She was too introspective, too sensitive; perhaps she was paranoid. It was vanity that made one see oneself in fictional characters. Adela Churchouse, or it might have been Roger Pallinter, had told her that when they used a real person to create a character, he or she never suspected, while people constantly saw themselves as the originals of characters based on others.

But when she came to type *Hand to Mouth* in 1984, she was no longer able to deceive herself.

10

The seahorse is unique among species in that it is the male who becomes pregnant and bears the young.

—HAMADRYAD

A FAMOUS ACTRESS, who had also been an acquaintance of Gerald Candless, recited the second half of Tennyson's "Ulysses." A rather less famous actor, but one who had occasionally stayed at Lundy View House, read Herbert's "Jordan." Ursula, in the front pew, with a daughter on either side of her, the younger in a huge black hat and weeping copiously, thought "Jordan" inappropriate for an aggressive atheist like Gerald, of whom it couldn't have been said that while he had his God, he envied no man's nightingale or spring.

Ursula didn't know, and had indeed never heard of, the soprano who sang a Hugo Wolf song. These were Hope's choices, and she suspected Hope had chosen what she would like at her own memorial service, if she had been able to contemplate having one. Roger Pallinter, thin in old age, arthritic and on two

158

sticks, recited one of his own poems. It was a surprise to Ursula that he had written any. Colin Wrightson, looking just as old and doddery, gave an address. Eulogy, thought Ursula. She also thought how very odd it was to listen to and look at a man who had once been one's lover and feel nothing for him but impatience and a faint distaste.

She would have liked to hold poor Hope's hand but could scarcely imagine what the reaction might be if she attempted to take it. Robert Postle, sitting behind her, had one of those noisy, spluttery colds that spray infection into a three-foot-long radius of atmosphere around their subject. She felt a spot of damp on the back of her neck and shuddered. While Wrightson droned on, his wife, on the other side of the church, put on her glasses and read the black-edged sheet Hope had had printed with the songs and poems on it and *Gerald Candless 1926–1997* in Times roman at the top. Perhaps she was as taken aback as Ursula herself had been at the Latin epitaph: *Vixit, scripsit, mortuus est.*

"He lived, he wrote, he died," Tessa Postle whispered throatily to her.

It made her shudder. She was going home on the 3:50, a train that would get her to Exeter by 7:00 P.M. From there, she would take another, reaching Barnstaple by some time just before nine. Both girls had asked her to stay the night, which amazed and touched her, though Hope's invitation had been grudging. Her sister, Helen, had asked her to stay, and perhaps she would have done if the prospect of getting from Carshalton to Paddington in the morning hadn't been so dire. Now it was all over and the organist was playing a voluntary, which Adela Churchouse was humming and to which she seemed to be executing a little dance in the aisle. London's literati drifted out into the courtyard, into Piccadilly.

Ursula was kissed by people she couldn't remember ever having seen before. Robert Postle, mopping his face with tissues from a box held by Tessa, said that they must meet; they must talk; there was the new book. . . . When would she come up again? When would she have lunch with him? "You don't need me," she said. A small crowd surrounded her by this time, but no one was shocked; no one was even surprised. It was her grief, her loss, the soul-rocking sorrow any woman would feel at the loss of such a man as Gerald Candless. To her surprise, Sarah came up to her, touched her arm, rescued her. She had a taxi waiting; she and Hope would accompany her to Paddington.

A red-letter day indeed, thought Ursula, who could hardly believe it. Once more, but this time in the taxi, they sat on either side of her, and she was moved by their presence, as nothing connected with Gerald could have moved her. He was gone, but she was still there; she was their surviving parent—Was that it? Was that what accounted for it? Something happened that hadn't happened for years and years. The tears came into her eyes, and not tears that stopped there, were blinked back, and quelled, but real gushing, pouring tears that spilled over and flooded down her face.

"Oh, Ma," said Sarah, "I'm so sorry, I'm so sorry."

Ursula hadn't felt so happy for ages. She hadn't felt happy at all for years, but now she did, because Sarah and Hope were being nice to her, were actually both of them kissing her good-bye. She couldn't remember Hope kissing her since she was a tiny girl. They were a threesome hugging, a great loving embrace; then the girls went, and happy Ursula, making sure they were gone, bought herself a poached salmon and watercress sandwich and a bottle of fresh orange juice in the sandwich shop for eating and drinking on the train, in the first-class compartment.

Sarah told herself that she had come to terms with her father's behavior, his assumption, for some reason or other, of a new identity. At least she was used to it. She could accept it. The difficulty was that her discovery had stopped her in her tracks; she was stuck as badly as if she had writer's block. Her father could have told her, though he never had, that if the first few chapters a writer has written are lifeless or have gaps in them, it will be very hard to proceed with any enthusiasm until that earlier part has been satisfactorily repaired. And if these repairs can't be carried out, the whole work may have to be abandoned.

She couldn't mend her chapter without the wherewithal for filling gaps. A great reluctance to go on had taken hold of her. How could she write about a man who seemed to have been born at the age of twenty-five? A man who had taken his first job at that age? The *Western Morning News* had replied to her letter. They had a record of Gerald Candless working for them in Plymouth as a general reporter from the summer of 1951 until late in 1957. She had even read a piece written by him on the Suez crisis of 1956 and soldiers leaving for Egypt on a boat out of Plymouth. But no records seemed to exist of his history before 1951.

The results of searching her father's study had been disappointing. He had not been a specially orderly man, but on the other hand, he hadn't been grossly untidy, either. There was no filing system, but neither were there drawers stuffed with rubbish. He had kept letters, still in their envelopes, but by no means all the letters he had received. In spite of what she had said to her mother, she read them and wondered at his choice of what to preserve, at last realizing—it was an unwelcome, even chilling, con- clusion—that he had kept letters from the rich and famous, from celebrities and from distinguished writers. Friends' letters had been discarded. It was impossible to escape the conclusion that he was look- ing to a posthumous future, when someone would write his biography and include those letters.

In that case, what had he expected a biographer to do about his banished childhood and youth? Not inquire perhaps. Assume, gloss over, pass on. Strange, then, that he had kept no sort of diary. Not entirely believing her mother, Sarah had searched for a diary, found only notebooks whose contents referred to the plots, themes, and characters of his novels.

All Saturday afternoon, she had worked in the study, but in the evening she had gone to the pub in Barnstaple and then on to a drinking club with a bunch of friends. Strangely enough, because there was no prearrangement, Adam Foley turned up among them once again. He was one of Alexander's friends, or an ex-boyfriend of Rosie's sister—Sarah wasn't sure which. His family had a weekend cottage in a village not far away.

Nothing was said about the phone call, coldly received and coldly terminated, but she thought he resented what had happened. It must be so. He spoke to everyone but her. He must remember her "No, thanks, can't, I'm busy." Too bad. She wouldn't talk to him, either. It was a shame he was so deeply, disturbingly attractive. His hair was black and his skin had a dark bloom. He was thin. She liked thinness and that peculiar grace with which he moved, very casual, laid-back, insouciant. But she had brushed him off.

After a time, she was aware, uncomfortably at first, then with mounting excitement, of his eyes on her. Not on her face, not meeting her eyes, but on her body. That wasn't what having a roving eye meant, but his eyes roved. While they were still in the pub, he went to fetch a round of drinks, then came back with glasses for everyone but her.

"What's poor Sarah done?" Rosie said.

He looked at her face then. "I didn't see you there."

It was uttered in an indifferent tone and as if she were too insignificant to be noticed. He must be paranoid if a woman's refusal to go out with him made him so rude. She could be rude, too. It would give her pleasure.

"Staring at an empty chair, were you?"

She got up, went to the bar, and bought her own drink. The place was so crowded, she had to push past him to get back to her seat. As she did so, his arm touched her thigh, pressed against her thigh. For some reason, she didn't walk out. She stayed and they went on to the club. It was in a cellar under a greengrocer's and called, of course, Greens. He pushed ahead of her; he let the door swing into her face. There was dancing on a little floor the size of someone's bathroom and he danced with Vicky and with Rosie. He danced with them and looked at her.

She was mesmerized by him. She began to feel a little sick. Of course, she had drunk too much. It must have been after one when they all left. Rosie asked him if he wanted a lift. He cocked a thumb in Sarah's direction and said in exactly the tone he might use about a taxi driver, "She's taking me."

And she did take him. Or he took her. He took the keys from her in silence, found her car, opened the passenger door for her, and drove a couple of miles. She was very drunk, but not too drunk to be aware that he had parked the car on the grass verge and gotten out. He came around to her side, pulled her out, put her in the back, and made love to her on the backseat.

Somehow or other, he and she had gone back to the cottage together and Sarah had stayed the night. With Adam, in Adam's bed, though members of his family were occupying the other bedrooms. And it had been exciting, like being a teenager again, creeping up the stairs, carrying her shoes, making no sound because Adam's aunt or grandmother or someone was sleeping on the other side of the bedroom wall. They had scarcely spoken. Early in the morning, the moment the old woman had gone off to Holy Communion, she had gotten up and driven home with a monstrous hangover.

Her mother had made no comment on Sarah's arriving back at ten in the morning, just asked if she'd had a nice evening. Sarah drank a lot of fizzy water and a fair amount of black coffee and took herself back into the study, where she expected to find nothing and where she made the only real discovery of the weekend.

It was in the last drawer she examined, lying on top of the sheets in an open pack of typing paper. She didn't know what it was and didn't know then that she had made a discovery, only that she was holding in her hand something peculiar that she couldn't identify and which seemed to have no place in a novelist's workroom. Not, that is, a novelist who was also an atheist. But she thought that later. After the memorial service, in fact, back in her own flat, where she showed her find to Hope and Fabian.

* * *

Their father had not only not believed in God but had been aggressively anti-God. (Their mother's attitude toward religion they had never inquired about nor thought important.) He had brought them up god-lessly, though without the ostentation of requesting they not attend school assembly. Religious ritual, he opined, would have no effect on them, and he had been right. Neither of them had ever read a line of the Bible, nor did they recognize quotations from it. They had been in church only to attend their cousin Pauline's wedding and their father's funeral.

Hope, therefore, had no more idea of what the thing found in the paper drawer was than her sister had. It seemed to be made of some fibrous vegetable substance, leaf or stem perhaps. A strip of this had been folded double, to which, two-thirds of the way up, a crosspiece, also folded double, was attached with a neat binding to conceal the join.

"It's a palm cross," said Fabian.

"A what?"

"There's atheism and there's ignorance," he said, "and you two are just plain ignorant. You don't have to believe in God to know something about religion. I mean a smidgen. If I asked you what is: a, a pyx; b, a creed; and c, Pentecost, you wouldn't have a clue, would you?"

"I know what a creed is," said Hope impatiently. "Anyway, never mind that. What's this thing? What's a palm cross?"

"It's palm leaf or reed or even a branch from a fir

tree made into the shape of a cross and given to people who attend matins or Mass, I expect, on Palm Sunday, which is the Sunday before Easter."

"I thought you were Jewish," said Sarah.

"I don't think you can be right, Fab," said Hope, "because Daddy would never have had anything like that in the house. Daddy *hated* religion. He said he didn't agree with anything Marx said except about religion being the opium of the people. And he used to mock religion, I mean make jokes about it. Jonathan Arthur was staying once and he was talking about Resurrection—he's religious—and Daddy upset him frightfully by saying that what went up must come down."

"I can't help that. It's a palm cross, known as a palm. Ask anyone if you don't believe me. Ask that fellow Postle, the one with the streaming nose; he's a Catholic."

"If I ask him, he'll want to know how the book's coming on," said Sarah, "and it isn't coming on. I don't know what to do next."

Fabian said, "Your dad had a London accent. I'm a latter-day Professor Higgins, I am; I know about accents. His was London, and I'd say with a faint undertone somewhere of East Anglia. So he's a Londoner, living alone, working on this newspaper, and something terrible happens. Discount something criminal; your dad wouldn't have done that, or so you say, so it's something that happened to him. Wife or lover died? Children died? Made some momentous discovery about his family—his real family, I mean? Some hereditary disease, murderer for a father—how about that?"

"I don't see why having your lover die would be all that terrible," said Hope.

"Thanks very much."

"I don't mean that, Fab. You know I don't. But why would it make you change your identity? A murderer for a father's more likely."

"I'm remembering something from long ago," Sarah said. "I once heard that funny old woman Adela Churchouse saying something to Dad about that. Oh, not about having a murderer for a father—I don't believe that—but about his accent. She said, 'You know, Gerald, sometimes when you get animated, the way you were just then, I can hear Silly Suffolk in your voice.' And Dad said there was nothing more likely, because he'd lived in Ipswich till he was ten."

If she had thought of that conversation at all since Joan Thague's revelations, it was to assume that everything he had said was a lie, just as she had assumed all references he had made to his origins were untrue. But suppose it hadn't been a lie? Suppose that, though not the Gerald Candless born to George and Kathleen Candless in Waterloo Road, he also had come from Ipswich and lived there long enough as a child to acquire an ineradicable accent?

The palm cross lay on the table, where Fabian had put it down on top of a copy of the *Spectator.* There was something about it that Sarah very much disliked and which she found deeply disconcerting. She didn't want to think about it too much, didn't want to confront its implications, yet to throw it away, to put it out with the rubbish to be collected by Camden waste disposal in the morning, seemed an extreme step, and one she might regret.

After Hope and Fabian had gone, she took out of the bookcase her copy of the *Shorter Oxford Dictionary,* put the palm inside it between *dynamicity* and *Earl Marshal,* and replaced the dictionary on the shelf.

11

*Times change and views do an about-face. Oliver's
grandfather would have been ashamed if his wife
had gone out to work, but Oliver was embarrassed
because his wife stayed at home.*

—HAND TO MOUTH

MR. AND MRS. JOHN GEORGE CANDLESS, put in possession of the facts, looked upon the whole thing with
suspicion. J.G. passed through three phases of doubt:
disbelief at first, then speculation, finally extreme
wariness. "Have nothing more to do with it, keep
away, ignore the girl's letter, or send back a sharp
negative response."

But Maureen said, "Suppose she puts it in the
paper or this book she's writing? Better be there and
find out what she's up to."

"All right," said J.G., "and tell her I shall be consulting my solicitor if you like."

Neither of them had ever previously heard of
Auntie Joan having a little brother who died. A little
brother called Gerald Candless. Why should they?
Auntie Joan wasn't really John George's auntie, but
something like his first cousin once removed, and it
had all happened so long ago.

"It's upset Auntie Joan a lot," Maureen had said. "I've never seen her tearful before. And now this girl's written and wants to see her again."

"There's bound to be some ulterior motive. She could be after Auntie Joan's money."

"She hasn't got any money, J.G."

"You never want to say that about anyone. The ones you say that about are the ones who are rolling in it."

So because Joan didn't feel like writing and didn't know what to say, Maureen phoned Sarah Candless and was careful to be offhand. She could come if she liked, but Mr. and Mrs. J. G. Candless would appreciate it if Sarah remembered Joan was an old lady and shouldn't be upset. She, Maureen, would make a point of being there just to keep an eye on things.

That made Sarah feel as if they suspected her of planning to steal the silver. She hardly knew what she was going to ask Joan Thague. If she asked about friends and neighbors at the time of the little boy's death, would that upset Joan? Would any reference to that time upset her? Suppose she asked for a photograph of the child? But how would that help? She remembered the fat photograph albums laid out, ready for scrutiny, but which had never been scrutinized. Did they take group photographs in those days? Of some university class or team, yes, but of the pupils at an Ipswich primary school?

She drove to Ipswich on the appointed day but lost her way and found herself in the center of the town. The place was full of churches and streets named for churches, so that once again she thought of the palm cross. She would have liked to imagine her father as a child in this town, walking with his mother and holding her hand, but it was impossible because so much must have changed, because the little shops of that time had been replaced by precincts and malls. But he had lived here—she was sure of that; she hung on to that, remembering the trace of a Suffolk accent Adela Churchouse and Fabian had detected.

When she eventually found her way to Rushmere St. Andrew, the front door of the bungalow was opened to her by Maureen Candless. She introduced herself brusquely as Mrs. Candless. She was a big woman, fat and heavy, somehow frightening in her charmlessness. Her face in repose was sullen and in animation a conflict of big jarring features—thick lips, overlarge teeth, a pointed nose with a tip that twitched independently of the rest of it.

"She can't tell you anything," she said. "I expect you'll have had a wasted journey."

This time, Sarah sensed, there was going to be no tea, no cakes on a plate with a paper doily. Joan Thague sat very upright and on the edge of an armchair made for the adoption of a more relaxed attitude. She looked uncomfortable and she was. She had been uncomfortable since Sarah's previous visit, having suffered repeated bad dreams for the first time in many years. And in the daytime, while apparently occupied with something quite removed from her family and the past, she had heard, as if a real child were in the house and a real child somewhere in pain, a thin, weary voice crying, "My head hurts, my head hurts." She'd been cooking a meal for her grandson Jason, standing at the stove, frying chips, when the child called her and she heard it, for she wasn't deaf to *that* voice.

None of this, of course, had been told to J.G. and his wife. They were given no details, only the bare facts. Joan was surprised they didn't know them already, and offended, too, hurt, rather, that J.G.'s mother had never said a word to him about Gerald and Gerald's death, had forgotten him or ignored him, as if he had never existed. Maureen was kind, especially in the matter of taking her to the Martlesham Tesco, but she didn't want Maureen there. She didn't want Sarah Candless, either. Or anyone.

And Sarah hardly knew how to begin. The two women were looking at her as if she were a social worker come to accuse them of mistreating a child. Joan Thague cleared her throat, brought her hands together, and looked down at her wedding ring. For the first time, Sarah was conscious of the smell in the house, a laboratory's attempt at re-creating the scent of daffodils and hyacinths. She thought she ought to preface her inquiries with some kind of apology for her father, and on the way here, she had rehearsed this, but it had turned into an apology for herself, for caring about a man who had manifestly been so false and so deceitful, and she couldn't bring herself to make it. Instead she said, "I feel that my father must have known your family. As a child, he must have lived somewhere near. He lived here till he was ten. And he had a Suffolk accent."

"Well, that's something no one in this family ever had," Maureen Candless said in a huffy tone and broad Ipswich.

"He had a trace of it," Sarah said. "That's been something for me to hold on to." She looked from one implacable face to the other, from Joan's wary eyes to the twitch at the end of Maureen's nose. "I'm sure you can understand." Why do we say we're sure when we mean we have the gravest doubts? "I wondered if you had a neighbor with a boy of your brother's age, Mrs. Thague. Or friends of the family. Or if he had school friends."

Joan Thague looked at her cousin's wife. For reassurance? Comfort? *Permission?* No, not that last. Joan Thague was, in the current phrase, her own woman. She said, "When you get old, you remember your childhood better than what happened yesterday. Did you know that?"

Sarah nodded.

"Gerald hadn't been at school long. The elementary school, that is. They didn't call them primary schools then. He was the only little boy in our street who went to that school. There weren't any other little boys. I know that, because Mother said it was a shame there was no one for him to play with."

"He had no one to play with?"

"He had me," said Joan Thague.

"Yes, but no one his own age?"

"We had these cousins, my mother's sister's chil-

174

dren. Two boys and a girl. Donald and Kenneth and Doreen." Joan had been thinking about it, racking her brain. "They used to come. My auntie brought them to tea once a week. She fetched the boys from school and brought them to tea and Gerald played with Don and Ken. Doreen was only little, too young for school. We had a special tea when they came. Mother made a sponge with chocolate butter icing."

It was a middle-class picture, not what Sarah had expected. She enunciated carefully, conscious that Joan needed to read her lips. "Your mother was a nurse. Did she go out nursing? I mean, did she go to people's houses? I thought there might have been someone she nursed who had a boy or a boy she nursed."

"My father would never have allowed my mother to work." Mrs. Thague was more than indignant. A flush burned across her face. "He was a master printer. It would have looked as if he couldn't support his family."

So why was she listed as a nurse on that birth certificate? Out of a struggling attempt, doomed to instant failure, on Kathleen Candless's part to assert herself as a person, not merely an appendage? This, at any rate, was how Sarah saw it. Not anxious to look into Mrs. Thague's face but knowing she must if the woman was to understand her, she asked about Don and Ken, the cousins, their ages, their fate.

"You can't expect her to know that," said Maureen Candless.

Because Maureen hadn't been looking in her

direction, Joan hadn't heard. The flush fading, the outrage subsiding, she said, "They were both younger than me and older than Gerald. Don would have been ten and Ken seven when—when my brother died. He was killed in the war, Don, I mean, in the desert at El Alamein."

To Sarah's astonishment, she eased her chair a little toward her, edging its legs across the carpet. She peered into Sarah's face. It was as if her outrage over what she took as suggestions her family might not have been comfortably off had cleared some obstruction in her head. Some inhibition had been broken down by a surge of anger. She leaned forward, her relative's wife forgotten.

"They weren't Candlesses. My mother was a Mitchell; she and her sister were Kathleen and Dorothy Mitchell and my auntie Dorothy was a Mrs. Applestone. So they were all Applestones, Don and Ken and Doreen. Not Candlesses. You understand that, don't you?"

"I don't believe my father was a Candless, Mrs. Thague. I'm sure he wasn't. I think he just took the name."

"That puts a different complexion on things," said Maureen, catching on at last. Her tone was lighter, relief mixed in it. She began slowly shaking her head, as if such iniquity as Sarah's father's had been was undreamed of in her philosophy.

"My cousin Ken," Joan Thague said, "Ken Applestone. I don't know what became of him. I left home, you see. When I was fifteen. The fact was, I couldn't stand being home after Gerald was gone. I couldn't bear it." She cast a glance at Maureen, perhaps to check the effect such a small display of feeling might have had on her. "I went into lodgings in Sudbury and worked in the silk mill. Then I met my husband and I got married—I came home to Ipswich to get married—and we lived there, over the shop on Melford Road, and he went into the army, and what with one thing and another, I lost touch with the family. With the Applestones, I mean, not with my family. I always wrote regular to my mother and she to me. That's how I heard about Don, through my mother."

"But no one mentioned Ken?"

"I know he was in the air force, went in when he was eighteen, in 'forty-three." She had looked down into her lap as she sometimes did when she was speaking, as opposed to the stare into the speaker's face she gave when listening, but now she looked up. "My mother died in 'fifty-one, but she'd have told me if Ken'd died in the war. I think he was alive and living—now, where did he live?—when she died, but after that—I saw Auntie Dorothy at Mother's funeral and I don't reckon I ever saw her again."

"Where did he live, Mrs. Thague?"

"Let me think. In Essex, I think it was. Chelmsford. Yes, it was Chelmsford, but that was forty-six years ago, and that's a long time in anyone's reckoning."

Emboldened by Joan's confidential manner, Sarah asked if she might see the photograph albums that had been displayed on her first visit but which

177

were absent now. Joan nodded and went away to fetch them. Once she was gone, Maureen got up and lumbered over to the window, stretching herself and rolling her heavy shoulders. Then she turned to Sarah and said coldly, "I wonder you aren't content to let bygones be bygones."

"I'm sorry?"

"If it were my dad, which frankly I can't imagine, I wouldn't want to bring any more to light. You never know what you'll find when you start looking under stones, do you?"

Joan Thague brought back three albums. They were the kind of thing Sarah knew families had but that were so conspicuously absent from her own home. Looking through the shoe box of photographs her mother kept in her bedroom, she had been rather taken aback by the paucity of the collection. It was on the day she had found the palm, and she had been holding that curious religious symbol in her left hand when she sifted through the snapshots—the single photograph of her parents at their wedding, baby shots of Hope and herself—and found the one picture that was of real interest to her. This was of a young Gerald, younger than in that wedding pose, slim, dark, stunningly handsome. He was standing against a seawall somewhere and in the background was an island and a wooded escarpment.

"He gave me that when we were engaged," her mother had said indifferently.

Sarah had identified the setting herself. It was Plymouth Hoe and that was Drake's Island, with

Mount Edgcumbe Park behind. Gerald Candless, firmly entrenched in that name by then, twenty-seven or twenty-eight, working for the *Western Morning News*. Now she looked at the pages Joan Sprague turned for her. Sepia photographs and then black-and-white photographs. Joan had to explain that this postcard-size shot of a man and a woman walking along an esplanade with two children had been taken by seaside photographers, something of which Sarah had no experience, though living by the sea for much of her childhood. But she looked closely at such a picture of George and Kathleen Candless with Joan and the small Gerald at Felixstowe and understood from this pictorial rendering what no words could entirely have told her: that these people could not have been her grandparents nor this child her father. DNA testing isn't the only answer.

George had been a little man, stunted perhaps by poverty in his youth. His wife was taller than he and broad in her striped Macclesfield silk dress, strap shoes, and small obligatory hat. Both had puddingy faces, small eyes, snub noses, he a large chin, she puffy cheeks, and what showed of their hair under their hats looked mousy fair. The little boy, Sarah perceived, could never have grown into her father. Even cosmetic surgery would not have changed that pudgy face with the close-set eyes and George Candless's chin into what she thought of and Hope had once called, half serious, half joking, all adoring, their father's noble countenance.

She turned to look at Joan Thague and cried out

involuntarily, "Oh, I'm sorry, I'm sorry!" for Joan was weeping, as Ursula had wept in the taxi to Paddington station, but somehow far more wretchedly and despairingly.

Giving birth to Hope had been hard. Ursula had never heard of a woman having a normal and easy delivery the first time and a cesarean the second. But it happens and it had happened to her. There was no milk and there was no joy.

She found that she had no feeling for the new baby. Gerald chose her name and, though he consulted her, she wasn't interested. She would as soon have named the child Despair. "Call her what you like," she said, and slept. All she wanted to do was sleep. She wasn't physically ill. Physically she recovered within a week and the scar was fast disappearing. That was in the days before they recognized or had a name for postnatal depression. Her mother came over to Hampstead and told her she had felt just the same after Helen's birth but that there was no use in moping; you had to pull yourself together and get on with things. After all, no one would do it for you.

There Betty Wick was wrong. The one who would was Gerald. But even he was hardly able to look after a baby and an infant not yet two on his own. He engaged a nanny. Ursula must have known her name at the time, though Gerald, as if he came from the upper class, always addressed her as "Nanny." Whatever her name had been, Ursula couldn't remember it now. She had always thought of her and spoken of her as "the woman."

The woman was highly qualified, very competent, brisk, and efficient. She knew her job. She despised Ursula and made that plain, but Ursula, from a distance of thirty years, from any distance, come to that, couldn't have accused the woman of stealing her children's love. Gerald did that. When she read *Hand to Mouth,* she understood that it wasn't an accident, that it wasn't chance, but a deliberate act. He said so in the book.

Sometimes she wondered whether things would have been different if she had managed to take Betty's advice and pull herself together. If she had asserted herself. But a black depression settled over her, as if a blanket had been dropped to envelop her; she retreated into its folds and curled up and shut her eyes.

The woman didn't sleep in the house, but went home to Edgware. There would have been room for her if Gerald had slept in Ursula's bedroom, but he had moved out so as not to disturb her, he said, when one of the children woke. He had Hope's cot beside his bed. Every morning, he took Hope in to see her, but he could detect her indifference to the baby, and later, looking back, she thought she could remember his satisfied expression, his *pleasure.*

She had made so many mistakes. But she hadn't thought it was a question of correctness or mistakes. It wasn't an examination. In her depression, she was so helpless. All interest in anything was lost, all desire to move, even to open her eyes. For a time, she wasn't even ashamed of how she felt; she was beyond shame, beyond love or guilt or hope. Her mother made her bathe or she would never have washed herself. She grew thin and weak.

Then the depression lifted. One day, she was in darkness, in despair; the next, she had come out of it and stood in the light. She felt better: Optimism returned and her strength came back. She was never able to account for the change. As she grew well again, able to get up and go downstairs, she tried to love Hope as she loved Sarah. But Hope cried a lot; she was a colicky baby who regurgitated a milky part-digested dribble of every feeding. Ursula's mistake, one of her mistakes and not the first, was to tell Gerald how she felt.

"*I* love her," he said, "so it doesn't matter."

"It's unnatural not to love one's own child. A little baby, Gerald. What's wrong with me?"

"Strange," he said, and he looked at her as he sometimes did, like a scientist scrutinizing a specimen. "I wouldn't call you a masculine woman, yet it's men who feel like that. Many men feel like that about their own children when they're babies."

"But not you."

"No, not I." (He would never have said "not me.") "Just as well, isn't it?"

It was love she had wanted, and reassurance. She wanted someone—him—to say, "You'll soon come to love her. Hold her every day, take her cot into your room, have her with you more, cuddle her, and kiss her." He only said she was strange. She was unnatural. What she would have liked was for them all to sit together, perhaps on the big sofa in the living room, with Sarah on her lap and Hope in his arms, but close, all touching one another, an entwined family group. And then it would get better. She would love her baby; she would be happy. If Gerald would love her, she would love them, all of them.

Out for a walk with Sarah, the little girl fell over, and when Ursula picked her up, she fought her and cried, "I want my daddy!"

Ursula plucked up her courage and asked Gerald when he was coming back to their bedroom. It took courage, and she knew that was ridiculous in a marriage, to have to rehearse for days beforehand the form of words you would use to ask your husband to come back and sleep with you. Would her mother have behaved like that? Would Helen? Would Syria Arthur? Sometimes she had the lunatic thought that marriage with Gerald needed *practice*, even that she should have been married before, that she should have been someone else's wife, to know how to manage this marriage.

The words she finally used were those words. Her tone was casual and friendly. She had wondered whether she could try a coyness, a flirtatious note, but in the end she had settled for this light, amiable inquiry: "Are you soon coming back to sleep in our bedroom?"

"I have to get up to tend Hope most nights," he said.

"We could hear her from our room."

He didn't answer. She thought he might just arrive one night. Even knock at the door and walk in and come over to the bed where she was, the way men in books did, though not his books. Reading the sex scenes in his books, rereading them as she found herself secretly doing, made her feel faint and her heart beat heavily. She wondered if he had done those things he wrote about. She could never ask him; she could ask him so little.

For a long time after Hope's birth, she felt no sexual desire. Perhaps it would never return. There was no one to ask. She imagined asking her doctor, Helen, Syria, but she never imagined asking her mother. When she was young—that was how she put it to herself, even though she was only twenty-seven—she hadn't looked at her own motives, questioned her thought processes, fears, hopes, but now she had become introspective. She had so little to do but think.

Although she felt guilty about it, she had lost interest in CND and never went to another meeting after Hope was born. If the Americans dropped a bomb on the Russians and the Russians retaliated, nothing she could do would stop them. Three months before Hope's birth, the bill making homosexual acts between consenting adults in private legal had become law. So Gerald had been right there, too, and change had come without any efforts on her part. She bought apples and oranges without noticing where they came from and never joined another campaign.

When the woman was gone, another one came to

clean the house, and Gerald was always occupied, endlessly busy. Writing, though he never wrote more than three hours a day, looking after the children, taking them for walks, playing with them, reading to them, bathing them. Already marked by those in the know as a distinguished novelist, literary but increasingly popular, he was one of the sights of Hampstead, pushing a pram up Heath Street with a baby at one end and a toddler at the other. Such an *unlikely-*looking man to be doing that, tall, growing heavy by then, with that thick, curly, longish black hair, those big sensual features—the fleshy lips, the hooked nose, the intense but ponderously lidded eyes.

Sometimes, looking at him, and she was always looking at him, she thought it an un-English face for a man born in Ipswich. More Spanish or Portuguese, owing something to Moorish genes. Or Irish. He never cared what he wore, choosing only the comfortable. If men of his age had worn denim at that period, he would have worn it. So he took the children to Hampstead Heath or to Whitestone Pond in old flannel trousers and a sports jacket with a greasy scarf knotted around his neck instead of a tie.

Alone at home, she read and thought. One day, Hope smiled at her and put out her arms, and Ursula fell in love. One of the things she had thought would never happen had happened. Unrequited love, though, may be worse than no love at all. Hope didn't dislike her, would allow herself to be hugged, fondled, kissed, but she infinitely preferred her father. As did Sarah. And Sarah, being older, vociferous, quite articulate for someone of two and a half, expressed her feelings whenever she was put out, especially when she was reproved.

"I don't want you. I want my daddy!"

They were beautiful children, with large, long-lashed eyes and flawless flower-petal skin. Hope had long dark curls that twisted naturally, as vines do, into ringlets, Gerald's full, curved lips and high fore-head. Both girls had her short, straight nose, and Sarah had her coloring, too, the freckled sandiness, the tawny hair. They would cling to Gerald, the pair of them, like kittens to a mother cat, nuzzling him, an arm thrown around his neck, a cheek pressed to a cheek. But he, with his curly mane and smiling muzzle, was a father cat.

Ursula was prey to strange suspicions. She had a dream in which Gerald figured, surrounded by children; he had been married before and had some unspecified number of children from this first marriage. The dream persisted as if it were fact, and later she brought herself to ask him, again rehearsing the question carefully, how he came to be so good with children.

"I like their company," he said.

"Yet you didn't have any brothers or sisters."

"I was not so fortunate," he said, using the cold and formal tone that was becoming habitual with him when he spoke to her. He no longer called her Little Bear.

And he didn't come back to sleep with her. Everyone said that a man's sexual desires were far stronger than a woman's; even people who never expressed opinions on this subject more or less said that, even her mother. What had happened to his desire? Or did his preoccupation with his children sublimate it? She started reading books on sex and popular psychology. Her own desire had returned and now began to torment her.

She was typing *A Messenger of the Gods*. The main character, the widow Annie Raleigh, had a voracious sexual appetite, which for a long time, given the time and the society in which she lived, she wasn't able to gratify. It surprised Ursula, and distressed her, to discover how much he knew about female desire and women's sexual needs. There was something uncanny about it, for it so closely paralleled her own feelings and situation. She asked herself why, if he understood, he didn't respond to her. It took years and two rereadings for her to understand that Annie Raleigh was herself.

An illustrated children's encyclopedia of the time showed Sarah photographs and drawings of thirties boys. *The Wonderland of Knowledge,* in twelve volumes, had been given to Fabian Lerner's grandmother on her tenth birthday. The boys wore short flannel trousers that reached to their knees, striped blazers, and striped ties. Unlike Richmal Crompton's William Brown (of whom Hope showed a surprising knowledge), none of them wore striped caps indoors.

The Applestone boys would have looked like that. Her father would have looked like that. She imagined the boys named Don and Ken going to tea in the house in Waterloo Road, a house in which there was no central heating, refrigerator, washing machine, dishwasher, television (though possibly a radio); no carpets, only rugs on linoleum; open fires and perhaps a gas fire; draft stoppers around the window frames; and once-weekly baths. Sarah had done her research, assisted by Fabian's grandmother. She had also looked for, and failed to find, a K. Applestone in the telephone directory for the Chelmsford area.

There were no Applestones at all. Applestone turned out to be a very uncommon name, while Appletons and Applebys abounded. But Kenneth Applestone existed in the records. Paying another visit to St. Catherine's House, Sarah found him born in 1925: Kenneth George Applestone, second son of Charles and Dorothy Applestone, née Mitchell. She started looking for a record of his marriage from 1943 onward, but there was nothing. Then she looked for a death certificate. No record of that, either. Joan Thague had no photographs of the Applestone boys, so it was solely Sarah's imagination that made her see Ken as a tall, dark boy with brown eyes and curly black hair.

At this point, she understood something. It was so clear and obvious, a child would have seen it, but she hadn't until this moment. Only if Ken Applestone was not to be found could she seriously begin to think of him as her father. The harder it became to find him, the more likely he was to be her father.

That evening, she phoned all the Applestones in

the London phone book. There weren't many. One of them, the last she phoned, said that her father had mentioned cousins called Donald and Kenneth and that the woman to get in touch with was another cousin, a woman named Victoria Anderson, who lived in Exeter. Sarah got this woman's phone number from directory assistance, then dialed it and encountered an answering service. She left her name and number and a brief explanation of what she wanted, and half an hour later the phone rang.

A voice said, "Ms. Sarah Candless?"

It hadn't sounded feminine, but still she said, "Victoria Anderson?"

"No, should it be? I sort of wish it was. My name's Jason Thague, and anything's better than that. I'm Joan's grandson."

It was three days since she had been to Ipswich, but she was sure he was going to reprove her. She imagined him saying, "How dare you come here and upset my gran? She's an old lady. She's not strong. Who do you think you . . ."

"What can I do for you, Mr. Thague?"

"Jason, please. I don't think anyone's called me Mr. Thague before. Ever." His wasn't a Suffolk voice; rather, the accent dubbed in the eighties "Estuary English." "It's more a case of what can I do for you," he said.

She hesitated. "Can you do anything for me?"

"I don't know. I hope so. My nan's told me about you and what you're doing. That was the first I'd heard of her having a little brother who died. The first my dad'd heard, come to that." He paused, then said in a stronger tone, "The fact is, I'm permanently strapped for cash. I'm a student, if you know what that means."

"I should," she said. "I teach them."

"Right. I thought—I'd *like*—to give it a go at finding your dad for you. Who he was, I mean. I think I'd be good at it. I'm in the right place, for a start. I know the place, worse luck. But I do know it. If he came from around here, I reckon I could trace him, and if there's any more to be gotten out of Joan, I'm the man to do it."

"You would want to be paid, of course?"

"I'm doing it for the money," he said simply.

She realized only now, late in the day, that attempting to find her father's origins had brought her a chronic distress. She hated it, the phone calls, the visits, the search through records. The excitement was all gone. Because it was her father, whom she had loved and honored and who, she had lately constantly felt, might not be worthy of even common respect.

"All right," she said. "Why not? Do you want some sort of contract?"

"I'd better. I'm tempted to take your word, but that wouldn't be businesslike, would it? You can send me a contract and all the info you've got about your dad."

The next day, she packed it all up for him: photocopies of her father's birth certificate and documents from the *Walthamstow Herald,* the *Western Morning News,* Trinity College records. In her covering letter, she gave it as her opinion—and it hurt her to write it—that some unknown man, probably twenty-five years old, probably a trained journalist, probably born in Ipswich and a resident there till the age of ten, had in the summer of 1951 assumed the identity of Gerald Candless.

He might have attended a university somewhere, though not Trinity College, Dublin. He might have served in one of the armed forces during World War II. He was the right age. His hair had been black when he was young. His eyes were brown. He had no scars or what used to be called on passports "distinguishing marks." She winced, writing these things to an unknown, brash young man with a common accent. She thought she could see him in her mind's eye, short and weedy, the puddingy Candless (the *real* Candless) face triumphing over Thague genes, spotty skin, round glasses, shaggy brown hair to his shoulders.

She wrote, "My father used to say he put everything that happened to him into his novels, these events being subject to the filtering process and subtle metamorphosis that operates with all novelists when using autobiographical detail in their work. I am sure you are aware of this." (She wasn't; she was far from sure. She thought of her own students.) "It may still be worthwhile considering passages in his novels as possible pointers to his identity. I would direct you to *A Paper Landscape,* in which he describes life as a member of a large Irish immigrant family who he writes about very tellingly. I mean by this that the reader can easily believe in this fiction as truth.

"It may be useful, too, to look at his first novel, *The Centre of Attraction.* Its early chapters are about World War II, when a young man of eighteen serves in the Royal Navy in Northern Ireland and later in the Far East. You may be a fan of my father's and have these books, but if not, I will, of course, send you copies."

When she returned from the post office, her phone was ringing. Victoria Anderson. Anderson was her married name. She had been born Applestone, the daughter of Charles Applestone's younger brother Thomas. Donald, Kenneth, and Doreen Applestone had, therefore, been her first cousins, though all much older than she. Doreen, the baby in Joan Thague's account, had been twenty-one when she was born.

Sarah quickly realized that here she had come across one of those family fanatics, as passionate about genealogical entanglements as she had been indifferent. Victoria Anderson would have her own personally created family trees, one for the maternal side, one for the paternal. It would be an ongoing irritation to her that she had failed, say, to get back further than 1795. She would be maddened by her inability to find the Christian name of a woman married in the 1820s or that of the child born in 1834 and destined to live only two days.

She reflected on all this while Victoria Anderson detailed the forebears of Mitchells and Thagues, digressing to catalog the eight children born to her cousin Doreen in two marriages.

"And Ken Applestone?" Sarah prompted her.

"He emigrated to Canada."

"When was that?"

"Ken? I thought it was Don Applestone you were interested in. Wasn't that what you said in your message? Well, one of us must have gotten it wrong. Don married in 'forty-one, you know. He was only nineteen, but he married and had a son called Tony before he was killed in Egypt. Tony's quite a lot older than I am, but we keep in touch. . . ."

"When did Ken emigrate?"

"Nineteen fifty-one." She must have been reading all this. Probably she had it on a computer, stowed under FAM.DOC. "He went to Canada in 'fifty-one. That's the year I was born."

"So you got all this from someone else?"

"Naturally. My mother told me about Ken emigrating, though she'd never met him. My father knew him, but my father died ten years ago. I did try to follow Ken up."

I bet you did, Sarah thought. "How did you try?"

"I had a friend in Montreal. She went through phone books for me." Victoria Anderson's voice dropped, becoming intense. "I didn't care to have a dead end, you see. He might have married and had children; he almost certainly did. It's quite personally upsetting to me to have gaps in my genealogical tables."

Not as upsetting as it is to me. Sarah said impatiently, "The fact is, then, that there's been no contact with Ken Applestone since 1951?"

"If you put it like that—well, no, I suppose there hasn't been."

Finding herself quite unaware of how to draw up a contract for Jason Thague that would be binding, she phoned Hope for advice.

"I'll do it for you," Hope said.

"Will you really? Thanks. I know you don't approve."

"Maybe not, but if it's got to be done, I'd like it done properly."

"Hopie, can you remember Dad ever saying he based a book on some actual event? I mean, I know he said everything he wrote had its source in his experience or his observation, but did he ever use a real event? Like people write novels about battles in the Crimean War or the sinking of the *Titanic*."

"*The Centre of Attraction*'s got the dropping of the atomic bombs on Japan in it. You remember what's his name—Richard—he feels guilty because the bombs probably saved his life; they stopped him from having to take part in an invasion of Japan. And then there's *A White Webfoot*. The critics said it was based on fact, although Daddy didn't."

"I was away when that was published. I was in America. Of course I've read it."

"The reviewers called it a thriller and said it was

based on the Highbury murder case of—let's see—1960 or 1961, I think."

"That would be too late. Ten years too late. And it hasn't anything in it about someone changing his identity, has it?"

"Nothing at all," said Hope.

12

Jacob Manley was not a forbearing man, yet when
someone died, he always said of him that he had
gone to his reward, never to his punishment.
                                    —EYE IN THE ECLIPSE

THIRTY YEARS HAD PASSED since Ursula had seen her
brother's first wife, Jean. She never thought of her,
except in one connection, and had almost forgotten
her. Jean had faded out of her life as in-laws do in the
event of death or divorce. In this case, it had been
divorce. And now she was dead.

Perhaps not too untimely a death. She had been,
after all, a few years older than Ian, which would
have made her over seventy. A letter coming from him
had surprised Ursula, the handwriting on the envelope, which at first she didn't recognize. They spoke
occasionally on the phone; they sent each other
Christmas cards, his second wife, the mother of his
children, writing them. He had phoned when Gerald
died but hadn't come to either funeral or memorial
service. But now a letter had arrived. It had to be a
serious matter to warrant a letter.

Ian wrote as if he cared, though not as if he

regretted. Jean had never remarried, had shared a house for years with her widowed sister. Death had come three weeks before; the funeral was long over. Ian hadn't attended it and he was sure neither Ursula nor Helen would have wanted to be there. Ursula, sitting at her kitchen table with the letter in her hand, tried to remember Jean, to see her face, to conjure up precisely her features and coloring, but that, she failed to do. She could manage only a pale blur that was somehow intense and strained, a tortured face, dark hair threaded all over with gray, hands that fluttered, then clutched each other. But she remembered with perfect clarity why Jean, who was seldom in touch with her, whom she could say she hardly knew, came to Holly Mount that day in 1968 and poured out the anguish in her heart.

Three years later, Jean and Ian were divorced and Ian married the woman on whose account Jean had come to confide in Ursula. Why Ursula? It was never made clear why she had been chosen. Perhaps because Jean's own family and friends were too close. Or perhaps it was that Jean, like Helen and even to some extent Betty Wick, looked upon Ursula, by virtue of her marriage to a novelist (a writer, an artist, a person from a different world), her entrée to elite and sophisticated circles, her home in that most elegant and least suburban of suburbs, as a woman of the world who would know answers and remedies in unfamiliar and indeed undreamed-of situations.

For infidelity was undreamed of among the Wicks and their connections. The sexual revolution that began in the sixties hadn't touched them, even supposing they knew that it was taking place. But it had touched Ian Wick, or something had, and led him into adultery. This was the news Jean brought to Ursula and *adultery* was her word. Ian had fallen in love with a young cashier at the bank, had spent nights with her, been away for weekends with her, and now wanted to marry her.

Ursula, of course, had no answers. And Jean's story of Ian's withdrawal from sex struck painful chords in her own recent experience. Jean came out with it all, no holds barred—Ian's refusal to share a bed with her, his unexplained absences, his apparent contentment, as if he had some other distant source of happiness. As he had, as he had. And as Ursula listened, helpless to console, she could think only of these parallels. When Jean had gone home (determined to take a taxi all the way to Sydenham at Ian's expense), she wondered she hadn't seen it before.

Gerald didn't want her because he had someone else. "Someone else" was Jean's expression until, her story progressing, she began using a name, and Ursula, with her newfound habit of questioning the words and expressions she used, found it absurd, almost comical, as if this combination of words could only properly apply to an illicit paramour. "Another woman" was almost as silly. Yet a woman there must be, a girl, a lover, a mistress, out there, a "someone else" intervening in her marriage. All the conditions of Ian's defection fit Gerald, except that of frequent absence.

When he was away from the house, Sarah and Hope were almost always with him. He had never, so far as she knew, taken them on visits to his publishers, but he seldom went to his publishers. Would he take her children to visit his mistress?

A Paper Landscape was published in 1968, and he had already begun writing his next novel. In that year, he also became deputy literary editor of a Sunday newspaper. The position brought books for review every week, and Ursula had plenty to read. She read so much fiction that she suggested to Gerald—jokingly, of course, but attempting to talk to him of things he knew about and liked—that they ought to make her a judge in the newly instituted Booker Prize.

"The other judges might have something to say about that," he said.

She hadn't understood. She hadn't wanted to. "Because I'm your wife, you mean?"

"Because you're hardly competent, are you?"

Another time, when he saw her reading a novel, his review of which had appeared in the paper the previous Sunday, he asked her if she really understood what she was reading.

"I think so," she said, tense already, expecting the insult.

He looked her up and down, the way he had recently acquired, the way a designer might view a model newly dressed in his latest creation. But he had no longer any interest in her appearance. He looked for something else, though she didn't know what.

"Should I," she tried, "should I try reading your critique?"

His face went dark with anger. "Critique," he said. "Are you French? Are you trying to impress me? It is a notice. A notice or a review. Can you remember that?"

Before he began his new novel, he had a title for it. When he had written two chapters, he asked her if she would type it for him. No taking it for granted this time, and she wondered why not. Was he for some reason placating her?

She had no room of her own in the house in Holly Mount. The house was really too small for them and he, of course, had the room intended as a dining room as his study. She was sitting in the living room, reading, and the children were asleep. He had given them their tea and bathed them and put them to bed. Often she had thought of asserting herself here, but to take these offices upon herself would have meant physically tearing the little girls from him.

Her heart quailed at the thought; she recoiled from it. He fed them, bathed them, told them their bedtime story, and began writing at 7:30. Just before ten, he walked in with his hands full of sheets of paper, paper whose edges weren't even aligned, but clutched in a bundle, held it out to her and asked her to "do what you have so kindly done before." She could hardly believe her ears.

"It's to be called *A Messenger of the Gods*," he said. "Would you get it into some sort of order for me, Ursula? Decode my scrawl?"

For the first time for months, he had used her Christian name. She stared at him, unsmiling, but put out her hand for the paper. There was an eagerness in his face that made him look younger, an enthusiasm. And she understood. He was pleased; he was happy. He had his title, and he had completed two chapters with which he was satisfied. This was his life; this was everything, this and his children. He told her because he had to tell someone. No doubt, he would prefer to tell that woman, the "someone else," his mistress, but she wasn't there.

"I'll start on it tomorrow," she said.

As the chapters came to her, she looked in the text, the story, for evidence of adultery. Already, at that time, she had heard him say—or, rather, seen him say, for she had read it in a magazine interview—that everything that happened to him went into his fiction. She found nothing. And then she realized something. He *never* wrote about marital infidelity. He seldom wrote about marriage, except peripherally, and although she had no means of knowing it then, this rule or inhibition was to prevail. He was never to write much about marriage or married life until the fateful *Hand to Mouth* in 1984, and even in that novel, though there was unhappiness and strife and incompatibility, though sex was important and sexual acts occurring, there was no unfaithfulness.

But then, when those chapters came to her in the early spring of 1969, this was still far in the future. This time, she encountered Annie Raleigh, shivered and trembled at his descriptions of her desires, looked in vain for adultery. But its absence might only mean that he was deferring the use of this particular experience, this perhaps new experience, until a later date, a later book. She typed his novel, she watched him, and she thought it coincidence that while she was tormented by sexual hunger, he had happened to write about a woman with a similar need.

She nevertheless repelled the advances of a young poet he invited to dinner and who followed her out to the kitchen while Gerald and Colin Wrightson and Beattie Paris discussed who would be candidates for the Booker. She kissed the poet back but stopped there and told him no, no, she wouldn't go out for a drink with him, see him again, no, no, definitely not. That night, though she had never before done such a thing nor knew how it was done, she masturbated. Otherwise, she would never have slept.

She watched him. She listened. It was the beginning of that fascination with him that was to replace love. She thought about him constantly. If the girls were taken to see "a lady," wouldn't they betray him? She even asked Sarah, though she hated herself for asking.

"Daddy takes us to see Miss Churchouse, silly," said Sarah.

Not Adela, who everyone said preferred women. Not Adela, who had threatened to chain herself to the Home Office railings over homosexual law reform. Jealous as she was, and made unreasonable by jealousy, as she knew, she still couldn't believe Gerald would sleep with that scatty fifty-year-old, she of the diaphanous garments and bead strings, who took out her "partial" in other people's bathrooms and left it grinning on the basin.

It wasn't Adela. She watched him and listened to him. She had taken to being present in the girls' bedroom while he told them their bedtime story, hoping to pick up some clue. If Sarah and Hope didn't want her there, they didn't say, only bade her keep quiet and not make a disturbance by moving about the room, picking up toys.

The stories he told them were serials. She couldn't remember now, twenty-eight years later, which ones he had told them that spring when Sarah was three and a half and Hope was nearly two, only that though Hope was really too young to understand, she seemed to follow it. That story quarter hour was the only time boisterous Hope was silent. What happened in those stories had disappeared almost entirely from Ursula's mind. She could just about remember that one involved an old man who sent messages by carrier pigeon to a little girl at the other end of the country and the other concerned a child who was sent up chimneys by a harsh master. This last owed a lot to Charles Kingsley's *The Water Babies,* not to mention Blake's verses in *Songs of Innocence,* but she hadn't read those then.

There was nothing in the stories about a "someone else." How could there be? How had she ever imagined there could be?

Gerald gave her plenty of money. They had a

joint account, and he never questioned what she spent. If he noticed what she spent, he didn't say, but she didn't think he was much interested in money. He wanted, he had sometimes said, a nice house to live in, a good house in a beautiful place. That was all he wanted to do with money. Foreign travel held no attractions for him. He disliked the theater and loathed opera. He bought books, but most of the books he wanted were gifts. One publisher had given him the *Encyclopaedia Britannica,* and another one gave him the complete unabridged *Oxford Dictionary.* Their car was a Morris station wagon, because that was more convenient for transporting children and their paraphernalia. Clothes were to keep him warm and keep him decent, and the watch he wore he had had for twenty years.

But she could have what money she wanted and do as she pleased with it. What she pleased to spend money on in the April of that year was a private detective.

Until the night he had died, she had never been in there. Sometimes she had thought it strange to have a room in one's house, a house one had lived in for twenty-seven years, that one never entered, whose shape one hardly knew, whose furniture one couldn't have described. Like a Bluebeard's chamber, which might contain nothing or might be full of bloody evidence. The difference was that she hadn't been curious. Once only, coming into the garden from the cliff path, she had walked across to that part of the house where his bedroom was and looked up at its windows, becoming aware for the first time—or else she had forgotten—that it was a corner room with one window facing north and the other west.

Daphne kept it clean. Daphne had changed his bed linen. A single woman, living with her sister, another single woman, and their mother, who had been widowed for fifty years, Daphne had never once commented on the fact that Gerald and Ursula slept in separate rooms. Perhaps it didn't strike her as remarkable. Perhaps she had no experience of how most married couples lived. She cleaned the room, sang "Dashing Away with the Smoothing Iron," changed the sheets, referred to it as "Mr. Candless's room," for though Ursula had become Ursula to her long ago, he had never become Gerald.

She suspected old Mrs. Batty of adhering to the Victorian principle of keeping out the night air, or, come to that, any air, for Daphne never opened windows, and she closed them if she found them open. Ursula opened all the casements in the room and leaned out of the one that faced west. The dark gray sea, an unrolled bolt of wrinkled silk, lay immobile, scarcely seeming to lap the pale, flat sand. It was misty, but the mist hung thin and distant, obscuring only the island and the far point.

Blinds at the windows. A bed with a quilt on it and a blue-and-white-striped cover on the quilt, two pillows in white cases, several hundred paperback books in a plain bookcase, a chest of drawers, an upright chair. The built-in cupboard she thought she remembered from coming in here nearly three decades before, but every bedroom had such a cupboard, so perhaps she didn't remember.

The two pictures, one facing the northerly window, the other opposite it, affected her unpleasantly. She had come a long way from that wide-eyed and optimistic girlhood when she would have said, had anyone asked her, that one should have pretty pictures on bedroom walls, if not puppies and kittens, certainly sunlit landscapes and Monet water lilies. But still she wondered at the taste and the mental processes of her late husband, who could have Piranesi's *Imaginary Prisons* on one wall and a painting of a lighthouse, a wild sea, and a sky of tumbling clouds on the other.

It was then that she remembered his clothes. He had been dead for three months, but it had never occurred to her to do anything about his clothes. She had forgotten their existence. She opened the cupboard and looked at them, the baggy trousers, shapeless jackets, two aged tweed suits, a heavy dark gray sheepskin coat. They smelled musty, of old wool. When someone died, you used to take their clothes to a rummage sale. Now you gave them to a charity shop.

She began taking them out of the cupboard. She laid them on the bed. When the cupboard was empty, she dusted the inside of it and closed the doors. She took the pictures downstairs, thinking them unsuitable for a guest bedroom, and read printed on the back of the lighthouse painting "*Korsö fyr* by August

Strindberg." She was trained as an art historian, but she hadn't known Strindberg had painted anything. She carried the paintings—the reproductions—downstairs and laid them against one of the walls of the study, replacing them with a still life from her own room and *Evening Light,* an innocuous and rather charming picture by Robert Duncan of a girl in white and geese in a rose bed, a picture that someone had given Hope when she was twelve.

The clothes were heavy and she had to make three trips. First to the kitchen. Later, she would put them in the boot of the car, then drop them off at Oxfam when next she went to the shops. Before you disposed of clothes, you had to go through the pockets. The idea brought her a wry amusement, because this was exactly the situation where the wife or widow finds the letter that reveals an unsuspected love passage. The mistress's assignation note from years before. Ursula smiled at the thought, because she knew she would find no letter, or anything else of that kind.

She postponed the search, put the clothes into a plastic bag and the bag into the broom cupboard, where there was no chance of the girls finding it.

Pauline immediately wanted to know why she couldn't have Sarah's room, where she had slept before, and seemed none too pleased when told both her cousins were coming.

"I didn't know you had a spare room up here," she said, no doubt recalling all those occasions on which she had either slept downstairs in the little room Ursula later took for her study or had shared with Sarah or Hope.

Ursula smiled but said nothing. It shocked her a little to realize, now, after all this time, that Pauline must always have believed Gerald and she shared a room, even shared a bed. Pauline stood inside and looked about her, approving, it was evident, of the view and *Evening Light,* but not especially of anything else.

"Those books will take a lot of dusting, Ursula."

She spoke the name with emphasis, preceding it with a small pause, no doubt to show that she had remembered the caution not to say "Auntie." Then she looked at her aunt, looked at her as if she hadn't seen her for a long time, as if they hadn't met outside Barnstaple station, traveled home side by side, and entered the house together.

"You've had your hair cut!"

"Nearly three months ago," said Ursula.

In the evening, after supper, Pauline reverted to her previous visit and to Ursula's proposal with regard to baby-sitting at the hotel. Ursula had forgotten whether she had told Pauline only that Gerald had stopped her baby-sitting or that she intended to do some baby-sitting now he was dead, and she realized too late that Pauline had known nothing about this activity of hers until she herself mentioned it.

"You actually did it!"

Pauline's tone couldn't have sounded more shocked and repelled, Ursula thought, than if she had confided her experiences as a prostitute in Ilfra-combe town center.

"I've thought a lot about it," Pauline said. "Brian often says I would have made a good psychologist. You weren't close to your own children really, were you? I suppose baby-sitting was a kind of compensating for that. What do you think?"

Ursula thought it surprisingly near the bone. They went to bed soon after that. Remarks of that kind, made late in the evening, were particularly unwelcome because they kept her from sleeping. She hadn't been back to the Dunes since the encounter with Sam Fleming, and she knew she would never go back. In spite of everything, in spite of her positive rejection of Sam, she had expected him to phone her. She had thought he would phone, if only to repeat his apology and explanation, but he hadn't. Though his grandchildren wouldn't be there, though they might never be there again, she would have gone back to baby-sit for others if he had phoned. It was an irrational, even absurd, way of going on, but it was the way her mind worked in this matter. And now the season was over, the hotel half-closed, to be shut up altogether for three months after the Christmas influx.

Ursula knew very well how a penetrating comment on the incongruities of one's behavior, a remark that brings home an unacceptable truth, arouses dislike for the one who utters it. She was filled at that moment with dislike for her niece, an antipathy that of course would pass but which she was aware of having sometimes felt on previous occasions. Pauline had seldom been as perspicacious as that, usually only liable to make personal remarks about people's appearance or habits, but even these, Ursula now recalled, had had a way of drilling into one's soft and sensitive parts. Ridiculous, because she had been a child then, and one should make abundant allowance for what a child says. According to Gerald, anyway.

Pauline had first come to stay with them in that fateful year, 1969. Ursula called it fateful because that was their last year in Hampstead, the year of her brother's separation from his wife, of *A Messenger of the Gods,* hailed by his publishers as the break-through for Gerald Candless from good to great fiction, the year of the private detective. Pauline came to stay because it was August, her school was on holiday, and Helen had to go into the hospital for a hysterectomy. Jeremy could stay with his paternal grandmother, whose favorite he was.

That year, Pauline was ten. She was coming up to the age when girls love looking after, playing with, and taking out small children. And she was a big, tall girl who looked at least two years older than her age, who perhaps felt older in some ways. Her mother was making her into a woman too early, letting her wear an unnecessary bra, cut off her plaits, and have her ears pierced. Helen believed that girls couldn't begin being feminine too soon.

Ursula hadn't seen a great deal of her since the incident of the engagement ring, when the small Pauline had brought the ring to her on the stem of a flower, and would hardly have known her. Gerald had no recollection of her at all. He put his foot down at once when Pauline wanted to take Sarah and Hope out. That was not to be; that was never to be. The danger, of course, involved the roads and the Hampstead traffic. No one thought about child molesters and rapists in those days. But he seemed pleased to have someone in the house to entertain the children, the possibility of their mother's doing this having been dismissed by him long before.

If Pauline hadn't been there, would he have taken the unprecedented step of being absent from home for a whole day and a night and half the next day? Would he have done this not once, but twice, if this eager, bossy, patient, and managing child hadn't been in the house to supervise the happiness of his daughters?

The private detective had been on Gerald's tail for a few months by then. He was expensive, and he had found out practically nothing. Ursula, who had expected some dashing gumshoe, a Philip Marlowe, asked herself what she was doing when she walked up the uncarpeted wooden staircase to the rooms over a theatrical costumers on the Soho fringes and found two middle-aged portly men in an office full of cigarette smoke and a bent white-haired secretary, at least old enough to be their mother. Later on, Ursula discovered this secretary was the mother of one of them.

Dickie Parfitt was polite, urbane, and knowing. Indeed, he was too knowing, for he assumed from the first that this was what he called "divorce work." Most of what he and Mr. Cullen did was in connection with divorces. Ursula had to explain that she wished to know only where her husband went, that there was no thought of ending her marriage. But afterward, as she walked back to the Tottenham Court Road underground station and the Northern line, she considered what Mr. Parfitt had said. He had put ideas into her head.

His first report reached her a week later. Gerald was referred to as "the subject." Better than Mr. X, Ursula supposed. Dickie Parfitt had followed him while he was out with Sarah and Hope and pursued him all over Hampstead while (like Shelley) he had made paper boats and sailed them on the Vale of Health pond, visited the geese and peacocks in Golders Hill Park, and bought ice creams in the Finchley Road. Another time, he went to Canfield Gardens in West Hampstead and was inside a house with the children for four hours. Mr. Parfitt was pleased with his find, but Ursula knew Gerald had only gone to the home of a university teacher and poet he knew named Beattie Paris, who, with his girlfriend, Maggie, had two daughters of similar age to Sarah and Hope.

That was before Pauline came. Pauline thought it amusing to see Gerald wheeling Hope about in a stroller, and she said so.

"My father says that's a job for a woman," she said.

Gerald laughed. He didn't seem to mind. He

treated most of Pauline's gnomic utterances as if she were the soul of wit. When she saw him sitting with Sarah on one knee and Hope on the other, an arm around each, she again quoted a parent.

"My mother says you can overstimulate children."

"Oh, can you now?" said Gerald, laughing. "And what happens to them when you do that? Do they break things or have fits? What do they do?"

Pauline said she didn't know, but she stared at him and his daughters with envy. A little later on, she went and stood by Gerald's chair. She leaned against the wing of the chair, then shifted herself to lean against his shoulder. Gerald was telling the girls his story about the chimney sweeper's boy. Installment fifteen or something like that, it must have been by that time. Pauline stood there listening.

The chair was big and Gerald was big. There was plenty of room. Gerald looked up into Pauline's wistful face.

"Come and be overstimulated," he said.

He hoisted Hope up onto the arm of the chair so that her cheek was close enough to his cheek to brush it, and he made room for Pauline on his knee. His arm went around both of them. Pauline perched there awkwardly at first, but eventually she relaxed. Ursula watched them. Probably few men today, in the nineties, that decade of lost innocence, would do what Gerald had done and take a tall, precocious ten-year-old girl onto their knee. Probably Gerald himself wouldn't. But no one thought anything of it then.

Except Ursula, and what she wondered was how it had happened that children all preferred Gerald to her, how it was that she was apparently no good with children, that even her own only suffered her, sometimes let her kiss and hold them, but wouldn't, she believed, have missed her had she been gone.

They missed Gerald when he disappeared for those two days. "I want my daddy" was the continuous refrain. But before that happened, Dickie Parfitt had followed him to an address Ursula didn't know, a house that belonged to no one she knew. Gerald had gone out alone, telling her he was doing research for an article he intended to write. When he went out, he always told her where he was going. Or, rather, he half-told her. That is, he would say it was for the purposes of research or to see his publisher or visit a library, but he never said what kind of research or why he had to see his publisher or which work of reference he required.

"I'm going out in about an hour," he said. "There's something I need to check."

Dickie Parfitt, alerted by a reluctant, near-nauseous Ursula, was waiting for him, lurking in the neighborhood of the underground station in Heath Road. He followed him into the train and changed with him on to the Central line at Tottenham Court Road. Gerald got out of the train at Leytonstone and walked westward along Fairlop Road, turned left into Hainault Road, and crossed into Leyton at Leigh Road. Ursula, reading Dickie's account, had no idea where any of these places were. She had barely heard of Leyton and

Leytonstone but had a vague idea of them as dowdy eastern suburbs.

The street for which Gerald was heading was called Goodwin Road, near where the London Midland railway line passed over Leyton High Road. It sounded unattractive, even slummy, though Dickie made no comment on the charms or otherwise of the neighborhood. Gerald stopped about halfway along the street and fixed his eyes on a house on the opposite side. A van was parked near where he was standing. It was empty. He positioned himself behind the cab in such a way, according to Dickie Parfitt, as to be able to see the house he was watching through the windows on the driver's side and the passenger's side of the cab, yet not be seen himself.

It was a fine day, and standing a hundred yards off, watching Gerald Candless watching a house, wasn't an unpleasant task for Dickie, who had done much the same thing in driving rain and snowstorms. But after half an hour, he began to wonder how long "the subject" would stick it out. Until the driver of the van returned?

Then something happened. The front door of the house under observation opened and a woman came out. Dickie gave no detailed description of her, but he said she was "elderly" and pushing a shopping basket on wheels. She was not, unless Gerald Candless's secret was that he was a gerontophile, his lover, but he took a photograph of her all the same. He watched her pass along the street in the direction of Leyton Midland railway station. Once she was out of sight,

Gerald began walking in the opposite direction, toward Leigh Road. He simply retraced his steps, got back into the underground, and returned home.

It occurred to Dickie that if all Gerald Candless wanted to do was watch a house, he could have done so far more easily from inside a car. This he bore in mind. Meanwhile, he had high hopes for Gerald's plan to be away for a day, a night, and half the next day. He followed Gerald into the underground once more. This time, he changed at King's Cross on to the Circle, getting out at Paddington, where, in the mainline station, he bought a first-class return ticket for Barnstaple. Dickie, behind him in the queue, bought an economy-class ticket.

By this time, Dickie confidently expected Gerald would be joined on the train by a "young lady," and he walked through to carriage H to check. But Gerald was alone, reading a book and eating a Mars bar. They changed at Exeter, but there was no young lady there, either, then commenced (Dickie's word) the long, slow journey to Barnstaple. And there Dickie, inevitably, lost him. For Gerald was met at the station by a man in a car, an ordinary sort of man driving a green Volvo, while Dickie waited in vain for a taxi.

The following week, when Gerald set off alone in the Morris, Dickie took a gamble and stationed himself on the corner of Goodwin Road, Leyton, to wait for him. It was as he had thought. The house could be the better observed from a car. Gerald soon arrived. He parked the car and watched. Or so Dickie supposed. He couldn't really see. But he saw and moved fast when Gerald got out of the car and approached the house, knocked at the front door, and finally let himself in with his own key.

Dickie Parfitt took a photograph, but the door had shut before he got much of a shot.

It was late on Friday evening that Sarah and Hope arrived in Sarah's car. This was unusual, for they seldom came together, but they did so this time, perhaps as a mark of solidarity, as a closing of ranks, when confronted by something as upsetting as the loss of a father's identity. Throughout the long drive, which they shared, they discussed Ken Applestone and their combined failure to find him.

"Or, rather, Jason Thague's failure to find him," said Sarah.

"Right. What steps did he take?"

"Some pal of his is Canadian. He got his father in Toronto to search through all the phone directories in the country. The man's retired; he's nothing else to do. Apparently, he loved it, made him feel useful."

"I wish this Thague didn't have to be involved," Hope said fretfully, taking off her large black hat and throwing it onto the backseat. "I hate the idea of strangers knowing about Daddy. You could have done all that—what he did, I mean. You've probably got a Canadian student, and you wouldn't have to tell her who Ken Applestone might be."

"No, I couldn't, Hope. I'm too busy. Term's started. I might as well say you could have done it."

"It's your book, though, isn't it? Have you thought

what you're going to do if it turns out Daddy did something dreadful? Poor Daddy, I know he wouldn't have meant to, but he could unintentionally have done something against the law. Imagine the tabloids getting hold of it. What are you going to do then?"

"I don't know," Sarah said, and she was silent for a while. Then she said, as the lights of Bristol began to appear below them, "The pal's father couldn't find Ken Applestone."

"You told me. But he found a John Applestone, didn't he?"

"He found a number. In Winnipeg. There wasn't any answer and no answering machine."

They stopped at a service station and bought two pork pies, two packets of tandoori-flavored chips, and two cans of Coke. Then Hope took over the driving.

"I don't know why you don't have an automatic car," she said. "This manual shift is *prelapsarian*. We should have brought mine. I did tell you, but you wouldn't listen."

"Eat your pie," said Sarah.

All conversation ceased while they ate. Outside Tiverton, Hope said, "You think Daddy was the son of someone connected with the Candlesses in Ipswich, don't you? Someone who was possibly in the house when the little boy died or was told about the little boy dying and told his own son, who was the same sort of age as Daddy?"

"Something like that. I don't think he was a complete stranger."

"It could be a tradesman, a caller at the house.

The grocer making a delivery, the milkman—that's an idea; why not the milkman? The postman, the baker, the knife grinder, a washerwoman."

"Hopie," said Sarah, "it wasn't Victorian England. It was the thirties."

Hope signaled left, pulled into a lay-by, and parked. She turned to her sister and said, "The doctor."

"You mean the doctor who would have come to the house to attend the little boy?"

"Exactly."

"There must have been one," Sarah said thoughtfully. "They weren't rich, but they weren't really poor, either. Would the child have been taken to a hospital in those days? Yes, maybe. But a doctor . . . Joan Thague would remember, surely."

"Ask the grandson."

"You can imagine the doctor going home and saying to his wife and children that he'd lost a patient, a little boy, that he'd died of meningitis. . . . The boy the same age as the dead boy. It would have made a great impression on him."

"Oh, yes, it would. Poor Daddy."

"Child mortality was quite low by that time; the doctor would seldom have had a child patient die. The doctor's own son would never have forgotten it. It might even have haunted him throughout his childhood. You can imagine him thinking, If that could happen to that boy, why not to me? He would have remembered the name—Gerald Candless. And then when the time came nineteen years later . . . You're quite brilliant sometimes, Hope."

It was after ten when they reached Lundy View House. Pauline, in a red afternoon dress with pearls, looked at Hope and said brightly, "Your hat is exactly the same shape as a coal scuttle we once had at home."

In the manner of a reclusive judge, the kind she sometimes had to listen to, Hope said, "What's a coal scuttle?"

Ursula might have said truthfully that they had never had coal fires either in Hampstead or in this house while the girls were growing up. But she said nothing. Sarah was already pouring a large whiskey for herself, and Hope had gone into the other room to answer the phone. The two of them, while loving Pauline when she was in her teens and they were little children, had later come to regard her with a kind of contemptuous tolerance. It was exactly the same feeling as she had for them. They thought she had never lived and she thought they had never grown up.

"Wrong number," said Hope, coming back and getting herself a whiskey. "A peculiar man with a very secretive manner."

Sarah wondered if it might have been Adam Foley. Next morning, she got up first. She usually did. She found her mother in the garden, deadheading the dahlias. Ursula asked her if she wanted another installment of life with Father—that was the phrase she used, trying to sound casual and cheerful at the same time—but Sarah said no, thanks, not this time, not this weekend, for there was something else she wanted to discuss. Then, to Ursula's extreme astonishment, Sarah kissed her cheek. She stood there with one hand up to her cheek and the other clutching the pruning shears for some moments before she felt the wind and realized she was getting chilled to the bone, out there without a coat.

The girls had been much nicer to her lately; they had been nicer, in fact, than they had ever been. It all dated from when she had cried in the taxi after the memorial service. Now she couldn't remember why she had cried, only that it wasn't because Gerald was dead. The girls thought it was, though, and perhaps that was why their attitude toward her had changed.

The phone was ringing as Sarah came into the kitchen. She glanced at the clock and saw it was just after 9:30, which she thought ridiculously early to phone anyone, so she lifted the receiver grudgingly. A man's voice said that he was Sam Fleming and asked if he could speak to Ursula.

Just at that moment, Pauline walked in and said that if she could take a car, any car, Ursula's or Sarah's, she'd like to go shopping in Gaunton. Yes, of course she could, Sarah said, covering up the mouthpiece, then uncovering it, looking out of the window to where her mother should be but wasn't.

"I don't know where she is," she said. "Can I get her to call you back?"

This Fleming man said yes and gave her a number, which Sarah tried to memorize, as there was no paper at hand. Pauline left and Hope walked in. They looked at each other and nodded, Sarah cocking a thumb toward the garden. Sarah said she was going to make French toast and asked if Hope wanted some, and while she was making it, Ursula appeared.

Ursula washed her hands at the sink. She started to feel nervous because both girls stared at her in silence and in a ponderous way. With her hair pulled back and screwed into a knot and wearing an old denim jacket and gray trousers, Hope looked a lot like Gerald sitting there. If Ursula had screwed up her eyes, it would have been Gerald she saw, Gerald about to say something cruel and devastating.

But what she and Sarah said, finally, wasn't exactly unpleasant, only unbelievable. Ursula found herself shaking her head.

"You didn't know anything about it?" said Hope.

"You told me he'd changed his name, but this . . ." What kind of a woman was it who could live with a man for thirty-four years and not know who he was? "Are you absolutely sure?"

"Afraid so."

And then, suddenly, Ursula found she could believe it. She could believe it all too easily. It accounted for so much. For the family life in his books and the unfamiliar people, the naval themes and the recurrent theme of poverty. The long procession of loving, self-denying mothers. The world of children, siblings big and small. In that kitchen, for a moment, she didn't see her daughters, both of them strangely solicitous, anxiously eyeing her. She saw the church where she and Gerald were married, the dearth of his relations, heard his incongruous laughter when she dropped the ring, and she saw Mrs. Eady, her gaunt, wasted body, her tragic face, and she recoiled from it. She got up and stepped back, holding her hands in front of her, pushing something away.

"Ma, are you all right?"

She felt very cold then, and she sat down heavily. Hope, who had never in her life done such a thing, reached across the table and took Ursula's hand in hers.

13

When he saw that the egress had been closed off,
Mark turned and retraced his steps back to where
he had entered. There, during the time he had been
in the passage, someone had blocked that end, too,
had sealed it with stone blocks set in mortar, and
the mortar was hard, as if it had been there for a
hundred years. He was enclosed inside a tube of
stone, and he knew that whatever the passage might
once have been, it was now deep in the earth, a
worm-cast tomb.

—A WHITE WEBFOOT

URSULA WENT FOR HER WALK as usual, taking her niece with her, though it was blowing a gale and the sea was a leaping mass of what Pauline called "white horses." When it was calm, she compared it to a millpond, or had done so until Gerald asked her if she had ever seen a millpond. While they were out, Sarah phoned Jason Thague and told him about Hope's doctor theory. He said he would be going to his grandmother's for supper and that he would ask her.

"Thanks for the check," he said.

"I've had this letter," she said. "May I read it to you?"

"Go ahead."

"It's from the widow of the former editor of the *Western Morning News*. Someone passed on my inquiry to her. She must be very old—the writing's a bit shaky. She says, 'Dear Miss Candless . . .' and then there's a lot of explanation, and then she says, 'I probably remember your father because he became famous later on. My late husband engaged him as a general reporter after interviewing him sometime in the summer of 1951 or 1952, early fifties anyway.' The writing's pretty illegible here but—wait, yes— 'My husband told me that on the day he started work, the new reporter asked to speak to him in private. He said he was writing a book, which he hoped to publish under another name. If my husband had no objection, he wished to call himself by this name from that time forward. I cannot remember what his name was, if indeed I was ever told it, but he wanted to change it to Gerald Candless.' "

"She can't remember what it was? That's great. That's all we need."

"She says she wouldn't remember any of this if the reporter hadn't become famous later on. Her husband told her about it at the time because he thought it strange. She goes on: 'But he didn't object to it. He said what he called himself was the young man's business. I never knew the young man as anyone but Gerald Candless. You probably know all this, but if not, I thought it might be of interest. Yours sincerely, Diana Birchfield.' "

"But his first book wasn't published for another four years," Jason said. "Not till 1955."

She was surprised and gratified that he knew. "No, but maybe he'd already started writing it. Besides, we think that stuff about the pseudonym was just an excuse, don't we? He wanted to change his name for some other reason; he'd probably already changed it."

She said good-bye to Jason as Hope came into the room and then she showed Hope the letter. She had no secrets from her sister, or not many, but she didn't tell her she would be meeting Adam Foley that evening in the pub. It was a strange business, this carrying-on (as she called it to herself) with Adam Foley; she had experienced nothing like it before. Whether he had set it up or she had was hard to say. Both of them, probably, unanimously, coincidentally, but without words.

Words were minimal between them. Strange for two highly educated, highly literate people. Once they were alone together, they spoke only about each other's appearance and what they wanted to do to each other. In the morning, either she got up and left first or he did, again without words, the other left sleeping. They both lived in London, both in Kentish Town, yet they never met there. He never phoned her, nor she him. She knew he would be in the pub with the others that night because Rosie had told her so. Rosie had asked her if she minded.

Hope was going to a school reunion. Six of them, while in the sixth form, had made a plan to do this every four years on the third Saturday in October. Hope couldn't remember why October or why the third Saturday or even why every four years, but she was going. Drinks, then dinner, then more drinks. Sarah had agreed to drive her to Barnstaple and she was going to take a taxi home.

The surface of the sand was ribbed by the action of a rough sea, the rippling and corrugating of a choppy receding tide. In the shallow wells lay white razor shells, upturned, their hollows full of saltwater. Buffeted by the wind, Ursula pressed on, determined to reach Franaton Burrows before turning back. Pauline had given up after a hundred yards.

"The woman who lives next door to Mother got Bell's palsy walking in a wind like this," she said at the foot of the cliff path.

"Why don't you go back, Pauline?"

"Her face never righted itself. It's permanently pulled down on the left side."

Ursula said nothing. At the next sharp gust, Pauline said she would go back, adding with a laugh that it seemed a shame to walk all that way down only to have to go up again. Ursula turned once to watch her climb the path, and when Pauline looked in her direction, she waved, not wishing to seem unkind. The beach was deserted. At the hotel, the shutters were closed on the upper windows and in its grounds the wind tore yellow leaves from the maple trees and the false acacias.

So Gerald was not Gerald and she might not, strictly speaking, even be called Candless. In that moment, she decided to revert from henceforward to her maiden name. Down there on the beach, in the sharp salty wind, she decided. She would be Ursula Wick and would immediately set about putting everything in that name. If he could change his, she could change hers, hers that wasn't hers and never had been.

What dreadful thing had he done? What offense or, more likely, crime had he committed that made him take a new identity? She told herself, angrily and aloud to the wind, that she could have believed anything of him. He was capable of anything. She wished now that she had never forgiven him, never overlooked so much for the sake of—what? She no longer knew.

In giving her the entire use of his money all those years, in leaving her the house and everything he possessed apart from Sarah's and Hope's legacies, in making her his literary executor, he was compensating for—what? For more than neglect and near ostracism, for more than contempt and the theft of her children. He was making up to her for the dreadful thing he had done and on account of which he had taken on the identity of someone's dead child.

She sat down on the turf in the lee of the dunes and wrapped her arms around her knees. The sea was half a mile away, a line of silver, a line of white foam, and between her and the tide edge, the lone and level sands stretched, bleak, pale, empty. "My name is Ozymandias, king of kings." The hand that mocked them, she thought, and the heart that fed. She would move; she would sell the house now, no matter what the girls said. "I don't want to know what he did," she said aloud. "I don't any longer ask why."

Once she had. Twenty-eight years ago, she still had wanted very much to know. She was young and she thought she knew. Yet the proof of it was a great shock. It is one thing to suspect your husband of infidelity, another to have his infidelity confirmed. This was how Jean must have felt when Ian confessed. Ursula knew Gerald would never confess to anything. If Dickie Parfitt had merely seen him go to a house, be let into a house, and spend time there, she would have thought very little of it, but Gerald had had a key. He had a key to a house in a street in Leyton and let himself into it with his own key, as a husband might. As an accredited lover might.

She had looked at Dickie Parfitt's photographs. The one of the old woman was clear enough, but she was just an old woman in a felt hat and a buttoned-up coat. The man in the other photograph might have been Gerald, but it was out of focus and no face could be seen. Perhaps he owned the house. What did she know? He might have lived there himself once, kept it when he moved to Hampstead, now allowed this woman to live there.

Ursula thought she would go to the house and see the woman who lived there, speak to her, find out the truth. But the idea was at first a dream, a fantasy; she would be terrified to do that. And then she asked herself if she really would be afraid. What was there to be afraid of?

Her mother had taken to coming over while

Pauline was with them. She had regularly paid a monthly visit to have tea with the children and to admire Gerald's "way" with them, but that August she came at least once a week. Ostensibly, this was to be with Pauline, the granddaughter she seldom saw because Pauline lived in Manchester, but her true purpose was to discuss her son's broken marriage.

In the world of Herbert and Betty Wick, divorce was so rare as to be practically nonexistent. To Betty, it had been something that happened in the lives of Hollywood film stars, and even there, she believed—or, at any rate, said—it was engaged in solely for its publicity value. Marriage was an absolute, as rock-solid and in a way as physical as birth and death. Love, compatibility, preference scarcely came into it.

She and Herbert had known each other since they were both fifteen, had married at twenty-one, had neither of them looked in anyone else's direction. If the question of marital discord was raised, she would say that so-and-so chose his or her partner and therefore should be content with that choice forever after. Minds that could be changed on almost any other issue—Betty sometimes said sagely that it was a woman's privilege to change her mind—must be adamant here, and the heart had no option but to remain true.

So Ian's defection had left her bewildered as well as horrified. To Ursula, she said repeatedly, "I don't understand it. I don't know what he thinks he's doing. He *chose* her, didn't he?"

If Gerald was present, he listened intently to what Betty said. He fixed her with his bright, dark eyes, frowning slightly, hanging on her words. And she was flattered by his attention and by the encouragement he gave her to utter further absurdities.

"Of course I blame her, as well. Marriage is a matter of give-and-take, and you have to work at it; you both have to work at it."

"It takes two to tango," said Gerald.

Betty wasn't sure about that phrase, having never heard it before. Nor had Ursula then, and for all she knew, Gerald might have invented it himself. But her mother liked the encouragement, saying, "Well, exactly."

Betty loved Gerald. He was the only husband she had ever come across who stayed at home all day and still earned money. Ursula thought then that Gerald had listened so intently to what was said because of his own adulterous behavior. He had an interest, as they said. Later on, of course, she knew why he had listened. He had been making mental notes and every sentence Betty uttered found its way into *Time Too Swift* five years later.

Betty said that as for the girl—Judy, who would become Ian's second wife—Herbert thought she ought to be horsewhipped.

"How about skimmity riding?" said Gerald.

Betty didn't know what that was, nor did Ursula then, the works of Hardy not being among her reading matter. In a grave but approving voice, Gerald explained how once in rural England women who misbehaved were made to mount a horse, sit facing its rump, and be driven around the town to loud music and the jeers of the populace. Betty took it seriously and said that those were the days.

She nearly didn't come the following week because Ursula told her Gerald wouldn't be there; he was going down to Devon again to do more research. Even Ursula couldn't believe he had a mistress in Devon and another one in London, so she accepted the research story and thought of the key he had to the house in Goodwin Road. She would go there while her mother was in the house, minding the children with Pauline's help. It was an arrangement to suit everyone.

But she was afraid of going. It happened to her often, at this stage of her life and later, to think of herself as she had been just a few years before, six or seven years before, and say to herself, This isn't me. I can't be doing this thing, these things. I can't have come to this. I can't have been treated like this, used like this; it can't be true. And she would look in the mirror, seeing herself as very much unchanged since the time she was twenty-three, her face still round and pretty, calm and composed, her hair still smooth, shoulder-length, sand-colored, her eyes still the same gray-blue. But perhaps the self-satisfaction that had been in them was gone.

So she said to herself, I must wake up and find myself at home in Purley, in my bed with the gauzy curtains springing from the golden crown and Cicely

Mary Barker's *Airymouse, Airymouse* on the wall and the southern suburbs outside the window. Work to go to in Dad's office, books from the library, watching television with Pam, getting ready to invite Colin Wrightson to the Library Users' Association . . . But she awoke always in her own bed in Holly Mount, to hear the children in the summer dawns talking and laughing in Gerald's room, and once to hear him, still in the dark, scream out a loud, terrible scream, so that she had run in to him without a thought. . . .

That was after she had been to Goodwin Road and seen Mrs. Eady and heard what Mrs. Eady had to say and so had no choice but to stay with Gerald. Of course, she had a choice, but it hadn't seemed like that then. It seemed as if he had done nothing, as if it was he who had to forgive her for her suspicions, while she must take him for what he was and continue to hope.

Was it the morning following her visit to the house in Leyton that he had woken screaming? It felt to her as if it was, and yet it couldn't have been, for he was away in Devon that night, house hunting, as she later knew. So it must have been a morning or two later, a dawn, rather, when the eastern sky had just begun to lighten.

She couldn't understand why it didn't wake Sarah and Hope, it was such a cry. A scream that burst from the big healthy lungs of a man in the prime of life, a howl of horror, the cry a prisoner might give who finds himself walled up in a doorless dungeon. And that was just what he had fancied he was in the

233

dream, which had been so real, so tangible, odorous, cold, that he thought it was true, that it was really happening.

When she got to him, he was sitting up, his mouth still open, his arms raised, his hands up, quivering, beside his head. Not thinking, not remembering in that moment those slights and rejections, she had gone straight to him and put herself into his uplifted arms. For a moment, he was still, petrified, and then his hands closed around her shoulders. He hugged her to him and she clung there, gasping. She hesitated for only a little while before getting into bed with him and holding him in her arms while he told her about his dream. There, two hours later, the astonished children found them fast asleep.

Ursula got to her feet and walked back along the wrinkled sand. Up in Lundy View House, someone had put lights on in the living room, though it wasn't even dusk yet. Tonight, the clocks would be turned back. The wind had blown leaves from the clifftop gardens down onto the beach, where they lay among the shells as if they, too, had been left stranded by the sea.

We never remember other people's dreams, only our own, but she remembered that one, Gerald's dream. He told her—she hadn't known—that it was recurrent, though sometimes years passed before it came again.

He whispered it all to her, and she was touched, moved, happy. He was talking to her as people who

234

were close did talk to each other, confiding, telling their fears and their pain. It was only later that she understood anyone would have done for him, any ear would have served, anyone's arms and anyone's warmth would have been enough for him. And there were some who would have been far more welcome than she. Dream people from good dreams that for some reason he could never find or keep or confront in reality.

He had been in a city street at night. Which city, he said, he didn't know and it didn't matter. He had entered a tunnel. Or, rather, a passage between streets of stone houses in some densely built-up ancient place. Small stone houses in back-to-back terraces that ran up hills and down hills in parallel lines. The passage was walled and the walls were of stone, damp and glistening, and it was roofed over with stone, from which drops of water fell. Only a very few drops, and they fell only occasionally, but with a soft, dull plop onto the stone floor.

It was quite a short passage, which should have come out into one of the streets, but when he rounded the bend in it, he saw that the way out ahead had been blocked by a smooth sweep of mortar. Where the opening should have been was a wall of man-made stone. He turned and retraced his steps back to where he had entered, and there, during the time he had been in the passage, someone had blocked that end also. Someone had sealed it over with stone blocks set in mortar and the mortar was hard and firm, as if it had been there for years.

He was enclosed inside a tube of stone. And he knew that whatever the passage might once have been, it was now deep in the earth, a worm-cast tomb. All around him, the stones sweated water, falling faster now, dripping softly, forming pools at his feet. He pushed at the stones; he ran to the other end and pushed at the curtain of cement that was covered with fan-shaped prints where hard hands had pressed it in—*from the inside.* Yet there was no one inside but him, and it was then that he screamed and woke screaming, holding up his hands in the attitude of the stonemason who was himself.

Sarah dropped Hope at the hotel where she was having her reunion, walked into the pub, and saw Adam Foley sitting there on his own up at the bar. He looked at her and she looked at him, apparently without recognition, and she walked past him and went into the ladies' room. When she came back, Alexander and Vicky had arrived and Alexander said, "I can't remember if you've met Adam."

"Once, I think," she said, and Adam said yes, once, but a long time ago.

Rosie came then and a man she'd brought with her named Tyger. Tyger with a y, as he told everyone, as if they were going to write him letters. Alexander got the drinks and they all moved to a table and Rosie said she had a conundrum to put to them. Suppose someone emigrated to North America and never came back home, or only came home on a visit and then went back again—it must happen to thousands of people—what became of the five (or seven or eight) hours they had gained? Everyone had answers for this: that time didn't work like that; that time wasn't a pathway, but a room; that the gain of hours was illusory, not real. Adam contributed and she contributed, but they didn't look at each other.

"Would you die five hours earlier than you would have if you hadn't made the journey?" Vicky asked, and Tyger said, "Or five hours later?"

Then they ordered food from the blackboard and Adam went to get more drinks. He brought drinks for everyone but her; it was the same performance as last time, and Vicky said, "Hey, what about Sarah?"

He looked and shrugged and Sarah sat silent, watching, wondering what the next move would be. Vicky pushed her white wine across the table, said, "Here, you have mine," and "For God's sake, Adam."

Of course Adam got Vicky a drink and the food came and Rosie said to him, "You and Sarah ought to come down from London together. Save petrol."

Sarah gave a tight smile.

"Well, you must live practically next door to each other. Don't you think it's a good idea?"

Sarah said, looking down at her plate, "Not really."

"Oh, I'm sorry." Rosie looked at Sarah's bowed head and Adam's stony face. "Have I said something I shouldn't?"

A silence fell. Sarah began to feel very excited. She hadn't known how easy it was to manipulate people, to create an atmosphere, to *change* things. Everyone (except Adam) was now embarrassed. Vicky began talking very fast about someone she knew who had gone to central Africa with a famine-relief mission and who had liked it so much that she had stayed.

"What, liked the famine?" said Tyger.

The conversation now turning to whether one should contribute to famine-relief charities, whether the money ever got to the starving, how much corruption existed, Sarah ate her fish and chips in tranquillity. There were three bottles of wine on the table, but she was going easy because she thought she should have her wits about her. She was very aware of Adam's presence and almost painfully aware of his attractions. Their like-mindedness slightly troubled her. No one she had ever known before had so closely shared her inclinations—tendencies that, until a few weeks ago, she hadn't known she had. Such compatibility threatened her freedom.

Which of them was to make the first move? The pub would close in half an hour and Alexander suggested they go on to Greens. Sarah said, "If I drink any more, I won't be able to drive home." She added, "I mean, not physically capable," lest anyone should think she was showing respect for the laws.

When she went into the car park, he would come to her—but suppose he didn't? Any message that could be passed, any eye signals, would spoil things. She scarcely considered them. She could drive alone to his family's cottage, but she knew she wouldn't. The others all got up. She heard Adam saying good night. He, too, had decided against the club. They made their way out onto the pavement. "Well, good night, Rosie. Good night, Alex," he was saying. "Good night, Vicky. Nice to have met you, Tyger. See you."

Sarah said, "You must be the most uncouth bastard in the West Country." Someone gasped.

"And you are quite a bitch yourself," he said.

She was trembling. "Good night," she said, her voice shaking. "Good night, Rosie darling. Good night, Vicky, Alex. Nice to have met you, Tyger." She rushed off around the back, under the old coaching arch, into the yard, into the car park. She stood by the car for a moment, for a whole two minutes in the cold. Then she got into the car, reversed, and drove out by the exit into a side street. She was sick with excitement, with terror, choking with it.

He was in a doorway, leaning against the wall, smoking a cigarette. She pulled across to him and he got into the car in silence. No kisses, no touching, no words. Why couldn't it always be like this? she thought. Perhaps it could. That made her draw in her breath with a sound, but he took no notice. After a moment or two, as if she were his hired driver, he told her to take Bishop's Tawton Road and there, about a mile out, to turn into the hotel that stood at the end of a long drive.

It was eleven at night and they had no suitcases, but the reservation was confirmed and no comment was made. Once inside the bedroom, he closed the door and locked it, then turned out all the lights but one small lamp. From opposite sides of the room, they moved toward each other, and, taking her face in one hand, he began to lick her mouth, her lips first, forcing them apart, then penetrating to touch her teeth, her tongue, as if he meant to eat her alive. But slowly, with infinite time and relish. With wide-open eyes, she looked into his cold, expressionless ones. Then her eyelids fell as his did. They touched and felt each other in silence.

Hope's taxi got her home half an hour later. Her mother and Pauline had gone to bed. She poured herself a large whiskey, thought about adding water to it but added a single lump of ice instead. For some reason, she thought the door to her father's study might be locked, but it wasn't. It smelled of him; it was full of him. She had continued to sit on his lap until a week before his death. Never mind what people thought. She sat on his lap and wound her arms around his neck and he put his arm around her waist and held her hand. Often she had come in here, knowing he would have finished work, and found him sitting in the big armchair, reading over what he had written. And she always kissed his cheek and sat in his lap, sometimes without speaking. If anyone had asked Hope what love was, she would have said what she had for her father and he had for her.

She sat down in his armchair in the dark. She kicked off her shoes, wrapped her coat around her, her warm coat, which she could fancy as comforting as strong arms. The tears began to fall, but she drank her whiskey, curled her legs up under her, and soon fell asleep.

14

NOT A DISAPPEARANCE, not a vanishing into another country, but a death. Ken Applestone had died of cancer four years before. His son had been expansive to Jason Thague on the phone, had talked for twenty minutes, offering unasked-for details, a painful description of his father's final year, the burnt-out lungs, the cigarettes snatched between the gulps of oxygen.

Sarah didn't want to hear that. It was disquieting to her even thirdhand. "He was quite old, surely." But her father, not much Ken Applestone's senior, had been too young to die. . . . "Did you ask your grandmother about the family doctor?"

"I asked her about all sorts of callers at the house," Jason said. "There was a chair mender. He came to redo the cane seats of chairs. A Mr. Smith—he's going to be a breeze to trace, isn't he? The vet came. They had a dog that got distemper—I reckon we'd call it something else, wouldn't we?—and the vet came, but it was no good and the dog was put down. She couldn't remember what the vet's name was. Or the milkman's or the postman's, if she ever knew. The doctor was named Nuttall. Dr. Nuttall."

"Did he have a son the same age as your great-uncle?"

"My what? Oh, right, yes, I suppose that's what he was, poor little kid. Or would have been. My nan doesn't know; she knows he had children, but she can't remember their sexes. Amazing to remember the name, don't you think?"

"Yes, I do." Sarah suppressed the rather unkind remark she had wanted to make, that Mrs. Thague would be unlikely to remember the name of someone who had come to the house yesterday. "So can we find this Dr. Nuttall?"

"He'd be at least a hundred if he was alive."

"Right, but can we find his descendants? Can't we look him up in *Crockford*?"

"That's not doctors," said Jason, "that's vicars. I'll find out what it is for doctors and I'll find him."

She was beginning to wonder. Perhaps her father's origins would never be found. A letter had come from Robert Postle, asking her how she was getting on and suggesting they should meet and discuss her progress, but she hadn't answered it. She didn't know what to say. After a tutorial the previous week, one of her students asked if she was "anything to do with" Gerald Candless, and she had said, yes, she was his daughter. But even as she had said it, she had this uneasy feeling about his name, her name, their claim to it. Would she ever feel right about her father, not just his name and his deception, but her *father,* if she couldn't find who he was? Would she feel content then?

She had begun rereading his books. If everything he wrote had its origins in historical fact, how much filtering, adapting, altering, twisting, distorting, flattering, debasing, glamorizing, and mutilating of that fact took place before it found its way onto paper? How could you tell? It might be that the ambitious artist daughter from the large Liverpool family in *A Paper Landscape* was a substitute or replacement for the ambitious writer son from a large Ipswich family, family size and the spur of fame being clues. Or that he had had a father or stepfather or uncle who was a religious fanatic, like Jacob Manley in *Eye in the Eclipse.*

But he might not have been writing about himself here, only about someone he knew. Was he one of the children uprooted from his home on the death of his father? Was he the man who married for the sole purpose of becoming a father? You might as well say he was the man who killed his lover in *A White Webfoot.* Or even imagined himself the dead man.

It was a beautiful book to look at, this one. Jacket designs, she thought, had taken such a turn for the better in the eighties, and this one with its painting of a silvery blue marsh landscape and white wading birds under a sky of clouds as delicate as feathers, the colors muted, the finish matte, was one of the finest examples. But the moth at the foot of the spine, incongruously black, made a sharp contrast to those watery shades. She wondered what had happened to the original—why hadn't he possessed it, as he had possessed the original designs for *Hamadryad* and *Phantom Listeners*?

She would ask Robert Postle, get in touch with him by the end of the week, say something to delay a meeting, make some excuse but not tell the truth. She wasn't going to reveal her father's secret to Postle, not, at least, until she had found out what that secret was. And if she had to abandon the attempt . . . Nevertheless, she would phone him. Something brought into her mind at that point the phone call made by a man called Sam something or other and that she had promised to get her mother to call him back. Still, it very likely wasn't important, and he would have called back if it was. She couldn't remember the number he had given her, anyway.

It might be better to write to Robert Postle, and perhaps go to Ipswich at the weekend. Not down to Devon. Adam Foley had revealed, while seeming not to be giving direct information, that he went to his family's weekend cottage only on particular Saturdays. Apparently, they had an arrangement, a rota, from which no family member might deviate. There would be no point in her going down to Devon.

The woman might be younger than she, although surely not much younger, more beautiful, better educated, more clever, wittier, more charming. There was nothing Ursula could do about any of that, but she would make herself look as good as possible. She dressed with care, in a pale green coat over a matching dress, made by Cardin, rather stiff, structured and with a lot of topstitching. Her mother would have asked where on earth she was going, got up like that, would have commented on her painted nails, her jade earrings, but she took care not to let her mother see her go. So far as her mother knew, she had gone out in a dirndl skirt and cotton blouse.

In the train, she felt overdressed, more as if it was a wedding she was going to; she fancied that people were staring at her, but by then it was too late. If she had gone back to change, she knew she would never have set out again. It was three in the afternoon and she had eaten nothing all day, fearing that if she ate, she might be sick. She felt sick even without having eaten.

Never once had she considered that the woman might not be in. She had assumed she didn't go out to work, because Dickie Parfitt had seen Gerald enter the house in the late morning. But that might be wrong; there might be no one in. She began thinking like this in the Central line train after she had changed at Tottenham Court Road. If there was no one in, would she be disappointed, or would she be relieved?

She had worked out her route from Gerald's London road plan. Fairlop Road, Hainault Road, Leigh Road. She had written these names down because she couldn't squeeze the heavy map book into her small bronze-colored handbag. Her bronze-colored stiletto-heeled shoes were not the most comfortable for walking in and she had about half a mile to go. The district reminded her of the hinterland of Streatham, of Crystal Palace, yet there was some indefinable stamp of north-of-the-river London on it. It was gray and Victorian, with patches of fifties architecture filling in where bombs had fallen during the war, and green with privet hedges. But as Leyton was reached, the neighborhood rapidly became rundown. Here, near the Midland railway arches, it was poor and mean, and it had always been so; you could see that the low red-brown houses had been frugally built when these streets came into being eighty years before.

Of all the journeys she had ever made, this was the one from which she most often thought of turning back. First, of getting out of the train at Camden Town because her clothes were too grand, then of crossing the bridge at Leytonstone and getting into the first train that came, then in Fairlop Road, in Leigh Road. But always she had gone on, pressed on, with the half-formed prevision that if she gave up, she would hate herself tonight, tomorrow, even more than she did now. And that, she couldn't bear. She already approached losing that sense of herself as a person worthy to be liked and admired; she was already developing what now, nearly thirty years later, was called "a low self-image," but which then was known as an inferiority complex. Once, though proud and flattered that Gerald Candless had wanted her, she would not have thought so poorly of herself as to assume that any other woman in his life must be better-looking and nicer and cleverer than she.

Goodwin Road was a double row of little red-brown houses, linked together into terraces. A train went by over the bridge as she turned into the street and its noisy passage shook the ground like an earthquake. The sunshine, which was strong, seemed full of hot dust. She stood on the corner for a little while, trying to calculate where the house with the number Dickie Parfitt had given her might be. There was shadow on one side of the street, unbroken sunshine on the other. It was her longest hesitation but her final one. She walked on and up to the gate in the wall that separated the mean little patch of a front garden from the pavement.

The front door and the window frames were painted green. Net curtains hung across the windows halfway up from the central bar. There was no doorbell, only a knocker that was all in one with the mailbox and made of a cheap chrome. Another train went by and the street felt the rattle of it, but more remotely. She lifted the knocker and let it fall, lifted it and let it fall again. Her throat had closed and her chest felt tight.

Footsteps sounded inside, as if from far away. Yet that could hardly be in this small house where the passage would stretch for no more than ten feet. She thought these things as she stood, listening. The sun had gone in and she was immediately cold. A feeling came upon her that some terrible thing was approaching the door, some monster that trailed and lumbered. She fancied she heard a choking sound from in there, a throatiness, and in that moment she knew she had been wrong, but not in what way or in what respect.

A bolt was slid back and something lifted and allowed to fall, a chain perhaps. Then the door was slowly opened. Not a monster, not a slouching grotesque, and not a pretty young girl, either, but a tall, gaunt old woman, the woman of the photograph, who stood before her with the door pulled wide, not an inch or two, but as far as it would go, her expression patient, gentle, and tragically calm.

Ursula met Mrs. Eady again in the novel Gerald published thirteen years later. That was *Purple of Cassius,* which she typed before the last one she ever typed for him. Mrs. Eady was in it as Chloe Rule, the protagonist's aunt, who brought him up when his parents were killed by a flying bomb. Deciphering his spidery zigzag handwriting, penetrating the web of deletions and corrections, Ursula brought Chloe Rule to light and recognized her for who she was.

Here she was in his pages and soon, more clearly and positively, on *her* pages, the living woman as real as the real Mrs. Eady had been, standing in that passage in the wide doorway. His description was accurate, down to the curiously luminous gray eyes and the big hands with a wedding ring on each of the third fingers.

By that time, she had grown a long way away from Gerald, almost as far as she was ever to be, but they still met at mealtimes, still made small talk across the table about the girls or the weather or something that needed doing to the house, and that evening, the first evening after her discovery, she had been many times on the point of asking him, of saying, "I recognize her. Who was she? Why did you go there? Oh, yes, I know you went there. Whom did you go to see and why did you? Why did you? Why did you go there and see Mrs. Eady and then, as if something was over or something resolved, uproot yourself and leave London forever?"

His silence silenced her. That evening at the table, she remembered, he had sat opposite her, reading a book, without speaking at all. She even remembered what the book was: *The Paston Letters,* in a new edition some publisher had sent him. He wouldn't have told her if she had asked—she was sure of that—and the next day, she went back to his scrawled and crisscrossed pages to meet in them a man not in the least like Gerald, a young, sweet-natured man named Paul.

Paul was sent by his friend to the friend's aunt, Chloe Rule, who kept a lodging house, and there he had his digs for years to come, becoming like a son to Chloe and watching her decline. It was a tribute to Gerald's powers, Ursula thought, and she had thought it reluctantly, that he could draw this woman as comparatively young, as no more than forty when Paul meets her, yet she, Ursula, the knowing reader, could recognize in the character the old woman she had met and met only once. For Mrs. Eady had been

250

old, had been deep into her seventies. Chloe Rule's black hair had turned white, her strong face had fallen, and the cancer that was soon to kill her had devoured the plumpness that Paul observed the first time he saw her. But she was the same woman, and Ursula thought with a shiver that she was someone Gerald had loved.

Not Leyton, but Hounslow; not a little red-brown terraced house, but a tall gray one; not six children, but just two; not the murdered son, the lost sons, the daughter consecrated to religion, but one son and one daughter, unimportant, distant characters, not figuring much in the narrative. Were those other children the family that appeared in *A Paper Landscape,* in *A Messenger of the Gods*? Perhaps. You could find out his whole life from his novels, yet not find it out at all, find out nothing.

The more she had known of these things, the less she had known him. That day, when she came home from Goodwin Road, it was to be weighed down with guilt. For she had misjudged him, falsely accused him. There was no one who could have entered that house but a woman from the next street, who had been given a key to the house to come in and keep an eye on things while Mrs. Eady was in the hospital having her operation. The woman had a station wagon and a husband, a tall, dark man, who might well one day have gone to the house in his wife's place.

Ursula understood that Dickie Parfitt had gotten it wrong. She had never had a high opinion of his intelligence. Guilty and ashamed of herself, she sat

251

down and wrote to the detective agency, ridding herself of its services and asking for its account. It was not until some time afterward that she understood her discovery really changed nothing. It didn't negate Gerald's visits to Goodwin Road; it provided no answer as to why he rejected her.

The following day, he returned from Devon and asked her a question. He was kind, almost jovial, somewhat paternalistic, faintly teasing, the way he had been in the days when he called her Little Bear. How would she feel about moving?

"Leave London," he said. "Go and live in the country. Or at the seaside."

"Don't you have to live in London?" she said.

"Why? I don't exactly work in an office."

"Is that where you've been?" she said. "Have you been looking at houses?"

Once she would never have—*dared* was too strong a word—never have quite brought herself to ask him anything so baldly. She was no longer afraid of him, no longer in awe.

"Is that where you've been when you were doing research?"

"In Devon, yes," he said. "North Devon. The most beautiful beach in England. A house on the cliff and a view of Lundy Island." He looked at her; his eyes flicked over her. "Should I have told you before? Are you going to be unreasonable?"

She said, like a woman twice her age, not like the Wicks' spoiled daughter, "I am never unreasonable."

"No, you're not, are you? I suppose that's something to be thankful for. Come on, Ursula, Little Bear, Constellation, be nice, be *pleased*." She had stared at him in astonishment and he had reddened. She had never seen that before, a blush on his face. "Come on," he said, "you come with me to Gaunton next week. We'll all go, and we'll go over the house. Won't you like that?"

She thought she might. She was flattered that he had asked. It would have been much more like him to have bought a house and then moved her into it. He disappeared one day before they left for Devon, but she didn't ask where he went; she didn't even care. Dickie Parfitt had been paid, had been a touch aggrieved, but had departed without a struggle. Then the tunnel dream came. It might even have been the night before they went to Devon, the very small hours of that day. And she went to him and comforted him and got into his bed.

Going over Lundy View House that first time with Gerald and the girls and the estate agent had made her feel like an ordinary, normal wife and mother. Like the beloved wife of a suburban man, the mother of loving children, whose husband has been given a promotion and can now afford their dream house. It was a fine sunny day at the end of August. On the previous occasion that he had been to the house, it had been fine and sunny. The couple who owned the house, who were reluctantly moving to a smaller place near their daughter in the Midlands, showed them the large airy bedrooms, all with views of the green wooded countryside and three overlooking the sea.

The garden then was full of the kind of flowers that last in bloom for months, hydrangea and helichrysum and statice, though Ursula didn't know their names then. They looked fresh and beautiful from a distance, a little worn close to. The lawn was yellowing in the heat, but the sea was blue as sea can ever be and the air so clear that you could pick out individual trees on the island and the striations on its cliffs.

Gerald said, out of earshot of the owners, "I could work in this room."

It was on the ground floor, protruding from the main body of the house like a small wing. Bookshelves already lined two of its walls. She could see him calculating where more should go. He had Hope in his arms, had carried her up and down the stairs, whispered to her which should be her room and which Sarah's.

Ursula's resentment at his high-handedness, his choosing a place, if not quite a house, without consulting her, was fading. The house itself helped dispel it. Besides, she had come to expect so little from him that she was flattered he had eventually asked for her approval. And she was even more astonished when, that evening in the Barnstaple hotel where they were staying the night, where they had been given a double room, he asked her if they should make an offer on the house.

"Shall we buy it?"

"Yes, let's." Her reply was spontaneous, eager. "I love it."

"My girls will have seaside every day," he said.

Three weeks later, she thought she might be pregnant. She didn't know whether she hoped it or feared it. Both, possibly. Another child for him to take away from her? Or a child for her to fight for and keep. In the end, she wasn't pregnant, so it didn't matter. And there wouldn't be any more chances; he had made that clear by locking his bedroom door in Holly Mount, so that Sarah, coming in as usual in the morning, had to rattle the doorknob and shout, "Daddy, Daddy, let me in!"

The Hampstead house was sold and they moved in December, the day after Sarah's fourth birthday. It was raining and the steely gray sea looked as if punctured all over by a million shining needles. Gerald's books filled twelve tea chests and he set about getting them up on the shelves as soon as they arrived. Next day, the fog came. The house, the garden, the dunes were swathed in it, muffled by it, and the sea was invisible. He reacted violently, saying he would never have bought the house if he'd known.

She had no idea what he meant. To her, it was just low clouds, a white wetness that left dew on the leaves and water drops on the windows. A neighbor, to whom she had already talked, told her the sea mists seldom lasted more than a day, and Ursula repeated this to Gerald. He said nothing, just retreated into his study, pulled the curtains, and put the lights on.

She was in the next room, the room Pauline was later to sleep in, getting it ready, making up the bed for the guest he had invited for the weekend, Robert Postle's predecessor at Carlyon-Brent, Frederic Cyprian, the editor who had "discovered" Gerald, who had been the first to read *The Centre of Attraction*. She would have preferred Gerald to have waited a week or two, but she had learned and was still learning that what Gerald wanted he got.

He came into the room where she was, holding a child by each hand, and said, "I want blinds put up in my room. Dark blinds. Can we get that done? How soon do you think it could be done?"

15

*Very little is more irritating than the speech
patterns of someone we know to be intelligent yet
who is ignorant of grammar and correct usage.*
     —A MESSENGER OF THE GODS

JASON THAGUE WAS VERY MUCH as she had pictured him. There was something uncanny about this, because we don't expect people to be the way we imagine them. Life isn't like that, but perverse and contrary. She had envisioned a short, skinny boy with a round, spotty face and glasses and long, curly, not very clean hair, so by the time she got to Ipswich, she knew she was going to see a heavyset, smooth-faced man with a crew cut. Her original idea was almost what she got, and it made her laugh.

Except that he was older. Nearly as old as she, perhaps, his face formed and set in its permanent shape, the spots departed, having left pits and scars. It was a hungry face, perhaps literally hungry for food.

He had a room in a terrace on the outskirts, the opposite side of the town from Joan Thague's outskirts. The house was Victorian, one of those Suffolk town houses of white brick without gable or bay on its facade, but still four stories high, and the room he had was on the top at the back. A room such as students have, dirty, a dump of paper and books, clothes and used cups and glasses, with an unmade bed, a view of rooftops, slummy backyards, and garbage cans, an Oasis poster on one wall and a Modigliani woman on another.

He offered her coffee, and she said yes so as not to be standoffish, but she winced when he found a mug under the bed and held it for a moment under a running cold tap. Unaccountably, he kept biscuits in a glass jar. They were chipped around the edges like old plates, and she quickly shook her head at them, too quickly perhaps, for she got a puzzled look before he began eating them himself. It was only later that it occurred to her he had saved them for her.

"Right," he said. "I'll tell you what I've found out."

"Dr. Nuttall?"

"He had two sons," he said. "He was easy to find, but of course he's dead. One of the sons is dead, too. Natural causes, I guess. He'd have been eighty if he were alive. The other one—his name was Kenneth— was born in February 1921."

"All these Kens," she said.

"As you say. It must have been the sexy name. These days, Kens are all Chinese cooks. But this Ken would have been a bit old to be your father. I mean, in 1951, when your dad changed into someone else, Ken would have been thirty, not twenty-five. D'you reckon he'd have taken on the identity of someone who'd have been five years younger than himself?"

"More likely than taking on the identity of someone five years older," said Sarah. "He'd want to be younger, wouldn't he? People always want to be younger than they are."

"Do they?" said Jason Thague, seeming unconvinced. "Could your dad have been seventy-six when he died?"

"I don't know. Maybe. People vary, they grow old at different rates. How would I know? I just accepted he was the age he said he was." As she had accepted everything else he said, as we mostly do accept. "Can we find this Kenneth Nuttall?"

"I don't know. It's not being able to find him that we want, isn't it? I can have a go. I will. His father, the doctor, died in Ipswich, and so did his brother. I can start with the phone book. Now, there's something I want to ask you."

She looked at him. Coming here, talking to Jason Thague, had brought her suddenly to a feeling that she must give this up. She couldn't account for it; it was illogical, absurd. The man was doing his best, had done wonders. But now it was as if she realized the impossibility of what they were trying to do. They had made too many assumptions, based everything on the tottering premise that the man who became Gerald Candless had known the dead Gerald Candless or known of him.

"Yes, what?" She sighed.

"Those books you sent me. I haven't read any of them yet."

Sarah shrugged. She was accustomed to the apparent paradox that students, who, of all people, have to do with the printed word and with learning, often make such heavy weather of having to read a book.

"I suppose you have your course work."

He didn't answer. "I haven't read them, but I've had a look at them. What's the point of that butterfly thing on their covers?"

"Butterfly? Oh, you mean the black moth."

"Is that what it is. Why's it there?"

She didn't know. She had never asked; she had never thought much about it. "That silhouette, he had it on the heading of his stationery, on his cards, and, of course, on his books. I don't know why. Does it matter?"

"It might. I'm in the business of looking for clues, aren't I? How do you know it's a moth and not a butterfly? I mean, I suppose there's a difference. I don't know what, but maybe you do."

"He called it a moth," Sarah said. "He used to talk of the emblem as 'my black moth,' but I don't know why."

"Could you find out? Ask your mother, maybe?"

"She wouldn't know. I suppose my sister might. Is there any point in all this, Jason? Shouldn't we just give up?"

He made a face. It was odd, but some women found that pockmarking attractive. Well, they must have, when you considered how many film actors had pitted faces. Of course, the actors didn't otherwise look like Jason Thague.

"Is that why you came here, to say we should give up?" he asked.

No, she had just thought of it, she said. It had suddenly seemed to her so hopeless. Without anything in his books, in the papers he left behind him—or in any memory of what he might have said—to provide them with a lead, what chance did they have?

She said, thinking aloud, "You're a bloke. What would you do? About changing your identity, I mean."

"I've thought of that. It was the first thing I did when I started on this. I'd do it legally. But that means it gets published in the papers. Your dad had some reason for doing it secretly. Now, I don't much like my name. I don't like Jason or Thague. Chasin' Jason. Facin' Jason. Hasten, Jason, with the basin. So I'd change to names I really like. Say Jonathan. If I ever have a son, I'm going to call him Jonathan, so I'd have that. And then I like monosyllabic surnames that aren't too common, so I'd have Dean or Bell or King. There you are—how about Jonathan King?"

"You're saying my father's favorite names were Gerald and Candless?"

"Not likely, is it? But Gerald must have been a favorite name with Kathleen and George Candless or they wouldn't have named their son that."

"If you're right," said Sarah, "we shall never get anywhere, because we can't know why. I mean, you don't know why you'd like to be called Jonathan King, do you?"

261

"I like the sound of it."

"There you are, then," said Sarah.

To Robert Postle, she wrote a cagey, cryptic sort of letter. Reading it in his office in Montague Street, reading it for the second time and reading between the lines, Robert thought she meant she was growing bored with the idea of the memoir. What else was meant by "presently insurmountable problems" and "difficulties in establishing a true picture of my father's ancestry"?

He had just returned from lunch with Sarah Candless's mother and Carlyon-Brent's publicity director. They would be publishing *Less Is More,* Gerald Candless's nineteenth and last novel, in January, and the publicist, Elaine Kirkman, wanted Ursula to help with its promotion. Ursula was in the publicity department with her now, talking about giving interviews to newspapers and magazines, attending literary lunches, and appearing on television. The aghast look on Ursula's face had told him of her disinclination to do any of this, of her shock at being asked. The poor woman probably thought she had been fetched up to London to talk about a design for the book jacket or whether Gerald's photograph should still be used on it.

He was far too discreet to have mentioned Sarah's memoir or her letter. Discretion apart, he had always had the impression that those two girls didn't get on too well with their mother. Spoiled to pieces by Gerald, they had been, both of them. Robert had his own beliefs about those who were excessively indulged in childhood, people who were extravagantly made much of. They started off as high achievers but never fulfilled their early promise. They weren't stayers. Besides that, they had no time for people who didn't think they were wonderful.

You had only to look at this letter to see it all there. And what did she mean by asking him why her father would have had a palm cross in his study? In the letter, she described him, Robert, as a Christian, which he hated. It made him feel as if he were about to be thrown to the lions. He was a Catholic, or a Roman Catholic, if you insisted. In his view, every-one in the Western world was a Christian, though many were lapsed or apostate. She had added a post-script, which seemed to him affected: "Have you any idea why Dad had that black moth emblem on his book covers?"

He didn't know. He had only become Gerald Candless's editor in 1979, when Freddie Cyprian retired. The fact was, she was chickening out of this memoir. And he had been fool enough to think he might see a first draft by Christmas and actually be publishing to coincide with the paperback of *Less Is More*. He thought of all the poor hopefuls out there who would give years of their lives just for a chance to get a book published! He put the letter on the pile and went downstairs to say good-bye to Ursula, who had said she wanted to catch the 3:30 from Paddington.

*   *   *

Ursula had never had much to do with the promotional aspects of Gerald's books. She had never before been in these offices, to which Carlyon-Brent had moved from Fitzrovia thirteen years earlier. He had changed his agent at about the same time, but she had met his agent only once and that was at a literary dinner. Carlyon-Brent's then publicity director, one of Elaine Kirkman's predecessors, had told Gerald that if he was never accompanied anywhere by his wife, gossip columnists would begin speculating that his marriage was unsound.

That, of course, was when it had reached its most unsound point, a position from which it was never again to waver. She went to the dinner and found herself not even sitting at the same table as he. She went to another dinner party, this time given by the American ambassador and very grand. The risk of gossip was presumably allayed, because Gerald didn't suggest taking her with him on an American tour or to an arts festival in Australia. When a new novel was published, he toured the country, going mostly to big cities, read from the new book, and signed copies of it for fans in bookshops, and he went without her.

Once, soon after they had moved into Lundy View House, he had done book-signing sessions in Devon and she had accompanied him. The whole publicity scene was quieter in those days, not looked upon as essential, particularly for a literary novelist. The booksellers gave them champagne and took them out to dinner afterward, even though Gerald sold no more than twenty copies of the highly acclaimed *A*

Messenger of the Gods in Plymouth and seventeen in Exeter. He had taken her with him, she thought, though she hadn't thought this at the time, to make it up to her for not sleeping with her. There was a lot of compensating going on at the time, mostly of a monetary nature.

Within reason, she could have any money she liked for the embellishment of Lundy View House, spend anything she wanted on help in the house and garden. She should invite her parents to stay, her sister, and Pam, her bridesmaid, now married and with children herself. Pauline must come during her school holidays. After the visit of Frederic Cyprian, Roger Pallinter came, and the Arthurs and Beattie Paris and Maggie. Gerald always spoke of these visits as supplying company for her. It didn't strike her; it was her sister, Helen, who remarked on the anomaly.

"Mostly when people get married, their friends are those who were the wife's friends. But the reverse is true of you and Gerald."

At that time, she still cared what other people thought, and she was afraid of Helen or the Pallinters or the Arthurs finding out that she and Gerald didn't share a bedroom. That was why she was so glad of that guest room on the ground floor. In the summer, their first summer, Colin and Sally Wrightson came.

When she was first married, Ursula had looked upon Colin Wrightson as having had a favorable and indeed almost-magical influence on her life. Without especially liking him, she saw him as her good angel.

Had it not been for his slipping on the ice and breaking his leg, she wouldn't have met Gerald. But now, nearly eight years later, she was beginning to see him as having done her an injury. She couldn't be in his company without thinking of that day when Sally had phoned to tell Betty Wick of Colin's mishap or without remembering her own dismayed excitement at the idea of Gerald's coming in Colin's stead.

Colin Wrightson was well known for his affairs. More so than for his historical novels, some said unkindly. Ursula said she didn't know why Sally stayed with him.

"Bread and butter," Gerald said.

"You mean she really stays on account of money?"

"Most marriages continue for economic reasons. Or, in other words, because women can't support themselves. That may change in the future, but it hasn't yet."

He talked to her—when he actually did talk to her—not as if they themselves were partners in a marriage but, rather, as if she were a casual acquaintance he had met in a pub. What she didn't tell him was that Colin Wrightson had once made a pass at her. She hadn't found it gratifying or amusing or frightening, and she certainly hadn't been affronted. But as well as not liking Colin very much, she didn't find him attractive. He was a few years older than Gerald and only a few years younger than her own father, red-faced, overweight, a lumbering, myopic man whose clothes smelled of cigarette smoke.

The Wrightsons had come, and on that Saturday

afternoon, Sally and Colin and Gerald had gone out with the children, leaving her at home alone. Why had she been alone? On account, perhaps, of a migraine. About that time, the migraines had started, though the one she had had that afternoon must have gotten better very fast or never have been that bad, because she wasn't too ill to do what Colin wanted when he came back unexpectedly.

To make an essential phone call to London, he said. Well, he had said it to Sally and Gerald. He didn't repeat it to her. He said a lot of other things that she would have been ashamed to say to anyone, that she would have been ashamed to say even then: that he couldn't get her out of his mind, that he wasn't made of stone, that he had only one reason for coming to Lundy View House. He sat on the sofa beside her, saying all these things, and after a while she got up and went into the guest room with him.

It was awful, electric, unexpectedly what she had longed for. With anyone, it appeared. Until she looked at his face, the texture and color of blackberry mousse and glistening with sweat.

"Go easy," he kept saying. "Go easy."

But she couldn't go easy—it had been so long.

"Hey, you're quite a girl," he puffed. "Go easy now. If you do that, I can't hold out. For God's sake . . ."

Probably he liked smiling, passive women. At any rate, he hadn't come back for more. She thought, madly, that she'd have killed him if he had, taken the kitchen knife with her and stuck it into his big belly.

She considered telling Gerald—just to see what he would say, what he would do. Instead, she asked him what it was she had done. It made her angry in later years to remember that she had put it that way. Not "What's the matter with you?" or "Why don't you want me anymore?" But "What have *I* done?" When the women's movement really got under way and she was reading about it and even excited by these new ideas, she understood she had been brought up like that, that her mother was like that and her sister, Helen, for they, too, had been conditioned to think that when things went wrong, the woman must be to blame.

He said, "Nothing."

Just like that, a bald nothing.

"We aren't having a real married life," she said, because she couldn't bring herself to use such expressions as "making love," or worse. "We don't share a room. Why don't we? That's why I asked what I'd done. Maybe I'd better say, where have I gone wrong?"

Then he told her. And she wished she hadn't asked.

"You were simply the wrong person. That's not as harsh as it sounds, because there is no right person and never can be."

She almost whispered it. "Was there ever?"

"No."

"Gerald, what do you want of me?"

"Nothing," he said again.

She had grown up a lot. She wasn't nearly so

afraid of him. "That's not good enough. I need more than that. I've a right to a better answer than that."

He sighed. She remembered—oddly then for her—a line from Shakespeare: "The heart is sorely charged." He sounded as if his heart were sorely charged.

"When we got married, I thought it would work. I thought I could manage." He didn't mention the children. This was fourteen years before *Hand to Mouth*. "It isn't my fault and it isn't yours."

"Why can't you tell me why?"

"I can. Up to a point." His sorely charged heart turned his face gray. "Long before I met you, I did something. Just a chance, rather daring something. Not wicked, not vicious. It destroyed my whole life. Later on, I tried to mend it, but it was too late. I'm sorry, but it makes me sick to talk of it. One day, maybe, I'll write it down. When I'm old. Perhaps."

"And that keeps you . . . away from me?"

He ignored that. "We dislike those we've injured. I know I've injured you—so there it is. If it's any consolation to you, I've been celibate. Entirely celibate."

She believed him. It wasn't a consolation. It just made her detective activities seem foolish. Her brother, Ian, had recently gotten his divorce, just in time to marry Judy and ensure the legitimacy of the child she was expecting. It had shown Ursula's family that divorce was possible without the world ending, that remarriage could happen. At the same time, Roger Pallinter's wife had left him.

"Are you asking me to stay?" she said, and it took a lot of courage to say it.

"No," he said. "No, I'm not asking you. I'm not even expecting it."

She waited for him to add that he would like it, though, that it was what he wanted. Instead, he added, "This is straight talking, so I may as well say I'm indifferent as to whether you stay or not. That's as you please. You have never shown a great deal of interest in the children, and they, of course, would stay with their father."

She was so shocked that she couldn't speak. It was easily the most brutal thing anyone had ever said to her. She seldom cried, but that night she cried bitterly. Next day, a Sunday, the first reviews of *Orisons* had appeared in the papers. They were the best he had ever had. The critics spoke of his compassion, his warm humanity, and of his ability to re-create on the page the magic that can exist between a man and a woman.

He had driven into Gaunton and bought all the papers. That was the only time he was really happy, when he got good notices, and they had never been as good as this. He pushed the papers across the table to her, read bits out of other reviews while she was reading, laughed with delight, once actually brought his hands together in a resounding clap of triumph. She was sure he had forgotten everything they had said the night before, or thought it of no particular account.

Now they wanted her to step into his shoes, so to speak, and publicize his new one. Walking across

Russell Square toward the tube station, she thought of the things that woman Elaine Kirkman had said, the possibility of her going on the radio, on *Kaleidoscope* to talk about his writing, of a television program called *Bookworm,* of being interviewed by the *Guardian* and the *Times.* She hadn't been able to bring herself to tell Elaine Kirkman or Robert Postle that the last book of Gerald's she had read or even looked at had been published twelve years before.

And now there was this business of his not being who he said he was. It had been clear that neither Robert nor Elaine knew anything about that. They couldn't, therefore, know how profoundly it had affected her, making the house and everything in it that was his horrible to her. Impulsively, she had decided she must sell it and move, and she hadn't changed her mind after letting the sun set on her panic. The sun had set and risen again and she was more than ever resolved on getting out.

When she got home, she would return to clearing out all those papers, continue the task she had begun and flinched from. The house should be made tidy and sterile, cleaned of him, and then she would put it on the market. She was thinking like this when she looked up and saw Sam Fleming walking toward her.

Her immediate instinct was a childish one, her reflex to the sight of him something she hadn't had since she was a child. She wanted to hide. Not be seen. Or pretend not to see him, slip past, eyes down. But he had seen her. He put out both hands.

"Ursula!"

She knew she had gone red. "Hello."

"Let me guess. You've been to your husband's publishers."

It wasn't so very clever of him. Where else would she have been but to Carlyon-Brent, unless it was to the British Museum? "I'm in rather a hurry," she said. "I've a train to catch."

"What time's your train?"

She told him, wishing immediately that she'd lied and made it half an hour sooner.

"Then you've plenty of time," he said. "Time to come and have a cup of tea with me."

Sitting opposite him in the café near the tube station, she thought she might as well say it. What had she to lose? In that moment, stirring her tea, she thought suddenly that she had nothing left to lose, for she had already lost everything.

"Why do you want to be here with me?" she said, and she looked him straight in the eye. "If you'd wanted it, you'd have phoned me. This chance meeting—are you just being polite? You don't have to be polite with me."

"I did phone you," he said. "I phoned you twice. The first time, I was told I had a wrong number, which I didn't really believe, and the second time, I left a message and my phone number."

"Oh. I see." One of those weekends, it would have been, when the girls were home or one of them was home. "My daughters, I expect. I didn't get the message."

"I'd hoped to make you understand that I didn't

want to know you because of your husband's books. Getting my hands on some first editions. That's laughable. I wanted to know you—I want to know you—because I like you. I find you attractive. I think we'd get on together."

"That's frank," she said.

"I still feel like that. I feel like it more. I see it as a tremendous piece of luck, a very happy coincidence, meeting you like this."

"Not such a coincidence," she said. "I expect your business is around here, isn't it? You walk across the square every day at this time. And one day, I was bound to walk across it, too." She felt a flicker then of that powerful desire that had afflicted her— oh, yes, it was an affliction—in the hotel that summer evening. His face, the sound of his voice, his enthusiasm, his eagerness to please her, so different from what she had been used to. "I must go and catch my train," she said.

"I'll come with you. I'll put you into your train. Isn't that what they used to say?"

She told him it wasn't necessary. She had only to go one stop to King's Cross and change to the Circle. He thanked her for telling him but said he was familiar with the configuration of the London underground and that he was going with her.

The train stopped in the tunnel between King's Cross and Euston Square and sat there for ten minutes. She had asked him how Molly was, and he was talking about Molly and the children and telling her how he thought Molly might marry again, when

Ursula realized she had missed the intercity train. It wouldn't now be possible to get to Paddington in time, and the next train was very late, too late to get a connection to Barnstaple. The tube train started with a shudder, but it was too late. She thought of asking Sarah or Hope if she could stay the night. One of them would say it just wasn't convenient, sorry, Ma, and the other would say yes, all right, but in a forlorn voice, and she thought she couldn't bear that.

The tears came into her eyes. He was looking at her, aghast. I know what this is, she thought. This is the start of some sort of breakdown. That is what will happen to me next. I shall break down, and that really means go mad, so to pieces.

"What is it?" he said.

"I've missed my train!"

"I know. Let's get out at the next stop." It was Baker Street, and on the escalator, he said, "We'll find you a hotel for the night. Then I shall take you out to dinner and you can tell me why you're so unhappy, because I don't believe it's missing your train or losing your husband."

"No," she said in a small voice. "No, it's not."

She thought he said that he would like to make her happy, but she couldn't be sure, because it was noisy in the tube station and he might have said something quite different.

16

When you think someone is listening to you he is probably only considering what to say next.

                                   —A MAN OF THESSALY

JASON THAGUE HAD FOUND Robert Nuttall's widow, Anne, living in the Cotswolds. Her husband had been a dentist in Oxford and they had retired to Chipping Campden.

"That makes me wonder about dentists," Sarah said. "I mean the Candlesses' dentist. They'd have had one."

"I don't think so. Most people didn't have dentists in the thirties, not a dentist you go to for regular checkups. You went to a dentist to have a tooth out when you had a toothache. Anyway, I asked my nan, and she said her father had had all his teeth out and false ones for a twenty-first birthday present."

"I don't believe it!"

"That's what I said. My nan's got dentures now, has had all my lifetime. She never went near a dentist till she was seventeen and living in Sudbury, and that was, like I said, to have a tooth out."

What would her father have thought of Jason's

pitted face and his voice and his accent? She said coldly, "So we've reached a dead end."

"Don't say that. There's still the knife grinder and the chair mender. Is my check in the post?"

Sarah had been fourteen when *Hamadryad* was short-listed for the Booker Prize, old enough to have some understanding of what that meant and young enough to be bitterly hurt and convinced of injustice when it didn't win. She had read the novel and believed that the young girl, Delphine, the protagonist, was herself. She asked her father and he said, "There's something of you in Delphine and something of Hope."

She had asked which "somethings," and he said, their beauty and their intelligence. What about the rest of her, then? What about Delphine's shyness, her goodness, her reclusiveness? No one, even then, could have pretended she and Hope were shy or retiring or even particularly good.

"That was someone I knew long ago," he said. "No, not a girlfriend." He had hesitated. "A relative."

She remembered that now. She was thinking of *Hamadryad* because Frederic Cyprian had still been her father's editor when it was published. After that, and before the next book, he had retired. Some said his retirement was directly due to *Hamadryad*'s failure to win. At the dinner, when the winning novel was announced, he had done something authors had been known to do but not publishers. He had gotten up from the table and walked out.

Sarah had met him a few times in the seventies

when he came with or without his wife to stay at Lundy View House. He was old then and his wife was older, and she had since died. Sarah had known, since moving into this flat, that he and she lived very near each other. For some reason, now forgotten, she had once looked him up in the phone book. It must have been simple curiosity, since she had never intended to phone him or visit him.

Now she had. If he was still alive, and Robert Postle had indicated he thought so, he was still there, around the corner, two hundred yards away. She walked down and looked at the house. Victorian, red brick, a steep flight of steps up to the front door. It looked empty, closed up. She hesitated only for a moment, then walked up the steps and rang the bell.

No one came. She rang again. The door was opened by a woman some ten years older than herself, but very different from herself. She looked worn and harassed and irritable and she was dressed in a dark purple shell suit.

"Yes?" she said.

"My name is Sarah Candless. Gerald Candless was my father. I wonder if I might see Mr. Cyprian?"

"Well . . ."

"He was my father's editor at Carlyon-Brent."

"I know that, Miss Candless."

The woman looked at her doubtfully. Sarah thought she recognized her from years ago as Frederic Cyprian's daughter. Jane? Jean? Or perhaps it was just that she saw something of him in this strained, intense face.

"I met your father," she said. "When I was young."

"That can't have been very long ago," the woman said dryly. "Won't you come in? I am Jane Cyprian. My father is very old and not well. More than that, but you'll see, you'll see." She added, "He may be quite lucid. He sometimes is."

Sarah felt the apprehensiveness that is almost fear and that comes at the threat of being confronted by someone whose control has slipped or been fragmented. She followed Jane Cyprian down the passage. It wasn't dark or in any way sinister, unless a profusion of pictures, ornaments, and clutter is sinister.

Outside the closed door, Jane Cyprian turned to Sarah and said, "I wish you'd phoned first."

"I was passing. I live very near."

A shrug, a glance of impatience, and the door was opened. The room on the other side of it held nothing to surprise a visitor of a hundred years before. It was perfectly but not self-consciously Victorian, even to the braided pelmet along the mantelpiece and the row of framed sepia photographs above it. The old man sat in front of the cold grate in an antimacassared armchair. In the years since she had last seen him, time had bleached and shriveled and drained him, had dried him up, like a fallen leaf.

"Dad," Jane Cyprian said, "there's someone to see you."

He turned his head, reached for the handles of the two sticks that rested against the arms of his chair, thought better of it, and extended one wavering hand.

"Ursula!"

Sarah shook her head. Jane Cyprian said, "That's not your name, is it?"

"My mother."

"Ah. He makes these mistakes. This is *Miss* Candless, Dad."

"Ursula," he said again.

Sarah made herself walk over to him and extend her hand. He looked at it as if it were some unfamiliar object, the likes of which he had perhaps never seen before, attached to her sleeve. His voice was thin and high, as if the vocal cords had shortened.

"That husband of yours never comes to see me anymore."

About to say Gerald Candless was dead, Sarah caught Jane Cyprian's eye and her faint shake of the head. She said nothing, feeling helpless. "I wanted to ask him about a sort of logo thing on the covers of my father's books."

"You can try."

But she couldn't. The old man with his papery face and his uncomprehending eyes brought home to her her own shortcomings. She hadn't been aware of them before, of this failure in herself to approach, to find any rapport with, the old, the unsound in mind, those who were different. An image of Joan Thague came into her head.

"I must go," she said. "I shouldn't have come."

"Perhaps not."

The woman despised her. Her contempt was palpable, and Sarah, turning to go, drew herself up indignantly. The old man's voice came eagerly, lucid now, "I'll take you up on that invitation when the weather's better. In the spring. I'll come down and see you and your little boys."

Outside, in the cluttered hall, Jane Cyprian said, "Alzheimer's, as you probably gathered."

"I'm sorry."

"Yes, well, you should have phoned."

Walking down the street, trying not to think of that woman and what her life must be like, Sarah found herself trembling. But a hateful woman. There was no need for such rudeness. I'll go and see Hope, she thought. I should have gone to her before. She's as likely to know about the moth as anyone. A taxi came and she got into it. Calling on Hope without phoning first would be almost unprecedented, and halfway there, she remembered her sister had said she would be staying with Fabian. Sarah gave the taxi driver Fabian's address at Shadwell Basin. It was a long way and there were cheaper ways of getting there. Am I really going because I want someone to talk to? Is it because, since Adam, I've felt more alone?

Fabian had two cousins from the country staying with him, accommodated in sleeping bags in the living room. Hope opened the front door, crowing with delight at the sight of her sister, which touched and slightly puzzled Sarah, until Hope said, whispering out in the hall, "We're in the middle of playing the Game."

"What, with the cousins?"

"Your arrival will demoralize them further. And

then they'll go out. They're going to the pub, but we won't. I've got plenty of booze."

They were a brother and sister in their late twenties. Hope held Fabian's kitchen scissors by their blades, passed them to the brother, saying, "I pass the scissors crossed."

The brother took them gingerly, opened them, and passed them to Sarah. "I receive the scissors crossed and pass them uncrossed."

Hope crowed, "No, you don't. That's wrong."

Sarah turned the scissors over, took them by the handles, closed them, and passed them to the sister. "I receive the scissors uncrossed and pass them crossed."

Fabian's female cousin opened the scissors, turned them over twice, closed them, and said, "I receive them uncrossed and pass them crossed" as she passed them to Hope. "Is that right?"

"Yes, but do you know why?"

"Because they're closed?"

"Wrong."

"It's the words you use, isn't it?"

Hope and Fabian laughed unkindly. The cousin then said it must depend on which way up the scissors were and her brother thought it was which way around they were. Neither guessed, though they played the Game for half an hour, Hope and Fabian enjoying themselves hugely and Sarah starting to cheer up. Fabian's male cousin thought he ought to have an explanation, but Fabian wasn't having any of that. The answer might get out and he and Hope would be deprived of this perennial source of amusement.

"Anyone coming down to the pub?"

Hope said a decisive "No, thanks," and as soon as the door closed behind them, she went to open a bottle. Not wine this time, but Strega.

"I shall get pissed," said Sarah.

"Good idea. You look as if you need it. Fabby's been doing some researches into the Highbury murder for you, if you're still interested. You know, the case they said *A White Webfoot* was based on."

"Fab has?"

"He's good at that sort of thing."

"Has it got anything remotely to do with Dad, Fab? I mean, first of all, do you think *A White Webfoot* really was based on it? And then, could it shed any light on Dad's past?"

Fabian rotated his glass, watching the pale yellow liqueur roll back and forth. He sipped it meditatively. "I've never read it." His tone made it plain he didn't intend to, either. "You'll have to judge. I've written it all down." He passed her a dozen sheets of paper in a green cardboard folder.

She said doubtfully, "It looks very businesslike."

"That's probably all it is."

"I've been wondering about the black moth. Does it have any significance. Why a black moth? Do you know, Hopie?"

"I've never thought about it."

"For a couple of women who had such an amazing relationship with their father, you seem to have been singularly uninterested in him. While he was alive, that is." Fabian grinned in response to Hope's mutinous look. "His ancestry, for instance. Women are supposed to be keen on that kind of thing. His childhood. And wouldn't the first thing you'd have asked when that moth thing appeared on his books—after all, you were in your teens; you weren't infants—wouldn't the first thing have been, 'Why the butterfly, Daddy?'"

"We didn't," said Hope. "We just didn't."

With the air of one just discovering a great truth, Sarah said wonderingly, "Isn't it a fact that you aren't much interested in someone who's very very interested in you? His interest in you takes up all the time, sort of occupies all the space. Dad was fascinated by us and we received his fascination, but we weren't curious about the . . . well, the bestower of it."

"That's all very fine," said Fabian, unimpressed, "but it's being a great nuisance to you now."

"He wouldn't have told us," said Hope, opening the Strega bottle for a refill. "Have you thought," she said to her sister, "of asking the woman who designed the jacket of *Hamadryad* if she knows about the black moth? She might. It was on *Hamadryad* that it was used for the first time."

"Ask her? I don't know her. I don't even know who she is. It must have been—oh, all of eighteen years ago."

"I know her," said Hope. "I mean, by sight I do. Her name's Mellie Pearson and she lives near you. That is, I expect she does, unless she was just visiting someone. I saw her in the street last time I was at your place."

*   *   *

Sarah wasn't going to make the same mistake twice. Mellie Pearson, who had designed the jacket for *Hamadryad,* lived not much farther away than Frederic Cyprian, and she passed the end of her street on the way to Chalk Farm Station. But this time, she would phone first.

"I remember my painting for Hamadryad very clearly. It was my first big job." She was a soft-voiced, slow-spoken woman who sounded as if she aimed to please. "And then the book was so . . . well, a best-seller and so talked about."

"And did you design the black moth, too?"

"The black moth? Oh, the little motif. Well, I suppose I did. I copied it, at any rate. Is it important?"

"It might be," Sarah said.

"Would you like to come over? You're not far away, are you?"

On the corner of Rhyl Street, she saw a taxi pull up and Adam Foley get out of it. The sight of him, so unexpected, though she knew he lived somewhere near, caught her up with an inner lurch. It was dark, but the street was well lit. She went on walking toward him, aware of her beating heart. His tall figure made a long, elegant shadow across the pavement. He paid the driver, turned, and saw her, then looked at her with perfect indifference. It wasn't even the glance of veiled admiration or hopefulness she was used to receiving from men who were strangers, but as if he barely noticed she was there. And she returned it with equal detachment, walking on at the same pace, not looking back.

The next weekend, he was due in Barnstaple and she would go down to Lundy View House. Anticipation ran through her body like a hot gush of steam. She was shut off from the outside world, enclosed in a strong, trembling excitement, so that she walked past Mellie Pearson's door and had to retrace her steps.

It took her a little while to bring herself out of the fantasy she had entered from the moment she had seen him. It took some deep breathing and hand clenching while she stood on the doorstep. And Mellie Pearson had opened the door before she could ring the bell.

"Couldn't you make the bell work? It doesn't always. I was waiting for you, anyway."

Sarah, restored quite quickly to reality, found herself looking at the original painting, not for the *Hamadryad* jacket, but for that of *A White Webfoot*. It had been placed on an easel, a watercolor of a blue, white, gray-purple landscape, the trees gray shadows in the mist, only the wading waterbirds clearly outlined.

"I did designs for four of your father's books," Mellie Pearson said. "He bought all the originals except that one. I don't know why, but he never much liked that one."

Sarah said, "You said you copied the moth. I don't know much about these things. Were you given a print of it to get into your drawing, or did you sort of stick it on later?"

Mellie Pearson laughed. "That's about it. I saw a print of it so that I could avoid its somehow clashing with my design. Do you see what I mean? If I'd done a very dark painting for *Hamadryad,* for instance, the moth wouldn't have shown up."

"What is it called?"

"The moth? I don't remember. I was given a photocopy of a print from an old book, *The Moths of the British Isles,* something like that."

"But you don't remember the moth's name?"

"It was eighteen years ago," said Mellie Pearson. "I do remember one of the moths was called Tanagra, because of Tanagra figurines. That's why I remember. You know, the terra-cotta figures discovered at Tanagra, in Greece. But it may not have been the one I drew for your father's book. Still, it doesn't matter. My not remembering, I mean. I've got all my notes and sketches for *Hamadryad.*"

"You've still got them?"

"I may not look it, but I'm really quite a methodical woman."

Photographs and sketches of waterbirds, avocets and whimbrels, goosanders and widgeons. For a moment, Sarah thought she had been given the wrong folder, and then she remembered the faint shapes of shadowy birds in the jacket painting for *A White Webfoot,* spindly-legged, gray-plumed. Next, she came upon a preliminary sketch for the jacket. No birds here, only marsh and mist, a blurred horizon.

Sarah thought back, seemed to remember her father rejecting an early design for this jacket as too misty, too vague. And the next attempt had also displeased him. Here it was, duck feet, goose feet, webbed and spread, making a pattern like fallen leaves on the pale opalescent background. Mellie Pearson's third attempt, with the birds and clouds and limpid water, the mist half-lifted, had been the one chosen. And this time, the moth was there, sooty black against the pastel bluish gray and gold.

It would be used again and again, on every novel Gerald Candless had published since that time, this small emblem placed above Carlyon-Brent's familiar logo of a winged foot.

Mellie Pearson had made notes for it in her artist's fine Italian hand from, according to the attached labels, *The Moths and Butterflies of Great Britain and Ireland* by A. Maitland Emmet, *The Moths of the British Isles* by Richard South, and *Butterflies and Moths of the Countryside* by F. Edward Hulme. She had been thorough and painstaking and rather more in love with words than Sarah would have expected. Under the heading "Psychinae," she had written, "Psyche, the soul, also a butterfly or moth from the analogy between metamorphosis and resurrection. The soul is the spirit of man liberated from the impurities of the flesh. Shrank says the name *Psyche casta* (chaste soul) may have been prompted by the fact that some members of this family refrain from sexual activity."

There was evidently more to moths than met the

eye. Sarah looked at the line drawings Mellie Pearson had made, exquisite, detailed, fine. Moths with patterned or striped wings and furry bearlike bodies, a coal black moth with splayed antennae, a tiny moth, fuscous, densely scaled. The artist had marked the bigger insect with a cross, the smaller with a question mark.

Sarah turned the page and came to a letter. It was a letter from her father, and the sight of the familiar handwriting in an unexpected place seemed to touch her heart and pluck at it. She had to look away and close her eyes. Then she braced herself and read it. The date was May 6, 1978.

Dear Miss Pearson,

I believe you are expecting to hear from me about the moth. My publishers will have told you I want to use a moth emblem on my books. However, it cannot be just any moth, but must be one of a specific genus: Epichnopterigini.

I have never seen this creature in life, only in pictures. I expect the Natural History Museum would help you to find it. They have an Insect Identification Department, I am told. The moth's name is Epichnopterix plumella. *One more thing—if this does not sound too pedantic and absurd, please don't confuse it with the larger* Odezia atrata. *This could easily happen, as you may find when you do your research.*

I look forward to seeing your drawing.

Yours sincerely,
Gerald Candless

What on earth did he mean? What was this business about confusing one Latin name with another? It all sounded so unlike her father, who had had scant interest in natural history and in the garden at Lundy View House hadn't been able to tell a fuchsia from a geranium. She said aloud, "Tell me the answer, Dad," and then added, "Tell me who you were."

A hint, not an answer, came from inside her own head. *Atrata* meant black, didn't it? *Post equitem atra cura sedet.* She remembered that—everyone knew about black care sitting behind the horseman. Her father had thought one black moth might have been confused with another. A big one with a small one? Were those two in Mellie Pearson's drawings *Odezia atrata* and *Epichnopterix plumella*? But why did it matter? What could it matter? And why did he want the smaller moth when the larger would have been more impressive? The small one—in the drawing, at any rate—looked less densely black.

"Tell me why, Dad," she said. "Tell me what all this is about."

Mellie Pearson evidently wasn't going to be able to do so. There were no more notes in the folder, only sketches. One of these, the final version of the black moth, had a piece of paper clipped to it on which she had written, "Approved by author." That was all.

Sarah asked herself how it was that her father had known about these moths. Somewhere, he had come across them in that dark, lost time before he became Gerald Candless. Their names seemed to mean nothing in particular, though for a few minutes she tried vainly making anagrams from them. Of course, it was always possible that the moth had played some decisive role in his destiny or his work, or, like Jung's golden scarab, had flown up against his window and distracted him from writing a letter that would have been fateful. Or, by burning its wings at his light, have shown him a course not to take.

In that case, she would never know. And perhaps it was unimportant. But she wasn't convinced that was so. The identification of this small dark insect contained somehow the solution to his identity.

Jason Thague always took a long time answering because the phone was downstairs in that tall old house and he had to be fetched or shouted for. At last, someone came, a woman who agreed grudgingly to summon him. But after Sarah had listened for some minutes to the sounds of the house, wind rattling the windows in Ipswich just as it was in Kentish Town, a door slamming, a radio blaring out soul music, the receiver was lifted.

"Ta for the check."

She winced. He had the voice of a disc jockey on a local radio station. "Can you find some moth or butterfly books and look these up for me? Or get hold of someone who'd know? You haven't got an ento-mology department at your university, have you?"

"I doubt it," he said. "Now, if it was business management or computer technology . . ."

"Well, it's not. These moths are called *Odezia atrata* and *Epichnopterix plumella*."

He said to spell, please, and she did, following

290

her father's rules, which they had thought so amusing and witty while in their teens: *E* for *epistemology, p* for *pomoerium, i* for *ichthyic* . . .

"Yeah," he interrupted her, "or how about *p* for *patronize* and *i* for *ignoramus*? Would you stop being clever for a moment and just spell it?"

It felt like an insult to her father's memory. She became stiff with him and cold, spelled the names clearly and slowly. "Have you got that?"

"Yeah, sure," he said. "I'll give it a go. What about *A White Webfoot* and the Highbury murder?"

"You can leave that for now. Concentrate on the moths. I'll call you from Devon on the weekend."

She would research the Highbury murder herself. She contemplated the green cardboard folder Fabian had given her, feeling an inexplicable unwillingness to look inside. But not perhaps so inexplicable. Moths were safe; moths were harmless—they didn't even sting. Murder, on the other hand, anyone's murder, was dangerous, she thought. Even to read about it could conjure ugly suspicions and speculations. There could be no question of her father's being involved, certainly no question of his having changed his identity on account of some involvement, for the murder had taken place years after he went to work for the *Western Morning News* and became Gerald Candless. But he had written a novel whose plot bore such strong similarities to the Highbury murder that critics had commented upon it and continued to do so even though he denied a connection.

He had waited more than thirty years before

writing that book. Did that mean he had waited until certain people involved were no longer alive? Or that it had weighed upon him and oppressed him so that at last he had to exorcise it, or attempt to exorcise it, by writing a novel with a plot similar to life? Get it down on paper, clear his mind of it. But of what?

Not of guilt—of that, she was sure. Of fear, then? Of pain? It is always helpful, when we have some dreaded task to perform, to tell ourselves that preliminary work must first be done, the ground prepared. Postponement could thus be entirely justified. Sarah, after the manner of her father when he had some paper or document, the very sight of which triggered apprehension, did as he always had and covered it up with something else, in this case the folder of Mellie Pearson's notes.

Out of sight, out of mind. At least for the present. She would prepare herself by rereading *A White Webfoot*. It was the story of two boys who had first met while at school in Norfolk, in the fenlands. Dennis's father was an agricultural laborer, Mark's the warden of a wildfowl sanctuary, before such places became commonplace, for the time period of the book was the aftermath of World War II and the fifties. The boys loved each other without knowing it, or at least without expressing their love in word or deed. Dennis understood his homosexuality, and that it was unchangeable, when he was very young, only fifteen. Mark denied his.

They were growing up in a world and under a legal system whose ideas had changed very little since the previous century. Homosexuality was still unmentionable in polite society. To reactionaries, it was evil, a crime on a par with murder, while the more liberal saw it as a sickness, a mental disease, invariably the result of the subject's weakness and corruptibility.

While some sort of life was possible for the practicing homosexual in London, in a country village, he was obliged to be either a eunuch or an unwilling, perhaps repelled, lover of women. Dennis chose the former course for a while, but left home as soon as he could, Mark the latter. Not that it was a choice—it seemed to him a bowing to a miserable inevitable.

As she read, the book came back to her. But she felt as she had the previous time she'd read it, that for the first time surely her father was writing of something quite outside his experience. And she looked again at Mellie Pearson's notes, reading once more of *Psyche casta,* the strange winged creature that for some reason abstained from sexual activity.

17

It is very hard to come to terms with the fact of someone simply not liking you.
—THE FORSAKEN MERMAN

THEY WENT TO A RESTAURANT not far from where Ursula was staying and over dinner she told Sam things about her marriage she had never told anyone. He told her about himself, and when these exchanges were over, he asked her what it was she wanted.

"What do I want?"

"Out of life. For your future. What do you want now?"

"To get rid of that house," she said. "To go back to the name I once had and to try to have a relationship with my daughters. Oh, and to forget Gerald. But that will be very hard."

"Perhaps you shouldn't try. The past may be less painful if the present gets better."

"I don't know. I think of the past a lot. I wish I didn't." She looked searchingly at him, experiencing as she had all evening the sexual pull she had first felt on the sands at Gaunton. With it came a sense of time wasted, of chances lost. "So tell me what you want?"

He said simply, "Oh, me, I want to be in love."

"What?"

"I liked it so much the last time. Well, that was also the first time. I want it again. Is that so strange?"

"It's not something people say," she said.

"No, they say they want sex or they want to find someone. I want to be in love. I want to be possessed and obsessed by it. I want the sky to change color and the sun to shine all the time. I want to long for the phone to ring and pace the room when it doesn't. I want to be breathless at the sound of her voice and tongue-tied when I first see her. I want to be her and make her me."

"You are an extraordinary man!" Ursula laughed aloud; she couldn't help herself. "Have you made many attempts?"

"Let's say I haven't succeeded. Come, I'll take you back to your hotel."

He left her in the foyer after they had made an arrangement to have breakfast together. He would come at nine. She went up to her room, had a bath, and, in the absence of nightclothes, wrapped herself in the terry-cloth robe the hotel provided. The next day, she thought, she would tell Sam about Mrs. Eady. It would be someone to tell; yet as she thought of it, she wondered what she would have to tell and whether that encounter would have meaning for anyone but herself.

And did it even have meaning for her?

*　*　*

She was so polite. She was so gracious. When she saw a stranger there, an overdressed young woman with a pale, anxious face, she said good morning and asked if she could help her. Ursula said who she was in a stammering voice. She could hardly speak. She had never in her life feared fainting, but now she did.

"I am afraid you're not well. Come in and sit down."

Ursula shook her head. If she was to harangue this woman's daughter, for it must be her daughter, she would do it on her own terms, in anger, in bitterness, not in the meek acceptance of hospitality. But those feelings now took second place to this overpowering faintness. She stumbled into the house, into the little front room, hardly seeing her surroundings, dazed and for a moment almost blind. This weakness, this feeble failure to cope with the house and its occupants, was something she hadn't anticipated. Or not on this level. Not that fear and shock would bring her to sink into an armchair, to hold her head down in her hands and remain there until gradually the sensation passed.

She felt a light touch on her shoulder and looked up, realizing then that she was being offered a glass of water.

"Thank you. I'm sorry."

"Sit quietly," the woman said. "You'll be better presently. I am Mrs. Eady."

She was perhaps in her mid-seventies, dressed in a dark sweater and skirt covered by an apron, the kind of sleeveless crossover overall, tied at the waist, that Ursula remembered her own grandmother wearing, not as protection against dirt or food stains but as part of a daily uniform. The skin on her face was red and shiny, but with an unhealthy, inflamed look, and her hands were red, too, large and spread and gnarled. A plain gold ring was on the third finger of her left hand and another encircled the third finger of her right. Her white hair was as brilliant as congealed ice.

Standing there, for she still stood, waiting to take the glass from Ursula's hand, she appeared to be a tall woman, almost six feet, somewhat bandy-legged, her strong, solid legs planted far apart, as if they had once supported an overweight body. It was gaunt now, the big bones prominent.

She said patiently, "There, that's better. You've some color come back into your face."

Ursula handed her the glass, thanked her again. She sensed that Mrs. Eady would never ask her why she had come, what she was doing there, would simply accept it. "Mrs. Eady," she said, "I am Ursula Candless. I am Mrs. Gerald Candless. Gerald Candless is my husband."

Of course she expected a flicker of something to cross that calm and steady face: the eyes infinitesimally to move, the lips to tighten, or the white head to bow a little. There was nothing. Then Mrs. Eady set the glass down on the table runner, a runner that held along its length a photograph in a silver frame, another in a tortoiseshell frame, a single rose in a green-speckled vase, and sat down in the chair opposite Ursula.

"I think I have really come to see your daughter," Ursula said. "I don't know her name. Your daughter, who lives here with you."

"I have two daughters," Mrs. Eady said, and she hesitated a little. But she went on, "They don't live with me. One of my sons lives nearby, but not with me. One of my daughters is married and lives in York and the other"—again the hesitation—"the other is a religious."

"I'm sorry? A what?"

"A sister. A nun."

Ursula bit her lip. Those words had the least expected effect of making her want to laugh. They were not the sort of thing people said. But the amusement, if that was what it was, died as quickly as it arose. She said, "Then someone else, some young woman, lives here with you. You have a"—she sought for the appropriate word—"a tenant, a boarder."

"No."

"Mrs. Eady, my husband was seen coming here, letting himself in with a key. Oh, I am sorry—it's embarrassing for me, too; it's shameful, I know. I am sorry. Perhaps I'm wrong. I hope I'm wrong—"

"I'm not embarrassed." She said it very quietly and easily, as if she had passed beyond embarrassment, had entered a world where social solecism is a trivial thing. "Would you tell me what you want of me, Mrs."—she recollected—"Mrs. Candless?"

"I don't know. I shouldn't have come."

"When was your husband seen coming here?"

"It was a few days ago, about a week ago. On a Tuesday morning."

"And he let himself in with a key?"

Ursula thought afterward that she must have imagined the points of light that for a moment appeared in the other woman's eyes, for Mrs. Eady said somberly, "I wasn't here, Mrs. Candless. I was in the hospital. I've been very ill."

"Oh, I'm sorry," Ursula said.

"I am very ill now—but we needn't go into it. While I was away, my son may have come in, but not till the evening, after his work. My neighbor down the street had a key to the house. To feed my cat and water my plants. I believe her husband comes in as often as she does."

"What does he look like?"

"He's a tall man, dark-haired, about forty-five. Is that where the mistake has been made?"

Ursula nodded. "I think so. I don't know." She looked at the nearer of the photographs, of a thin, very handsome boy in jeans standing by a motorcycle. "Is that him? Is that your son?"

At once, she knew she shouldn't have asked. She hardly knew why she had asked, for it wasn't Gerald who had come to this house, and it wasn't this skinny boy, but the neighbor. If light had come into Mrs. Eady's face, it was now overshadowed by pain, the lips compressed as if to keep in a cry. It took her a little while to speak.

"That *was* my son. I had four sons, Mrs. Candless. That was Desmond. He was . . . killed. My son who lives here is James, and Stephen is a teacher on the other side of London."

"Killed?" Ursula faltered. She said it because she didn't know what else to say in the face of this naked acceptance of grief.

Mrs. Eady stood up. "For a long time, I kept his photograph in a drawer, but then . . . It's the worst thing in the world to lose a child, an unnatural thing. Yet even that passes." Ursula's anxious, almost hungry look must have forced the words from her. She said, "It can't interest you. It's not connected with why you came," and then she added, "Desmond was killed; he was murdered." She clenched her hands. "Beaten to death, yes." She added with courteous formality but in a strained voice, "I mustn't keep you any longer."

"Oh, no, no, I must go."

A painful flush had spread across that gaunt face. Mrs. Eady regretted having said so much, and it showed. Now she was making a polite effort. "Once, a long time ago, I knew some people in Ipswich named Candless."

"I expect they would be his family. He came from there. Good-bye."

When the house was left behind, she ran. She liked the rhythm of it, the freedom of running, and in Hainault Road, she did an unprecedented thing: She took off her shoes and ran on the warm pavement in her stocking feet. A few people looked at her. She ran on, full of hatred for Dickie Parfitt, who had nearly wrecked her life.

Instead of telling Sam Fleming this story at breakfast the next morning, she talked about her daughters and how she believed that, now Gerald was dead, she might manage to get on better with them. And she recounted the incident of the embraces in the taxi and of Hope holding her hand.

"Why didn't you take a stand when they were young?" he asked. "How could he make them love him and not you, unless you let him?"

"I tried, but I didn't try hard enough. And he had that advantage over most fathers—he was always there. Short of physically pulling them away from him, there wasn't much I could do. If I'd ever been alone with them . . . but I never was. He married in order to have children; that is the plain truth of it. And when he got them, he was going to extract every ounce of love and pleasure and . . . well, richness out of it."

"And you were expendable?"

"I was expendable, but I couldn't be spent, so to speak. I think he'd have liked me to go and leave the children, only I wouldn't go. Perhaps I stayed because he wanted me to go."

She said she would like to visit the British Museum. He looked incredulous when she said she had never been there, but he took her, and he took her out to lunch. She wouldn't have said another word about Gerald if he hadn't asked. Asked and pressed her and shown an interest that wasn't feigned.

"He hadn't anything else, you see. He only had the children."

"He had his work," Sam said.

"Yes. He had his work. I don't know which was more important to him, his writing or his children. About equal, I expect. I thought he had other women; for a long time I was sure of it, and then, quite a bit later, I thought there might be . . . men. But I don't think so now. He said he had no sex life, and I believe that. I think he was always perfectly faithful to me— for what that's worth."

"Often not as much as many people think."

She had never before talked like this to anyone, but now she was telling it all, or much of it, to Sam Fleming, knowing by some instinct she must recently have developed that it would be quite safe with him. He listened, but he said very little. Sometimes he smiled or raised his eyebrows. He made no final comment. She thought she had never known a man, in conversation with herself, look less bored.

He took her to Paddington in a taxi. He talked about their next meeting as if it was something previously firmly decided on. There would be a next meeting. The question was only of when and where.

"Come back up here. You say your daughter's going down for the weekend. Get a lift with her and come back on Sunday night."

"I wonder if I could," Ursula said. "Why not? I don't suppose she could exactly say no."

"That's the spirit," said Sam.

He got out of the taxi with her, lifted her hand and kissed it, then drove away again quite quickly. In the train, instead of reading her book, she thought of all the things she had said to him, relived what she had said and felt comfortable about it. He hadn't been impatient and he hadn't swamped her with sympathy. She reflected on the last thing she had said to him, before they left the restaurant where they had lunched.

"It's very hard to come to terms with the fact of someone simply not liking you."

Gerald had written that, in one of his books. She hadn't fully realized the truth of it until she had spoken it aloud. From soon after Hope was born, she had known Gerald didn't love her. The effect of this realization was a profound sense of loneliness and a sinking of her self-esteem. He didn't love her; he had no desire for her. Yet somehow, for years, she clung to the statement she had made to Roger Pallinter, that she and Gerald were friends. They were companions on an equal footing. She transcribed his handwriting and typed his manuscripts. With her, he shared his income entirely. She knew precisely what he received in royalties and, indeed, it was she who corresponded with his accountant and from 1973, when value-added tax was introduced, kept the VAT book.

In this way, she deceived herself. They might no longer share a bed, but they shared what was more important—the maintenance of a family, the running of a household, the entertaining of friends, decisions as to the children's welfare. And then one evening, after he had been more than usually silent all day, she asked him if he had another chapter completed for her to deal with the next morning. He was reading, not a book, but some journal, the *Spectator* perhaps— she couldn't remember—and he looked up, barely looked up, and, frowning, waved one hand in a dismissive gesture. Don't bother me, it said; leave me in peace. Can't you? Why do I have to put up with this?

And in that moment, she knew as plainly as if she had read it on the page that he didn't even like her. It wasn't a positive hatred; it was worse than that: a mild dislike, composed of utter indifference combined with resentment. Don't bother me; leave me in peace. Why can't you just do my typing and cook my food and manage my money?

That was when she began walking every day on the beach. A mile one way and a mile back, rain or shine, mist or clear. Out of his house, away from his children—though they were at school by this time— along the pale black-streaked sand, watching the flat sheet of lapping water or looking inland at the hummocky moon-landscape dunes. At first, on these walks, she dwelled on whether she should go or stay. Divorce, with the new law, would soon be easier, geared in women's favor. She would get custody of the children. He would have to keep them all financially.

It was that very day, or perhaps the day after, that he had taught Sarah and Hope the Game—I Pass the Scissors. It was more a test or an ordeal than a game. She had looked up *ordeal* in the dictionary and found it defined as "any severe trial or distressing or trying experience." At first, seeing the three heads bent over a table, she supposed them to be playing cards. Then she saw the kitchen scissors going from hand to hand. They wanted her to join in, a rare event.

But by that time, the girls had caught on, or Gerald had whispered the answer to them. Was it possible those two little girls of nine and seven had solved the Game in ten minutes? She was never to know and never to learn how herself. In the meantime, they wanted her as their stooge.

"I pass the scissors uncrossed."

"No, you *don't*, Mummy."

"You don't see, do you, Mummy?"

"All right. Try again. I pass the scissors crossed."

"Wrong again," said Gerald. "That's enough for today. Come along, my little lambs, we're going on the beach."

Could she take his children away from him?

He wasn't like an ordinary father. Not only did he worship the girls, but he had done everything for them. She had been like an upper-class woman whose children are cared for by nannies. If she took them away, it would ruin his life; it might kill him. Did she care? Strangely, after everything, she found that she did, still did.

Also, she would have to earn her own living. She would be morally bound to do so, if not actually. If I could have foreseen such feelings ten years ago, she thought, if I could have imagined at my wedding the person I'd become in this short time . . . She could type. She had no other skills. Even if she stayed with Gerald, she ought to do something more with her life.

The first thing that came out of those beach walks was a decision to educate herself, and the next day she signed up for an art history evening class. She told Gerald, but she didn't think he heard, and if he noticed she was out on Tuesday and Thursday evenings, he certainly didn't miss her. Later, of course, she knew he had heard, had been busily making notes.

At art history class, she met new people and made some friends. Until then their friends had been Gerald's, but now she saw the possibility of having her own. But at the same time, she withdrew even more from her children. It seemed the natural result of their indifference to her, their overwhelming preference for their father and their tendency, Hope's especially, to ignore her. Perhaps she should have persevered, treated these clever, bright girls as if they were handicapped children who needed constant stimulus and the knowledge of unquenchable love. But they got that from their father, and she couldn't compete, scarcely knew how to, lacked the heart. Instead, she turned to her new friends, and to one man in particular.

It was at about that time, a few days before Easter, that she found the newspaper cutting in Gerald's study. He had gone to Exeter to give a lecture at the University of the Southwest. She went into the study to find the chapter he had written the day before, part of *Time Too Swift,* with the character spitefully based on Betty Wick. It was lying on his desk, the usual higgledy-piggledy pages of scrawled, crossed-out, margin-scribbled prose, indecipherable to all but her.

She picked it up and in doing so lifted too much, a letter from a reader that lay underneath it, an invitation to take part in an arts festival, and under that the cutting from a newspaper, probably the *Daily Telegraph,* though all that appeared at the top of the row of columns was the date: Monday, April 16, 1973.

These were deaths. He hadn't told her that a friend of his had died. But he told her so little. Only a fraction of the death announcements was there, for the paper had been cut, not lengthwise but across, to leave only the top entries in each of the first two columns. Baker, Brandon, Bray, Burton; Daynes, Denisovic, Docker, Durrant, Eady . . .

Eady, Anne Elizabeth (née O'Drida), April 12, age 76, beloved wife of the late Joseph Eady, mother of James, Stephen, Margaret, and Sister Francis of the Order of the Holy Paraclete, and grandmother of Amanda, Leo, Peter, and David. Funeral April 18 at the Church of Christ the King, Leyton, E.10. "Precious in the sight of the Lord is the death of his saints."

She read it over and over. It aroused in her a powerful, undirected, almost-hysterical rage. Without knowing what she was doing, acting on angry impulse, she began tearing the newsprint into pieces. She saw, as she cooled, that she had torn it into scraps like confetti. She swept them into her hand, then into an envelope, took the envelope to the kitchen, and thrust it into the bottom of the waste bin.

If he noticed the absence of the cutting, he said nothing about it.

18

The greatest fallacy is that good looks are an essential ingredient of sexual attraction.
—HAND TO MOUTH

IT MUST BE SOMETHING out of the ordinary for Jason to phone her at college. She was surprised he knew where she worked, because she couldn't remember telling him. Perhaps he had set himself to find out things about her.

"I'm in London," he said. "I've just come from the Natural History Museum."

"You sound excited."

"You will be, too, when you hear. Can we meet? I want to tell you face-to-face."

She sighed. He must have heard the sound. "What time is it?"

"Just gone four."

He would want to come to the flat. Then she would have to have him there again—obviously enjoying the unaccustomed luxury, the warmth, the drink. And once more have to remind him of his last train, once more pay his taxi fare all across London.

"I'm not very far away," she said. "Why don't we meet somewhere for a drink? Say in an hour?"

"Could we meet for a meal?" he said.

"You can't get meals at five in the afternoon."

"That's all you know," he said. "If you go to cheap places, you can get meals all round the clock."

She would have much preferred a pub. She liked pubs. The place he chose was hardly a restaurant in her eyes, more a café that dispensed nothing more select than hamburgers and pizza. At least it was licensed. That was the first thing she looked for, cautiously stepping inside. Bottles of wine from Chile and what supermarkets rather oddly called "the New World" were lined up behind a counter with a till on it and doughnuts in cellophane packets.

The place was very warm and quite crowded for the time of day. Jason was already there, sitting at a table by the window, without even a drink in front of him. He looked gaunt and pale. She hadn't previously noticed how thin he was, but she saw now that he was a thin, almost-emaciated man. The incongruous thought came to her that if he had a girlfriend, she would find it very uncomfortable to sit on his knees.

"Let's have a drink," she said, and when the waitress came over, she said, "We'll have a bottle of the Chilean Semillon."

"Not unless you'll drink it all yourself," he said. "I'm going to have a beer." He directed his next request to Sarah. "And please may I have the pizza

310

casalinga and chips and some bread first, bread and butter?"

"Pizza casalinga and a side order of french fries?" said the girl, looking from one to the other of them. "Ciabatta or focaccia?"

"Not for me," said Sarah. "I don't want anything at this hour. I'd better just have a glass of wine, a large glass."

He looked at her. "You can take the cost of the pizza off my next check if you like."

"For God's sake. You said yourself it was cheap." She opened and shut her hands impatiently. "Now, what have you got to tell me?"

"You're going to like it. It's the first real step along the way to knowing who your father was." He took a small notebook from his jacket pocket. "You know how we thought of all those people who might have come to the house, regular callers who'd know about the little boy's death?"

"Of course I do. The butcher, the baker, the candlestick maker. The milkman. The doctor. The dentist who never was. But I thought you were researching moths."

His beer came and her wine. She drank greedily. Waiting until she had set her glass down, he said, "I was. I have. This is about the moth. It's the moth that gives the clue to your father's father's occupation, or that's what I think. See what you think. There are two moths, right? Both black." Jason referred to his notes. "The big one, *Odezia atrata,* is blacker, and

311

one of the books about them says of the little one, *Epichnopterix plumella,* I quote: 'It is not quite true to nature, however, that he should be less densely black than his master, since the latter would ordinarily see to it that his fag did an abundant share of the work, and the boy-nature of the latter would consider even a modified cleanliness as somewhat of a weakness.' "

"Should I know what you're talking about? When was that written?"

"In 1903."

"What fag? What master?"

"These moths don't just have Latin names; they have common names, too. *Odezia atrata* is commonly known as 'the chimney sweeper,' and *Epichnopterix plumella* as 'the chimney sweeper's boy.' How about that?"

She had never appreciated what "tucking in" meant until she saw Jason eating his mammoth pizza. He passed her the basket of chips, but she shook her head. Another glass of wine was more necessary. Wine to blur despair and wine to settle excitement.

"You're saying, aren't you, that Dad's father, my grandfather, was a chimney sweep? That somewhere he'd come across this moth and been amused by its name, by the appropriateness of its name for someone who actually was the sweep's boy, the sweep's son."

"Right."

"You're brilliant, Jason, you really are. I don't know what I'd do without you."

He had demolished half the pizza. He looked up at her and grinned. When he smiled, you could see the outlines of his skull under the stretched pocked skin. "Is there anything you can remember to . . . well, back it up, if you know what I mean?"

"There is something. My father used to tell my sister and me this story. The hero—well, the boy in it—used to go up chimneys. The story was about his adventures. When I was older, I thought it came from Kingsley's book *The Water Babies,* and I'm sure it did in part, but I think some of it was based on fact."

"Your dad wouldn't have gone up chimneys, not in the 1930s he wouldn't."

"His father would have. His father did. Or stuck his brushes up chimneys, or whatever they did. And he was his boy. The black moth was a secret joke."

"One he didn't share with you."

Sarah disliked being reminded of that. The picture she formed of her father discovering this insect, its Latin name and then its common name, his amusement, perhaps a wry amusement, his decision to have it on his books as an emblem, esoteric, intensely personal, utterly private—all this was displeasing to her. Silently, to herself, she admitted she was jealous. Jealous of an insect?

"Jason," she said, "your grandmother would remember the sweep, wouldn't she? She'd know his name, maybe a lot about him?"

"I'll give it a go," he said.

*   *   *

313

Lundy View House was empty. Never before had Sarah arrived to find it empty. It was a piece of luck she had brought her key. The central heating was off and the house was cold. She found it all rather unnerving. It had begun to rain, the wind was getting up, and a high tide pounded against the foot of the cliffs. She checked the garage, saw that her mother's car was gone, and thought about road accidents. Then a sense of grievance overpowered mild anxiety. She had never before come home with no one to welcome her, offer her a drink, food, ask about her week. If her father had lived . . . Immediately, the tears threatened. She rubbed her eyes angrily and poured herself a stiff whiskey. Then she switched on the heat.

At any rate, she could now phone Jason Thague without an audience. And Ma could pay for the call, which would be a long one. She took her whiskey and the phone and sat down in "Daddy's chair." But it was a little while before she dialed the Ipswich number.

Since the discovery of the black moth's common name, she had felt both closer to her father and further away. Closer because of the thought processes his connection with this small black emblem revealed, because, knowing him so well, she could imagine his researches, his perhaps grim amusement, and his response to those who asked why. "A private matter," he might have said. "An in-joke shared only by myself with myself." What would he have said if she had asked? If Hope had asked? This was what distanced her from him now, the secret he had hidden from her and hidden so successfully. She touched the arms of his chair. His own hands had worn the velvet almost bald. Her hands lay for a moment where his had lain, and then she picked up the phone.

It rang so long, she thought no one was there to answer it. She was on the point of putting the receiver down when his voice said, "Hello?" Absurdly, she thought he should have sounded breathless, should have exerted himself to get to the phone. But his voice was calm, almost indifferent.

"I've asked my nan. She remembers they had the sweep, but she can't remember his name. It's a bit much to expect her to remember."

"She remembered the doctor," Sarah said.

"Look, she's a marvel, considering. I just hope you and me'll have our marbles the way she has when we come to wrinkleland."

"Okay, okay, I'm not knocking your grandmother."

He spoke to someone in the house where he was, some fellow tenant. "Will you turn down that radio? Sorry, but I can't hear myself speak. Sarah, she's going to try and think. See if there's any way she can check. If she can't remember his name, there are a lot of things she does remember. Hang on, will you, and I'll get my notes."

Sarah hung on. The radio, which no one seemed to have turned down, was providing the sort of music companies play to callers awaiting attention. She half-expected a voice to say, "Our agents are aware of your call and will attend to you soon." The music tinkled out "Für Elise." Jason, she thought, why was it such an awful name? Jason was a hero; he captured the Golden Fleece, gained a kingdom, and married Medea. David, who was also a hero and whose name was almost an assonance of Jason, didn't sound ridiculous, nor did Adam. . . .

He came back. "I was telling you what she remembers. For instance, that the day her brother died was April twentieth, a Wednesday. He was taken ill on Monday the eighteenth and died on the Wednesday. The doctor came several times, but he wasn't taken to the hospital. He died at home.

"On Thursday, the twenty-first, the sweep came. He was booked to come. The winter fires were over and Kathleen Candless, my great-grandmother, that is, wanted to start her spring-cleaning, which she couldn't do till the chimneys were swept. Nan says he came to the door at eight on the Thursday morning and she was sent to tell him to come back another day. Then her dad came out and told him his son had died the day before and that he should come back the following week."

"If she doesn't know his name, does she know whether he had children?""

"She doesn't know much about him except that he was a man who was usually black with soot and who rode a bike. He carried his brushes with him on a bike."

Sarah had started to say that they must find out this man's name, that there must be ways, when Ursula walked into the room. She changed her tone to one more brisk and businesslike. "I've put your check in the post. I'll phone again tomorrow or the next day." The gentle smile on Ursula's face made her unreasonably indignant. She said like a hectoring parent to a child, "Where have you been?"

Ursula started to laugh. She and Gerald, united for once, had made a point of never asking the girls that question. Sarah looked peevish and her compliment sounded grudging.

"You look wonderful. You look ten years younger."

"I've been in London to see Robert Postle. I met a friend and decided to stay on another day."

"Have you had something done to your face?" Sarah peered closely, decided she was close enough for a greater intimacy than interrogation afforded, and planted a kiss on her cheek. "You must have been having a great time. The house was absolutely freezing. I did phone yesterday—well, I phoned a lot of times, but you weren't here."

"I'll get us something to eat, shall I?" Ursula had been disarmed by that kiss, found her spoiled child amusing, felt at once lighthearted. She looked at herself in the mirror, at her flushed face, the brightness in her eyes, the upturned corners of her mouth, and was inspired to ask, "Can you take me back with you on Sunday? To London, I mean. I have to go back."

"Yes, if you want." Sarah was staring. "Ma, I think Dad's father was a chimney sweep. Does that mean anything to you?"

Ursula nearly said she didn't know and she didn't care. But, as always, she remembered her daughters' great love for Gerald, and how the knowledge of that love always checked her, so that she was ever prevented from derogation of him.

"Let's go and see what there is for supper," she said.

He was sitting at a table with Vicky and Paul and Tyger when Sarah came in. She had dressed herself up in total black, a minimal black skirt, fishnet stockings and knee boots, and a black sweater that was too small for her and which she had found in Hope's room. Tyger looked her up and down and said, "Going on somewhere, are you?"

"You have to be meeting someone, sweetheart," said Vicky, "done up like that."

"I felt like it," Sarah said, and gulped her wine rather fast. "I felt a bit wild."

He didn't say a word. Alexander came in and then Rosie. They were all for going on to the club at once; they were tired of this pub. You could eat at the club and drink till forever and it was raffish and pretty. Everyone drank up and Vicky put her coat on. Sarah also put on her coat, which was a hip-length black mock marabou and also Hope's.

"You'll be lucky if they let her in," Adam said suddenly. It was the first time he had spoken. "She looks as if she's on the game."

Vicky gasped. Sarah turned her eyes on him coldly. "What did you say?"

"You heard. I grew up in this town. Some of my

318

family lives here. I can't afford to be seen about with whores."

"For God's sake." Alexander put out one hand, interposing it between them, as if he feared their coming to blows. "What's with you? What have you got against Sarah? This isn't the first time."

"He hasn't anything against me," Sarah said. "He's a shit. He talks like that because he's too fucking stupid to make normal conversation."

"And you, woman, are a university lecturer who is too ignorant to manage invective without lacing it with obscenities. No wonder education is in the state it is. Do you let your students see you dressed like that?"

"Now, come on," Vicky said. "For God's sake, cool it. Are we going on to the club or aren't we? I think you ought to apologize to Sarah, Adam."

"Over my dead body," said Adam.

He picked his jacket off the back of his chair and walked out. Sarah was almost too excited to move. Her speech was choked. The others thought she was upset, that once more his rudeness had cut her.

"I think I'll go, too," she said.

"Oh, come on. You shouldn't let it affect you. It's Saturday night."

"No, I'll go home. I'll see you all in a couple of weeks."

She ran out the back way, staggering. He was leaning against her car. She looked at him, said, "Where are we going?"

"Caravan site. I've borrowed someone's van. The cottage is full of family. But a field first. I can't wait."

"Will you drive?"

"No," he said. "You must drive. I want to touch you while you're driving."

19

*"There's no knowing why we remember some things
and forget others," Laurence said. "If Freud had
been right, we'd block off all the bad things and our
minds would be storehouses of bliss."*
—PURPLE OF CASSIUS

FEELINGS AND MEMORIES she thought forgotten were
revived by these photographs. Apart from that quick
glance at her wedding album, it was years since Joan
Thague had bothered to look at these records of the
past, but now she had begun. The young lady whose
name couldn't really be Candless had done that for
her. She and, through her, Jason. These past few days,
she had made a perusal of the albums an evening
ritual.

Jason wanted a memory, though he didn't know
which one. A name, the name of a long-dead man.
She thought she had given him all her memories, but
now she was no longer sure. The most unexpected
things came back to her. She would sit down with the
album, not on her knees, but open on the table in
front of her, study a photograph, then close her eyes
and let all the associations of that picture flow into
her mind.

She had begun with her grandparents and, as a result of studying this formal studio portrait of them at their golden anniversary, recalled her visits to their cottage, the two old people facing each other from armchairs on either side of the graphite range, the sight, always daunting, of their gnarled hands like tree roots in a picture book, for both were arthritic, even the smell of the place, a compound of stewed food and lavender. Looking at the photograph brought back their voices, the rich Suffolk speech, and the strange words: *pytle* for "meadow" and *sunket* for "a sick child." Her grandmother, she remembered, had called poor Gerald sunket when she came over and saw him that Monday morning.

Joan looked at the picture of her parents' wedding, her mother and Auntie Dorothy, her bridesmaid, in satin hobble skirts. Her mother's wedding dress hung for years in the wardrobe in a calico bag, to be looked at by special permission but never to be used for dressing up. When Gerald was dead, though there seemed no reason for doing such a thing, Kathleen Candless took the dress out of the wardrobe and had it dyed black. As if she could have worn a fifteen-year-old wedding gown for mourning. She never did wear the dress, and Joan had no idea what had become of it.

Here was the beach photographer's snapshot Miss Candless had stared at so . . . well, rudely, in Joan's opinion. She had had a very good idea of what the girl was thinking—that these people looked poor and old-fashioned and ugly and their children clodhoppers. It was that as much as anything that had made her cry and had, at any rate, moved the girl to say she was sorry. Joan wasn't going to cry now. She looked calmly and sadly at Gerald's round, happy face, his curls, his bright eyes, his hand in their mother's hand as he skipped along. There was another snap of him on the next page, or rather, a snap with him in it, for the Applestone boys were there, too, all sitting on the low wall of a front garden. Was that the Applestones' house, dark brick, with small windows, and steps up to the front door? She couldn't remember.

Noticing for the first time that all these photographs had been taken outdoors, she realized what she must once have known very well. In those days, an ordinary camera couldn't cope with interior shots. There was insufficient light. A flash mechanism didn't exist, or if it did, it wasn't available to the likes of them. You depended on sunlight, as her father must have when he had taken this shot of her mother and herself and Gerald on a day out by the sea. The background looked like Southwold, but she couldn't be sure. How had they gotten there? No car for them, of course; she couldn't remember anyone her parents knew having a car. Probably they had gone in a charabanc, as coaches were called then.

It was the last picture taken of Gerald, though eight or nine months before his death. You took photographs in the summer then, on your holidays; a camera was a luxury. She studied the little boy's smiling face, wondering how he would have looked if he had lived and grown up. If, for instance, he had been able to come to her wedding. And then she thought, with a little inward tremor, that if Gerald had lived, she might never have met Frank, let alone married him. For it was only because the house and its surroundings had been so hateful to her without her brother that she had left home and gone to Sudbury in the first place.

Joan closed her eyes and slipped into a reverie. When she was young, people told you not to dwell on painful things, to forget them, put them behind you. Unpleasantness must be buried, or at least hidden from public view. So she had never talked to Frank about Gerald's death or even allowed herself to think about it. She had shut it off when it arose in her mind unbidden. But it had always lain there, asleep yet menacing, and now she had awakened it, or the pictures and the girl who wasn't called Candless had. And Joan understood with relief that it was better for her and somehow better for Gerald now that she could confront it and remember.

When he was dead, they let her see him. For hours and hours before that, twenty-four hours, she hadn't been allowed in his sickroom. Dr. Nuttall came and went and came and there was talk of a nurse. But her mother had been a nurse and wanted no other. Outside his room, unseen, Joan sat on the top stair of the steep flight. It was dark there; it was always dark until they lit the gas. She listened to the murmur of the doctor's voice and the higher-pitched sound of her mother talking, and then Gerald's cries—"My head hurts, my head hurts." When he shouted with the pain, she put her hands over her ears, but when he began to scream, she ran downstairs and hid in the hall cupboard among the brooms. The long silence that followed was broken by the old lady coming, though she talked in whispers. She came to lay out the body, though Joan didn't know that then. Dr. Nuttall came back and then Joan's father took her into the room where her mother was and the doctor was and where Gerald lay, his closed eyes looking up to the ceiling, his face white as a wax candle. They told her she could kiss him, but she wouldn't; she shook her head wordlessly. Later, when she was grown and had children of her own, she thought they shouldn't have asked her to kiss a dead boy.

It was evening, night perhaps; it must have been. They hadn't drawn the bedroom curtains. The sky over Ipswich now was a bronzy red color, but then it had been a deep dark blue with stars. Gerald was going to lie there till the morning while her mother sat at his bedside. Joan couldn't remember the night or what her father did, no matter how hard she tried. But she remembered the morning and her mother there in the kitchen, getting breakfast for the man of the house, as she always did, as she would have if she herself were dying.

The undertakers were to come and take Gerald away. Had someone told her that? Surely not. She must later have known it was what would have happened. But no, for when there had come that knock at the front door, her mother had said it must be the undertakers; she had said the undertaker's name, though Joan had forgotten what it was. Just as she had forgotten the chimney sweep's name. The knock at the door, and her mother had said it was the undertakers, then recalled they weren't coming till nine and it was only eight. She had sat down heavily, the teapot in her hand, looked at Joan's father with such black despair, such hopeless grief, and said, "It's the sweep. I can't be doing with the sweep today, not today."

Joan had never seen the slightest sign of demonstrative affection between her parents, not a kiss, not a touch. But now her father went awkwardly to her mother, took the teapot from her, and laid an arm around her shoulders. He stood there with his arm around her, his hand patting her shoulder, and said to Joan, "Go and open the door, there's a good girl, and tell him he can't come today. You tell him why. You tell him about your brother and to come back another day."

She had gone and had gotten the door open, but her father must have thought better of it, for he came himself and talked to the sweep while Joan stood by and heard for the first time the word *meningitis,* a word that was to have a special dreadful meaning for her forevermore, worse than the worst expletive or curse, a significance of evil and pain and loss.

The sweep must already have cleaned one chimney by that time, for his face was blackened and his clothes were sooty—they looked as if soaked in soot—but his brushes were clean, the tools of his trade, somehow shaken and wiped free of chimney dirt after every use. He had left his bicycle resting up against their fence. Thieves didn't steal bicycles in those days, the way they did later on. She could only see its handlebars, but somehow she knew now, because she had seen it before or seen it afterward, that along a metal sheet fixed to the crossbar was painted in black letters on white, or white letters on black, his name, with his initials and his trade.

Remembering what that name had been was another thing altogether. She tried and tried, but failed. Yet she could still hear her father saying, "Meningitis, meningitis" and the sweep saying he was sorry and that he'd come back another day, next week, whenever they said. And she could remember another caller that day: the sweep's wife.

It was in the afternoon. They had taken Gerald's body away by then, hours before. Auntie Dorothy came and brought Doreen with her, but not the boys. Young as she was, Joan knew that though men went to funerals, death itself was somehow for women and girls to concern themselves with, not for men, just as birth was and marriage was. Doreen was only two, but she was a more appropriate person to be there than Ken or Don. Neighbors had been coming to the door all day to pay their respects and offer their sympathy, and her mother thought it was another of them when someone knocked after Auntie Dorothy had been there half an hour.

Auntie Dorothy went to the door and came back

with the tall lady. She must have said her name, or perhaps she only said whose wife she was, for that was what Joan remembered. Her husband had come home after his work and told her and she had come to say she was sorry; she wanted to express her sympathy for Mrs. Candless's great loss.

Joan's mother or Auntie Dorothy, one of them, had offered her a cup of tea. Joan remembered that clearly and she remembered the lady talking to Doreen and Doreen immediately taking to her the way little children do to people who show an interest in them. But she had refused the tea and said why—and now her reason came back to Joan in a flash of illumination. She had said she couldn't stay, that she must go at once, because she had brought her children with her, or some of her children, and left them outside. It wouldn't have been fitting to bring them in, it wouldn't have been suitable.

Any impression she might once have had of those children was almost entirely lost, though she had gone to the door with the lady, had been sent to see her out. She had opened the door herself and had glimpsed those children—three of them, was it, or four?—standing outside the gate where that morning their father's bicycle had leaned. Boys or girls? How was it possible not to remember a fact like that?

Then Joan, opening her eyes and returning to the album, recalled that she had from that time forward felt a liking for the chimney sweep and his wife, a kind of mild gratitude for their kindness, and that this had led to something or other. She had done something or arranged something because of that liking, but what?

The recovering of memory tired as well as gratified her, and these evenings she went early to bed. But on the following day, after she had had her tea, she was back with the photographs, to her marriage and the war and the children. And she was carried away by them, by herself with Frank on their honeymoon, Frank in his army uniform, Peter, her first-born, in his pram. There was a photographer who hung about outside the clinic and took pictures of the babies when their mothers wheeled them out and down the steps. He must still have been there two years later, for here was just the same sort of photo of Anthony.

Quite forgotten until now was the studio portrait of the whole family taken a year after Frank was discharged: herself sitting down and holding the baby, Patricia, a little boy on either side of her, their father standing behind. She was more enthralled by their young faces and by the clothes that still seemed to her desirable and elegant than she could have been by any television program. It was days now since she had even turned the telly on. But even as she was transported into the past and immersed in the emotions of the past, she was aware that this was not the way to find what she was looking for. Clues to it didn't, couldn't, lie in the early years of her marriage or in the family she and Frank had created.

She was afraid then that those clues, if clues there were, must have lain somewhere in the sparse and few photographs taken in the years before Gerald's death. But she had been through them and found little or nothing to help her. It was the chimney sweep, after all, that Jason was interested in, and the purpose of this search of hers had been to find something that would trigger the memory of his name. Again she closed her eyes; again she rested her head back and transported herself back to that day, the day after Gerald's death, to the sight of the sweep on the doorstep, the handlebars of his bicycle showing around the end of the hedge, his dirty face and clean brushes. To his tall wife with her kind face and her sweet way with Doreen. Mrs. something, they must have called her, her mother and Auntie Dorothy. Will you have a cup of tea, Mrs. something? Good-bye, Mrs. something.

Unless the pointer to the name lay somewhere in the past, before Gerald died, or even in the future, after he was dead. The sweep must have come every April to sweep the chimney before spring-cleaning, but Joan could recall no previous visit. Perhaps she had been at school when he came. And afterward?

It wasn't much more than two years later that she went away to Sudbury. The sweep must have come in those two years, but she couldn't remember his visits, only the emptiness of the house without Gerald and the loneliness. Perhaps the chimneys hadn't been swept again, for her mother lost interest in the house and the cooking and her husband and her daughter and for a long time retreated inside herself, into that

330

place where perhaps her dead child still lived. Because of this, her father was always out, at his men's club. And Joan went to live twenty-two miles away, a distance that would be nothing now but was considerable then, the other end of the county.

Four years passed before she came back, and that was for her wedding in 1938. She opened the last album, the one she hadn't looked at because she looked at it so often. Those photographers always began with a picture of the church, and St. Stephen's was pretty enough, if not on par with the one she had wanted in Sudbury. Then came the shot of herself on her father's arm, walking up the path to the door. She was holding up her white taffeta train with one hand and clutching her bouquet with the other. Her father looked happy enough, and in the later pictures, her mother looked happy. They were back to normal; they were over it. They had recovered, or recovered as much as they ever would.

What was she looking for? She had half-forgotten. The photographer's series that she had looked at so often before passed gently before her eyes, the wedding, the bridesmaids, the group on the steps, the departure for the reception. The month of May and a glorious day. Happy is the bride that the sun shines on. . . .

Happiness, yes, but surely she had wanted luck, as well? Joan felt a constriction in her throat. What had she done for luck? Worn something old, yes, something new, something borrowed, and something blue. . . . She was nearly there; she sensed it. She turned to the last photograph in the album.

It hadn't been taken by the professional, but by Frank's best man. Joan couldn't remember his name now, but he hadn't been a very good photographer. Why had they stuck this picture in with the good ones? Because Frank had wanted it, because Frank for some reason had liked it. Usually, when she looked at her wedding album, she stopped before this page or else allowed her eyes to flicker swiftly over it.

Now they rested on it. And she saw herself and Frank arm in arm and the man who stood smiling at the front of the little crowd with his brushes in his hand and, behind him, leaning against a tree trunk, his bicycle, with his name clearly written in white on black on the metal sheet triangle attached to the crossbar.

J. W. RYAN, CHIMNEY SWEEP.

Ursula's lover was named Edward Akenham and, in a way, he was the only lover she had ever had, for Colin Wrightson didn't count, and though some husbands can also be lovers, Gerald had not been one of them. Edward was a painter with a cottage in Clovelly, but in order to live, he taught art history at an evening course in Ilfracombe.

From the first, she had known the kind of man Edward was. She had no illusions, perhaps because she had had so many about Gerald and all had been rudely smashed. Chronically poor, permanently unsuccessful, splendid to look at, if a little worn, Edward made a point of having an affair with one of his art history students each term. Occasionally, such a relationship lasted two terms, and Ursula was one of the two-term women.

He was honest. He told his girlfriends he had no money to spend on them, that he had never been married and didn't wish to be. On the other hand, he was free. He had a place to take them, a cottage of exquisitely picturesque appearance, with the advantage of being next door to a pub. And he would make love to them nicely, with care, perhaps with passion. For a while, he would give them his devotion. What love he had to give, and within limits, he would give them. He was an honest man.

For nearly a year, he made Ursula feel desired, beautiful, sexy, and needed. In all that time, she never had a migraine. And Edward paid her a compliment very close to what Gerald had said to her on their honeymoon.

"You are the kind of woman most men dream of making love to."

But June came and the end of the art history course for that year. Edward went off to Spain to stay with an equally impoverished friend, first saying an unequivocal good-bye to her, coupled with another compliment, of a sort. "It" was among the best he'd ever had. She minded, as she had known she would, because she was more than a little in love. But that, she had also known to be inevitable, for how could you live the life she lived and not fall in love with the first kind, clever, handsome man who paid attention to you?

She had read somewhere, perhaps among the pieces of advice given by an agony aunt, that if you have a love affair your husband hasn't found out about, it is wiser and kinder not to tell him. But that, she felt, didn't apply to husbands like Gerald, who wasn't really a husband anymore, but someone she shared the house with, a not very congenial kind of landlord. So one Saturday morning, when her Thursday migraine was over, when Sarah was out riding and Hope was at her dancing class, she told him about Edward Akenham.

He looked up from the *Times*. "What do you expect me to say?"

It was terrible how she had learned to talk the way he did; she had learned his kind of repartee. "What you've just said." It was true. "No other comment?"

"Not so long as you don't get yourself in the newspapers," he said. "I refer to your association with me, of course."

She pondered his words: "your association with me" not "my wife."

"And I don't want my children witnessing any primal scenes."

"There is nothing to witness. It's over," she had said.

"No doubt there will be others."

There never had been. Until now.

"Why did you tell him?" Sam Fleming asked her.

"I don't know," she said. She had told him all of it, that and much more. "I mean, I didn't know at the time. It wasn't revenge or some sort of wish to hurt him; I knew it wouldn't hurt him. Afterward, I thought about why, and I think I told him in the hope he'd throw me out. I hadn't the strength to leave, you see, and I couldn't bring myself to take the children away from him and go, but I think somewhere in my unconscious was the wish that he'd leave me or force me to leave. He'd do it for me."

"He didn't, though."

"He didn't care enough. It looks as if he must have needed me in some way, and he did, but not in the way any woman would want to be needed. And by then he was beginning to be very well known. He was giving interviews to newspapers and getting pieces about him in the Sunday supplements. It suited the persona he'd created to have an apparently stable marriage, a serene family life. And his children had to have a mother—I don't think he ever considered the possibility that they might not have a father—even if they didn't care much for her. She had to be there so that they had a mummy and a daddy, like the other girls at school. It's different now, but most children did live with both natural parents then."

"It was a few years later that he wrote *Hamadryad*."

"The young girl was a kind of amalgam of Sarah and Hope, older than they, of course, and idealized—

at least the dryad girl seemed idealized to me. Perhaps he saw his daughters like that."

"The hamadryad," Sam said, "dies when the tree she inhabits dies. Did he mean his daughters couldn't exist without him, without his support?"

"God knows what he meant. It was sometimes hard to know with him where reality stopped and symbolism began. Maybe we have to remember that a hamadryad is also a kind of snake. But I'm talking too much. I haven't talked so much for years."

"You can talk as much as you like with me," Sam said. "I like to be talked to. I'm a good listener."

She smiled at him. They had been together almost continuously since the Sunday night when she arrived at the hotel where she had stayed before and booked into again and where he was waiting for her in the lobby. The drive from Devon in Sarah's car had been uneventful and their conversation of the bland small-talk kind, broken by long silences, until the western outskirts of London were reached and Sarah asked her where her friend lived.

Ursula had often noticed that when a woman speaks to others of a friend, the assumption will always be made that that friend is female. She had wondered if things had changed among the young and if this rule no longer applied, but apparently it still persisted, for Sarah said, "If your friend lives this side of London, I can drive you to her place."

"It's his place," Ursula said.

"I'm sorry?"

"My friend is a man, Sarah. He lives in Bloomsbury and I am staying in a hotel. You won't want to go so far east, so if you'll drop me somewhere on your way, I can get a taxi."

"It was all rather absurd," she said to Sam the next day, "because surely most daughters would have asked about this mysterious man, would have teased their mothers about a thing like that, made some comment. It made me realize, if I hadn't known it already, what a thin sort of relationship we have."

"Perhaps she didn't want to probe."

"No, it wasn't that. She didn't care. She was thinking about something else."

"It's made you unhappy?"

"No," she said, "not at all. Because when I got here, you were here, and that was wonderful for me. It made me forget her. I forgot all about it till now."

He had been there, waiting. He had put his arms around her and kissed her as if they had known each other for years. Yet there was none of the custom and indifference of years. They had a late supper in the hotel and drank a lot of wine and he took her up to her room and kissed her again. And the next day, she went to the shop with him and looked at his books, saw Wrightson and Pallinter and Arthur first editions among his books, and these brought her a strange feeling that was a combination of familiarity and extreme distance. There was no Gerald Candless among them, and he said that at present he hadn't a single copy in stock.

Lunch was in the restaurant next door and in the afternoon, which was fine and unseasonably warm, they went for a walk in Victoria Park. She had barely heard of Victoria Park and hadn't known where it was. He had grown up near there at Hackney Wick and kept a sentimental affection for this park, which was the biggest in London but which people shuddered at for its location between Homerton and Old Ford. He laughed at her when she said she had never been on a London bus and he said that in that case, they would go on one.

The grass in the park was a true emerald green and the scattered lakes looked a clear blue on this fine day. He took her arm and hooked it into his—and that, too, was something new for her, to walk arm in arm with a man. But she didn't tell him so, for he was already making her feel, by introducing her to these simple and ordinary pleasures, that up to now, she had hardly lived at all.

He lived on two floors over the shop and there he cooked their dinner. No more restaurants, not that night. Later, she couldn't have said who made the first move, for there had been moves all evening— her hand suddenly clasped and held, his arm around her waist, laughter between them, so that she spontaneously turned and hugged him. A light kiss and then another, and that one changing its character and deepening into a conjunction, a special kind of sexual act. By the time they went into the bedroom and into his bed, they had already made love, quite naturally and easily and as if from long-established habit. Nothing like those early couplings with Gerald or the excitement of the weekly renewed adventure with Edward Akenham.

But the second time, in the early hours, was quite different, and afterward as they held each other and she was still amazed and wondering, it no longer occurred to her to make comparisons.

"Nan asked him to come and stand outside the church when she got married," said Jason. "For luck. She'd forgotten, but the photo brought it back."

"She did *what*?"

"It was lucky for a bride to see a sweep on her wedding day, and sweeps earned a bit extra by appearing at weddings. They got paid for it. She'd liked this guy Ryan for some reason, so when she got married, she asked him. Great-granddad gave him five shillings—that's twenty-five pee, but it was a lot then. And Nan had met his wife and his kids—well, she'd seen his kids. His wife came over to say she was sorry about the boy dying, and her kids were with her. Left out in the street."

Sarah felt a thrill touch her spine, like a cold finger running down the vertebrae, tapping each bone. One of those children had been her father. The chimney sweep's boy.

"How long was that after the little boy died? Her wedding, I mean."

"About six years. She was nineteen. But now comes something that'll interest you. He died, that sweep, that J. W. Ryan. The following year. Nan remembers now. Her mother told her. He died of tuberculosis, or maybe it wasn't that; maybe it was some disease you get from inhaling soot. And the family moved away."

The shiver touched her again. "Jason, it's in *A Messenger of the Gods*. You haven't read that, have you? It's the novel where the father dies of silicosis and the mother's left to bring up this family. And it's in *Eye in the Eclipse,* too. They're taken in by an uncle, the father's brother. He lives in London; he's a widower. How many children did the Ryans have?"

"Nan saw three that day, but she says there were more. Five or six."

"Jason, I love you. I really love you. You're a marvel. Your check's in the post. You're going to find out where they went and what happened to them, aren't you?"

Their conversation restored her excitement at the prospect of her book. She imagined herself writing the moving story of the Ryan family, their undoubted poverty, the father's premature death. Perhaps she would need to put in some research into chimney sweeping. A short history of chimney sweeping would have its place in maybe chapter two. That kind of research was what gave her pleasure, not all this tracing of births and deaths in registers, but a genuine investigation in libraries, a trawling through old works of literature, a returning through the distant past to sources.

To match this history with the theme of *Eye in the Eclipse* would give an added literary dimension to her memoirs, something she thought her readers would expect from her. And, of course, she would use also in that first chapter, perhaps even as her opening paragraph, Gerald Candless's own happier version of *The Water Babies,* which he used to tell to her and Hope when they were little.

"Once upon a time, there was a chimney sweep who had two sons. . . ."

20

Insensitive people are powerful and the thoroughly thick-skinned are the most powerful. They make the best tyrants.

—HALF AN HOUR IN THE STREET

SARAH LET HERSELF IN to Lundy View House at ten on Friday night. Ursula came out to her, came into the hall, and, emboldened by recent demonstrativeness, put out her hands tentatively. Sarah gave her a very practical but very light kiss on the cheek.

"How have you been?"

Ursula might have said she hadn't been there very much. She might have said that while she had been there, she had gone so far as to look in at the windows of two estate agents without actually going inside. But a habit of wariness is hard to break. With a glass of whiskey beside her, Sarah settled herself in an armchair. The paperback that lay open and face-down on a small table beside "Daddy's chair" was evidence that she had been sitting there before Sarah arrived.

"You're reading Titus Romney," Sarah said.

"Yes. It's rather good."

"Ma, have you thought any more about what Hope and I told you about Dad?"

"About his changing his name, do you mean?"

"Not just his name. His identity. His whole life."

"I can't see much point in my thinking about it, Sarah. I didn't know about it. If it happened, it was before we met."

"That's all very well, but it's your name, too, you know."

Ursula sighed. It was one of those sighs that often precede "speaking out." "Not any longer. I am reverting to my maiden name. I'm calling myself Ursula Wick."

Sarah was shocked. "But why?"

"As you said yourself, it wasn't really his name, so I'm under no obligation to go on using it myself. He took it. I am dropping it." That wasn't the real reason, but it would do. She said, "I think I might have a drink, too."

"I'll get it for you."

This was an offer Ursula couldn't remember either of her daughters ever making to her before. Sarah had remembered, too, that she drank only white wine and had poured her a glass from the fridge.

"Ma, does the name Ryan mean anything to you?"

"I don't think so. It's an Irish name and quite common, I would say. Why?"

"I wondered if Dad had ever mentioned the name or ever wrote to a Ryan or had letters from a Ryan."

"I'm sure not, Sarah. Why?"

Sarah told her. Trying to look interested, Ursula found herself rather repelled, unwilling to know.

"The family moved to London in 1939," Sarah said.

"The year the war started. Most people would have moved away from London if they could have."

"They couldn't. They were poor. Ryan's widow had this offer from a relative and she took it; I suppose she didn't have a choice. Anyway, I think they went to London a few months before the war. It started in September, didn't it? They may have gone in the summer. After the sweep died, Ryan, Dad's father."

"If he was his father."

"Oh, I think he was. Because of the book and the story he used to tell us. If anything about a Ryan comes back to you, you'll tell me, won't you?"

Instead of the pub, they were meeting in Greens, and the meeting time was later, nine o'clock. According to their unexpressed rule, she was prevented from speaking to Adam Foley, so she was quite unprepared for what happened. On her arrival, she went straight to the ladies' room and was joined there after two or three minutes by Rosie. During those minutes, Sarah made adjustments to her appearance she wouldn't normally have thought of: put more gel on her artfully tangled hair, painted her mouth a richer, darker red, and pulled in her stomach as hard as she could so that the waistband of her black leather trousers fitted more smoothly.

In some doubt about it, she had taken off the black velvet choker with the gold spikes and, having second thoughts, was putting it back on again when Rosie came in. Rosie looked over her shoulder, waited till the door closed, and said she was delighted to see her, had thought that after what had happened last time, she wouldn't come, but that she need not worry, because Adam Foley wouldn't be there. That was the point of meeting at Greens. He didn't know—no one had told him—so Sarah could relax and enjoy herself.

Wild thoughts of going to the pub ran through Sarah's mind, to be almost immediately driven out again. They had gone too far last time; they should have realized. She wondered how she was going to get through the evening.

Upstairs, in the small stuffy room, dimly lit as an American bar and smelling of air freshener with an undertone of cannabis, Tyger told her in a confidential tone that they had all been disgusted by Adam Foley's behavior. Alexander said he had been offended and even more appalled that he had refused to apologize. With an air of someone imparting a piece of entirely original information, Vicky said that Adam Foley was the rudest guy she had met in all her life.

They went on like that for some time. Sarah wondered if it would have helped if one of them had told her beforehand that Adam didn't know the change of venue. But what could she have done about it if they had? It then occurred to her that she would have to take some care, a moderate amount of care, as to how much she drank, because she would have to drive home at midnight instead of the next morning. And what she now wanted was to get very drunk indeed.

There was some dancing and a female impersonator—Rosie swore it was a woman impersonating a man impersonating a woman—came on and told transvestite jokes. Sarah was casting caution aside and drinking one of the club's champagne cocktails when Adam Foley came down the steps and walked up to their table. It was a cold night and he was wearing a greatcoat that reached almost to his feet.

He said, to Sarah's consternation, "I've come to apologize."

There was an expectant and somewhat excited silence.

"I'm sorry. I apologize. I bitterly regret my behavior. Will you forgive me?" He didn't wait for her to speak. "That's all right, then. Scene over. Fight unnecessary. Now can I sit down and have a drink?"

No one said anything. Adam Foley took a glass and helped himself from the red wine on the table. Sarah, who had long abandoned her evening as a waste of time, now felt herself beginning to tremble. His presence—he had sat down next to her—made her feel almost faint. The silence was broken by Alexander's asking if anyone wanted to eat. Either at the Scarlet Angel or a curry house somewhere.

This led to a discussion of food and eating places. Adam Foley turned his back on Sarah. She had been sitting next to one of the cuboid Art Deco pillars that held up, or appeared to hold up, the black-and-gilt ceiling, and by moving as he had, still inside his voluminous big-shouldered coat, he managed to force her back into an alcove and exclude her from the company.

Her position was made worse by his sliding his chair back so that it pressed against her knees. She was actually squashed against the wall, in a certain amount of pain. For a while, she didn't know what to do. And no one else—from what she could see of them—seemed to have noticed. That she had no idea what particular game he was playing this evening added to her excitement, but all that would be lost if she was actually made ridiculous. If she was squeezed out of her corner onto the floor or forced to call for help. If he crushed her so that she was physically injured.

Then he stood up. The coat swept against her face, a thick muffling mass of tweed. She let out a cry and pushed at him. He stepped aside, looked at her, and said, "Good God, how long have you been there?"

As if he had been totally unaware of her. As if she were insignificant, not a woman, not a human being, of no account. He had spoken to her as if she were someone's small dog trapped behind a sofa. And for an instant, she doubted. It was as if all that had been between them and all they had done had never been done. But only for an instant. Still, she couldn't answer him; he had deprived her of her powers of repartee.

They were going off to eat somewhere. Or some of them were. She heard him say, and her heart seemed to revolve, return to its place with a bump, "Curry it is, then."

At the foot of the stairs, he stepped back to let Rosie and Vicky pass ahead of him and then walked on up, leaving her to follow. Her throat was dry and blocked at the same time. On the back of his coat, at about waist level, her mouth had left a dark red blurred imprint. She asked herself then what she had never before asked: why she liked this, why it excited her so much, and why did the doubt add to her excitement. If she had been drunk, she was no longer, but she still walked slowly, dragging herself up the stairs.

The street door swung back. She had to put up her hands to keep it from striking her in the face and she heard the doorman or bouncer or whatever he was mutter something like "That's a right bastard."

Out in the street, they were gone, all of them. She imagined him telling them she'd said to say good-bye for her, that she'd gone home. Bitterly, she thought that by now they must be used to her leaving early and chagrined perhaps that for once he wasn't. The car park was dark, almost empty of cars, a great pool of oil lying in the middle of the asphalt. She skirted around it, looked for her car, then saw a single point of red light.

It was his cigarette. He was sitting on the rear fender, and when she came up, shaking and speechless, he took the cigarette from his mouth and with thumb and forefinger put it into hers with a lingering touch.

* * *

At nearly thirty-two, which was young for this to happen, Sarah saw in herself signs of developing eccentricity. Of her curious relationship with Adam Foley, she preferred not to think, for thinking would, if not spoil it, interfere with its remote and emotionless nature. But that decision in itself was an eccentricity, as the relationship was. Another was her growing dislike of admitting anyone else into her home. She had asked her mother to stay, both immediately after her father died and more recently, but her relief at her invitation's being refused was disproportionate. After each refusal, she had come home and luxuriated in her solitude, drinking too much and falling asleep fully clothed on the hearth rug.

Ideally, she understood herself to feel, she would never let anyone else in here ever again. That went for Hope and Fabian, too, she discovered to her surprise. She amused herself for a while thinking of things she could do that would make it impossible for people to be invited here. These were few, but they included displaying hard pornography on the walls, never cleaning the place, and taking all her clothes off the moment she got in the door.

None of it was possible this evening because Jason Thague was coming. Sarah groaned at the thought of it, adding making faces in the mirror to that other bizarre but quite frequent habit of hers—talking aloud to herself. He was coming because he was in London on her business and had invited himself as a matter of course. Why not? It could be done on the phone and it could be done by letter, but why not face-to-face, since she lived in London? He had phoned her at college just as she was off to give her Wednesday-morning tutorial—and what could she say but yes? He probably didn't notice how grudging a yes it was.

He couldn't help his acne scars or his clothes or, come to that, his accent, but he could have washed himself and washed his hair. The ancient Colin Wrightson had told her some months before in a burst of self-pity that along with arthritis and a diminution of hearing, he had lost his sense of smell. Sarah felt this wouldn't be such a bad deprivation when Jason came into her flat. Her own sense of smell was acute. It registered an earthiness about his clothes and a staleness coming from his skin and hair.

She offered him a drink and sat a long way away. He had been most of the day at St. Catherine's House, checking on the Ryan family, and had found them, had found all the children born to John William and Anne Elizabeth Ryan and followed the history of some of them. Noticing that he drank his drink rapidly and somehow furtively, as if he was afraid someone else might get to it first, she offered him another. He shook his head.

"My nan keeps brandy for medicinal purposes," he said. "I try to faint sometimes." She didn't smile. "It's a long time since I tasted gin. I don't want to get carried away. Can I get myself some water?"

"I'll get it." She fetched Perrier from the fridge. "Tell me about the Ryans."

"They were married in 1925. In Ipswich. Her name was O'Drida. The first child was John Charles, born April twentieth, 1926."

She felt a stinging behind the eyes as if she was going to cry and was surprised to hear her own voice so steady. "Was that my father?"

"I'd think so, wouldn't you? He was three weeks older than Gerald Candless."

She talked to maintain that steadiness. "The death of the little boy his own age would have stayed with him always. You can imagine that, his father coming home and saying what had happened, that the Candlesses had lost their only son, and Mrs. Ryan going over to the house with her children, her own little boys—oh God, she was my *grandmother.*" This time, her voice broke—she couldn't help it—but she managed to cough the tears away, dip her head, fists to forehead.

"Hey, come on," he said. "This won't do," and he went over to her, sat down beside her, and put an arm around her shoulders.

If anything could have banished emotion, it was this. She exerted herself not to shake him off, not to scream at him to get out. Almost worse than the arm and the greasiness was the handkerchief proffered to her, a gray crumpled object smelling of dirty pockets and dried nasal mucus.

She jumped up. "I'm fine now. Thanks. Let me get you another drink. Some ice."

He nodded happily. She couldn't help noticing his glass was heavily marked with sticky fingerprints and salivary ellipses. "Please go on," she said. "I'll be all right now."

"They were Irish Catholics. Nan remembers her mother telling her that. There were five other children. James Robert and Desmond William were the next." He was reading from notes he had made. "They were probably the ones left outside the gate along with"—he looked warily at her—"your dad, because Margaret wasn't born till August 1933 and the other two, Mary and Stephen, not till 1935 and 1937, respectively."

"Then Stephen can't have been much more than a baby when the father died."

Jason referred to his notes. "Ryan, the sweep, died in April 1939, when Stephen was—let me see—nineteen months old. Your dad would have been just thirteen. And sometime after that but before the start of the war, I think—I don't know, mind—the family moved to London. Mrs. Ryan, with John, James, Desmond, Margaret, Mary, and Stephen, moved to somewhere in London to the home of a relative."

"What does 'relative' mean?"

"It doesn't mean brother," said Jason. "O'Drida is a very uncommon name. I've looked in a few phone books for various areas and not been able to find one. I found Anne Elizabeth O'Drida in the records as born in Hackney in 1897 and a sister Catherine Mary O'Drida born in 1899 but no brothers."

"And your grandmother can't be more specific?"

"I've tried 'uncle' on her and 'brother-in-law,' but

it doesn't ring any bells. I reckon she's told me everything she knows." He grinned at her. "If I persist, she may tell me more than she knows."

"Is Hackney significant?"

"Maybe. But there's no O'Drida in Hackney in the phone book. And why would there be? It's a hundred years ago we're talking about."

"So what happens next?"

Instead of answering, he said, "Your dad wasn't a Catholic?"

She shook her head, then remembered something. It was still there, in the dictionary, between *dynamicity* and *Earl Marshal*. She held out the palm cross to Jason. "He never went out on a Sunday morning. I'd know; I was almost always there."

"But maybe he went out on a Saturday night. Lots of Catholic churches have Mass on Saturday evening."

"What a lot you know," she mocked him, suddenly angry.

Jason looked at his watch. "I guess I'd better go home."

He said it with a kind of drawn-out reluctance, a shrug, and a heavy sigh. He looked at her as if waiting for her to suggest an alternative. Perhaps he thought she would put him up in a hotel?

"Have a last drink," she said, and on an impulse, while filling his glass, she added, "I'll give you your taxi fare to Liverpool Street."

"Thanks. I've missed the ten o'clock, but there's a last train at eleven."

"You have a lecture in the morning?"

"I don't exactly go to classes anymore." His eyes avoided hers. "I thought you might have realized. I . . . well, I dropped out. That is, I never went back after the Easter break."

"I see." She didn't quite. "So your grant—what are you living on?"

"You," he said. "You've been a godsend." He looked at her then. "In more ways than one."

She went into the kitchen and found her purse, came back with two ten-pound notes, a good deal more than his taxi would cost—but what the hell.

He took the notes gratefully. "Nan doesn't know. I reckon she'd stop feeding me if she did—just when I need it most. And giving me baths. I ought to make myself wash in cold water, but I guess I don't have the willpower, as Nan would say. My parents don't know. They think I'm still trying to cope with psychology. But something'll happen, I reckon. Something usually does."

She thought with distaste that anyone these days can keep himself clean. Heat water in a kettle, have a stand-up wash, go to the launderette. If she told him so, he would only tell her she'd never experienced it. Which would be true.

"Look, I thought I'd keep on at the O'Drida angle," he said. "I'll keep at it."

She saw him to the door, then, on second thought, went down with him to the street and waited until a taxi came. From the window, he waved to her with enthusiasm. She returned upstairs, shivered at the stuffiness in the flat, and began opening windows.

Absurdly perhaps, but with a real distaste, she didn't want to touch that glass, but at last she did, having first put on a rubber glove. Even so, she picked it up gingerly between thumb and forefinger and carried it out to the kitchen at arm's length, the way one might remove a dead spider.

A bound proof of *Less Is More* arrived the next day from Robert Postle. The cover design, as Carlyon-Brent pointed out on the back, was not that which would appear on a finished copy. An empty city street by night, a photograph, not a drawing—it looked more like somewhere on the continent than London. The back cover of the proof also bore quotations from highly laudatory reviews of the author's previous works and commendations from Malcolm Bradbury and A. N. Wilson.

At the foot were a few lines informing the reader that publication would be on January 29, 1998, the price £16.99 in hardback, its size 51/2 by 81/4 inches and its length 256 pages, all this followed by the ISBN number. A short biography inside told Sarah a few things she now knew to be false about her father, such as his status as an only child and his education at Trinity, and something painfully true, that he had died in July 1997.

The dedication, as so many dedications had been in the past, was to her and her sister. "For my daughters, Sarah and Hope." Tears prickled Sarah's eyes once more. She remembered his asking the two of them for their permission.

"As is proper," he had said, and then added, "may I have the honor of dedicating the new one to you?"

A Messenger of the Gods, she remembered, had been dedicated to Colin Wrightson, another one—was it *Hand to Mouth?*—to Robert Postle, and *Time Too Swift* "In memory of my mother," while the early books had no dedications. It occurred to her then to wonder why not a single book had been dedicated to his wife, to Ursula. And why hadn't she noticed that "In memory of my mother" before? He hadn't been remembering Kathleen Candless, but Anne Ryan.

Did that mean Anne Ryan had died around the time of *Time Too Swift?* Or had died when he began to write it? Sarah went to her collection of her father's works, found that novel, and saw that its publication date was 1975. She had been nine or ten at the time, but of course she had no clear memory of the book's being published. Come to that, though she had read it, as she had read all his works, she couldn't recall anything about it. She must read it again, as she must reread all his books before writing her own.

Perhaps Anne Ryan had died in 1973 or 1974. If he knew of her death, it must be because, to some extent, he kept up with his true family. From a distance, he had made himself aware of what happened to the members of that family. Had he also known some of his O'Drida connections? Ryan and O'Drida—her father had been, in anyone's estimation, an Irishman. And was that why, when choosing a university for himself, he had picked Trinity?

Sarah wrote a note to Jason Thague, asking him if

he could trace the record of Anne Ryan's death in the early seventies and to find if there were O'Dridas in the Dublin telephone directory.

When Sarah's letter came, Jason was in his room in the tall white brick house in Ipswich, reading *A White Webfoot* in the paperback edition she had sent him. Both letter and book smelled of Sarah, of a musky and faintly bitter French perfume. The cover of the book also reminded him of her, though he would have had difficulty in saying why, as the design on it was an impressionistic painting, streaks and veils of white mist half-covering a pallid blue sky and a blurred white sun, while Sarah invariably dressed in black.

Jason could have done without all these long descriptions of fenlands and wildfowl sanctuaries on the Suffolk coast. It began to get better when the story moved to London and sex raised its more attractive head. One of the young men the novel was about apparently lived by prostitution and enjoyed it and had entered into the whole gay life with verve and gusto. Dennis had a steady boyfriend who kept him and a great many others he picked up, mostly in public conveniences in parts of London unknown to Jason. And he had his old school friend, Mark, a man who refused to admit his own sexual orientation and who underwent all sorts of treatment aimed at turning him into a lover of women.

The idea of homosexuality as a disease was common at the time. Some saw it as a moral sickness to be resisted by greater self-control, others as a curable mental disorder. Jason looked back a couple of chapters and found that the date when the action was supposed to be taking place was 1960. While Mark entered treatment, first by being given massive doses of estrogen and later by aversion therapy in a mental hospital, Dennis, who regularly had secret encounters with a string of young "rough trade" boyfriends, was moving into an apartment paid for by his lover. The guilty feelings of one man and the carefree brashness of the other were starkly contrasted.

Mark became a voluntary patient in a psychiatric ward in South London. There electrodes were attached to his body and shocks administered each time a picture of homosexual erotica was shown on a screen. The treatment had no effect but to make him deeply miserable and to contemplate taking his own life. Jason was very taken aback by all this, wondered if such things could really have gone on in his own parents' lifetime. How had Gerald Candless known about it anyway?

Earlier, when they were boys, there had been some kind of encounter between Mark and Dennis, though the details of this were never spelled out. Mark, fresh from his failed treatment, met Dennis again by chance, discovered the kind of life he was leading, and became obsessed with the idea of a confrontation between them, an explanation. Was Dennis to blame for his fate or he for Dennis's? He knew he must either thrash this matter out or kill Dennis, for while he lived, there could be no peace for him.

Jason gave up for the time being, saw to his surprise that he had been reading for three hours. Two evenings before, he had gotten out of the cab just around the corner from Sarah's place and, ignoring the expostulations of the driver, taken the tube to Liverpool Street station, thus keeping for himself most of the twenty pounds. Just enough now remained to buy half a bottle of gin or some food. He went downstairs and around to the corner shop, where he thought of Sarah, rejected the gin, and bought a pint of milk, a pizza, a bumper packet of minitortillas, and a pound of cheddar cheese.

21

"Remember that if you tell a man you love him,"
said Mrs. Rule, "you may forget it, but he never
will, and he will cast it up at you for the rest of
his life."

—PURPLE OF CASSIUS

THE LAST TIME PAULINE EVER CAME to stay during Gerald's lifetime was in the long, hot summer of 1976. Gerald was writing *Half an Hour in the Street,* the least successful and certainly the least acclaimed of all his books. Perhaps he was affected by the heat or just didn't apply himself. They spent most of the time on the beach, not the great stretch of sand that spanned the seven miles to Franaton Burrows—it was too crowded there—but in the little cove around the north headland, where there was no one but themselves. It was so quiet there and so isolated that quite often the tide came in, went out again, and returned once more over virgin sand no foot had trodden in the meantime.

Pauline was seventeen and had a boyfriend. He was the only boyfriend she had ever had and later on she would marry him. Brian was his name. Sarah wanted to know about him and got Pauline to talk about him all the time, which wasn't hard to do. Hope wasn't interested. She was still at the sand-castle stage. Gerald built the most beautiful sand castles on the beach, fortresses with moats and crenellated walls and keeps and towers. When Hope was younger, all she had wanted to do was knock them down, but Gerald hadn't minded; he had only laughed.

Ursula swam every day, but Pauline couldn't swim and didn't want to learn. She talked to Sarah about Brian and about the possibility of getting engaged to Brian and her mother saying she was too young, but it was Gerald she looked at and Gerald's sand castles that she admired. Her future might be with Brian; it was Gerald she was in love with, however. Ursula didn't know how Hope, aged eight, could know this, but she did know it and she sat even more frequently than usual on her father's lap, twining her arms around his neck and casting at Pauline sly, challenging glances.

The fine weather came to an end before the school holidays did. One morning, there was no beach to be seen and no blue sky, only the all-enveloping mist, a white fallen cloud. Gerald shut himself up in the study with the blinds down and the lights on and got back to work on his novel. After that, the mist came down every morning, sometimes staying all day, and at the end of the week, Pauline went home because school was starting the next day. But before that, the day before she left, something happened between her and Gerald, though Ursula never knew exactly what it was.

In any other marriage, she thought, a husband who wasn't unfaithful and didn't want to be—she was quite sure of this; she knew this—would have told his wife when a woman made an advance to him and he rejected it. Ursula had an idea that a man would want to tell, would be proud of telling, because it would be a kind of insurance for him. Whatever he had done before or since, *that* time he had resisted. He had been good; he was good. And he would want to tell his wife because it would make him seem strong-minded, impervious, and therefore attractive.

Gerald said nothing to her. Of course, it was inconceivable that he ever would talk to her about anything verging on human relations or sex or his personal feelings. But she knew Pauline and Gerald had had some sort of confrontation. Pauline's face, which had no mark on it, no tearstain, nevertheless looked bruised. She was silent and her eyes, which had rested so constantly on Gerald, now wandered everywhere, while he seemed relaxed. It was impossible for him to be more attentive to his daughters, but perhaps he was more than usually demonstrative.

What had Pauline done? Gone to him in the study, Ursula thought, where the blinds were down and the mist pressed against the windows outside, and in some childish, clumsy way offered herself to him? His reaction was beyond her imaginings. She hoped only that he hadn't been too unkind. When the time came for leave-taking, he had kissed Pauline, as he always did, and Ursula, who was used to seeing her rapturous response, noticed how she seemed to shrink into herself like someone out in the cold wind and inadequately dressed for it.

The customary thank-you note arrived ("Dear Auntie Ursula") but the last line, which had become requisite, was missing. This time Pauline hadn't ended her letter with a "Hope to come back next summer holidays" and an exclamation mark. As she always did, Ursula passed the letter to Gerald across the breakfast table and he read it, as he always did, in silence. The only comment came from Sarah.

"Is there anything in it about Brian?"

Both Ursula's parents died the following year, her father in the spring, her mother at the end of the summer. Their house and their savings went to Ian and Helen and Ursula, to be divided equally. Apart from what she had got from the sale of her engagement ring, it was the first money of her own Ursula had ever had, and though it didn't amount to a great deal, it was enough to escape on. It would buy a flat and supply the means of living for a little while. The guilt she might feel if she left Gerald and lived on his money would be assuaged. Even before she got the money, knowing she would get it and having a fair idea of what it would be, she thought about this prospect. She thought of it at her mother's funeral, her eye on Ian and his not-so-new wife, Judy, the woman Herbert Wick had wanted to horsewhip. They had two children now and Ian had never looked so well and happy. A man must be doing well for himself if he looks happy at his mother's funeral.

Pauline came up to them afterward with a tall redheaded boy in tow. "This is Brian, Auntie Ursula. We're getting engaged at Christmas."

She bestowed a big smile on Gerald. You see, somebody likes me; somebody wants me, desires me. Gerald didn't say a word, but he, too, smiled. Shaking hands with the boy, he smiled his Mephistophelian dead-eyed smile.

Walking on the beach every afternoon, Ursula thought of taking the girls out of the good schools they loved, away from this house and this seaside, away from their father. The nearest she came to going was when she broke off from typing *Hamadryad* and wrote him a long letter of explanation for her departure. Later, she tore up the letter and put the money she had inherited into their joint account. Instead of going, she thought of going in the future, and to that end or partly to that end, she applied herself to the Open University's art history course.

Hamadryad got rapturous reviews and was named by various celebrities as their book of the year. It was one of the six short-listed for the Booker Prize and Ursula went with Gerald to the Booker dinner. If he was disappointed at not winning, he didn't show it. Frederic Cyprian had pushed back his chair with a flourish and a clatter, stood for a moment, and marched noisily out, but Gerald had only lifted his shoulders and slowly dropped them. A journalist asked him how he felt. Wasn't it true that he had been asked to change the end but had refused?

Gerald could be pompous. "Like Pontius Pilate

and Strindberg," he said, "I told them that what I have written I have written."

"Maybe you should have done what they suggested," said the journalist.

"And maybe you should get back to subjects you know about. Like rock and cannabis."

There was a scene in the novel that Ursula took particular note of while she was typing it. A young girl, friend of the Sarah-Hope heroine, makes an advance to an older man, who turns her down. In the man's words and the girl's turns of phrase, she heard Gerald and Pauline. His economical wit was there and her naive platitudes. It was a cruel piece of work. Her fear was that Pauline might read it and recognize herself or someone else might recognize her in it and tell her.

She was nearly certain this never happened. In those days, Pauline never read anything. Her father died the following spring, her wedding was postponed, and when a date for it was finally fixed, she wrote asking Gerald if he would give her away. Sarah, aged sixteen, said it was disgusting, a woman being given away like a cow or a bushel of wheat, but Gerald only laughed and said he would.

"Why not? I may as well. I'll never get the chance with you two liberated souls. You're more likely to give *me* away."

Which only led, of course, to hugs and passionate denials. But Sarah and Hope were happy enough to be bridesmaids, in pink-and-purple tulle, while Ian's little girl wore pale lilac. Helen called them sweet pea colors. A picture of the wedding got into a Sunday paper because of Gerald, whose *Hamadryad,* adapted by himself, had just been shown on television under the title *A Young Girl,* and Pauline was enraptured. At the wedding reception, after quite a lot of champagne, she threw her arms around his neck and told him he was the best uncle in the world. All, apparently, was forgotten, or at least forgiven.

Ursula worked hard at her art history. She went on a trip to Florence to see the Uffizi and another to Madrid to visit the Prado. Since her honeymoon, she had rarely been abroad, been anywhere really. Gerald didn't like holidays, unfamiliar places, upheavals. If you lived by the sea, he said, you didn't need holidays. Besides, around that time, he was doing author tours, one in the United States and one in Canada, and a four-day promotion in what was then West Germany. She went to Berlin with him, chiefly because she wanted to look at the Wall, but when Robert Postle suggested she accompany Gerald to New York, Washington, and Chicago, and then to Canada, she said no. Gerald just turned his head and glanced at her.

"Don't you like flying, Ursula?" Robert Postle asked.

"That depends on whom you're flying with," she said.

He thought she meant the airline. Gerald knew. She could see it in his eyes and see something else, too, something that brought her a chill. He liked it when she spoke like that; he enjoyed her dislike, a bit of spirit. It relieved the boredom. She turned her back

366

on him and told Robert she couldn't leave the children. Sarah wasn't old enough to be left in charge of her younger sister.

No one argued with her about her European trips. No one cared. Daphne Batty, recently engaged by Gerald on account of her name, would look after them. Ursula didn't know, wouldn't have guessed, though she knew him so well, what mental notes (and actual notes, probably) he was making for future use of the things she said about the hotels she would be staying in, the pictures she would look at, the sightseeing she would do. It was to the girls that she said these things, but he listened.

And he listened when she came back and told them what she had seen and where she had been. One day, she found an essay she had written on Vasari and left beside her typewriter now slightly out of alignment, crooked, instead of lined up against the desk edge. But then she had no idea why he should be interested in what she studied or wrote. He concerned himself with her minimally, so why this?

But before she typed the next chapter of *Purple of Cassius,* she put her essay away in a drawer and locked it.

She told Sam none of these details, only that she had been to Florence.

"Let's go there," he said.

"You and I?"

"I love the way you say 'you and I,' whereas everyone else says 'you and me.' I bet when someone rings up and says, 'Ursula,' you say, 'This is she.'"

"Gerald made me," she said. "That was one good thing he did for me, taught me grammar. Did you really mean we could go to Florence?"

"We could go anywhere," he said. "Within reason."

He was staying with her at Lundy View House. When told he was coming, Daphne Batty had asked if she should make up a bed in "Mr. Candless's room," and Ursula, who doubted if she would have been as bold if the girls had asked, said, "No, thanks. He'll be sleeping with me."

Daphne said, "Why not," then started singing something about two sleepy people in dawn's early light and too much in love to say good night. She had simpered at Sam and winked when she thought Ursula wasn't looking.

"I'd like to go to Rome," Ursula said. "But I don't suppose we could."

"We'll go tomorrow," he said. "I'll fix it. I'll go into Barnstaple and fix it."

"Can you do that?"

"Of course I can. Anyone can. We'll go for a long weekend."

Fleetingly, she thought of the girls. It wasn't Sarah's weekend. Hope hardly ever came. "I feel happy," she said, "the way a child does. Simple, innocent happiness."

Hope and Fabian were coming over for a drink, and when the doorbell rang, Sarah thought that was who it was. She didn't know why they were going to the Odeon at Swiss Cottage, since one of them lived in

Crouch End and the other, when they weren't under the same roof, in Docklands. But they had said they would drop in after the film, and she had told herself that her reclusiveness shouldn't apply to her sister.

The doorbell rang at 9:30, which was a bit early for the last showing to be over, but Sarah thought only that perhaps they hadn't liked the film. But when she picked up the intercom, the voice of the speaker on the doorstep was Jason Thague's.

She felt a surge of impatience, of almost-wild protest. Didn't he appreciate the sanctity of one's home? Just because he hadn't one of his own . . . She wanted very much to tell him to go away and not bother her, but he was her researcher, her detective; she had to be pleasant. Still, when he appeared, she did tell him that she was expecting her sister and she didn't say it in an inviting way.

"It'll be nice to meet her," he said, his eye on the bottles and glasses Sarah had set out on the table.

"Would you like a drink?"

"Not just yet," he said. "Maybe just some water for now."

That alarmed her. How long did he mean to stay? Spots had erupted around the cleft in his chin. It occurred to her, for no reason that she could think of, that Americans called them "zits." The idea of it made her shudder. Zits. As she poured gin into her glass, she was aware that he smelled better; he smelled quite nice and he had washed his hair.

"I wish you'd phoned first," she said.

"It's not easy phoning, you know. I expect it's

another thing if you've got a mobile phone. I have to find a call box and then find change. I'd probably have to wait in a queue. It just seemed better to come here."

Not for me, she thought. "Have you got something to tell me?"

"Yep. And it's quite exciting."

She settled down, resigned herself to it. If it really was exciting, it would be better to get it over before Hope came.

"You found an O'Drida?"

"Better than that," he said. "I've found your uncle."

"My uncle?"

"That's what I said. Your father's youngest brother, and he's very much alive."

For a moment, a frightening instant, she didn't want to know. She wanted to stop. There was something dreadful waiting, a dark, shapeless thing that hovered behind a door, and now the door was opening; she had her hand on it, pushing it outward. Children dream of such things living in cupboards; she had dreamed of them, and screamed for her father. He had always come and always comforted her, but now he wouldn't come. She reached for her drink and had it to her lips when the bell rang again. Hope and Fabian. Jason watched her go to answer it, conscious, it seemed, only of his own triumph.

Hope was wearing a large chocolate-colored velvet hat. She and Fabian were still laughing indignantly about the hat and the trouble it had caused in the cinema. The woman behind Hope had said she couldn't see and had asked her to take it off, and Hope had pointed out that the cinema was three-quarters empty and the woman could go and sit somewhere else. She kept her hat on because it was cold. The woman said she had a right to sit where she liked and a right to an uninterrupted view of the screen, while Hope had no business to keep an enormous hat on under those circumstances.

At this point, Sarah introduced Jason. Hope acknowledged him vaguely in passing. She obviously hadn't realized who he was. His name wasn't enough to recall to her his function in Sarah's memoir.

"Oh, how do you do?" She barely looked at him. "So Fab started telling her the law on rights to sit where one likes and that sort of thing. It was hilarious. And then a guy in the row in front turned around and told us that if we wanted to talk, we should stay at home and watch the telly, and a great swearing match started, and in the middle of it I quietly took off my hat, and it was amazing—everyone just shut up and went back to looking at the movie, which was the great bore of the year, anyway, wasn't it, Fab?"

"Jason is doing research for me for my book," Sarah said.

Perhaps it was that which did it. Sarah remembered too late that Hope had said she didn't care for the idea of strangers rooting about in their father's past. And now she looked at Jason like one who rather dislikes animals might look at the dog curled up on a friend's sofa.

"May I have an enormous glass of that red?" she said, and then, smiling, opening her eyes wide, added, "Are you a professional researcher?"

"I don't know," Jason said. "I don't know what that is."

Hope raised her eyebrows, looked down, put on her Mrs. Justice Candless look. She said to Sarah and Fabian, "Let's get him to play the Game."

"What, now?"

"Why not?"

Sometimes Hope could be very clever. It never did to underrate her. Sarah poured the wine and went to look for scissors. The kitchen pair had disappeared, so they settled for the silver-handled nail scissors that had been part of a manicure set inherited by Sarah when Betty Wick died.

"What is this game?" Jason said.

"You'll see. Give him a drink. He's going to need it."

"Will you?"

"You could put some gin in this water. Just a little."

"You have to pass the scissors crossed or uncrossed," said Fabian. "There's a way of doing it right, just one way. We'll tell you when you get it right, but you have to show us you know why. Okay?"

"Yep. I guess."

"I pass the scissors uncrossed."

"I receive the scissors crossed and pass them uncrossed," said Sarah to Fabian.

"I receive them uncrossed and pass them uncrossed."

Hope took the scissors. "I receive them un-crossed and pass them uncrossed."

"I receive the scissors uncrossed," said Jason, turning them over and opening them, "and pass them crossed."

"No, you don't," said Sarah. "I've just seen something. It's easier for women, isn't it?"

"Daddy noticed that when he was only a little boy. He told me. But he had a brilliant mind. I bet he got it at once. He never said, but I bet he did. I receive the scissors crossed and pass them uncrossed."

Jason, who had been leaning forward with his legs apart, crossed them, said, "I receive the scissors crossed and pass them crossed."

Hope said, "You do, but do you know why?"

"Sure I know why. It's your legs. When your legs are crossed, you pass the scissors crossed, and when they're not, you pass them uncrossed. Simple, my dear Watson."

Hope turned pale. "I don't believe it."

"Why not? It's obvious. It's a game meant for kids, isn't it? Surely everyone soon gets it."

"No, they don't. It takes them years. How long did it take you, Fab?"

"I don't know, weeks. But I'm not very bright. Typical lawyer, I am, good memory but no brain."

"I can't believe what I've just seen," said Hope.

It occurred to Sarah while Hope was putting her hat back on that she might get them to take Jason with them; Fabian might even be induced to drop him off at Liverpool Street, but then she wouldn't hear about the O'Dridas. And suddenly, she wanted to know. Her fear had passed, the monstrous thing behind the door had retreated, and a new respect for Jason had replaced it. No one, after all, had ever gotten the point of the Game so fast.

"I'll never believe you weren't shown it as a child," Hope was saying. Ungenerously, Sarah thought. "You've probably got repressed-memory syndrome."

Jason shrugged and smiled. Fabian said, "Can we drop you somewhere?"

"No, he mustn't go. He's got something to tell me." Hope's lifted eyebrows angered Sarah. She said defiantly, "I'm going to give him another drink and hear our family's secrets. Off you go. I'll phone."

Jason waited until the front door had closed. "Your sister shouldn't have made such a song and dance about that hat. It's antisocial, that kind of behavior."

"Maybe. Tell me about—did you call him my *uncle*?"

The notebook was brought out. Jason looked at it, glanced up, said, "You got upset last time. It's all a bit emotional, this, isn't it? Will you be okay?"

"Of course I will."

"All right, then. Here goes. There's just one O'Drida in the Dublin phone book. He's eighty-five years old and Anne Ryan was his half sister. She and her sister were born in Hackney, if you remember, but when the mother died—Mrs. O'Drida, that is— the father went back to Ireland, leaving his daughters

374

with their maternal grandmother, who lived in Ipswich. She brought them up. O'Drida settled in Dublin, remarried, and had several children, and the last remaining of them is this Liam O'Drida, whom I talked to. He told me all that. He's quite compos mentis."

"But he isn't my uncle; he's my . . . well, my great-uncle maybe."

"I'm coming to your uncle. Bear with me. Liam O'Drida never knew his half sisters. He was much younger, for one thing. But he did know or know of James Ryan. Liam's daughter came to London as a student nurse in the sixties, and while she was there, she looked up her aunt's son or her half aunt's son. He was the only person in London she had any connection with. She visited him and his family a few times."

Sarah said thoughtfully, "This was the next brother to my dad, my uncle James?"

"Was. He's dead, according to Liam. The sisters are alive, Liam thinks, Margaret and Mary. He says there was something odd about Mary, but he doesn't know what, or can't remember. It's the youngest one, Stephen, I mean when I say your uncle."

"And he's still alive?"

"He was sixty this year. Born in 1937 and nineteen months old when his father, the chimney sweep, died. All Liam could tell me about him was that he was a schoolteacher in Plymouth."

"In *Plymouth*. But then he and Dad . . . Look, Dad, all of us, we lived in the same county; Plymouth's only about seventy miles away. And Dad worked in Plymouth at one time."

"Maybe. So what? I don't know any more than I've told you. I haven't gotten around to looking Stephen up in a phone book. I could go to Dublin if you want, but it'll cost you, and I don't think I'll get any more from Liam. Stephen is the next step."

"How about Margaret and Mary?"

"Liam didn't even know their names, only that there were two sisters and one of them had done something peculiar or different or whatever. He knew James and Desmond were dead and he thought John was, too. Oh, and he said the mother, his half sister—"

"My grandmother."

"Your grandmother, right. He said he thought she'd married again."

"Where in London was it the student nurse came to when she visited James?"

"Liam can't remember. The girl herself—well, she's fifty-five now—she married a Canadian and went to live in Nova Scotia."

Sarah sat in silence for a moment. She was thinking of her father's visits to Plymouth, notably a time when she was a child that he had been there to give a talk and sign copies of a newly published novel in a bookshop. If Stephen had gone there, would he have recognized his brother? Plymouth was a big city with a large population. How many people would have attended her father's talk? A hundred, if he was lucky.

All this put a strain on her, seemed to take hold of

her emotions and wring them out. "I'm going to open another bottle of wine."

"Not for me," he said, and then, astounding her, he added, "You drink too much."

"I beg your pardon? That's rich, coming from you."

"I know I drank your gin, but it's only when I'm with you I actually ever get a drink. But you don't just drink when you're with me, do you? Well, obviously you don't. You drink like this all the time, and you shouldn't—it's bad for you. You're beautiful and you'll spoil your beauty."

The only part of that she really heard—the earlier sentences passed over her—was the last. So that was how he saw her? She was surprised. But she didn't open the wine. "I was forgetting—you have to get the last train."

"I've missed it," he said. "It went at eleven. Can you—I mean, could I kip down here?"

He had shocked her as much as if he had started taking his clothes off. Her instinct was to say a violent no. No, no, of course you can't. Go to a hotel; I'll pay. She got up and took the glasses to the kitchen, stood thinking, but thinking of nothing much except how she hated the idea. Then she walked back into the room and said, "Yes, yes, of course you can." She made herself smile and even managed to pat his shoulder. "Of course you can stay—what else?"

If only she had two bathrooms. Suppose he used her toothbrush? But no one would do that. She said good night and to please turn off the lights, rushed into the bathroom, then rushed out again and into her bedroom, clutching her toothbrush.

It was better when her door was shut and much better when he put the lights out. She could pretend she was alone as usual. She got into bed. It was quite silent in the flat, with no sound but the occasional distant hum of traffic. The proof of *Less Is More* was on the bedside cabinet and she began to read her father's last book.

Perhaps more than anything else could have done, the plot of this novel distracted her mind from the unwanted guest in the next room. Gerald Candless plunged directly into this narrative of a man who abruptly leaves his family without explanation for his departure, takes on a new identity and profession, and makes for himself a new life. In a series of flashbacks, he had his protagonist recall that former happy existence, the closely united family, the loving parents.

Overcome by his memories, Philip knows he must at least once return to the family home and experience its atmosphere, absorb what he is sure it still has but what he has lost. All these years, he has retained a key. He watches from the opposite side of the street, in a surge of emotion and pain sees his mother go out, and, once she is out of sight, lets himself into the house.

Sarah had reached this point when she fell asleep. It was more a dozing off, and she jerked herself awake again, turned the page, read another paragraph and then another. But she knew that if you are tired, it matters very little how interested you may be in something or how intensely you want to go on with it, sleep will get you. She had learned that in her student days. In a way, she was relieved, for if she could feel like this, the presence of Jason Thague in the flat couldn't be seriously incommoding her, and that was her last thought when, having dropped the proof on the floor and turned off the lamp, she fell asleep.

At first, she thought it was a dream that woke her. Something heavy and alive lying beside her, an arm around her waist, a mouth against her cheek. She came back to consciousness, felt real skin, a real hand. . . . She sat up, screamed, "Get off me!"

She shoved him with all her strength, though strength wasn't needed, he was so thin and light. She jumped up, kicked him, stood on the mattress kicking him, leaped off, pulling the quilt around her, cocooning herself in it.

"Get out of here, you fucking rapist," she yelled at him. "Get out of my flat. Get out."

One of them put the light on. It must have been Jason. He sat on the bed, blinking.

"Get out. Now."

"I wouldn't rape you, Sarah," he said. "I wouldn't know how to rape anyone."

"Just go," she said. "Please just get dressed and go."

"I thought you liked me. You said you loved me. On the phone you said it, but I knew it was a joke. I'm not a fool. But I did think you liked me, and when you said I could stay, I thought you might—well, maybe not do much the first time, but something. . . ." To her horror, he began to cry. He put his head in his hands and sobbed.

"Oh God," she said. "Oh God."

"I'm so lonely, Sarah. And I'm hungry. When I played the Game and got it right I thought I'd proved myself to you. I'm so bloody lonely and I'm starving to death."

"You don't expect me to feed you, do you? Just get out. Get out now."

22

"Those who marry to escape something," Oliver remarked, "usually find themselves in something worse."

—HAND TO MOUTH

DRIVING HER UP TO OXFORD, Gerald told Sarah the story about Cardinal Newman, whose father's decision as to the university he should attend depended on which way the coachman chanced to bring the carriage around that fateful morning. If the horses had faced eastward, it would have been Cambridge, but, in fact, they faced westward, so it was to Oxford that Newman went.

Such last-minute decisions had for a long time not been feasible, Gerald said, though there had, of course, never been any doubt that his daughters would have the pick of any seats of learning available. Ursula, sitting in the front for form's sake while Sarah and Hope were in the back, thought it unfortunate for a girl of seventeen and a girl of nearly sixteen to be exposed constantly to this kind of flattery, but it would be useless to say so. It was probably too late, anyway, and the damage, if damage there was, was done.

She was working hard for her own degree from the Open University. Gerald and the girls knew about it and Sarah and Hope had at first shown some curiosity. What did she want it for? Was she going to get a job? Why art history? Gerald, on the other hand, appeared entirely uninterested. He seldom watched television, making an exception only when the adaptations of *Hamadryad* and later of *A Paper Landscape* were broadcast on BBC2, and when Ursula took over the downstairs spare room for herself and moved the set in there, he said merely, but in a tone that was more gratified than disapproving, "That will mean we can't have anyone to stay."

On the return journey to Devon, though Gerald and Hope talked exhaustively about academic matters concerning her future and the glowing A levels she would get, with occasional reference to Sarah's prospects, Pauline's dismal abandonment of education, and Robert Postle's double first, no comment at all was made on her, Ursula's, art history endeavors. Still, nothing was said about Gerald's own academic achievements at Trinity, either. And Ursula didn't mind. She would rather have nothing said than the casual contempt that was the probable alternative.

Gerald had been occupied in writing a script based on one of his earlier novels for a feature film. Ursula had no typing to do for him and was left free to get on with her own work. But in the early spring of the following year, he began writing a new novel. Sometimes he found his title before he had written more than a few pages, and it was so in this case. He called it *Hand to Mouth.*

Since Sarah's departure, things had been rather better between them. Hope, too, was much occupied with school, seemed always to be out pursuing after-school activities, and their rapprochement, if it could be so called, might have been due to their being much alone together. Ursula supposed it was because she was his only companion that he was obliged to talk to her, but whatever it was, there was no longer any evidence of the dislike he had once more or less expressed for her.

On one occasion, very early in the morning, when she was watching a filmed lecture on the Italian Renaissance, he came into the room and sat down beside her on the settee. At the film's close, he asked her questions, seeming genuinely interested. Another time, he asked her about the class she had attended in Ilfracombe. She expected mockery and jibes, but none came, nor did a suggestion that she had only chosen art history as her discipline because Edward Akenham taught it.

Trying to account for his approaches to her—conversation at mealtimes, signs of consideration, even an inquiry after her health—she wondered if it might be his age, if he was settling down, resigning himself to her and his fate. In May of that year, he would be fifty-eight. Inevitably, he would soon be alone with her, both his children departed.

*　　*　　*

Gerald handed her the first chapter of *Hand to Mouth* one wet day in March. It was raining too hard for her to go for her beach walk and so she settled down at once at the typewriter. It wasn't until she was given the next two chapters that she began to see what was being done to her. She still remembered thirteen years later, with almost the same physical sensation, her increasing sickness, her actual nausea, as she deciphered this narrative of a man choosing a young naive girl from a suburb to be the mother of the children he so much wanted.

By the time the novel began, she had become a silly woman in early middle age. Her name was Una. She was married to a distinguished musician with a full and productive life, and because she had no talents herself and no inclination for good works, she spent her time in acquiring an education. The early chapters were about the turn academe had taken in the late seventies and early eighties, about cranky degree subjects, low standards in polytechnics, evening classes in obscure crafts and Oriental martial arts, education by mail and education by television.

Flashback chapters told of Una's youth in Golders Green. The only daughter of the prosperous owner of a department store and his wife, she grew up ignorant, spoiled, and sheltered. It was at the only concert she had ever attended that she met her future husband, a composer on the lookout for a healthy, undemanding bride.

Two sons were born to them. They lived in North London, in Highgate. Una was never able to hold her own in the conversations her husband had with his intellectual friends and she turned out not to be as good a cook and housekeeper as he had hoped for and a less than adequate mother. At the same time, her pretensions grew, and when the family moved to Somerset, Una began investigating the possibilities of further education in order to keep up with her husband.

When she got to this point, Ursula walked into the study and asked for an explanation.

"You can do the explaining," he said. "I don't understand what this is about."

She told him and he denied it. Una had dark hair, she was forty-six to Ursula's forty-four, she lived in Somerset, her husband was a composer younger than she, and she had sons, not daughters.

"It's still based on me," Ursula said.

"Nonsense."

"Why did you do it?" She corrected herself. "Why are you doing it?"

"It is you who are doing it, Ursula. Still, it's a recognized phenomenon. People wish to identify themselves with characters in fiction, still more to find characters they can allege are based on themselves. I don't know why, but it's probably vanity. Vanity and a desire to be the center of attention."

She asked him not to publish it. He laughed and told her she was imagining things. But he did change Una's name to Imogen, Ursula and Una strictly being the only two English Christian names for women beginning with a *U*. He also made Imogen childless and her studies in social sciences rather than fine arts.

Ursula had typed six chapters but broke off in the middle of the seventh. She told him she would do no more. She would never type another line for him, and she waited for him to ask how, then, she justified her existence as sharer in his income. But he never did. That wasn't his way; that was the last thing he cared about.

No one else could have read his handwriting, so he went into Barnstaple and bought himself a type-writer. As a journalist all those years before, he had been a two-finger typist and he managed. The result wasn't fit for his agent's eyes or Robert Postle's, and Rosemary, who typed for a living, was found to take on Ursula's job.

Hand to Mouth was published in the autumn of 1984. The reviews were disappointing. Ursula waited for some friend or acquaintance or even gossip columnist to point out the similarities of character and way of life between Imogen and herself. But no one did.

"I've read *Hand to Mouth*," Sam said, "and I wouldn't have said Imogen was a portrait of you. She's not in the least like you."

"Her life was like mine was then. You didn't know me then. She used my turns of phrase. She dressed as I dressed."

"There's a story about Somerset Maugham and Hugh Walpole," he said. "Maugham based a charac-ter directly on Walpole. The self-opinionated critic Alroy Kear was Walpole to the teeth, barely a feature or a character trait altered. When *Cakes and Ale* was already in print, at proof stage, Maugham gave him a proof, and as Walpole sat down to read it that same night, he recognized himself in every cruel detail. There was nothing to be done except sue, but he didn't sue. It was said to have ruined his life; he was never the same again, never got his confidence back. And he had thought Maugham his friend."

"Well, I'd thought Gerald was my husband. I never really spoke to him much after that. That was the end."

They were at the top of the Pincian Hill because Sam said it was the best place to watch the sun set over the city. The dome of St. Peter's seemed to melt into the growing dusk as the Angelus began to ring. As the sky changed from red to violet, they began to walk down, pausing to look through the bars of the gate at the ancient garden.

"Hold my hand," Sam said as they descended.

"I think I'm too old to hold hands."

"Hold my hand. Please."

So she held his hand and he told her how this was the only section of the Aurelian Wall that Belisarius had failed to repair, for the Romans told him St. Peter himself would defend it against all assault. A young man and a girl were walking ahead of them, also hand in hand, and when the man turned around to look back over his shoulder, his dark good looks reminded her of Fabian Lerner. He was very much like him, almost his double, or his double as Fabian had been twelve years before.

Hope had brought him home to Lundy View House. It was December and their term at Cambridge, where they had met two months before, had just ended. Publication day of *Hand to Mouth* had also been Hope's eighteenth birthday. Fabian had turned eighteen the previous June.

She could remember so clearly their arrival, the sound of Hope's key in the door just when Gerald's nerves were starting to get the better of him and he had begun to pace. She was half an hour late, or half an hour late in his view, for she had certainly not given any arrival time. The key in the lock and then her voice calling, "Daddy!"

That was when Hope had begun wearing those hats and the one she had on was her first black velvet cartwheel. She threw it onto the sofa and rushed into her father's arms. Ursula said hello to Fabian, shook hands, waited for the greetings to be over.

Hope said belatedly, "This is Fabian."

Gerald looked at the boy then. But he quickly disguised, veiled, obscured, the indefinable flash that leapt in his eyes. She saw it later, when, thinking himself unobserved or perhaps that observers would fail to interpret, he allowed his gaze to rest on Fabian for a long moment—of what, Ursula hardly knew. Briefly, his whole face changed; his eyes darkened, and his flesh seemed to swell. He passed his tongue across his lips. And then, swiftly, he collected himself. He sat up straight. He smiled.

She squeezed Sam's hand, looked up into his face.

"Ten thousand lire for them."

"I was thinking of my daughter Hope's boyfriend. That boy looks like him."

"I don't like you to think of boys," Sam said. "I want you to think of me."

Sarah had lain in bed in the dark, unable to sleep. The black misery she had felt when her father died descended once more, but this time it wasn't definable; she didn't know why she was plunged into such deep unhappiness. It had nothing to do with Jason Thague, who was a fool, who misunderstood everything, but who hadn't, of course, tried to rape her. Perhaps it was the same old misery from the same source, because her father was dead and wouldn't come back and be there.

If he had been alive, she would have gone to him and thrown herself into his arms, talked to him and been comforted. There was one man in the world she thought could comfort her, hold her and kiss her and tell her all was well, but even as she thought it, she saw the folly of that. His might be the first name to come to mind, but it should have been the last. Her relationship with Adam Foley depended on mutual rudeness and antagonism, with no place in it for tenderness.

She imagined phoning him. It made her shudder. If you were really close to someone, you ought to be able to phone him at any hour of the night and unburden your soul, but there had never been anyone like that in her life except her father. No contemporary, no lover. Violence and abuse aroused her, and she didn't know why. They were the antithesis of what she had had from her father. But she didn't want to think about that; it bit too hard at the bone. She would think about Adam, sex with Adam, which she did more or less rewardingly, and at last she fell asleep.

That had been nearly two weeks ago, and in those two weeks she had done the things Jason might have done but which she could no longer ask him to do. She sent him a check—the final check, she thought it would be—without a covering letter, then set about finding Stephen Ryan herself. It wasn't difficult, because he was in the Plymouth phone book, the street where he lived recognizable as in that district of the city called Mutley. She didn't know Plymouth well, but she knew that much.

Phoning J. G. Candless had been one thing; this would be quite another. She had been naive then; she had believed she knew exactly who Gerald Candless was. Besides, this Stephen was her uncle. She couldn't just pick up the phone, dial his number, say who she was, and tell him he was her uncle. Instead, she wrote. It took her a long time, that letter, and when she had finally finished it, she balled it up, threw it away, and wrote simply: "Dear Mr. Ryan, I believe I am your niece, your lost brother John's daughter. I am writing a book about him. May I come and see you?"

It was only after she had posted it that she realized she hadn't said her father was dead.

23

On the subject of relatives, Louisa Manley used to
say that blood being thicker than water may be the
problem. Blood clots and water does not.
—EYE IN THE ECLIPSE

INSTEAD OF A PHONE CALL, a letter came addressed to
Mrs. S. Candless. "Dear Mrs. Candless . . ." it began.
It puzzled her for a moment and then she understood
he must suppose her to have been called Ryan and
that Candless was her married name. He wrote that
he would be happy to see her; he was generally at
home in the evenings from five onward. Although
she hadn't asked for it, he gave information about
himself.

He was a widower, his wife having died four
years before, and their three children were all married and had children of their own. His son also lived
in Plymouth, one of his daughters in Cornwall, the
other in York. He was a teacher, just sixty, he had
turned sixty in September, and he hoped to be able to
work until retirement age, five years hence. The book
she planned to write interested him, as he had himself written two books, one on walks on Dartmoor

and the other purporting to be the journal of a parson who had spent his summer holidays fossil-hunting on the Dorset coast. If Mrs. Candless would like to name a day for her visit, perhaps she would leave a message on his answering machine, as he was at work during the day.

Sarah thought that he, too, was wary of this meeting, rather shy, nervous of confronting her, and determined not to speak to her until he could also see her, but she might have been reading too much into what was perhaps a routine instruction he gave everyone. Whatever the reason was, this initial remoteness suited her, too. She picked up the phone at eleven in the morning, when she knew he would be at school, and told him she would like to visit on Friday in the late afternoon.

Adam Foley would be at the family cottage in Barnstaple on the Saturday.

The tall finger of stone on the hill, the Wellington monument, meant she was coming into Devon. She relaxed a little. It had seemed a longer drive than usual.

No word had come from Jason Thague. She hadn't expected anything, but his silence made her angry just the same. He could have acknowledged the check. He could have written. It wouldn't have hurt him to have apologized to her a bit more formally. But what could you expect from someone with his background and antecedents? Her father had been a snob and had made her one, and she knew it, but the knowledge didn't change her.

She remembered Joan Thague with a shudder. At least the woman hadn't turned out to be her aunt, and that was something to be thankful for. And now an uncle, who might be just as bad, awaited her, no more than twenty miles away. She had just driven along the coast road and through Dawlish and it was already getting dark. December, her thirty-second birthday next week, a couple of weeks to go before the shortest day, then Christmas. The first birthday without her father and, unthinkable, the first dreadful Christmas. She wouldn't go home for it, that was for sure, and Hope wouldn't. Would Adam?

It was just after five when she approached Plymouth. All the lights were on and Sainsbury's supermarket with its roof of sails gleamed like a fleet of white ships. Up to the right for Mutley. She drew the car into the curb where there were no yellow lines, parked, switched off the ignition, and looked at her face in the rearview mirror. This was something she never did, repowdering her face and relipsticking her mouth like an old woman, like her grandmother Wick used to, but she did it now. And she ran her fingers through her hair and tossed it and ran a wet finger under each eye in case there were mascara smudges.

For an old schoolteacher. She must be mad. If they took a sample of her DNA and his and compared them, they would be able to see a close relationship. As close as to her father, she thought, or was that wrong? And those children of his who had children of their own, they were her cousins. She might have seen that woman in the street in Fowey or Truro and never known. The one who lived in York—Sarah had done some of her postgraduate work at York University and could have passed her every day, met her eyes, even noticed some vague, unlikely resemblance.

His house was part of a Victorian terrace. It was all late Victorian up here, biggish houses or small, three up, two down, a bathroom, a kitchen, and a scullery. Sarah had had a school friend who lived near here and her grandmother had called it a scullery, the dark hole of a minikitchen with a copper in it. All the rows of houses had gardens behind and alleys running between them, parallel to the streets and linking them as the streets did, flagstone passages with high stone walls. Something struck a chord in her mind. Where had she read recently about a stone passage, a tunnel in someone's dream? It would come back to her.

The houses themselves were dark gray granite, solid as the rock itself dug out of Dartmoor. She went up the path and rang the bell. Immediately, a light came on in the little porch. She expelled her breath heavily. It was ridiculous to be so nervous. She tried to relax, drop her shoulders, loosen her tense hands. The door was opened and she saw what she hadn't anticipated, what she had forgotten she might see, something that had never crossed her mind.

It might have been Gerald Candless standing there.

* * *

Younger, of course. He was Gerald as he had been when Sarah herself was twenty-one, his hair nearer to black than gray, his thick, curly hair. This man was lighter, thinner, even a little taller. The massive impression her father had made—the bearlike figure, heavy shoulders, big head—that was absent. But his features, the wide, curved mouth, the big hooky nose, the broad forehead, all framed by that bushy hair . . . For a moment, she had a dazed feeling of faintness; the little hall seemed to spin. She clenched her hands, swallowed, then said too brightly, "It's good of you to see me."

The voice was a little like her father's. "You look as if you've seen a ghost."

"Yes," she said. "You're like him."

He took her into what probably had once been a seldom-used parlor but was now part of a room extending from the front of the house to the back. He had lit a coal fire and the place looked comfortable, somewhat untidy, lived in by someone busy and interested. She turned to look at him again, noting that he even dressed like her father, the same baggy cords, check shirt, Fair Isle pullover.

"Why didn't he come himself?"

She remembered then that she hadn't told him. Would it be a shock? Hardly, after forty-six years. "My father's dead."

"Ah," he said.

"He died last July."

"Yes. Well. I'm sorry. For you, I mean. How old was he?"

"Seventy-one."

"I shouldn't have to ask. He was eleven years older than I am."

"It was a shock."

He nodded. "Come in. Sit down."

She sat on a sofa that had a stack of books on one arm, the *Guardian* and a left-wing periodical on one of the seat cushions. "What do I call you?" she asked.

"Not Mr. Ryan. Not Uncle. God forbid." He smiled. "My friends call me Stefan. My wife was Polish, you see, and that was her name for me."

Constructing her image of him, a compound of Joan Thague and Frederic Cyprian, she had half-expected to be asked to call him Uncle Steve. "I am Sarah. But you know that. And it's not Mrs. Candless."

She hesitated, looked around the room. The wall facing her was lined with bookshelves, but she turned her eyes quickly away from it, from trying to detect one of her father's books from the color of a spine or that tiny black moth logo. This man would know; somehow she understood that. The name would not bewilder him as it had those others.

"I'm Sarah Candless," she said, "and my father, your brother, was Gerald Candless."

"The same name as the writer. Is that why he picked it?"

"He *was* the writer."

He drew in his breath, said, "My goodness," then added, "the novelist? You mean the novelist Gerald Candless?"

"Yes."

"Gerald Candless was my brother?"

"Yes."

He got up, walked across to the window, then turned back to face her. "How amazing."

"I know."

"I've read most of his books. I've got most of them—well, in paperback. Oh—wait a minute; this is really extraordinary—my daughter wrote her M.A. thesis on his work."

"He would have been very pleased if he'd known."

"How did it—I mean, how did John Ryan get to be Gerald Candless?"

"I'm hoping you can tell me that," she said, and then she told him all about her father, everything she knew.

"It's your turn now."

He nodded. "I'm going to give you a drink and get myself one. We'll go out to eat, if that's all right with you. But I'll start the . . . the family history first."

He was outside a long time, much longer than it took to open a bottle of wine and put glasses on a tray. She read an article in his *New Statesman,* had a look at his books. The fire needed making up. She had never made up a fire in her life and that suddenly seemed odd, given the fact her grandfather had been a chimney sweep. There were logs on the hearth and she picked one up gingerly and then another and put them on the dying embers. He came back as the fire began to crackle and flame.

"Sorry to have been so long. I found I needed to be alone for ten minutes and I thought you'd understand."

"I did."

"I was thinking about him," he said, "and about what I could tell you. Let me give you a drink."

He turned off the overhead light, left on the two table lamps. They sat in a dimmer, golden, less revealing light. At first, she didn't look at him while he spoke—he looked too much like her father.

"I was a baby when my father died," he began. "He had tuberculosis, a form of tuberculosis. Lung damage from the soot, I suppose, though apparently the doctors wouldn't admit it. It's hard to imagine what it must have been like for my mother. She had six children, the eldest thirteen. She was a Catholic; we were brought up Catholics. Your father was an altar boy. It's a wonder really that she didn't have more children. We lived in a rented house, more a cottage. She went out cleaning; that was our only income. Of course, I know all this from her and from what my brothers told me.

"She used to say to the children, as a joke I suppose, when they were being trying, that she'd had enough, that she was going to put her hat on and go and throw herself in the Orwell. That's the river there. Well, after my father died, she said she really thought of doing it, that it was a punishment for making such a wicked threat. She was very religious, my poor mum was. Of course she didn't do it; she had six children to think of."

"Can you remember the Candlesses?" Sarah asked.

"I'm not sure I understand you."

"There was a family in Ipswich named Candless. My grandfather"—she smiled as she said it—"swept their chimneys. You don't remember?"

He shook his head. "That's where he took the name from?"

"Their son died. He was the same age as my father."

That made him pause for thought. "Yes. I see."

"Tell me, Stefan"—she managed to say the name, and it didn't seem absurd—"tell me, how did you all get to London?"

"My mother's cousin offered her a home. She hadn't been very close to him, I gather. He was closer to her sister—"

"That would be Catherine O'Drida?"

He laughed. "You've found that out. My aunt Catherine told him about her sister's . . . plight. He wrote to her and offered her a share in his house, her and all her children. Out of pure Christian charity and kindness of heart, I think. He was a good man, if a bit stern and remote. Conscious of his virtue, I could say, though of course I wasn't aware of that for years and years.

"His name was Joseph. We little ones called him Uncle Joseph. He was a widower and childless. I'm inclined to think I shouldn't have said that about his conscious virtue—still, too late now, I've said it. If it hadn't been for him, John would have left school at fourteen, probably would never have attended a school in London at all, and I and my sisters would have been denied our education. Really, he saved us all."

"That must have been just before the Second World War started."

"A few weeks before, yes. Leyton isn't exactly inner London, but it suffered a good deal of bombing. My three brothers and my elder sister were all evacuees—that is, they were evacuated to the country with their schools. Mary and I and Mother and Uncle Joseph, we stayed where we were. There wasn't any choice about it; we had nowhere else to go."

She had picked up on one name. "Leyton?"

"In East London. E-ten. That was where our house was, in Goodwin Road, Leyton."

Her expression must have told him what she wouldn't say. He said quickly, "You're thinking it was hardly 'our' house. It was, though. Uncle Joseph and my mother got married. Later on, years later, after he was dead, my sister Margaret told me they got married because in those days it wasn't considered the right thing for a man and a woman to live under the same roof without being married. People would have talked."

"Victorian," said Sarah.

"Yes, well, it was only with the war that things began to change much. I don't know if my mother loved him or he her; he wasn't very lovable, though he was good."

"He was a cousin, but he wasn't a Ryan or an O'Drida, was he?"

"His name was Joseph Eady. My mother was Anne Elizabeth Eady."

They went out to eat at an Italian restaurant two streets away. Stefan said to the proprietor, "We'll have a carafe of your house white. We've something to celebrate."

Sarah, catching sight of her own face in the mirror behind Stefan's head, thought again that she looked like her mother. It was Hope who was like Stefan, and suddenly she understood how much like. Some reconstructing process in her mind put long dark curls on him and makeup and—of course—a big black hat. That made her laugh. He put up one of Hope's black circumflex eyebrows.

"I was thinking how much like you my sister is."

"So there are more of you?"

"One more. Two years younger. She's a solicitor."

He nodded. He seemed momentarily to have gone away into thought, and revelatory thought at that, for he smiled to himself, then looked up at her. There was something of wonder, of growing amazement, in his eyes.

"You may not believe this—you may think it's hindsight—but in many of your father's books, when I read them, I used to come across familiar things, things that reminded me of my family. I never made the connection—I'm not saying that. I never for a moment thought it might be my brother writing. It was rather that I felt so much in sympathy with this author. He became pretty well my favorite author. He seemed to look at things the way I looked at them and write about the kind of people I knew. Chloe Rule, in *Purple of Cassius,* you know, she was so absolutely my mother, and Jacob Manley in—I can't remember the name. . . ."

"*Eye in the Eclipse.*"

"That's right. *Eye in the Eclipse.* He was so like Joseph, and then, of course, the first novel, The *Centre of Attraction,* the chap who joins the navy. I can't remember his name. . . ."

"Richard Webber."

"Right, Richard Webber. He did all the things my brother John—your father—did, served in Northern Ireland, went out to the Philippines, believed his life was saved by the dropping of the first atomic bombs and suffered terrible pangs of conscience afterward."

"That was my father?"

"Well, wasn't it?"

"I don't know. I want you to tell me. But he came to Plymouth, you know, did a signing and a reading in a bookshop. About, I don't know, twelve, fifteen years ago."

"I know. I meant to go to it, but I was away on holiday with my family."

"Would you have recognized him?"

Stefan shrugged. "When he . . . disappeared, I was fourteen. We didn't have any photographs of him—well, maybe a couple of snapshots. Thirty years do a lot to a face, and I wouldn't have had any reason to suspect. I daresay I might have thought he was rather like our family, but then, so might any passerby be."

She drank her wine, remembered that sometime tonight she would have to drive right across the county, then decided not to think of that now. Their food came. Stefan refilled her glass.

"Were you"—she had been going to ask if he had loved her father, but she couldn't—"fond of him?"

Stefan was bolder, less inhibited than she perhaps, despite the difference in their generations. "I loved him very much," he said simply, and then added, "He was like my father."

"But you had Joseph."

"No. No, I didn't. Not really. Joseph was good to us. He spent what money he had on us; he made sure we went to church, that we were properly fed and dressed and went to school, that we 'minded our books,' as they used to say. But I don't think he liked children's company; he had nothing to say to us. He did his duty." Stefan smiled. "He was Jacob Manley."

"And my father did more than his duty?"

Stefan laid down his fork. He broke a piece off a roll and picked at it, making crumbs. "He loved children. All of us. You know the eldest of a big family sometimes feels it unfair to have to do so much child-minding, resents it because the children aren't his—they've been thrust upon him. John—your father—wasn't like that. He was completely different from James, for instance. That was the brother closest to him in age. James couldn't be bothered with Mary and me—we were babies—but John never had enough of us—well, all of us. He used to tell us stories, wonderful stories." That spark of revelation came back into his eyes. "Yes, of course, I see now. Did he tell you stories?"

"Oh, yes."

"He adored us. That was what made it so strange, so terrible, that he went away from us."

"You're not eating," she said.

"No. I'm finding this too . . . emotional." He drank some wine, ate a piece of bread, then shook his head and laid his knife and fork side by side across the plate. "I'm remembering what it was like when he . . . went. It's forty-six years, but all very clear when I talk about it. Painful. I'm sorry."

She waited, allowing him to recover himself. He drank his wine carefully, as if it had been measured out, as if it were medicine. Then he shook himself, his head, neck, shoulders, the way a cat does when it has landed from a height and readjusts its balance.

"He wasn't living at home, of course," he went on. "He hadn't been for two years, and between 'forty-three and 'forty-five he'd been away in the navy. But just the same, he was always at home—he was always there, to be with us."

"Did he—did he go to a university?"

Stefan seemed surprised. "Not unless he did after he disappeared. When he left school at seventeen, he went to work for the Press Association as a telephonist."

"A *telephonist?*"

"The telephonist would go out with a reporter to phone in his copy. No recording devices then, no E-mail."

"And that's what he did?"

"It was a way of getting started in journalism. But he left to join the navy. We missed him but—well, I suppose we vaguely knew where he was and we knew he'd come back. And he did. He lived at home with us and got a job on a local newspaper. I remember my mother was very proud of him. He was the first member of our family to have a—I don't know if you'd call it a profession, not to work with his hands, anyway, to have what the Americans call 'a white-collar job.'"

"Was it the *Walthamstow Herald*?"

Stefan shook his head. "The *Herald* was their rival paper. John worked for the *Walthamstow Independent*. He was a general reporter. He used to cover courts, local meetings, county councils, that sort of thing. His shorthand was very good, very fast."

"Was it?" she said wonderingly, reflecting that she had very little idea what shorthand actually was. "I didn't know."

"He used to come home and tell us his adventures. Some quite exciting things used to happen, even in Leyton and Walthamstow. Then he left home and got a room in Walthamstow."

"Why did he do that if he was so fond of you all?"

"My brother James got married. He was only twenty-one, but his girlfriend was pregnant."

She looked blankly at him, as one who is confused by what seems a total non sequitur. That made him laugh. It was cathartic laughter, and when it was over, he seemed freed of some burden. He even looked younger. Color had flooded his face.

"My dear Sarah, the world has changed so much. How can I explain? It was very disgraceful; it was still disgraceful in 1949. I was only twelve, but I was made to feel the disgrace of it, the shame. Joseph, not my mother, explained to me what had happened and what must happen: James and she must be married as soon as possible. They didn't like the girl; even James didn't much like the girl, but that had nothing to do with it. They had to marry and come back and live with us. There was an acute housing shortage, and they had nowhere else to go.

"John—I suppose I should call him Gerald—said he'd move out. He was the only one who didn't make a big tragedy out of the situation. He even laughed about it. He said to me that this was something that happened all the time and I was to remember that; it wasn't some exceptional sin that every right-thinking person condemned.

"It's funny how clearly I remember our conversation, but I do. I remember him saying that there were some things that were sins, crimes that could never be forgotten, but that wasn't one of them, whatever Joseph might say. The most important factor in all this, he said, was the unborn child. A child deserved two parents and a sound family background; that was all they should be thinking of. A family was a sacred thing, he said. To break up a family and destroy it, that was a sin. I've always remembered that."

"What did he mean, sacred?"

"I don't know, Sarah. I was only twelve. The most

important factor to me was that a strange woman would be moving in and my brother, who was nearer to a father, would be moving out and I couldn't stop it."

"But he came back often to see you?"

"Three or four times a week, and at the weekends he sometimes stayed over and slept on the settee downstairs. Even without him, we were crowded. James and Jackie and eventually the baby took over the front bedroom, which had been my mother's and Joseph's, while they had their bed down in the erstwhile dining room, Margaret and Mary were in the back bedroom, and I had the tiny box room with two bunks in it." He looked up at her. "Would you like anything else to eat?"

"Just coffee," she said.

"Just coffee. And shall we have another half carafe?"

"Why not?"

What she wanted to ask him wasn't relevant, but she very much wanted to know. Of course she knew that those who have had a happy childhood—and many of those who have not—see their parents as sexless beings, physical relations between them being unimaginable. And her father, while so extremely physical, had seemed more asexual, as far as she could tell, than most. She couldn't remember seeing him kiss her mother or even touch her hand. And then there swam into her consciousness a memory from Holly Mount days, of going into his bedroom, as she always did in the very early morning, and of finding him not alone but with her mother, the two of them in the bed with their arms around each other.

"Did he have girlfriends himself?" she asked Stefan abruptly .

They were walking back from the restaurant, up the hill in the lamplight. He pursed his lips, shrugged.

"There was a girl. I think she worked on the newspaper, too. Sheila? Shirley? I was too young to know about these things, but I don't think it amounted to much. He never brought her home. I don't know now how I knew she existed. Maybe I saw them out together in the street."

"Tell me about when he disappeared."

Stefan unlocked the house door and let them in. It was 9:30, according to the clock in the hall, which struck a single note as they went back into the living room. He said, "Can I get you anything? A drink?"

"I mustn't. I've got to drive." Her head was already swimming, but she thought longingly of brandy. "Well, a very small brandy, if you have it."

"Sure I have it."

She sat thinking about her father and his youth and his love for these brothers and sisters and knew she wouldn't be able to sleep. There was no point in hurrying home to sleeplessness. She might as well stay and hear the rest, not postpone it till another day. He came back with the brandy, an amount no one could call small, in a balloon glass.

"Thanks," she said, and, out of character, raised the glass. "The Ryans!"

He smiled. "Well, there are some of us left. My children. James's two and Margaret's two."

"Mary didn't have any children?"

"Mary became a nun."

Sarah made a sound she hadn't uttered for twenty years. "Wow!"

"Wow indeed. I'm used to it, but it still seems a little strange. She had a true vocation, I suppose you could say. One could say. Joseph certainly could and did say. He was overjoyed. She's dead now; she died five years ago. We're not really a long-lived family. But I was going to tell you about when John disappeared."

"Yes."

Stefan sat down opposite her. He leaned back for a moment, contemplating the ceiling, then sat up rather stiffly, as if bracing himself for an ordeal. "It was in the summer. The summer of 1951. Mary's birthday was July the second and John came over for that. He wouldn't have missed something like that. She didn't really have a party—we couldn't afford it—but she had two of her school friends to tea. She was sixteen. We were all there—well, James was working nights, but Jackie was there and their baby, Peter. John, your father, he came along at about eight, after he'd been to cover the annual general meeting of some society or other. I can't, needless to say, remember what.

"He brought Mary a present—well, two presents. A box of chocolates—chocolate was still rationed, so it was a great treat to have a whole box—and a book called *Young Pegasus*. A book of poems. It was in the house for years. We didn't have many books, so I remember that one.

"And I remember we all played a game. Even Mary and I were a bit old for it, but we always played it; I couldn't remember a time when we hadn't. And we played it to try it out on the school friends, see if they could get the point. It was a ridiculous game; it went like this. . . ."

"I pass the scissors crossed," said Sarah very quietly.

"Ah." He nodded, thought, nodded again. "So he taught you, did he?"

"Yes."

"As I taught my children and Margaret taught hers. Somehow I have my doubts about James. By the way, Margaret is still very much alive, but James is dead. He died as your father did, of heart disease. So we're all gone now but Margaret and me. Now, where was I? Yes, the party.

"That was the last time I ever saw your father. He said good night to us all and went to get the last bus back to Walthamstow. Not many cars about then, you know. We didn't know anyone with a car. He went, and he was quite cheerful and normal. It was a Monday, and he said to Mother that he'd see us on Wednesday, that he'd come for his tea before he went to cover something or other. Maybe a meeting of the Leyton council, I don't know. Oh, and he said he'd something to tell us but that it would keep; it would keep for a couple of days."

410

"Something to tell you?"

"We never found out what it was. He didn't come. John never broke promises; he was a most reliable person. They are the ones that cause the worry, the reliable people, the ones who never let you down, because when they do . . . My mother was worried from the first. And when he didn't come the next day, she was desperate."

"Didn't she phone him?"

"We didn't have a phone, Sarah. John didn't have a phone, not in his room. On the Friday, she got James to go to the *Independent* offices—well, it was a printing plant—and ask for him. They hadn't seen him, either. He had left without warning, though they weren't much surprised. He had given in his notice there weeks before, as it happened, and had only a few days left. My mother thought that must have been what he meant when he said he had something to tell us, that he was leaving, that he was perhaps going to some other newspaper and that one a long way off."

"He was," she said. "When did you come here to Plymouth, Stefan?"

"It must have been in 1971. Why?"

"My father worked for the *Western Morning News* in Plymouth from 1951 till 1957."

"Not as John Ryan?"

"As Gerald Candless."

"Ah," he said again. For a moment, he was silent. Then he said, "Joseph reported him to the police as a missing person, but they weren't much interested. A young man, you know, not living at home, not a person in any sort of danger."

"Did you—any of you, I mean—did you try to find him?"

He said rather dryly, "We weren't the sort of people who were equipped for finding someone. No phone, for a start. And no know-how. Joseph—I don't think I told you—Joseph was a postman. James was a motor mechanic. Margaret and Mary and I were too young to know what might be done. Besides, Margaret was preparing to go to university—another wonder for Mother and Joseph. I think, eventually, we all just accepted that he'd left us. We were sad, and we mourned him in a way, but there was nothing to be done. I believe—well, I know— that later on Margaret wrote to several provincial newspapers to inquire if he might be working for them—that is, if John Charles Ryan might be, but she always got negative replies. No wonder, in the light of what you've told me.

"And that's all I know. I've told you everything about your father I know. It was all forty-six years ago and I never saw him again. None of us did."

"So far as you know."

He looked at her in surprise. "Well, yes, that's so."

It was time for her to leave. She would come back, of course. There was a lot more to say, a lot more to know about the family after her father's departure, but it, too, would take hours to tell. She had been in Stefan's company for six hours. He was tired, his face drawn with fatigue and strain and the pain of remembering. A small hammer banged in her head. She had drunk too much and now she had to drive all those miles across the moor to Tavistock and Okehampton and Bideford. But there was one more question. She was standing up, being helped into her coat.

"You've mentioned all the family but one, the third brother, Desmond. You haven't said a word about Desmond."

"No," he said.

"He's dead, I gathered. You said they were all dead but you and Margaret. What happened to Desmond?"

He went to the door with her. He opened the door and took her hand. She thought he was going to kiss her, but he didn't. "I can't tell you tonight," he said. "I'll tell you next time. We're both too tired for it. Good night."

"Good night, Stefan," she said.

24

"Sunsets aren't red," she said. "The sky turns red only after the sun has gone down."
— A Man of Thessaly

THERE WAS FOG ON THE MOOR. Pockets of fog hung in the dips of the narrow road and scarves of it drifted suddenly across her windscreen. She drove slowly and shakily, uncertain how much of her loss of control was due to drink and how much to the unleashing of emotion. It seemed that for hours now she had held a quantity of unshed tears throbbing and prickling behind her eyeballs. At the same time, she was growing very afraid of falling asleep at the wheel, skidding, involuntarily letting her foot slip off the brake, of plunging into fog and thence into some stream or pool or through a gate.

She had probably drunk almost a liter of wine, for Stefan had certainly not drunk more than the contents of the small carafe. And then there had been the brandy. Jason Thague's words came back to her and she thought, But if I don't drink, how will I get through my days? How could I have gotten through this evening? Oh, I want my father, I want him. I never drank so much while my father was alive.

It seemed an interminable journey. Once or twice, she thought of parking the car under a hedge, of lying down to sleep on the backseat with her coat and the car blanket over her. She would be afraid in this wild, deserted place. It was strange, because she never was afraid of the dark or who might be out and about in the dark or of being attacked. What she had learned this evening had made her vulnerable. A skin had been pulled off her and the tender places exposed. She drove on, glad when, as occasionally happened, she saw the lights of another car, the lights of the empty towns as she passed through them.

Lundy View House was in darkness when she reached it, the sea a shining pan of ink, a glittering expanse between invisible headlands. A tiny segment of moon showed between bluish swollen clouds. She let herself in and went straight upstairs in the dark, in the familiar place, her father's house, where no light was needed to find her way.

Ursula came up to her and kissed her. It was an unprecedented act in the morning, and though she knew she should have been more trusting, she was suspicious. A favorite phrase of her father's, quoting from *The Taming of the Shrew,* came to mind: "I wonder what it bodes."

"I am thinking of selling the house," her mother said when breakfast was coming to an end.

"This house?" Sarah knew that was stupid, as though her mother possessed several houses.

"I don't want to live here alone. It's too big for me, for one thing."

"And for the other things?"

Ursula didn't answer. "I don't think it means much to you without your father."

"What about Hope? It means a lot to her."

"Hope has been here only a couple times since your father's funeral."

Sarah, who had considered telling her mother all the things she had found out, now changed her mind. If the house was sold how could she go into Barnstaple and meet Adam Foley? Ursula didn't read her thoughts, but it seemed as if she did.

"I know children always think of their parents' house as their home. Even after years away. But I don't want to be condemned to living alone on the edge of a cliff above the Bristol Channel for the rest of my life."

Just because you and Hope might occasionally want to come here, Ursula had been going to add, and use it as a hotel, for Sarah's fourteen-hour-long Saturday-night absences hadn't escaped her notice, but she didn't say it. The habit of conciliation and gentleness took a long time dying, would probably live on in its present moribund state.

"Where will you go?"

Ursula wasn't lying. She really wasn't quite sure yet. "I don't know."

"Have you put it on the market?"

"Not yet. I wanted to tell you first. And I want to

say, while you're here, will you have a look around and see if there's anything you want? Furniture or ornaments, of course, and anything of your father's. There's a big box of his reviews in the study."

Black velvet from head to foot. She varnished her fingernails midnight blue and when her face was done, painted far more thickly and elaborately than it ever was in London, she unscrewed the top from the silver-flecked midnight-blue lipstick and sat there holding it in her hand. You will be thirty-two next week, she said to herself. Thirty-two was young, but not young enough. She had a swift nightmare vision of horror, undefined, shapeless, a gnarled hand in it, a grinning face, and she put the lipstick away and found a red one instead.

Hope had a long black cloak in her room. Sarah put it on, took it off. Batwoman. She saw her mother looking at her fingernails but knew she wouldn't say anything; she never did.

"I thought I'd wear Dad's sheepskin. It's so cold. Is it in his room?"

"I'll get it for you."

The coat that had been a jacket on him was almost full-length on her, dark gray, the sheep's wool lining curly gray, like his hair. She snuggled into it, closed her eyes, and felt as if her father were hugging her. In the hall, Ursula was on the phone, talking animatedly. Sarah just raised her hand, mouthed that she didn't know when she'd be back.

* * *

After Sarah had gone and she had finished talking to Sam, Ursula went back to the kitchen and once more opened the broom cupboard. She had completely forgotten about the bag of Gerald's clothes in there until Sarah had asked about the sheepskin coat. Sarah had better keep that coat. The rest of the clothes, she would put in her car boot now.

A search of the pockets yielded two crumpled handkerchiefs, a five-pound note, the stub of a pencil, a receipt for petrol, and a key. The shape of one's own house keys are imprinted on the mind. Close the eyes and the outline can be seen, the silhouette. Ursula didn't recognize this key. But she knew what it was and which door it opened. It was the key to the house in Goodwin Road.

So it *had* been he whom Dickie Parfitt saw. Twenty-eight years ago, but yesterday all the same. She would never know why he went there and now she no longer cared. A black floater swam across her vision, the beginning of pain following it. She would have a full-blown migraine by nightfall.

They were all in the pub but Adam. Rosie admired Sarah's nails and said she'd thought of having hers done with a pattern, designer nails, or whatever it was called, but really she was too old. Rosie, Sarah happened to know, was thirty-three. A discussion ensued as to what they should do, where they should go.

"Why can't we just stay here?" said Sarah, looking at the clock.

"It's so boring here. And the club is boring."

Someone Alexander knew was having a party. A thirtieth birthday. He had been invited, so they wouldn't be crashing it. What, five of them? Rosie said. That "five" made Sarah uncomfortable, because she suddenly thought they must wonder why she always came alone, that she never brought a man, that she apparently had no man.

"We'll have another drink here," said Vicky, "and then we'll go to this new restaurant that's called the Trawl or something and have fish and chips and then we'll go to the club. How about that?"

Sarah said as casually as she could, "But will Adam find us?"

"He's not coming, you'll be glad to hear. He hasn't come down from London."

She was dazed and stilled, as if a gray net had been thrown over her. He wasn't coming. He hadn't come down from London. Those two sentences repeated themselves in her head. The whole evening stretched ahead of her as some rare childhood evenings had for her and Hope, notably when Auntie Helen was visiting or her grandparents, gray panoramas of boring grown-up talk, until her father had come and rescued them. He couldn't rescue her now. No one could. She looked at her ridiculous fingernails, down at her knees in skintight black velvet jeans. They made it quite difficult to walk, something she had felt as sexy before but now knew was absurd.

She drank her second drink, went with the others to the restaurant, aware that her quietness must be remarked on but finding nothing to say. The reason

419

for his absence was no longer a mystery. It was deliberate, of course, the ultimate rudeness, the titillating, exciting rudeness. Now she would never know when he would come back, had no way of knowing, since other contact was forbidden in their unwritten laws. He was challenging her, or was he seeing how far he could go, if he could draw her down here week after week on the off chance? She shook; she couldn't eat. Nausea came up in her throat.

"I won't go to the club with you," she said. "I'd better go home. I'm not feeling well."

It was the first Sunday down here since her father had died that she hadn't woken up bludgeoned by a hangover, hadn't had to drive back to Lundy View House with a throbbing head and shaking hands. She got up early and dialed Stefan's number. His answering machine was on and she left a message on it. If he wasn't busy this afternoon, could she come and hear the rest of it?

Perhaps now was the time to tell her mother. Or would it be better to wait until she had heard what else Stefan had to say? I shall be here again next Saturday, after all, she said to herself. And then she realized what she had said and was as quick to deny it. Adam mustn't be allowed to rule her. She wouldn't return until the fourth Saturday in the month, until after Christmas.

"Did Dad ever go out on a Saturday night?" she asked abruptly.

"Possibly." Ursula seemed indifferent. "Occasionally. To take a manuscript to Rosemary perhaps. Why?"

"I think he went to church. I think he went—at the end, he went back to the church."

Ursula's sudden bark of laughter shocked Sarah. Contrition followed: Her mother said she was sorry, and then added, "If you and Hope want to come here for Christmas, I'll do my best to see we have the nicest time we can." She hesitated. "Fabian, of course, and there's a friend I'd like to ask, and we could invite—"

"Oh, no. No, I couldn't. And I'm sure Hope couldn't. It would be terrible—can't you see it would be terrible?"

"Perhaps. If you say so."

"You'll be all right, won't you? You can have your friend and . . . well, anyone else you'd like to ask."

"I can have my friend," said Ursula.

After lunch, she tried Stefan again, and again the machine was on. Had he said he was going away? Had he said something about visiting his son? She couldn't remember. She left another message that she would like to see him the following Friday. That way, she would have to come down; she would be here on Saturday. . . .

Afterward, she hardly knew what had made her phone Hope. She never phoned Hope from Devon. Even before she made the call, she knew she wouldn't tell Hope their mother meant to sell the house. She'd be *afraid* to do that over the phone, afraid of Hope's explosion, her wail of wrath and misery. But now she had Hope on the line, she had to say something to her.

"I'm bringing some stuff of Dad's back. D'you know why he didn't keep any reviews of *A White Webfoot*?"

"He didn't like them. The critics said he'd written a thriller. You won't remember. You know you were away."

"You told me it was based on the Highbury murder."

"That's what they said, the Ryan murder case."

"The *what*?"

"The murder of Desmond Ryan. I don't know if it was. That's what they said."

That evening, when she got back from Devon, she went straight to Hope. Fabian wasn't there and for once her sister was alone.

"It was years before we were born," Hope said. "One of the critics said 1960, I think."

"He was Dad's brother," Sarah said. "One of his younger brothers," and she told her sister about Stefan and the Ryan family. Hope listened, not interrupting. The color came up into her face, burned her cheeks, then faded away as fast as it had come.

"You're saying that after all those years, Daddy based a novel on his brother's murder?"

"It looks like it."

"But if that's true, Daddy had left his home and all of them behind for almost ten years before Desmond was murdered."

"He'd still have known about it, wouldn't he? If it was in the papers. D'you know the circumstances?"

"I don't know anything about it," Hope said. "I've read *A White Webfoot*—of course I have, and so have you. But that won't be a faithful reporting of the case; it'll be the way Daddy always did it. The filtering process, the changing to disguise it and make a better story. I don't really understand why you want to know. You're going to write about Daddy, aren't you, not his family?"

"He is his family. I can't leave them out."

"*I* would. You know who he was now, his real name, and that he took the new one in 1951—isn't that enough?"

"I don't know why he did," Sarah said.

"Well, it wasn't because his brother got himself beaten to death or whatever nine years later, that's for sure. Ma phoned me this afternoon—did I tell you? No? She says she's going to sell the house. I wasn't surprised; I thought she would."

"Don't you mind?"

"It's funny," said Hope, "but I've been thinking about it a lot. I mean, before she told me. I even thought that maybe you and I could raise the money, get huge mortgages or something, and buy it from her, and then I thought, What's the point? I couldn't bear to be there. I can't bear the place. I can't bear to be in the rooms. Not without Daddy." She looked at her sister, with tears streaming down her face. "I loved him too much, you know. I loved him too much for my own good."

The FOR SALE sign was discreet, white with austere black Gothic lettering. But passersby stopped to look at it. There weren't many on foot at this time of year, but even cars stopped. The estate agent had asked what Ursula would think of advertising the house as the former home of Gerald Candless. "Anything that sells it," she had said recklessly.

The study was empty of his papers now. The books remained. It looked, she thought, like the room in a writer's house that has been preserved as a museum, the rows of reference works, the shelf of his own books facing the desk, the typewriter uncovered. She had laid a sheet of A4 paper beside it and a fountain pen across the paper, then taken them away again. Stupid game playing—what was the point?

Sarah had taken the first edition of *Hand to Mouth.* She was glad to see it no more, the black moth on its yellow spine, the woman on the front cover that the artist had given black hair and a full red mouth but in whose face she could always see her own. The rest of them, the four that Hope didn't want, she intended to hand over to Sam. *A Man of Thessaly* was the next one Gerald had written and the patient typist in Ilfracombe deciphered. She remembered, with distaste for her own pettiness, the quiet pleasure she had taken in witnessing his struggles with the unwieldy mass of paper, scrawled all over as by a planchette needle gone wildly out of control. Once a week, he had grabbed handfuls of it, stuffed them into giant brown envelopes, and driven off to Ilfracombe.

He had never said a word to the girls. Nor had she. And they had never known, as evinced by Sarah's surprise that her mother hadn't read *A White Webfoot*. Gerald went on tour to the United States for *A Man of Thessaly*, but she stayed at home. He told anyone who cared to know that his publishers weren't prepared to pay her airfare.

The angina began the following year. He had never walked much and now he walked even less, for any climb left him fighting for breath. While at the hospital for tests, actually during a cardiogram, he had a heart attack. Not much of a one, but alarming.

Once again, nothing was said to the girls. The woman who no longer cared about him bore the brunt of his health problems, while the women who loved him were left in ignorance. As far as they knew, their father might live for twenty years.

The year of *Phantom Listeners* was the year he got the OBE. She went to the palace with him and sat in the audience next to Robert Postle. Afterward, he told Robert that the queen had asked him how many books he had written and whether he was working on one now. They had lunch in Charlotte Street and Robert asked what he had said to the queen about writing another book, as he, Gerald's publisher, would very much like to know.

"I may give up writing," Gerald had said. "I may retire."

"Writers don't retire. Not at sixty."

"Some should when they're thirty," said Gerald.

Robert hadn't taken the threat seriously. And that was wise of him, because Gerald had begun work on *A White Webfoot* the following week. Ursula hadn't known its title and hadn't cared to find out, but the girls knew and talked about it. There was no escaping involvement with his work in that house.

He bought Sarah's flat when she had her first job in London, and Hope's a year later. South Kensington or Bayswater was what he would have liked for them, but they had to settle for Kentish Town and Crouch End, the best he could afford. Not that they had been anything but rapturous, touchingly grateful; they realized their own luck, aware of their friends' mortgages. The new book progressed slowly. She wondered if he was ill, if he lay on the sofa in the study, racked with angina pain, instead of writing. Something was making the process very slow for him, as if the pages he produced were not the result of a melding of invention and imagination, but of a hand-to-hand battle with a demon that must be daily wrestled to the floor. And when he finally appeared, to sit reading in the living room or come for his meal, he looked gaunt and ghost-ridden, his eyes staring, black shadows under them like inky fingerprints.

For a few weeks, they had reached a point where they ceased altogether to speak to each other. Total silence between people who share a home might have been possible on his side; it wasn't on hers. Gradually, they began once more to exchange remarks about their children, the weather, the condition of the sea and his health.

One evening when she was coming out of a racking migraine, she looked at him and thought he seemed worse than she was. "You are very ill," she said.

"It's in the mind," he said, "only in the mind," and then he laughed, presumably at that "only."

"If I were you, I'd make an appointment with the doctor."

"And if I were you," he said, "I'd want me to die. The sooner the better."

It took him two and a half years to complete his new novel. Within a few months of its reaching Robert Postle, a rough of a proposed jacket design arrived. The white, gold-shot mist—rather, the dazzling whiteness barely broken by streaks of saffron and blue—reminded Ursula of an Impressionist painting, a Monet without a motif. Gerald hated it. His feelings about it, violently expressed, came near to generating a real conversation between them. He sent it back to Mellie Pearson, the artist, with demands for change, but even the final version, with birds and a sun and a pale waterside, was always to be a cause of deep dislike that almost amounted to phobia. The original in a pastel gray frame, presented to him at the novel's launch party, he afterward returned to the artist.

The critics called *A White Webfoot* a thriller. One newspaper had its crime-fiction critic review it. Another described it as "a murder story dressed up in Dostoyevskian pretensions." Gerald Candless, said the *Evening Standard,* no longer able to dredge up plots out of his own imagination, had based his new novel on the Ryan case, a notorious and sordid murder that was of interest today solely because of its place in the history of the campaign for homosexual-law reform.

Gerald had had very little experience with bad reviews. Even *Half an Hour in the Street* had met with nothing like this. He didn't want his daughters to see the newspapers, but he was powerless, in Hope's case, to prevent it. Sarah, as it happened, was out of the country. Hope, of course, flew to her father's defense and would have written impassioned letters to several newspapers if Gerald hadn't gently persuaded her that this would do more harm than good.

His last book, the last, that is, before the one that would be posthumously published, he wrote in four months. No one could have called *The Mezzanine Smile* a thriller (Gerald said) and no one did. Reviewers wrote four hundred words about it rather than the established eight hundred and it passed quietly into number twenty on some newspaper's best-seller list. Ursula, in tune with her resolve of nine years before, didn't read it.

"And I still don't know what it's about," she said to Sam, taking the book down from the shelf and handing it to him.

"A man who works on a provincial newspaper but who gets up at five to write plays and a woman who loses her chance of marriage because she stays at home to look after her old parents."

"You can take them to London with you. I must stay here for Sarah at the weekend and then I'll come up and maybe . . ."

"You won't go back?"

"I shall have to tell the girls, Sam. I don't think they'll mind. They're not very interested in what I do. Shall we go for a walk on the beach?"

The sea was a dull slate blue, its color the reflection of dark clouds with gaps of clear sky between them. Mussel shells, ground into powder by the tides, made chevron streaks on the pale, flat sand, and the razor shells lay everywhere, some split and splintered, others perfect open blades. The air was clear and cold, the sun a pool of yellow light between bulges of cloud low on the horizon.

"Have you ever noticed," she said, "how sunsets aren't red? The sky never goes red until after the sun has gone down."

"Your late husband pointed that out in one of his books."

"Did he? You know his work better than I do. But I'm not surprised; he pointed everything out. Somewhere he said that people never shiver from fear or emotion, only from the cold, though writers are always saying they do."

"Hold my hand," he said.

They walked along the water's edge, where the sand was firmest, hard as setting mortar. Gerald had never written about this sea that for twenty-seven years had been under his windows. He had enjoyed it only on the finest days. She thought, as the trickling tide crept close to her shoes, as she stepped aside and he jumped aside, laughing, I will do my best never to think about Gerald again; I will try to shut off my past.

At the gap in the dunes, they turned back. The hotel, which had been dark for long weeks, now had lights in many of its windows and, as they watched, more came on. They were going to eat their Christmas dinner up there. It is where we met, she thought, turning her face to him, smiling. He bent over and kissed her.

She wanted to ask him something. She remembered what he had said soon after they met, how he wanted to be in love, and she knew that if she asked him, she would get an honest answer. Why am I so greedy for punishment? Haven't I had enough? She asked herself those questions but asked him nothing, and they watched the sun go down and the red color gradually seep across the sky.

25

WITHOUT ANY GROUNDS FOR HOPE, she had half-expected a letter from Jason to be waiting for her when she got back, an apology, a request for more work. There was nothing, and on an impulse, she sent him a check for the amount she had been paying him weekly when he was still her researcher. He was loathsome and clumsy, but his cry of hunger sometimes still echoed in her head. She considered a covering letter, something to the effect of hoping he was all right, but she couldn't find suitable words, and in the end, she put the check by itself into the envelope.

In his absence, she had to do it herself. She went to the British Newspaper Library in Colindale. Hope had given her the approximate dates. It was a slow business, finding the appropriate newspapers, waiting for them to be brought to her, and it made researches at St. Catherine's House seem simple. But at last, when she had been there more than two hours, she found what she was looking for.

The death of Desmond Ryan had taken place in the autumn of 1959. In October. The *Evening News* was the first newspaper to carry a report of it. A body had been discovered that morning by a friend who had a key to a flat in Highbury Crescent. It was identified as that of Desmond William Ryan, twenty-eight, of that address. Police were treating the case as a murder.

The following day's papers all carried similar accounts. All were brief, cagey, somehow veiled. It didn't take a particularly suspicious mind to detect a contrived cover-up. The local weekly, the *Waltham-stow Independent,* was less reticent. On the following Friday, when it came out, it carried a much fuller story and a long article about what it described as a "perverts' ring" and a "network of corruption." Its tone was one of almost incredulous moral outrage. The word *homosexual* was never used, nor was *gay.* Perhaps *gay* hadn't come into use then, Sarah thought vaguely. The piece told of large-scale investigations by the police and the uncovering of a "web of vice" unparalleled in British history.

"Perverts" and "inverts" got in touch with one another through elaborate codes in film and porno-graphic magazines. Accounts followed of recent prosecutions, the imprisonment of a clergyman for what the chairman of a quarter sessions had called "one of the most terrible offenses in the world." Public conveniences were a notorious meeting place for these "sick men," and there they even indulged their disgusting and degraded practices. Such behavior was common across the metropolis, though it seemed to have begun in Soho, and to have spread its "abominable tentacles" outward, through Finsbury, Islington, and Highbury, Lisson Grove, Kilburn, and the respectable northern suburbs.

Sarah couldn't see where Desmond Ryan came into all this until she reached the proceedings at the central criminal court, the accounts of the trial of George Peter Givner for his murder. Here, in the national newspapers, the process was again heavily veiled under prudery and euphemism, but she could make out Givner's role and Desmond's. Givner had been his lover, had rented the Highbury Crescent flat for him and occasionally lived with him there. On the evening in question, according to the police, Givner had arrived at the flat, let himself in with his key, and found Desmond Ryan there with another man. There had been a violent quarrel, during which the other man fled and which culminated in Givner first striking Ryan with a table lamp, then using an eighteen-inch-high marble statuette of a male nude to beat him to death. Much was made in the report of this bronze figurine of Apollo.

The next day, the witness, the other man in the flat, James Henry Breech, a private soldier, gave evidence of Givner's arrival, his verbal abuse of Ryan, and the quarrel. He had not witnessed the murder, but he had seen Givner pick up the statuette and strike Ryan with it. Then he had fled, run down the stairs and out into the street. He denied a sexual relationship with Ryan, describing the two of them as "close friends," but the police found letters from him to Ryan in the flat, misspelled, punctuation-free effusions of love combined with offers of payment for favors.

Among these letters was one other, a literate piece of work, written in a spidery, sloping hand and signed only with the letter *J*. It was dated one week before, but there was no address on it and no clue as to the sender. This letter was read in court just as Breech's letters were and the newspaper gave them all in full, the soldier's, Sarah suspected, for the pleasure of offering its readers examples not so much of the man's depravity as of his brutish ignorance. J's letter was quite another matter.

Desmond,
You will know who this is from. I need not explain.
It has taken me eight years to find the courage to
write it. I have hated you and I have blamed you.
Through you I lost everything that mattered to me.
I think it may be possible you can understand why,
after what happened, I could never go back. But it
was no more your fault than it was mine; it was no
one's fault. And now I need to see you and talk to
you and see if we can forgive each other and teach
ourselves to forget. So I am asking you to let us
meet. I will phone you in a week or so. J.

The court seemed to regard this letter simply as further evidence of Desmond Ryan's propensities and no great weight was attached to it. The prosecution's next witness was the man who had found the body the following morning, and who described the wreckage of the room, the smashed furniture, a rug dyed almost entirely red, and the blood splashes on the walls. After that, the court adjourned until the following Monday.

Sarah looked in vain through the following Tuesday's newspaper for the progress of the trial. Instead, in the next issue, she found a paragraph to the effect that George Peter Givner had committed suicide in his cell. During the Sunday night, he had removed his shirt and his underclothes, torn them into strips, plaited them into a rope, and hanged himself.

The file on Gerald Candless, alias John Ryan, now had the thickness of a telephone directory. Sarah added her newspaper photocopies to it and sat down to read the rest of *A White Webfoot*. She had abandoned it a month before because it seemed to have so little relevance to her father's situation, and she had had the more recent *Less Is More* to study. Opening the earlier novel again, halfway through, she felt frightened by disturbing pictures, the white walker, half beast, half bird, and its webbed prints in the snow, and she was aware of real but ridiculous fear, the shiver of the child reading a ghost story in an empty house. Then she came to the dream, the man in the tunnel who finds the exit ahead blocked and who, on turning around, is confronted by a stone wall where the entrance had been.

It got dark so early at this time of the year. After a while, when she reached the chapter in which the murder happens, she put more lights on. She went to fetch herself a bottle of wine and drank the first glass straight down.

She could see what the critics had meant when they called the novel a thriller. In none of his other books had her father so graphically described violent death. Here was the battle between George Givner and Desmond Ryan—Harry Merchant and Dennis Conlon in the book—one man armed with an object that might have been designed as a weapon, the other defenseless but for the cable, a lamp cord, the author put into his hand. Gerald Candless, with characteristic Candless imagery, compared the two to Roman gladiators, the man with the sword and the man with the net.

Sarah flinched from it as she had never before recoiled from her father's work. When the blood was described, flying like red birds smashing into glass walls, she had to look away from the page. The damage to Desmond-Dennis's beauty dismayed her, the long, painful, passionate dwelling on his ruined face, the bloody cavern in his skull, his broken hands. She skipped paragraphs after that, then came to the discovery of the body and at last to Givner-Merchant's piteous self-inflicted death, the lonely suicide, the long, cold hours that passed before the dead man was found.

No mention of letters, Mark the boyhood friend not mentioned for two chapters, then described only as reading an account of all this in newspapers. Just as she herself had done. The thriller element of the novel soon disappeared. There was no more suspense, no mystery, only a long examination of Mark's guilt and conscience, as he blames himself for Dennis's death.

Sarah had been refilling her glass as she read, and by the time she reached the last chapter, she was fuddled with wine, the print starting to dance. She had learned nothing new, only that her father must have been made to suffer painfully from his brother's death. She fell asleep in the chair and the book fell to the floor.

By the time Ursula was prepared to work and qualified to work, there were no jobs. It was the late eighties. And Gerald, if not exactly ill, had a heart condition, which meant he needed to care for himself and be cared for. She learned to cook the right sort of food for him; she encouraged him to take a walk around the garden, on the level ground, every day. If he had been able to climb the cliff, he could have joined her in her beach walks, but climbing the cliff would probably have killed him.

Not a word to the girls. He was insistent about that.

"They love me," he said. "I am blessed in that two beautiful, brilliant women love me. What have I done to deserve that? Am I to reward them by making them unhappy?"

Ursula thought that he had done plenty to deserve it. Gotten up in the night to tend them, hugged and kissed them, told them stories, given them everything they wanted, spent large sums of money on them, bought them their homes, but she didn't say so. He drove himself to the hospital for regular checkups, dropping off chapters of *The Mezzanine Smile* at Rosemary's. Ursula wasn't allowed to drive him; he didn't think women made good drivers, Sarah and Hope necessarily being the exceptions.

An angioplasty was proposed. It was a method for unblocking an artery by inflating a kind of balloon device that had been passed into it by means of a catheter. Gerald liked the idea because the process could be carried out without surgery. It failed. The artery was impenetrable.

Ursula drove him home and he said nothing about her driving. He was deeply depressed. For most of his life, he had enjoyed robust good health and now his strength had been taken away, like Samson's. For most of his working life his books had been received first with enthusiasm, later with rapture. But the critics had disliked *Half an Hour in the Street,* sneered at *A White Webfoot,* and damned *The Mezzanine Smile* with faint praise. Worse, they had given it short paragraphs at the foot of pages.

Back at home, he did no work. The strong medication he had been put on had a side effect of bringing him dreadful dreams. He said only they were dreadful, not what their content was. She wondered if he still had that recurring dream in which he was in the stone tunnel and first one end, then the other, was blocked, but she didn't ask.

She felt nothing for him. No pity, no interest, of course no love. One good thing was that, mysteriously, she never felt him to be an encumbrance or a nuisance. He was her fate. She looked after him with great care, keeping him warm, comfortable, and suitably fed, as she might an aging once-loved pet animal. While in her company, he was dull, spiritless. He had done that himself. By a long process of attrition and occasional bouts of violence, he had worn away her love and even her liking for him, had silenced her, made her wary of speaking to him, and the result was that he had nothing to say to her. Symptoms of illness were occasionally discussed, the weather, the state of the tides.

Of those writer friends of his, Roger Pallinter was dead, Jonathan Arthur's wife had died and he had married again and gone to live in France, and Adela Churchouse was too mad to go out alone. Frederic Cyprian was reported as being in an advanced state of Alzheimer's; Beattie Paris had written his autobiography and died the day it was published. Only the Wrightsons still came. Gerald saw few people but his faithful daughters. They came every weekend, and Robert Postle occasionally came, talked publishing gossip to Gerald, and walked with her on the beach.

Sometimes she felt she must escape, get out, but she had never in all her life been to a cinema on her own and she wasn't going to start now. She had had her fill of evening classes. Gerald hadn't been precisely rude to the neighbors (one family at the top of the cliff road, two others in houses below the hotel), but he had left them in no doubt that he was humoring them, was bored, and they were afraid of him. They wouldn't come again and they wouldn't ask her without him.

Well before the height of the season, the hotel advertised for baby-sitters. When she told Gerald she had thought of doing a baby-sitting stint once or twice a week—to get out of the house, to escape—he flew into a rage. That was a job for peasants, for the likes of Daphne Batty. It was scarcely a step up from being a charwoman. She had never heard him use the word *peasant* before. His heavy, dark face was suffused with blood. The veins stood out on his forehead and temples like purple roots. She said if he felt like that, of course she wouldn't do it. But she wondered later what that "peasant" and "charwoman" talk had meant.

She knew very little about his parents; he never talked about them. He had told her their names, that they were dead, that his father had been a master printer and he was their only child. Now she wondered if his mother had gone out cleaning—or was she being too "psychological"? But she didn't wonder much; she didn't really care.

Then he started his next novel, the one that was to

be his last, *Less Is More.* The difference in him was startling. He was happy, looked younger, regained some energy. He wrote every day, completed the manuscript in six months. When his publishers wanted him to accept the invitation to attend the literary festival at Hay-on-Wye, he agreed happily, looking forward to meeting acquaintances there and to reading aloud, something he enjoyed and did well.

The days when she might have gone with him, when he might even have asked her, were long gone. He never rang while he was away, though the girls sometimes had long telephone conversations with him. On his return, he said nothing about the festival, how it had been, whom he had met there, and, contrary to his usual practice of taking a rest, then devoting time to research, he immediately began a new book.

Or so she supposed. He didn't tell her what he was doing. And this in itself was strange, for, no matter how bad their relationship had been in the past, even after the fracas of *Hand to Mouth,* he had always announced to her his commencement of a new novel. He hadn't been able to help himself, she had often thought, he was so happy on that day, those days, that first week. His energy overflowed. If there had been anyone else there to tell, he would have, but there was only herself, so it was she he told.

"I started the new one today."

And she had never quite been able to find it in her heart to say, "Who cares?" Or "So what?" His enthusiasm touched her, in spite of everything.

"It's going well. I've made a good start. I'm pretty pleased with it."

Of course, as time went on, the anxieties began and the doubts, the self-torment. She could see it in his face, though he seldom expressed it. Since she had stopped typing for him, he never spoke further about what he was writing, only occasionally of the practicalities. He was running out of paper. He was going out to take his manuscript to the typist.

But this time, after his return from Hay, though she could tell he was working frenetically, he said nothing about starting a new novel. She wondered if it wasn't a novel, if it was his autobiography, though he had once said he would never write one. About the same time, he told her he had invited a man called Titus Romney and his wife for a weekend. Romney was a writer he had met at Hay.

"A fan," he said.

"Of yours, you mean?"

"Of course I mean that. I'm not likely to be a fan of his, am I? I'd never heard of him till a month ago."

She shrugged. Then she remembered who Romney was. Robert Postle had mentioned him. Wasn't he one of Postle's authors?

"You needn't worry—they won't stay here. They can go to the hotel. I suppose we can give them lunch? My girls can come down and have a bit of fun tormenting him."

"How very pleasant."

"Oh, for God's sake," Gerald said. "He's a wimp."

At his next checkup, the cardiologist recommended a coronary bypass. It was possible that two arteries would need to be bypassed. If Gerald didn't want that, they could put him on stronger medication and his life would be indefinitely prolonged. But it was unlikely in that case that much exertion would ever be possible for him, and there might be unpleasant side effects—bad dreams, sleeplessness. While, with the bypass . . .

"I'll have it," Gerald said. No doubt he remembered the bad dreams he already had. "When can you do it?"

She had been there with him. They must have presented to this heart doctor the picture of the long-married, devoted couple. The wife much younger, anxious but practical, a capable nurse.

"I'd like to tell you," said the surgeon, "how much I admire your books."

Gerald hadn't known the man knew who he was. "Thanks very much," he said.

The health insurance would pay. He could have the operation the following week. A nurse told him the healing of his leg, from which the veins would be taken, would be more troublesome than the site of the main surgery.

"I'm sure," Gerald said. "It'll be a real breeze. I can't wait." In the car, on the way home, he said to her, "Not a word to my girls."

"I'm not hearing this."

"Yes, you are. You heard."

He worked on whatever it was he was working on. Every morning and half the afternoon. She waited for him to say he was taking the manuscript to Rosemary, but he didn't; he seldom went out, apart from taking a walk around the garden and to the cliff edge. He was typing it himself, of course, as he had typed all his work since she had refused to do it, but his typing was inadequate to pass muster. She heard from outside the study door the clatter of keys, and heard his muttered swearing when he made mistakes and had to do a line of x's.

It must be that he didn't want Rosemary to see it. Would he want *her* to see it? She asked herself why she cared. Until recently, she had been quite indifferent about what he did, how he was, even if he lived or died. But then, at that point, she had almost offered to type his manuscript for him, to forget the pain and humiliation and perform this service for him as if *Hand to Mouth* had never happened. She hadn't done that, but she had watched him and, to some extent, waited on him in a way she hadn't for years.

His operation was to be on the Thursday. He accepted, knowing, without asking and without her telling him so, that she would accompany him to the hospital on Wednesday afternoon. And then she would go through all the motions of the anxious, loving wife, make the requisite phone call on the Thursday evening, be told he was "comfortable," phone again the next morning, visit as soon as they said she could.

She had forgotten the Romneys were coming. He hadn't. But such visitors were no trouble. She always cooked a roast for him and the girls, and it would only mean a larger joint of meat. He sat with the proofs of *Less Is More* on his knees and the *Encyclopaedia Britannica* on the table beside him, a man with a bad heart, a man who, given what he was and the mind he had, must dwell sometimes on the journey his blood made throughout his body, squeezing its way through constricted passageways, on each rotation still reaching its destination, escaping again, once more penetrating the infinitesimally narrower passages.

Until the thick-walled tunnel closed at both ends.

"Do you think pity is akin to love?" she said to Sam when he was back with her at Lundy View House. "It's what they say."

"It's what they used to say," he corrected her. "All those eighteenth-century heroines pitying their lovers. That was just a way of saying they loved them but not using a word that betrayed their own weakness."

"You mean, if you pity someone, that means you're stronger? I think I was stronger than Gerald in his last days. I did pity him, and that's what it was, pity; it wasn't love."

"What was it he was writing? This *Less Is More*?"

"No, it can't have been," she said. "He'd already gotten the proofs of that by the middle of June. He was correcting them when he died. I don't know what it was. I looked for it after he was dead and I looked some more when I was sorting out all those manuscripts." His puzzled look made her smile. "You'll want to know how I could tell it wasn't there. His typing. It was so bad. There wasn't a messy manuscript among them; they'd all been typed by Rosemary or me."

He had destroyed it himself, she decided. Whatever it was, autobiography, new novel, amalgam of both, he had gotten rid of it. With no means of burning anything that size in summer, he could simply have dumped it in his wastepaper basket for Daphne to empty.

"I'm glad I felt something for him at the end," she said. "It wasn't love; it was just a little warmth, a little pity."

"Did you hope he wouldn't die?" Sam asked.

"I didn't think that far." She was suddenly visited with courage, the nerve to ask him. It was all this talk of love and pity. And he was looking at her with such tenderness, from which all sentimentality, it seemed to her, was absent. "Sam," she said, "you said to me when we first met that you wanted to be in love. Do you remember?"

He nodded.

"So I'm asking you . . . well, I'm asking if it's happened. With me, I mean."

She held her breath. She needed to because of his hesitation. If he hesitated, wasn't it all up with her? Wasn't this an indication that everything was at an end?

"I'm not in love," he said at last. "And you're not, are you?"

"I don't know," she said very quietly.

"I think I'm too old. Or I've had it before and can't have it again. Something like that. It was absurd to expect it. I do love you; I do want you to live with me. I want to live with you, I think spend the rest of our lives together. Is that good enough?"

"Yes," she said.

26

*It is easier to excise letters cut in stone than to
unsay what has been said.*

—A Paper Landscape

"You haven't read *A White Webfoot*?"

"No," Stefan said, "I don't know why. When was
it published?"

"Nineteen ninety-two."

"Ah, then I do know. That was the year my wife
was so ill. I didn't read much. I certainly didn't read
reviews, so I wouldn't have known about it. And
when the paperback came out—would that have been
the following year?"

Sarah had checked that morning, before leaving
for Plymouth. "Hardback publication was in October
1992, paperback in October 1993."

"That was the month she died." He was silent,
then smiled at her. "You said he lived at Gaunton,
didn't you?"

"A house on the cliff, yes."

"My sister Margaret went to stay at Gaunton in
the summer with her daughter and her husband. At
the Dunes Hotel. Is that anywhere near?"

"Next door," she said. "A hundred yards away."

"It was July. They might have seen each other and not have known."

"Or have known," said Sarah. "You wouldn't know exactly when, would you?"

"I know they left the hotel on July the sixth, because they all came to see me here before going home."

He had had a shock. She remembered the look on his face, the dazed look. The sleepwalking look. Before he went across to the hotel with those Romneys, he had been his normal self, and when he came back, the shock was there. A sight had stunned him. He had seen his sister and recognized her after forty-six years. She hadn't known him, though. She would have come back with him if she had. The shock had gone to his heart. Had broken his heart?

"Tell me about your brother Desmond," she said.

"All right. Would you like a cup of tea?"

"I don't want anything," she said.

Her father looked at her out of Stefan's eyes. Their voices, that at first she had thought alike, really weren't at all similar. Her father's had been very deep, rich, with that underlying faint burr. Stefan, of course, had left Suffolk when he was only a little over two, when he must barely have been able to speak, and his voice was educated London. He watched her, looked away, then turned to her again as if making calculations.

"Desmond," she said gently.

"Well, Desmond," he said, "I think you know he was murdered."

"Yes."

"When John disappeared," Stefan went on, "Desmond was twenty and living at home, as all the rest of us were. That is, James and his wife and baby, Margaret and Mary and I, and, of course, Mother and Joseph. Desmond and I shared a room. We Ryans were a very good-looking lot, tall, dark, regular features—not me, I was the ugly one—but Desmond was the best of us. People used to say all the girls would be after him, and maybe they were, but it wouldn't have been of much interest to him."

"He was gay."

"Yes." Stefan looked at her inquiringly. "You've been reading about the trial?"

She nodded.

"I didn't know, of course. Not then. None of us did. It's impossible to imagine what Joseph's reaction to such a thing would have been. You, at your age, probably don't realize how the general public felt about homosexuals in the fifties. And I, at mine, just have a sort of muddled recollection of horror at the very idea. This was many years ago, before the act that made homosexual relations between consenting adults over twenty-one legal, and feelings were as strong as they had been at the time of the Oscar Wilde case."

"I didn't know. But I've read some newspaper accounts since then."

"Then you'll know judges and magistrates were describing homosexuality as the worst evil known to man, as a hideous crime, and, above all, as a deliberate, calculated viciousness. The most liberal, the really enlightened, took the view that it could be cured, that it was a kind of madness or sickness. Right on during the sixties, men were being put into mental hospitals and given aversion therapy to 'cure' their disease."

"There's a lot about that in *A White Webfoot*."

"Is there now? I knew nothing about homosexuality until my brother Desmond came up in court in 1955. He was found guilty of an act of gross indecency in a public lavatory and sent to prison for six months."

Sarah wanted to ask what gross indecency was but as quickly decided not to. Instead, she said very tentatively, for she was bewildered, "You don't mean with a child, with a minor?"

"He was twenty-four and the other man, so far as I remember, was over thirty. It was a crime in those days, Sarah, with anyone of any age. Fortunately—I think I can fairly say fortunately for him—Joseph was dead before it happened. He had died the previous year. National newspapers were quite reticent about cases of this sort, but local papers weren't, and it was all in the *Walthamstow Independent,* which my brother John had worked for. All there for my mother to read."

"What did he do for a living? Desmond, I mean."

"He had had various jobs. He'd been a messenger

and worked in a shop behind the counter. A gentlemen's outfitters. He'd been a barman, and at the time of his arrest he was working as a receptionist in rather a dubious sort of hotel in Paddington. But he always had money, far more money than he could have earned by the sort of work he did. We never noticed or we never made the connection. We were innocent.

"After he came out of prison, he didn't come back to live with us. He got a flat of his own. It was in Highbury and he was set up in it by the man who killed him. There was no question of my mother not wanting to see Desmond; she wasn't like that. None of us would have rejected him, but he just didn't come back. And I don't think he ever again had a regular job. He'd call in sometimes to see her and he'd bring her presents. He was always well dressed. And he was always happy."

"Happy?"

"You might think there wasn't much for a homosexual man to be happy about in the fifties, but he was. *Gay* wasn't in any way a misnomer for him. In fact, *gay* in its older sense really described him; gaiety expressed him. He was nice and sweet and lovable. I don't think he was in the least bit ashamed of the kind of life he led. You might say, why should he have been? The answer to that is that everyone was always telling gay men they should be ashamed, that they were sick, that they were vicious, that they'd either chosen their way of life or else they were mentally disturbed."

Sarah considered. "Did he talk to you about it?"

"You have to understand that we didn't meet much. I went away to university in 'fifty-five, the year he went to prison, and I wasn't home much after that, except for the holidays. But he did talk to me on a couple of occasions. That's how I know he wasn't ashamed. I'm sure people would have said then that in telling me these things he was trying to corrupt me—the powers that be were very big on corruption in those days—but of course he wasn't. He wouldn't have wanted me to follow his way of life—why should he? He was he and I was I and we were different. I think he recognized, even then, that some are born gay and some straight, just as some have blue eyes and some brown. He never went into physical detail, anyway, only told me about love affairs he'd had. And he talked about clubs he went to and baths."

"You mean steam baths, Turkish baths?"

"He was very big on that. I think he enjoyed showing off his body. He liked the old men who went there looking at him. He never mentioned Givner to me—not by name, that is. It was quite simple and straightforward, you know. Givner loved him, provided him with that flat, spent money on him, and he was unfaithful to Givner. What else did the man expect? He must have been living in a dream world. You've read about the trial, you said?"

Sarah nodded. "Givner hanged himself in his cell while on remand."

"Yes. It was a terrible thing for my mother. The

loss of Desmond, the trial. Everyone knew, of course. The neighbors knew."

"If Desmond had been a respectable heterosexual with a wife and children, she'd have gotten sympathy, but because he was gay and things had come out about his way of life, it was quite different?"

"That's right. By that time, James and Jackie had two children and had moved into a house a couple of streets away. Mary was serving her novitiate. Margaret and I were both teaching nearby and both living at home. But it was John my mother wanted. I've told you how we tried to find him. We advertised for him, but we didn't get any response. And Mother said we never would; she knew she'd never see him again."

"And eventually you came down here?"

"I didn't think I'd actually get the job. It was a good school, a better school than I could have hoped for in London. And I loved the place, not so much Plymouth as the countryside around it. So I left and Margaret stayed. She stayed because someone had to. She was a prime example of the single woman who sacrifices herself for a parent."

"*The Mezzanine Smile,*" said Sarah.

"Well, yes, maybe. Yet Mother didn't want it; she didn't expect it. Margaret was engaged, and she kept the man she was engaged to waiting for seven years. Then Mother insisted, said to go and get married, to leave her, and in the end, Margaret did."

"What became of your mother?"

"She died of cancer in the spring of 1973. She was ill for a long time, was in and out of the hospital;

she had a mastectomy and a hysterectomy. The cancer went to her lungs. It was an awful death. If John—Gerald—if he'd known, perhaps he might have . . . But there it is—he didn't. Why did you want to know if I'd read *A White Webfoot*?"

She wished now that she had brought a copy with her. She had taken it for granted that such a self-confessed fan of Gerald Candless would have the paperback in the house. It was half-past six. If it had been earlier, they could have gone out and bought a copy. In the bookshops in the shopping center above the Hoe, they would be bound to have *A White Webfoot*. Still, it was too late now.

"It's about two boys growing up in the fens," she said. "They have some sort of sexual encounter at school; it's rather glossed over, no details. They grow up—one becomes a practicing and promiscuous homosexual and a happy one; the other is haunted by his . . . his orientation."

"Ah," said Stefan. "I begin to see. Why is it called that?"

"*A White Webfoot*? It's a quotation from something, a poem—I can't remember what. Mark, who's one of the protagonists, has a recurring memory of web-footed creatures walking in a marsh. And he has a dream of being in a stone passage with one end sealed off, and when he turns around, the entrance has also been blocked. I suppose it's a trap dream, an expression of a need to escape while knowing there's no escape. Mark is married; he has a sympathetic wife and two sons. He sees Dennis and observes him, follows him, but they never meet. When Dennis is murdered by his lover and the lover kills himself, Mark blames himself for both their deaths. He feels sure that if he had told Dennis the truth years before, that he loved him and wanted to live with him, none of it would have happened. The rest of the novel is about guilt and self-realization."

Stefan was silent for a moment. "And you think this is based on fact?"

"All his books were. He said so. But facts changed, were filtered, *processed*. The places were changed and the names, of course, and the relationships of one character to another. You can never quite tell what is fact and what is imagination, but you can always be sure the emotions were real. He had felt them or someone he knew had." Sarah got up, went over to the bookcase, and brought her eyes close to the row of her father's paperbacks, the line of black moths, chimney sweeper's boys. She turned around quickly to look once more at this man who was her uncle. "I think my father wrote the letter the police found."

"The letter?"

"Among Breech's letters was one from a man who signed himself J. It was read in court."

"None of us went to the trial. While it was on, we wouldn't have newspapers in the house, for my mother's sake. Then Givner died and that was an end of it."

"The letter seemed to be saying J wanted some sort of reconciliation. It's not very explicit, but it does seem to suggest that J wanted to come back to his family after an absence of eight years and could do so only by talking to Desmond. Does that mean anything to you?"

"No, it doesn't. I wish it did."

"He says in the letter he'll phone Desmond after about a week. The letter was dated a week before the murder. Perhaps he did phone. Perhaps a date had been set for a meeting. But then Givner killed Desmond."

"I wonder what he wanted to talk about."

"Perhaps he wanted to tell someone why he had left, where he'd been, why he'd changed his name. Perhaps he wanted to prepare the way via one family member for returning to the family. But he does say that he and Desmond had somehow done each other a great wrong."

"Are we ever going to know what that was, Sarah?"

"I don't know. Somehow I feel we aren't."

She thought, but didn't say aloud, If he had met Desmond and talked to him, would he have reverted to being John Ryan, gone home again to Goodwin Road, been reunited with his family? Terrible questions reared up. Would he ever have written another book? Or if he had, would he have written the books he had written?

Would he have met her mother and married her? Would she, Sarah, ever have been born?

On the doorstep, saying good-bye, Stefan wished her a Happy Christmas.

* * *

457

In her headlights, the FOR SALE sign gleamed whitely. No one bought houses in the midwinter, though; there was time yet. It would be a long time before a sale happened. Before the house was no longer there, she thought, for that was how it would feel when it was gone from them and owned by others, as if it had disappeared. As if a mighty spring tide had come and swept it away, drawn it off the cliff into the depths of the sea. Like another Lyonesse or Dunwich, it would lie down there, intact but unreachable, inaccessible to anyone.

A foolish fantasy. Her mother had gone to bed, though her bedroom light was still on. Sarah thought that there must be people of her age, perhaps most people, who under these circumstances would have opened that bedroom door, put a head out, said something cheerful, pleasant, inquiring, or gone up to the woman reading in bed and kissed her. She half-wanted to do some of that, but she couldn't. She stood for a moment outside the door, hesitating, in a dilemma about something so trivial, so absurd, then finally called out, "Good night!" and ran into her own room.

Psychologists said that it is best if a child models itself on the parent of the same sex. She and Hope had modeled themselves on the parent of the other sex and couldn't undo it now, wouldn't want to undo it now. How unhappy he must have been, her poor father, she thought as she lay in bed. While he was alive, she had never thought of his happiness or unhappiness, only of him as her father and sometimes, often, of her luck in having this father, so clever, so talented, so successful, so generally admired, so good to her and Hope, so generous and so loving.

But he carried with him always some terrible thing. Oh, why didn't he tell me? Once we were grown-up, Hope and I, why didn't he tell us? We would have comforted him; we would have made it better, because we loved him so much.

There was nothing to do the next day. If only she had thought of that, anticipated it, she wouldn't have come down until this afternoon, would have stayed in a hotel in Plymouth. It was too cold to go out unless going out was essential, as it would be in the evening. Her father's study was stripped and emptied. It was painful to be in there. She thought of a line he had quoted somewhere: "The flesh, alas, is sad and I have read all the books." It was true about the books, but her flesh wouldn't be sad tonight, no matter how cold it was, and how much she reflected and wondered and mourned.

The rapport she and Hope had seemed to establish with their mother a few months back had faded. She hadn't kissed her and thought she never would again. Whatever burden her father had carried through life, her mother should have helped lighten it. Sarah was sure she hadn't. She had left him to bear it unhappily alone while pursuing, like the woman in *Hand to Mouth,* her own selfish and petty interests.

Overnight, her heart had hardened against Ursula

and it was with wonder and some self-disgust that she looked back on her journey of the evening before across the moor, when she had speculated on the single state of Stefan and her mother and had considered the possibility of bringing them together. The deceased husband's brother. Once, and not so long ago, historically speaking, marriage between them would have been against the law, would have counted in some bizarre way as incest.

She had nothing to say to Ursula and said nothing. In the afternoon, a rather wonderful thing happened. Vicky phoned. She sounded embarrassed and rather nervous. Adam Foley was down for the weekend and wanted to join them in the pub, but she had wondered how Sarah would feel—he was for some reason so antagonistic to her, could be so rude—and if it would spoil Sarah's evening, she, Vicky (her voice strengthening and growing indignant), was quite prepared to call him back and tell him no.

"I'll be fine," Sarah said, and she grew tense with excitement. "I don't mind, you know. I hope I'm tougher than that."

The outrageous dressing was becoming a habit. She no longer had so many doubts. This time, she painted her mouth blue as well as her fingernails. She plundered Hope's wardrobe for black stockings, not tights, a skintight miniskirt that would show those stocking tops if she bent over. The shoes, with four-inch heels, were her own. She couldn't imagine why she had bought them but was glad now that she had. It would be better if her hair were extravagantly long or shorn to her shapely skull, but that couldn't be helped now.

It was still only half-past six. She sat in her bedroom, reading the one book of her father's his house now held, the copy she had brought with her, *Purple of Cassius*. His family was in there—she knew that now—not only Chloe Rule, who was his mother, but Peter, who must be Stefan as a child and perhaps James as an adult, Catherine, who was an amalgam of Margaret and Mary, and the strict God-fearing neighbor, who was another version of Jacob Manley, another face of Joseph.

It wasn't possible to concentrate on what she was reading. Sexual desire drives out everything else, she thought, takes over, fills the body and expels the mind, turns the blood into some steamy substance, changes the heartbeat, sets the skin on fire.

Ursula looked at her mouth and her shoes, said nothing. She said nothing at the sight of her bent over at the drinks cupboard with her stocking tops showing. But when Sarah poured two inches of whiskey into a tumbler and took a swig of it, she did speak.

"Sarah, are you sure that's wise when you're going to drive to Barnstaple?"

"I can take care of myself," said Sarah. "Don't you worry about me."

Tyger wasn't there. Rosie had a new man, Neil, or perhaps he was just a new companion for the evening. From the moment she got there, from before she got there, Sarah was afraid Adam wouldn't come.

That Rosie had said he would made no difference. Not coming after all might only be the next step in the game of tease and rudeness, disappointment and renewed expectation, the ultimate playing of hard to get.

She kept to whiskey. Her mouth left a blue imprint on the glass. After half an hour, she went to the ladies' room and, looking at herself in the mirror, thought she looked like someone who has been too long in a cold swimming pool, white-faced, lilac-lipped. When she got back to the table, she told herself, he would be there. She delayed, pushing her fingers through her already-tangled hair, applying more blue lipstick. But when she got back to the table, he would be there. He wasn't. Vicky had begun talking about where they should go on to. Barnstaple was such a hopeless place. Why didn't they all move to London? If they were in London, where lucky Sarah lived and lucky Adam lived, there would be a hundred places to go to; there would be infinite choice. Someone suggested a wine bar that stayed open till midnight. Someone else came up with five fresh drinks on a tray. Alexander said, "Why not eat here?" and everyone started consulting the menu. Sarah couldn't face food.

Their plates came, the usual pub possibilities, a plowman's, fish and chips, chicken and chips, all crowded onto the too-small table with sauce bottles and a basket of chopped-up French bread. Sarah picked at the bread, poured herself more wine, then more. She began thinking of what to do if he didn't come. It was nearly ten. She hadn't spoken for an hour, apart from saying yes and no. If he didn't come, it would just be a repetition of last week. But she couldn't face the lonely drive back, the dark house, her mother there and not her father.

Perhaps there was something Adam expected her to do. Go to the cottage, ring the doorbell, be insulted by him, turned away, then meet five minutes later outside in the dark. Or perhaps he was driving her to do the dreadful thing, the humiliating thing, go home and try again the next week and the next, be driven to phone him in London. But how long could she do that? And wouldn't such compliance with his wishes defeat the object, since it was antagonism and hostility that he desired as much as she?

She looked up and saw him come in by the side door. In a single moment, a second, her fear and doubt were gone. Heat flooded her, rushed up to her head, so that the beating blood sounded in her ears like the waves of the sea. One rational thought did come, that it was strange, inexplicable, how the sight of someone, not his voice or his touch or his presence but just the distant sight of him, could bring such arousal. She was almost afraid of her own body, so nearly out of control, behaving as it should not now but only later, in his arms, under his hands. For the first time that she could remember, she was aware of gasping involuntarily. Alexander looked at her, raised his eyebrows.

She kept herself sane enough to be thankful they must think her reaction one of trepidation at Adam's arrival. He came up and stood at the already-full table, said a general "Hi." He didn't look at her; she knew he wouldn't. Rosie moved to the left, Vicky to the right; he pulled up a chair between them and sat down.

"This is Neil," Rosie said.

"Hi, Neil."

"We were talking about where to go on to."

"You always are," he said.

"Right. Have you got any ideas?"

"There isn't anywhere."

"There's the club. There's that new wine bar."

"It won't affect me, anyway," he said. "I can't stop. I only came in for a quick drink."

He turned upon her a cold, indifferent glance. She returned it. She was so sick with desire that she wondered if her legs would carry her. When he had drunk that drink, he would go and she would have to follow him. The licensee would call time. Suppose she couldn't get up, couldn't walk? His cold eyes met hers again. He wanted her to begin. She was to start the exchange that would grow more and more acrimonious, insulting, unbearably exciting.

She said, surprised that she had a voice, "Have you got a date, Adam?"

"What?"

She repeated it, "I asked you if you'd got a date." He shook his head. It was a movement that implied the impossibility of understanding her, the total mystery of her thought processes. The others had become tense. To her astonishment, she felt Rosie reach for her hand under the table and squeeze it. Adam did the entirely unexpected. He felt in one of the pockets of his voluminous greatcoat and pulled out a book, a paperback, which he threw onto the table. A glass fell over and red wine trickled between the plates, dripped onto the floor. Vicky started mopping it up with a handful of paper napkins.

The book was one of her father's, *Phantom Listeners.*

It was dog-eared, the cover with its design of huddled ghosts alarmed by the dawn, curled at the corners and bruised. The wine had splashed its spine, leaving blood-colored drops on the black moth. Sarah put her hand up to her mouth, as if warding off a blow.

"I picked it up off a stall in the flea market," he said, "for thirty pee. If any of you want to read it, you're welcome. If you can get through it. I couldn't." He slowly turned his head and let his eyes travel from her face, where a blush was mounting, down her body. "You, of course, will already have had that dubious experience."

She was stunned, had nothing to say, felt the tightening pressure of Rosie's unwanted, unneeded hand.

"The renowned novelist was something of a pompous old git, wouldn't you say? Something of a pretentious nerd? I suppose there's a kind of distinction in writing nineteen books, each one more boring than the last."

Alexander said, "Adam."

Simultaneously, Vicky said, "Look, this is embarrassing. Didn't you know Gerald Candless was Sarah's dad?"

"There wouldn't be much point in saying it if he wasn't, would there? She doesn't look much like him, though. He had a face like a lizard with whiskers. It's a wise child that knows its own father, isn't it?"

"Of course he was my father, you bastard," Sarah said.

"Charming. Thank you. I hardly suppose it's anything you're proud of. I'd keep quiet about it if I were you."

"Adam! Stop it." Rosie was on her feet. "We can't do this anymore. We can't have you here with us like this. It's awful; it's unbelievable. . . ."

"What, because I tell a woman what she knows already, that the darling of the literary establishment was a clapped-out hack who wrote shit? Who called it art and had the cunning to get others to do the same?"

Sarah wrenched her hand free from Rosie's. She got up, pulled her father's sheepskin around her, and, hardly knowing why, picked up the paperback from the table. Holding it in her two hands, she made for the side door to the car park. Vicky's voice called out, "Sarah, wait . . ." She didn't turn her head.

Pain spread across her shoulders and up into her head, settling on the top of her skull like a too-tight hat. It had been hot in there and she was shivering.

The night was damp and dark, a black mist hanging above the cars, leaving water on their surfaces in clustered glittering pustules. She unlocked the car and sat in the driver's seat. Her breath misted up the glass, enclosing her in opaque walls.

She knew it would be no more than five minutes before he opened the passenger door and got in beside her. He would be there in five minutes. It was, in fact, three minutes. The interior light came on and she saw her face in the rearview mirror, ravaged, aged, the mouth blue, as from hypothermia.

He got into the car, closed the door, put his hand on her knee. The light went out and deep darkness came. He took her hand and touched the palm with his tongue.

As if she was very tired, as if she was ill, she said in a weary voice, "It's no use." She took her hand away and pushed his hand away. "I can't. Not tonight. Not ever."

"What do you mean?"

"You know."

"I do not."

"The things you said."

She could see his face only as a vague blur, but she caught the gleam of an eye.

"That was a game," he said. "You know that. That was the game we play. You like it; I like it. It turns us on."

"No."

"You liked it before. It's happened before." He

was urgent. He was panicking. "For God's sake. I didn't mean any of it. I love his writing. I loved that book. You must know I didn't mean those things."

She tried to be calm, articulate, partly succeeded. "You said them. I don't suppose you did mean them. But that doesn't matter. They were said and they can't be unsaid. I would never forget them. I will never forget. I can't help it."

"I'm sorry," he said. "I apologize. I'm deeply, truly sorry." He sounded it. He sounded how she would have hated him to sound at the beginning of it, humble, penitent, afraid. "Please let me unsay them. Come back all I said, can't we say that?"

"I would if I could." What's done cannot be undone, she thought.

"Then say it. You can."

"I can't. It was the one place you shouldn't have stabbed, that's all."

"Sarah, I don't understand you."

"I'm going home now. Good-bye."

He began to protest. She got out of the car, went around the front, opened the passenger door, and stood there, waiting. It took him a moment, but he got out. She didn't look at him, though he was quite clearly visible out here in the lamplight. Back in the car, she started the engine, pressed the switch to demist the windows. By the time she had driven out into the street, he was gone; he was nowhere.

Her head hurt behind her eyes. She needed some relief for pain, but she didn't know what. Rain began when she was halfway home. The rhythmic swish of the wipers passing to and fro, to and fro, signified a dreadful meaninglessness. She carried the book into the house. It was only a few yards, but she and the book were soaked. She hadn't cried for years, but she cried when the front door was closed. She dropped onto the floor in the hall, weeping in the dark, her father's book, a wet, soggy pulp, pressed against her face.

27

What did Scheherezade do after she had told the thousand and first story? Did safety kill the creative impulse in her? Of course not. She began to write. One day the stories she wrote down will come to light and they will be a great improvement on the first thousand because security nourishes talent better than peril.

—HAMADRYAD

THICK FOG PERVADED Sarah's dream, but she was somewhere in the country, not on the beach, and there was no color. It was like a black-and-white film, or gray and dark gray. They walked toward each other, she and Adam Foley, emerging out of the fog, met, stood apart. He said, "I never said those things. That was my double saying them." "You haven't got a double," she said, and she felt nothing for him, no desire, no challenge. The fog had condensed and clustered on her arms and hands. She looked down and saw that her whole body glittered with water-drops like glass from a shattered windscreen.

"He hasn't a double. There's no one like him," her father's voice said. Then she saw her father where Adam had been. She knew it was her father, but he was young; he looked like Stefan and perhaps also like someone she had never known, someone who died horribly before she was born. "I put it behind me, or I tried," her Stefan-Desmond-father said. "But it was always in the mist that I saw him."

She was lonely, with no remedy. She asked herself if she wanted Adam and had to answer honestly that she didn't; she never wanted to see him again. The house would be sold and she would never go back; she would never see Rosie and Alexander and Vicky again. Or the white mist that came in from the sea. Or the rhododendrons and the white razor shells, the black mussel-shell sand and the island lying becalmed on the flat gray water.

Did she have any friends? Masses of acquaintances, yes. Other lecturers. A sister and a sister's partner. An uncle, who had his own life, his own children. An aunt she would never meet and cousins she had no wish to know. As usual—and she acknowledged this—she left her mother till last, had almost forgotten her mother.

The file on Gerald Candless was complete. Or as complete as she could manage. She leafed through the material, newspaper photocopies, her notes, photographs she had brought from Lundy View House, synopses she had made of her father's books and her own attempts at beginning her book, Jason Thague's reports, the Candless family tree, the Ryan family tree. She knew everything about him except why. She knew of his childhood, his parents, his stepfather and his brothers and sisters, his school days, his first job and his war service, his job after the war, his moving out of his family's home, and his disappearance.

What she didn't know was why he had disappeared and why he had taken on that new identity.

Her memoir would have to be written without that knowledge. With a week to go before her new term started, she sat down at the word processor early in the morning and began. When she had produced two thousand words, she broke off and wrote a letter to Robert Postle. She told him she was sorry about the long delay, that she had had to do research, but now she had made a serious beginning and had set herself a deadline of May. The end of May, she added.

While she was writing Carlyon-Brent's address on the envelope, her mother phoned. Sarah thought she must be at Lundy View House and asked if it was snowing. Somewhere or other, she had seen snow forecast for the West Country. Ursula said no, not unless it also was in Kentish Town. They sorted it out and Sarah was more interested by the coincidence of her mother's being in Bloomsbury while she was addressing a letter to the same place than by her reason for the call.

But then it occurred to her that Ursula ought to know what she had discovered, should have information about all these new relations. To be fair, she should have advance warning of what she would read in the memoir.

"Look, if you're in London for a bit why don't

you come over here tomorrow evening? I'll get Hope, too. I've got something to tell you."

It came to her that mothers always took that to mean a forthcoming engagement or even a marriage. Something sexual, anyway. Sarah was so preoccupied with thinking she would never be sexual again that she didn't take much notice of Ursula's saying she had something to tell her, too.

"You haven't sold the house?"

"Hardly. It's only been on the market two weeks."

Hope arrived with her head tied up in a scarf because Fabian had said her fur hat made her look like Boris Yeltsin.

"I'm sure Ma will think I'm going to announce my engagement."

"You're not, are you?"

"Whom would I get engaged to?"

Opening the bottle of wine she had brought, Hope said that she and Fabian were thinking of getting engaged.

"You always are. You've been thinking of it for ten years."

Hope sat down, looking closely into her glass as if into a crystal ball. "If we got engaged, it would be a sort of signal for us to move in together. And then, maybe, in a year or two, if it works out, we might get married."

"You really believe in rushing into things, don't you?"

Ursula arrived, wearing the kind of fur hat that might not have looked good on Hope but suited Ursula. As far as Sarah could tell, she was dressed in new clothes from head to foot. Her hair had been cut once more, and cut a good deal better than they had done it in Barnstaple.

She, too, had brought a bottle of wine, but hers was champagne.

"Have you sold the house or something?" said Hope.

"I've had an offer. The agent phoned me this morning."

"I don't know what the champagne's for." Sarah had kissed her mother. More because, as she told herself afterward, she smelled so wonderfully of Biagiotti's Roma than for any other reason. "But can we have it in favor of your wine, Hope?"

"If you look at the bottle," said Hope, "you'll see you've drunk all my wine already."

Their father had been very good at opening champagne. He had always done so without spills or explosions. Hope managed fairly well, fetching a cloth from the kitchen to mop up the table.

"I want to tell you what I found out about Dad."

"It's not horrid, is it?" Her sister, Sarah thought, looked just as she had twenty years ago and more, when a picture anticipated in a book threatened terrors or when one of their father's stories took a turn around a frightening bend. He had always promised nothing bad, nothing to alarm, and always kept his promise. "It's not going to upset me?"

"I don't think so. I'm sure not."

She couldn't give his guarantees. But she told them the whole of it. Hope's mobile face registered every emotion. Once she put up a hand to cover her mouth, once put her head in both hands. She made a little sound that might have been distress or might have been protest. But Ursula sat impassive. She hadn't touched her champagne. Sarah drank hers and had more, aware by then that her voice was thickening.

Hope said, the words bursting out of her, "But why? Why did he?"

"That's what I don't know."

"But you must know." Hope spoke to her mother as if she were a policeman and Ursula a suspect in an interview room. "You can't have been married to him for thirty-five years or whatever and he not have told you."

"No. Yes, I should say, I was. I never suspected he wasn't who he said he was. Why should I?"

"The thing is," said Sarah, "shall I tell Robert Postle about it or not?"

"Tell Postle? Why the hell should you?"

"I'm writing a memoir of Dad, remember? He was Dad's publisher and he's mine. That's why. Do I tell him in advance that Dad was really called John Ryan and all the rest of it or do I wait till the memoir's finished?"

Ursula said nothing. She listened in silence. She picked up her champagne glass and drank a little from it. Reaching for the bottle, Hope said, "If you tell him now, it'll get out. He'll be very excited—he's bound to be—and he'll drop a word to someone. If only to that wife of his. Or a secretary will see it. Don't forget *Less Is More* is due to be published in a few weeks. Somehow, there'll be a leak—there always is—and it'll get into one of those diary columns in a newspaper and we'll all have reporters on the doorstep."

"I think that's a bit unfair to Robert, but I see what you mean. Not a word, then, until he gets the manuscript. Is that agreed, Ma?"

"Yes, of course, if that's what you want. The reporters will turn up when it's published, though."

"We'll all be prepared by then," said Sarah, without explaining how they would be prepared, without knowing how.

She sighed. She had expected the telling to be a relief, to make her feel better, but it hadn't. She was aware, suddenly, that her sister and her mother would go away soon, would leave her alone; she would once more be alone, and she had never felt quite like that before. The drink that always helped hadn't helped. When they were gone and the bottles were empty, she would find what drink she had in the flat. She would put herself out for the night.

Ursula said, "I said I'd got something to tell you, Sarah. You and Hope."

Had she? Sarah couldn't remember. She must mean the offer on the house. Was that what the champagne was for?

"Do you remember when you brought me to London that time I told you I'd be seeing a friend?"

"That's right. I took you to a hotel. Where you are now."

"No, I'm not there. I'm staying with someone, that friend. You said, 'Where does she live?' and I said, 'It's not a she; it's a he.' Don't you remember?"

Sarah nodded, because it was easier than arguing.

"I'm staying with him. No, I'm living with him. His name's Sam Fleming and I'm going to live with him. Perhaps in his place or perhaps we'll buy somewhere together when the house is sold. I don't know. But I'm living with him—now."

"Why didn't you tell us?"

"I often tried to tell you, Sarah, but you didn't listen. You don't listen to me. I tried to tell you when you took me to the hotel. And when he phoned me and you answered. So I thought in the end that I'd have to come here and tell you both. Like this. And I have."

Her mother had grown quite breathless. She was flushed. She said, "I didn't mean that about you not listening to me. I know you have your own worries and things to think about. Why should you listen? Anyway, I've got you both listening now. I want you to meet Sam soon. He wanted to come with me tonight, but I said no, not this time."

Sarah was so intent on her mother's flushed face, her mother's unexpected awkwardness, and, above all, her words, that she didn't look at Hope. She had, for the moment, forgotten Hope's existence. So that when Hope yelled, she jumped.

"You can't! You can't do that!"

Ursula retreated a little into her chair. Her warding-off hand came up. Sarah thought for the first time how often in the past she had made that particular gesture, but always at something their father had said. Now it was to defend herself from Hope.

"I can't see how it will affect you much, Hope. You knew I was leaving the house; you were happy about that."

"I wasn't happy!"

"You were content with the arrangement. I'm going to live in London with a man I'm very fond of. I shall be near you; we could see each other. . . ."

"See you? I never want to see you again as long as I live. You were married to *Daddy*. Have you forgotten that? To *Daddy!*"

Ursula's awkwardness gone, her flutteriness gone, she said in a strong, bitter voice, "You know nothing about it. What do you know about other people's marriages? No one knows what goes on in a marriage. You know nothing, *nothing.*"

"I know I hate you." The tears streamed down Hope's face. "You were Daddy's wife, and now you're going to live with this man. He must be awful to want you. You should be dead like Daddy. You should be dead instead of Daddy."

She was eight years old again. Her face had puffed up into childish contours. Sarah was frightened. She was at a loss, but she got up and went to her sister, her arms out. Hope struck out at her.

"You're not to!" she screamed. "I forbid you to do it. Daddy forbids you."

"As you say, Hope, your father is dead," Ursula said.

Hope pulled on her coat, stumbling, scrubbing the hair out of her eyes, wiping at her eyes with her fists. Sarah did nothing. She didn't speak. Ursula lay back against the cushions, white-faced. Hope got the door open and pulled it shut behind her, crashed down the stairs. The front door slamming rocked the house.

Sarah rubbed her arm where Hope had punched her. She looked at her mother, wanting her to sit up and smile and say something about how childish Hope could be and she didn't know what had got into her and it would all soon blow over. But Ursula said none of those things. She looked deathly ill. The brightness of her appearance when she had first arrived, the gloss of new clothes and freshly done hair and, yes, of happiness surely, all that had faded and she looked stricken. It was as if lightning had passed through her, felled her, deprived her of some vital force.

"Ma," Sarah said, and then said, "Mother."

Ursula moved. She raised her shoulders, dropped them, made a wincing face. Then she shook herself, or perhaps she shuddered. "I must go."

"Look, she didn't—" Sarah had been going to say that Hope didn't mean it, but she remembered that was what Adam had said, and his saying it had made no difference. "I mean, she did mean it at the time, but she'll get over it. Are you okay?"

"No. But I will be. One day. I, too, will get over it. I must go."

"Would you like me to call you a taxi?"

All at once, Ursula became articulate, calm. "I can get a taxi in the street, Sarah. I don't think that's difficult, though I hardly know, I've been here so seldom. But I can get a taxi or I can walk to the tube station because I don't want to stay here any longer. I don't want to talk anymore, not now. There's just one thing I want to say to you. I've never said it and perhaps I shouldn't now, but I'm going to. I was deeply unhappy with your father—it was no marriage; it was nothing. He rejected me in every way after Hope was born, and if he never abused me physically, he—he struck me daily with his tongue. I'll go now."

Sarah stared at her. She got up mechanically and helped her mother into her coat. Ursula turned, her face close to Sarah's, her eyes tired and sad. Sarah put her lips up to a cheek that was cold and rigid. The kiss wasn't returned. Nothing more was said until they were downstairs, Sarah realizing too late that she had offered her mother no congratulations, no good wishes for her happiness. It was too late now.

"Look, Ma, I'll be in touch. I don't even know where you're living. I haven't got a phone number."

"I was going to give you that, both of you," said Ursula. "It can wait awhile, don't you think? Good night."

Upstairs in the flat, Sarah looked down into the street from the window. It was early yet, only nine. She saw Ursula walking along under the bare tree branches and then the rear lights of a taxi as it came out of a side turning. Her mother was out of sight by

480

then, too far away for Sarah to see if she got into the taxi or not, and when the doorbell rang five minutes later, it seemed as if she must have come back. She had forgotten something or regretted her parting words. Sarah picked up the intercom, said, "I'll open the door for you, Mother."

There was silence, then a crackle, then a voice said, "It's not your mother; it's Jason."

"I thought maybe you wouldn't let me in," he said.

Like her mother, he had had his hair cut. He looked healthier, as if he had been eating. The spots had gone. He handed her an envelope.

"It's your check. I'm giving it back. I didn't do the work, so you shouldn't be paying me."

"Do you want a drink?" she said.

"I brought a bottle of wine. It's what's in my pocket—I haven't suddenly gotten fat. I've got a job—well, it's part-time, on account of I've gone back to school."

"You've gone back to college?"

"I will have. When term starts. Not in Ipswich, here in London. Have some wine?"

She had had too much already. She shook her head and he smiled, his eyebrows up. "You keep it for tomorrow then. Did you find out why your dad changed his name?"

She told him about Stefan, showed him the file, then the two thousand words she had written. He said, "There isn't going to be any more to discover, is there?"

"I don't think so."

"You're never going to know why. D'you want to know what my nan said when I told her? She said that he must have done something terrible to a member of his family. Or one of them had done something terrible to him."

Sarah nodded. She said in a stifled tone, "If anyone had ever told me I'd be pleased to see someone who called his grandmother 'my nan,' I'd never have believed them."

"You're a snob, Sarah."

"I know."

He laughed. "I'd better go. I'm still living in Ipswich for another week, and my last train's at eleven."

She hesitated, thought of them all suddenly, her dead father, her mother, Hope, Adam Foley's hurtful insults, and she said in a small voice, not looking at him, "Would you like to stay the night?"

28

---

*Plagiarism is more often the outcome of
desperation than of villainy.*
> —THE BRIDEGROOM'S DOORS

MANUSCRIPTS FROM TWO OF HIS AUTHORS arrived on
Robert Postle's desk on the same day in the first week
of August. The one that came through an agent, he
hadn't expected for a month or more; the other, which
was sent to him directly, he had almost given up hope
of ever seeing.

Thankful Child: A Memoir of My Father seemed
about twice as long as *The Spoiled Forest,* which
would suit Robert's requirements very well. Titus
Romney's manuscript was the novel expected as the
second under the terms of a two-book contract. At
first glance, it looked as if it wouldn't make two hundred pages, but Robert was gratified to note its early
arrival just the same. When last he had spoken to
Romney on the subject, the author had told him he
was bereft of ideas and suffering from writer's block.
But that, Robert reflected, not altogether happily, had
been nearly a year ago. Time flew.

He didn't much care for Sarah's title. She was

playing with that line from *Lear,* of course. "How sharper than a serpent's tooth it is/To have a thankless child!" A couple of months ago, she had hinted to him that the memoir would make a sensational impact. Her father hadn't really been called Gerald Candless; he had changed his name and identity at the age of twenty-five. There had been a lot more in the same vein, but Robert wondered, as he had wondered at the time, if Gerald Candless had been sufficiently a celebrity for the tabloids to get excited about it. Perhaps. It would depend on what she had found out and had written. Anyway, that would be a problem for Carlyon-Brent's publicity department, not him.

Ursula had sold Lundy View House and was living with a bookseller in London. Robert had expected to meet the man at Hope's wedding, but he wasn't there. More to the point, Ursula wasn't there. If some people asked why not, Robert hadn't been among them, but a woman called Pauline told him Hope had fallen out with her mother and the breach wasn't mended yet.

"Personally, I'd have expected Auntie Ursula to show more respect for my uncle's memory."

Then Sarah had introduced him to a man she called Stefan, who seemed rather too old for her, but that was all right, because, later, while she was explaining to him yet again that the book wouldn't be done by May, after all, a much younger chap turned up who was obviously her boyfriend. One of those awful names, Gareth or Darren—no, Jason.

That was when she said the memoir would be sensational and the Jason chap laughed and put his arm around her and said that was an understatement. Now that he had the manuscript there before him, he began to feel apprehensive. No, that was an understatement. He was afraid of it. Of course, this wasn't an unfamiliar feeling; he was quite used to having it. Publishers are habitually afraid of possible libel, defamation, ludicrous mistakes, gross inaccuracies, and blatant falsehood from their authors. Not to mention plagiarism. It seemed possible that all those causes of fear might be found in Sarah's book, and therefore he was afraid.

The two cardboard folders that contained it, fastened together by an elastic band, looked innocuous lying there. Only paper, after all, five hundred sheets of paper with words printed on them. But paper and print always look innocuous. Nothing in this world was more deceptive when you considered what the printed word could and did do.

He was going away on holiday on Saturday. With his wife and those of the children who still lived at home. Carlyon-Brent's senior editors were expected to take their main holidays in August, the silly season. One of those manuscripts he would read now and the other take with him to the Luberon. Which?

Perhaps obviously, one read the shorter first, the less welcome, the one to be gotten out of the way. Using a phrase of Freddie Cyprian's, he said to himself that a couple of hours would wrap it up. Then Sarah's, later. On a hotel terrace in the warm shade or at a table outside a café . . . Was there a photograph in existence of Gerald with his two girls when they were small? He seemed to remember one Carlyon-Brent had in its archives. It would do admirably for the jacket.

He put Titus Romney's *The Spoiled Forest* in his briefcase and after dinner, after the nine o'clock news on television, took the manuscript out of its cardboard folder and began to read.

29

1

The forest might be green and wild to the north,
a real woodland of grassy dells, but here it was
dusty, it was shabby, and even in spring the trees
looked weary of the struggle to remain standing.
Along a path, into the depths, it grew quieter, a
little more like the country. The sound of traffic
from the conjoined roads faded; the light was left
behind. The sky was a luminous gray, not really
dark, a mass of broken, shining, variable cloud,
from which the moon emerged and retreated and
appeared again.

John was quite near home. Both his own
home, where his mother was and his brothers and
sisters, and the house he lodged in. One house
was in a street half a mile to the west, the other
a little farther away to the south. He decided he
was far enough away. They wouldn't come here,
any of them. Only one sort of human being came
here after dark, the sort he had come to find.

The directness of this thought caught him up,
frightened him. He told himself he should not

have put it so boldly, even to himself. He had come merely to look around, to see if what he had heard said was true. On the paper, in the office and the press, the rumors moved around. He had no idea where they came from, but they were there, mentioned by the older men with worldly wisdom or sniggered at. Not, of course, if girls were present. He had listened to the stories and he, too, had sniggered or cast up his eyes in the required way. But he remembered, he stored up his information.

The forest, they said. Up by the reservoir. Forest Road, Grove Hill, around the back there. That's their stamping ground. You go up there, lad, and you want to keep your back to a tree.

Only he didn't want to. He didn't want to express it, either. He had just come to take a look around. Because it was a possibility for the future, something to think about and consider the pros and cons, whether this way of life was for him. The others were not possibilities. Not the baths—probably not the baths—and never, never, the other choice. As soon as he'd known about those subterranean places, as soon as that boy at school had told him, he had stopped ever using a public lavatory. He never went near one after that. It was no problem in the navy—there were other problems, God knows!—but since becoming a reporter . . . He always had to go home or use the one in the office or go into a pub, or if all else failed, go behind a tree somewhere.

He had come, here, to the only option. Now he was in the depths of this triangle of spoiled forest, in the middle probably, approaching the little cluster of ponds, he asked himself how it would be for him if nothing happened. Would he feel relief or disappointment? Must it even be one or the other? What he could not face was going on as he was. Taking Sheila about, squeezing his eyes shut before he kissed her, imagining always something quite other, fantasizing. Looking at his brothers, envying James his *normalcy,* his desire for his pregnant bride, envying Stephen for being still a child. And what of Desmond—what did he feel for him? Speculation. Doubt and certainty. Wondering always if Desmond, so young still, so handsome, might be the same way inclined?

It was sequestered in here, yet it was open, the trees scattered, the ponds so many bright eyes, looking back at the sky. The seat, no more than a bench, was in the open but with the enclosing woodland behind it. You go up there, lad, you want to keep your back to a tree. It was silent and still, no wind, but he was aware of movement somewhere. Nothing he could hear—rather, a vibration through the earth, a sense of not being alone. He might have been imagining it.

He sat down on the bench. For the first time, now, he looked about him, really looked. Across the water, behind him through the trees and between their trunks into the darkness, ahead, up to where the path met an intersecting ride. The moon had sailed out into a clear patch of sky. Up by the ride was another bench and a man was sitting on it. A person, anyway, but it wouldn't be a woman. Not a woman in here, alone, at night.

After a moment or two he turned his gaze away from the figure on the other bench. He lit a cigarette. He would give himself ten minutes, the time it would take him to smoke that cigarette. Then he would go. Not to his room but back to the house down by the Midland arches, see them all, lie down to sleep on the settee, and, before he slept, decide. What to do. Never to go out with Sheila again, that was the first thing, the kind thing. It wasn't fair on her, the way he had been behaving, because he could never, never . . . Never again. Those times in the Philippines came back to him and he banished the memory by a physical effort of clenching his hands, opening them, pressing his fingers against his head. He drew long and deeply on his cigarette.

He would go to the doctor. Not his doctor, of course, not the doctor where Mother went and the boys and the children. Whatever doctors might say about the sacredness of patients' confidences, he would never trust to it. If anyone told his mother, he would kill himself. Another thought to be suppressed, crushed, deadened. He would go to a doctor not in the National Health and pay him and the doctor would send him somewhere to be cured. The cigarette was more than half-smoked. He looked across the water, the smooth surface of the ponds, each of them reflecting a picture of that tumbled sky. And then he became aware that the man on the other bench had moved.

How was he aware of it? He hadn't looked. He had sensed only a disturbance of the space to his left, just as earlier he had been warned of another's presence by a vibration through the earth. Now he looked. The man was coming this way. Perhaps he should go. He put out his cigarette, ground the stub into the clayey soil, looked down at his own knees. The man would come up to him and ask him something, ask him for a light most likely. And he would get out his lighter and snap on the flame and in it see a young face. . . .

Instead, the man sat down on the bench, the far end from him. John looked at him and quickly away. The clouds had massed and darkened and the moon had gone behind them. He couldn't see much. When the man lit a cigarette, the flame seemed very bright. John lit another. They sat at opposite ends of the bench, smoking, and John thought again, When this cigarette is finished, I'll go; I'll leave then and go home.

The man leaned back. He left his cigarette in his mouth, hanging from his lip. John's eyes were accustomed now to the new darkness and the light from the two cigarettes helped. He saw the man begin massaging himself. His eyes were closed, so he couldn't see John looking, but John knew he knew he was looking. He saw him put his hands inside his trousers and those hands slowly moving, expertly moving, he thought. He didn't know what to do, though do something he must. Going home now was impossible. It was as if to go home now would be an abnegation of everything, a denial of all hope and possibility, an absolute death. He must do something, so he began to do what the man was doing.

He had done it before but never like this. Never in company. Never had he even dreamed of this, of two men sitting at opposite ends of a bench, their cigarettes extinguished, the silence more profound and telling than any sound could be, their hands rhythmically busy. The man had turned his head and opened his eyes. They gazed at each other.

"Let's go over there."

John got up and followed the man in among the trees. He would take the other's lead; he would do nothing on his own initiative; he would learn. The man was young, in his early twenties, ordinary-looking, thin, smelling of soap. The voice had been rough working class. John thought he would kiss him. That was how you began with girls, with a kiss, always with a kiss.

Dark in the wood, warmer. Eyes looking at him for a short moment, what light there was caught on their glassy convex surfaces. Then the lids falling, hands touching him, no kiss. He began to do with his hands what the man was

doing with his. Prostitutes don't kiss, they say—
kissing is too intimate—but somehow he knew
that wasn't the reason the man didn't kiss him;
there must be some other. He thought those
things while he could think, before the power of
thought slid away into a deep mindless well of
sensual pleasure.

2

The world was a different place. He was more
alive than he had ever been, and more afraid. One
evening in the spoiled forest had done that. There
could be more evenings, and once he went back,
looking for the man whose name he didn't know.
He sat on the bench and looked at the water and
at last someone did come. People came. Two
policemen.

They were walking side by side. They stopped
by the bench and one of them came over to him.
"You waiting for someone?" the policeman said,
and when John said he was just sitting there, he
was just out for the evening, the policeman said,
"Get along home now, son." The other one said,
"You've been warned."

John went home. Later on, he understood he
had been lucky. They had been kind to him. The
police used agents provocateurs. If they had
known why he was there and what he hoped for,
they might easily have set him up with one of

their own. For John knew now that if he had met a man and that man asked him back to his room, he would have gone. Happily, delightedly. But the two policemen had only warned him and sent him home.

It wasn't long afterward that he was sent to report a case at quarter sessions. Two men, one very young, the other in his fifties, charged with gross indecency. While awaiting trial, the older man had attempted suicide in his cell. Both were sent to prison, though the offenses had been committed in the total privacy of the older man's isolated house.

One of the results of this case and others like it was that John's editor set him on researching homosexual activity. It alarmed John at first because he thought he must have been picked for a specific reason, something about his appearance or speech, some mannerism unknown to him but which betrayed him. But he was soon reassured. The choice was made on grounds of experience and his good qualities as a reporter alone. Some of the others in the office commiserated with him and there was more advice about keeping his back to the wall. One of them had recently interviewed a biologist who had produced homosexuality in male rats by segregating a group of them from females. This proved that men only wanted to be "queer" when they didn't mix with women. Everyone in the office, including John, fell about laughing.

Perhaps only John's was genuine derision. He had tried mixing with women but preferred now not to think of it, to forget it. He started his research by going to coffee bars the editor said he'd heard queers frequented. The only queer he had ever spoken to was the man in the forest and then only to say "Yes" and "Thanks" and "Good-bye." He wondered if he would know one when he saw him, but in fact he had no difficulty. The two men at the next table were what someone later told him were known as "screamers." It was easy to see why. They had shrill voices, affected manners, and made exasperated gestures when they talked. John wondered if he ever made a similar impression on people, and he resolved to be more careful, to restrain his laughter, to keep his voice down and be more low-key.

At home with his mother and stepfather and the children, it was a different world. In that house, in spite of the overcrowding, everything was orderly, neat, bright. It seemed always as if truth were spoken and words transparent in their honesty. Anyone who derided family life, called it, for instance, a cover-up of ugly secrets, skeletons in cupboards, should have to come to see their family. More than anything in the world, he would have liked to make such a family for himself. One day. To have that sanctuary, that peace, the absolute safety.

All that was strong and powerful and big about his mother was her physical size. Her spirit—

495

once, he would have said her soul—was gentle and tender, timid and innocent. He was as nearly sure as he could be that she had never heard of men loving men, that if told, she would barely believe it. Experts—so-called experts, doctors, psychologists—were saying that it was strong, dominant women who made their sons into homosexuals. They ought to see his mother, humble, quiet, compassionate, deferring to the male viewpoint, yet she had two sons who were queers.

He was sure Desmond was. Just as he knew his eldest brother was not and his youngest brother was not. The youngest was only fourteen, but still he could tell. He would have been able to tell if he were only eight or only six. Did it matter? Not if it could be hidden and the hiding be maintained, if not forever, for years. So that his mother need never know and Joseph need never know. In the climate in which they all lived, keeping it secret was obligatory, anyway. He was beginning to find out that it would be preferable for him to have syphilis or be certified as mad than to admit his homosexuality.

3

The consultant in contagious diseases he went to interview at the local hospital called himself a liberal. He told John he was opposed to anything that might curb prostitution because that would turn more men toward homosexuality. John asked him if he thought of homosexuality as an illness and, if so, whether it was one of the diseases he was a specialist in.

"Venereal disease is my subject," the man said none too pleasantly. "But, yes, I do think of inverts as sick men. You notice I call them 'inverts' and not 'perverts.' In my opinion, they are to be pitied, not condemned. Our task is to cure them, not send them to prison."

"How will you do that?"

John really wanted to know. If there was a possibility, he wanted it. In a curious way, from observing him, watching him, he thought Desmond wouldn't want it. But he did. He wanted to feel for Sheila or some other girl, any girl, the desire he had had for the man in the forest.

"How will I do it? I shan't. I'm a physician. We must pin our faith on the psychiatrists. Aversion therapy is the up-and-coming thing."

The psychiatrist John talked to was convinced a failure of family background was responsible. Many homosexuals were fatherless or their mothers didn't know how to be mothers. As a result, boys grew up as feminine souls in male bodies. John thought of his own family, of the mother he thought of as perfect, the woman who had remarried solely, he was sure, to give her children a father.

He wondered what the psychiatrist would say if he told him the truth, if he could possibly imagine telling anyone the truth. But he knew the answer. He would be told it only looked that way to him, that his mother wasn't really passive and gentle, Joseph wasn't really strong and dominant, and the family members weren't really happy, but suppressing their true feelings. That was the way psychiatrists always talked. They had an answer for everything.

Next day, he went back to the coffee bar. The "screamers" weren't there, but other queers were. He could tell. He should have felt at home among them, but he didn't. A woman was staring at the two at a corner table, at their longish hair, their tight trousers and too-sleek sports jackets. John thought, If one were a dwarf and put to live on an island where there were only dwarfs, would one feel better about things or worse? He didn't know. But he knew a solution to all this was possible. If you could live and be yourself and do what you wanted and everyone else accept and even like you and be pleased. Of course it was ridiculous, impossible; it would never happen.

Abnormal, sick, mad, filthy, wicked, resistant to a caring society's desire to cure you, that's what you were and would always be. Why wasn't Desmond weeping and distraught for the blow fate had dealt him? Why was he *happy*?

John ordered a coffee and a cheese roll. Seeing those others affected him in a way far from the editor's intention when he had set him on this assignment. It made him want to go back to the spoiled forest. Of course he couldn't go back there, because police patrolled it. But there were other places, the London parks, Victoria Park, for instance, the nearest one to where he lived. There were public conveniences. He hated the thought of that because it put what he wanted to do on a par with peeing and shitting. Love shouldn't have his mansion in the place of excrement, as someone ought to have written but hadn't.

Almost without knowing it, at least without thinking about it first, he moved his seat to the empty table next to the one where the longhaired men sat. They would think he had only moved to be nearer the window. He ordered another coffee. He was afraid to be seen looking at the men and he only gave them a covert glance, but it was long enough to see that one of them had plucked his eyebrows. Sheila had started doing that, but you could hardly imagine a man . . . John began to feel excited.

He was very near them. He could hear everything they said. One of them was a hairdresser; the other worked in a men's outfitters. They talked about customers and clients and not in the way heterosexuals would have. A sentence made him shiver.

"All those beautiful butch men in there naked."

He hadn't heard everything they said,

evidently. He'd missed what led up to that. They couldn't have meant the hairdresser's or the clothes shop, that was for certain. Then, rapidly, after more overheard words, he knew.

"Take care. They wouldn't let people with permed hair within miles."

"I'll have to grow my eyebrows."

"Oh, do. And we'll go, shall we?"

John didn't stay any longer. He had a curious feeling that he needed air. It had been quite fresh in there, smelling sweetly of coffee and pastries, but he had felt as if he were being choked. He stood outside, taking deep breaths. It was a long time, all of half an hour, before he allowed himself to think coolly of what they had said, the place they had named, the venue they were going to. Where he could go. If they could, why not he, too?

It was the perfect place. Anonymous, they had said. You could be invisible, or almost invisible. And the beauty of it was you could go there for a . . . well, legitimate purpose. Many did. Perhaps most did. Not a park or an open space where the police walked, not a sordid place of excrement. The reverse of that really.

A place of absolute cleanness. Of purity. Nothing you did there could be dirty or squalid because, by definition, all dirt was washed away in those surroundings. There, in that whiteness, you would be whiter than the snow.

The piece he wrote for the paper was too sympathetic, the editor said. It turned homosexuals into misunderstood men or even sick men, putting them on a par with sufferers from a congenital disease. That frightened John. He thought the editor seemed suspicious of him and, rewriting his article, he put in a lot of statistics of the number of men convicted of "grave and degrading" homosexual offenses.

Still, the editor wasn't satisfied. "You don't seem to understand what the filthy buggers do. Do you know, I heard of one of them who put tomato ketchup on his privates to look like a woman with her monthlies."

"You're not asking me to put that in, are you? Aren't we supposed to be a family newspaper?"

"I'm not asking you to put it in, Mr. Ryan, I'm just giving you an idea. You write about them as if they've got TB, poor sods."

But that was enough for John. He was more disgusted with himself than with the editor. He was betraying himself and his kind, his nation, and he'd heard the cock crowing once too often. He said he'd done his best, could do no more, and someone else must be found to write it. By then, he didn't much care, even if he was putting his job on the line. He had a job move in view. In fact, he had two possible jobs in his sights.

That same day, from his office, which was no more than a partitioned-off area of the printing-press room, with a phone in it and a typewriter, he put a phone call through to the Mile End Public Baths. The door was shut. Not that it mattered. If anyone overheard, they would only suppose he was pursuing his research for the wretched feature they all still thought he was writing.

A cockney voice answered. He knew they had men's days and women's days and he asked which days were for men only. Tuesday, Thursday, Friday, and Saturday. Did he need to bring towels? No, and no soap or shampoo, either.

Tomorrow was Tuesday, but that was too soon. Besides, he had a council meeting to cover. Someone with good shorthand was needed for that, and John was proud of his. Thursday? He wouldn't go in on Thursday but would use the evening to watch. Find the place and check out its environs, see what was in the wind.

On Wednesday evening, he did what he always did when he wasn't working, went home. Had his evening meal at home. The concept of the high tea was going, he sometimes thought, being replaced by a cup of tea and biscuit in the afternoon and something you either called dinner, if you had pretensions, or supper, if you were what George Orwell had called upper lower middle class. John had written a leading article about changes in mealtime and meal customs for the paper. It had provoked plenty of readers' letters. But at home, they still had high tea, and he loved it. Those meals were by far the best of his week. Tinned fruit to start with and evaporated milk, ham and tongue (chicken for a great treat) and hard-boiled eggs and lettuce and tomatoes, thin-cut brown bread and butter, then ginger cake or a Dundee cake, maybe Bakewell tarts, biscuits, and a chocolate bar for everyone.

His mother was the best cook in the world. He liked to tell her that and see her pleasure. She had had a hard life. But her big family of loving children was her reward. There must be plenty of women, he thought, who would like to have a lot of children if only they could have them already big and sensible and independent. She had brought hers up the hard way, six children, never much money, and, after his father died, perhaps not much love. Well, not much of that sort of love. You only had to look at Joseph to know that.

Joseph was at home; he always was. John couldn't remember a single evening when Joseph had taken his mother out anywhere. They stayed at home with the children, who weren't Joseph's but might as well have been. He treated them as his own. Stephen, Mary, Margaret, Desmond, James, and himself. Aged fourteen, nearly sixteen, eighteen, twenty, twenty-two, and the one who had been away and seen the world and come back, oh, so thankfully.

Joseph said grace. He was a devout Catholic

but behaved more like a nonconformist, reciting "For what we are about to receive" and reading the Bible every evening. Desmond wasn't there. At work, his mother said. Desmond worked in a London hotel, doing what, John didn't know, perhaps as a porter. He was always vague about what he did. John missed him; he liked everyone to be there.

James's wife of a month sat between him and Mary. Her pregnancy had begun to show. John thought he longed for the coming baby almost more than its parents did, perhaps really more, for James and Jackie had had to get married and very likely wouldn't have if she hadn't been pregnant. But he knew his mother rejoiced in the prospect of her first grandchild and Joseph did, too, after his first anger was over.

It had been left to John to explain things to Stephen. He was going to use this evening to do that, take him aside after tea and have a quiet, reassuring word. Joseph had made Stephen feel the disgrace of it. He had spoken with his customary measured gentleness, but the words he used were harsh. James and Jackie had committed a sin and now must make restitution, must marry, never mind their feelings—those had nothing to do with it. They had to marry and come to live with James's mother and stepfather, inconvenient though it might be, crowded though it would certainly be, for they had nowhere else to go. Sin, Stephen was told, must always be paid for, and the payment was unpleasant and painful.

John, of course, took a different line. They went up to the bedroom Stephen shared with Desmond, ostensibly for John to look at Stephen's cigarette-card collection. There, first of all, he told Stephen to remember he owed Joseph a lot; he must always love and respect Joseph. But he need not take everything he said too seriously. This wasn't the big tragedy Joseph said it was and it certainly wasn't some exceptional crime that every right-thinking person condemned.

"Uncle Joseph called it a sin," Stephen said.

"I know. But, believe me, this is something that happens all the time. Some of the strongest feelings we have when we're young are our sexual feelings and they are the hardest to resist. I think Uncle Joseph has forgotten that. James and Jackie couldn't resist their sexual feelings and the result is that they're going to have a baby. That doesn't sound like a crime, does it?"

Stephen asked thoughtfully, "What would be a sin, then?"

"To harm someone or to betray him, to tell lies, to be unkind. The most important in all this is the baby who's going to be born and that he or she has a family and plenty of people to be loved by. We've had that, haven't we, all of us?"

Stephen nodded.

"A family is a sacred thing, Stephen. To break up a family and destroy it, that's a sin."

John believed all that when he said it, knew it was true, but when he spoke about sexual feelings, he felt his voice begin to falter. He had consciously to keep it firm and strong. Later that evening, when he was back in his rented room, he had never before been so powerfully aware of the pressure and insistence of a desire for sex. He did what he had done with the man in the forest, his eyes closed, imagining the man there with him in the dark.

Would he always close his eyes in the act of sex? For him, while mostly enjoyed in solitude, it was always the act of darkness. He was twenty-five years old and he had only once had sex the way he really wanted it, with a man, and then it had been incomplete. It had been a glimpse of something that might be wonderful, and then the curtain had fallen.

5

His interview with the editor of the newspaper that might or might not offer him a job was the next day. It was on the outskirts of London, a highly regarded paper, but still only a weekly. The other one, the one he was still waiting to hear from, was a daily and prestigious, but a very long way away, in the West Country. Being away from them all in the navy had been bad enough. Could he face it again? The train journey took five hours; he would be cut off from them for weeks on end, would maybe come home for a weekend once in every four. . . .

Still, he hadn't yet heard from that one, while the editor of the weekly wanted to see him that afternoon. It was a mere bus ride away. Was he damaging his career prospects for the sake of his family? Perhaps, if he had a career in newspapers at all, if being a journalist was really what he wanted. He thought of his half-completed novel lying in a canvas bag under his bed, the novel he could never make time to finish.

He was nearly late for the interview because before he left he had to check up on a story about a Leyton man who planned to row across the Atlantic, get a photograph, have a look at the boat. Nearly late but not quite. The editor seemed impressed by some of the things he had done and by his shorthand note. But he didn't offer John the job there and then, only said he would let him know. John went back by tube instead of on the bus, and when the train came to the Bank station, he got off and changed on to the Central line. He had a job later, no more than picking up the details of a residents' association meeting from the secretary, but it was in Leyton and he thought of going to see his mother first. And maybe Desmond would be at home. It was a couple of weeks since he had seen Desmond. But instead of going on to Leyton, he got out of the train at Mile End.

507

All day long, he had forced himself not to think about the baths and the things those men had said in the coffee bar. He had constantly deflected his thoughts, and that hadn't been too difficult with the job question uppermost in his mind. Now, in the train, it had come back. He told himself he was only going to have a look. He would look at the outside, case the joint, see who went in, check, for instance, if it really was men only this evening.

The baths were easy to find. They were where the man on the phone had said they were. Opposite, on the other side of the wide arterial road, was a little café with an uncurtained front window and glass panels in its door. John checked that a window table was free and went in.

He had to eat, after all. He couldn't expect his mother to feed him every evening. He asked for a cup of tea and sat at the table in the middle of that quite big window, from which the baths could clearly be seen. It was a long building of brown brick with a flight of wide steps at the front leading up to swing doors. He ordered shepherd's pie with peas and carrots, apple crumble and custard. If he saw any obvious queers going in, he'd eat his food and go and never come back.

The first man went in after about five minutes. He was tall and heavily built, wearing an old blue pinstriped suit and a shirt without a collar. John could see plainly from his window. Another man with his hair cut very short all over his head, the way the GIs' had been, was next. Both of them looked like ordinary, normal men, husbands and fathers. But John couldn't eat. He was too excited, too keyed up.

Three more men went in, two of them quite old. John hadn't expected people like that, not elderly men with bald heads and big bellies, one of them with a white moustache, the other in a long overcoat, even though it was June and warm. Their seniority reassured him, though. They seemed to make the place respectable. These were municipal baths, after all, people went to them for all sorts of reasons. He wasn't sure that he wanted respectability; indeed, in a way, he knew he didn't, but he wanted things to look proper, to look as if this was what all normal men did, like going to the pub.

He paid for the food he hadn't eaten, crossed the road, and approached the steps. It was nearly seven o'clock and he had to pick up the residents' association meeting agenda at eight, so it was too late to go in. Or he told himself it was. He told himself that he'd go another time. When he had more time. His heart beat with a heavy rhythmic plodding, the way it had in the forest. He began walking around the building, down the street on the left, looking up at windows far too high for anything behind the glass to be seen. Along the street behind where the facade was, there was a plain high brick wall, slightly sinister because it

509

was windowless, up the right-hand street, and out
again into the main road. Next week, then. Next
Tuesday or Thursday. He went back to the tube
station.

6

The way to manage it was by not thinking. Or by
thinking of other things. Forcing it. He thought
of the possible jobs. The editor of the weekly had
written, offering him the job, and he had accepted
it. Anything to get away from the *Independent*
and those sniggerers and that rabid editor, the
hot, stinking press, the rush and panic. Of course,
it might be as bad in the new job, but at least it
would be different.

And then there was the West Country daily.
They had written suggesting Saturday for an
interview. He had liked that, because it meant
they understood he had obligations here, couldn't
simply get on a train when he chose and travel
220 miles. They were allowing him a weekend.
That might well mean they were keen to have
him. And in spite of telling the weekly he would
join them in July, he was keeping his options
open. He wasn't obliged to take the job just
because he had accepted it. That sort of thing
was standard practice if something better turned
up. But could he contemplate going 220 miles
away from them all?

These speculations served very well to keep his mind off the baths until he was on the steps, walking up toward those swing doors. Then a torrent of feelings descended, of fear, and a very real sense that he might be undertaking something that would damage him, that he would always regret. But he pushed open the doors and went in.

He was in a hall or foyer. On the left was a cash desk and above it a hanging sign that listed the price of a bath, the use of the swimming pool, the steam bath, and the days which were for men and those for women. A woman of about sixty sat at the receipt of custom. He hadn't expected women here, and the sight of her made him feel better. She wasn't in the least like his mother—she was older and much shorter and fatter—but he fancied she had a motherly look, placid, sensible, calm. She wore a blue sweater and a checked crossover overall.

He paid for the steam bath. She gave him a ticket and directed him toward a pair of green rubber doors. On the left was an opening like a serving hatch. A man, the very man with the crew cut John had seen the previous week, was handing in his ticket, so John did the same. It was easy when you knew how. Would all of it be easy?

Behind was a very big room in which stood three long wardrobe rails with wire baskets on hangers swinging from them. On each basket was a metal disk with a number on it. The crew-cut man went into a changing room and John followed. Out of sight, he pressed his hand against his heart and felt the steady, rapid pounding. But as he held his hand there and breathed deeply, the pulsation slowed.

He copied what the other man did, took off his clothes, put them into the basket, his jacket over the hanger, his cigarettes and matches into one of his shoes, the change from his pocket into his handkerchief, which he knotted twice and put into the other shoe. The towels he had taken he arranged as the other man did, one around his body up to his waist, sarongwise, the other draped across his head and shoulders. An attendant had appeared, and when John turned away from his basket, he told him to keep the disk on its band with him, either as a wristband or on his ankle. John put it around his left wrist.

The next room was full of chairs made of Bakelite or perhaps one of the new plastics, brown-and-white chairs. People sat about having cups of tea. That was another sight which surprised John, these old men decorously toweled, sitting chatting and smoking, drinking tea out of thick white china cups. He had expected something like a cross between the school swimming bath and a Roman orgy.

The place was lit by greenish fluorescent strip lights and the walls, tiled in white, had turned grayish, or perhaps the harsh light had discolored them. But it was pleasantly warm. The way it had been most of the time he was in the Philippines, warm and close and damp. The old men had horrible bodies, all bulges and folds of flesh, the skin mottled white like a fish on a slab, their legs seamed and knotted with dark gray veins. But they brought him reassurance. It couldn't be for sex that they came, and when he saw one of them looking at him, he put that covert gaze down to simple interest at the sight of a newcomer.

Another hatch had a tea lady behind it, younger than the other one, but middle-aged and respectable-looking. He would have been disconcerted by some dizzy young blonde. You could buy buns and sweets as well as cups of tea and this was where you bought your soap and shampoo.

More doors, one with STEAM above it, another labeled MASSAGE, SHOWER, COLD PLUNGE. When the left-hand door opened, steam billowed out, clouds of it accompanying the young man who emerged, making for the next room. John followed cautiously. More old men here and some beautiful young ones. The atmosphere of respectability was fading. John felt it recede, to be replaced by a sense of danger, of tension.

The man he had followed, who was about his own age, also had a towel wrapped around him and he walked erect, slowly, showing himself off, heading for the cold-water pool. A group of onlookers watched. Not one of them could be under sixty. What went through their minds?

Did they think a man like that proud walker could be in search of a father figure? Some hopes!

The young man let his towel drop to the floor and stepped into the cold water. John couldn't take his eyes off him. It was all so unlike what he had expected. The young man had white skin and light hair, butter-colored. He came out of the water, picked up his towel, and went into the shower room, followed by another man, older but still young. John went in there, too. He told himself he must do something, have a shower perhaps, something innocent.

The blond was washing himself with soap on a loofah. His companion—if he was his companion—said to him, "Want me to do your back, mate?"

A towel was spread out on a bench and a vigorous soaping began. Was this a pickup or did all men, normal men, behave like this at the baths? Perhaps. John took a shower. When he came out, the loofah massage was still going on. The older one said, "Was that okay, mate?"

"Great, thanks," came the answer. "You want to get done?"

They went together into the shower. John moved away. But they weren't long. One said to the other, "Fancy a spell in the hot room?"

John followed them in. In a quarter of an hour, he felt he had received more education than could ever have come to him from advice or books, if such books existed. The hot room was like a kind of amphitheater. Or he thought it must be. He couldn't see the highest levels of the terracing, for the steam was too thick up there. The two young men had disappeared into the mist.

It was like walking into a hot cloud—at ground level, the pale mist of a summer's morning, but up there it was white, dense, rendering everything invisible. Then, with a return to that heavy beating of his heart, he thought he could discern up on the fifth level, in one corner, a sensuous movement. No more than that. No one was on the fourth level, though there were one or two on the third.

Somehow, he knew he mustn't hesitate too long. Two old men sitting on the second level were gazing at him with hope; he could tell it was that. They were hoping he would come over, pass near them. It was a new world he had entered, something he had no idea existed. Quite slowly, with a deliberate tread, beginning to enjoy this, he walked toward the old men and, starting to mount the steps, passed between them. Each step was at least two feet six and the old men couldn't climb them, couldn't ascend beyond the second level. He felt their eyes following him, deriving a sensuous pleasure and a bitter pang from the sight of his movements as he climbed into the thick white fog.

There was no stopping him now. The steam was like burning cotton wool. He spread one of his towels and lay down on the fourth level. Would someone come to him? He didn't know whether he wanted this or not. In a way, he felt he had done enough, learned enough. He lay on his back, with one leg stretched out onto the step below, the other bent, his right arm behind his head, his left resting lightly across his body. The other towel covered him decorously—temptingly? He closed his eyes. In the heat and the dense white fog, with his eyes shut, he thought how wonderful it would be were someone to approach, to be there looking at him. To touch him.

All the time he lay there, he sensed that he was watched. Not just by the old men on the lower levels. He doubted if they could even see him. The young and the beautiful watched him, just making out his shape and his youth through the veiling, titillating whiteness. A net, a gauze, an all-enveloping disguise.

After about half an hour, he got up and descended the steps. Perhaps because he had made up his mind that nothing would happen, nothing would happen this time, he was surprised and a little shocked when one of the old men reached out a hand as he passed and touched his leg. He bent down and pushed the hand away. He showered again, dropped his towels into the bin, dressed, and left.

Once outside in the air, he felt cold, though it was a mild night and getting on for midsummer. He also felt tired, exhausted as much by the assimilating of new experience as from the heat. Next time, things would happen. If there was a next time.

Robert had been absorbed by Titus Romney's manuscript and hadn't noticed the time. Now, at the end of chapter six, he saw that it was midnight. The rest must wait for tomorrow and he would finish it the night before he was due to go away.

On his way up to bed, the strange ideas that his reading had aroused all returned to him for review. If he hadn't been sent this by Titus Romney's agent on behalf of Romney, he would have guessed it to have been written by the late Gerald Candless. He wouldn't have put it among Gerald's best work; he wouldn't even have put it among Gerald's *finished* work. He would have placed it, because much of it read like a synopsis, as a first draft or even an experiment.

As far as he knew, Titus Romney and Gerald Candless hadn't known each other. They might have met at some publisher's party or a book festival, but that was all. So was Romney, consciously or unconsciously, aping Gerald's work? Had he perhaps read *A White Webfoot* and been powerfully influenced by that book?

Robert got into bed beside his sleeping wife but lay awake a long time, thinking about the two novelists and remembering suddenly that Titus Romney had said in an interview in the *Radio Times* that his problem was not the writing but finding something to write about.

7

The impression he made on the editor was a good one. He could tell. He wouldn't have been surprised if he was offered the job there and then, but this didn't happen. It was the usual "We'll let you know," and in a way, John was relieved. What would he have said if told to start in two weeks' time?

After all, he had accepted the other job. His aim was to get to Fleet Street, that or become a novelist, a real full-time novelist, and he thought he could attain either or both as well from a weekly on the outskirts of London as from a provincial daily. But still he wasn't sure. He kept thinking of his family.

This reminded him that his sister Mary's birthday was in just over a week's time. Monday, July the second. She would be sixteen. He had already gotten her a box of chocolates, having saved up his coupons. Chocolate was still rationed, even though the war had been over for six years, and a box of Black Magic was a rare treat. But she ought to have something else, as well. With seven pounds a week coming in, he wasn't poor and could have gotten her a sweater or a dress length, but Mary wasn't interested in clothes. On his way to the station and the London train, he went into a bookshop and bought her a book of poetry called *Young Pegasus*.

He dreamed that night. But he dreamed every

night now, falling asleep to the rhythm of a fantasy and sliding from visions of beautiful young men to dreams of them, so he hardly knew where one ended and the other began. All were either in the dangerous darkness of the spoiled forest or in various versions of the baths. Their naked bodies were spread on ziggurat levels or temple steps or they walked, proudly and sensuously, down the inclines of pyramids, and they were veiled in a mist that deepened and thinned, moved, lifted momentarily, swung back in a descended cumulus cloud.

Sometimes the mist closed in so completely as to blind his waking or dreaming eyes. He would be suspended, sightless, in a blank whiteout that was not only opaque but stifling, too. A woolpack, a cloud bank. And then, when he thought he must lose consciousness and cease to breathe, the vapor thinned and lifted, disclosing once more beauty and youth, clearer now than before, no longer merely display and promenade, but embracing, enfolded, and, in the later dreams, passionately conjoined.

He knew somehow that he would be an involved participant in these fantasies and dreams only when he had himself, in reality, done everything they did. And he was ready for that now, aware that the time had come. All ideas that maybe he wasn't really homosexual, that there was a way out, some avenue that could be taken where you learned to be a lover of women, all those ideas were gone. He felt committed. He had set his foot on this path, not that one, and he couldn't go back. As soon as the chance came, he was returning to the baths.

The difficulty was when. It sounded like one of his old excuses, born of fear and self-doubt, but it wasn't. They were busy on the paper and he didn't have the time. It didn't occur to him that leaving as he planned to leave, about to give in his notice, he could neglect his job, not bother. He pursued the stories he was doing with his old zeal. Tuesday was when he could have gone to Mile End, but every fourth Tuesday the housing committee met and he had to be there. No one else had his fast shorthand.

He went home to tea on Wednesday evening, just dropped in really, because he had a school play to cover. He wouldn't have bothered to be there except that a once-famous actress and friend of the headmistress was coming down to attend the performance. Desmond was at home, too, had come back from work to change before going on somewhere. He was tremendously well dressed, in a light gray suit and jaunty trilby hat. They walked as far as the bus stop together and, leaving him, Desmond winked and said he had a date. John saw him get into a taxi.

On Thursday, he thought the time had come and he could make it that evening. It was either now or waiting till next Tuesday, because the women's days were out and he couldn't go on

Saturday. He had promised to take Mary and Stephen to the zoo. The paper went to press on Thursdays and it was a busy day because all the reporters took a hand—it wasn't a union shop—and journalists handled the lead, putting headings into the dummy, and photographic blocks, too. One of John's jobs was to set up the weekly chess problem.

He was doing this when the chief sub came over to him and asked if he could go out to Woodford at seven and cover a political meeting. The man who usually did Woodford was off sick. Sylvia Pankhurst would be speaking. John said he thought Sylvia Pankhurst was dead, but the chief sub said no, that was her mother, and he was afraid there was no question about it—John would have to do it.

Why didn't he say, "Do it yourself; I'm leaving"? He could have. He should have. He was going to write his letter of resignation tomorrow, anyway. Instead, he shrugged, said yes, okay.

A refusal would have saved his life, but how was he to know that?

The letter from the Devon daily paper, offering him the job and with a much higher salary than the weekly one, came on Friday morning. He had almost definitely decided not to take it, but to take the other one. He wrote his resignation and posted his letter on Saturday morning, on his way to his mother's to pick up the children.

His mother put her arms around him and kissed him, which naturally didn't happen each time he went home. She said he looked tired, a bit strained—was anything worrying him? It was then that he nearly told her about his change of job, but he didn't because he hadn't quite decided which one he was going to take.

On their way to the tube station, Mary said her friend's mother had told her she had been on elephant and camel rides down the Broad Walk of Regent's Park and could they do that? John said, "If it's possible," but when they got to the zoo, they found the rides in the park no longer happened, though both children got to sit on an elephant. A tall, thin young man was feeding the lions. He had lion-colored hair and tawny eyes, was shaped like the statue of the discus thrower, and that night he came into John's fantasy and then his dreams, wearing only a loincloth, which he dropped onto the marble as he stepped down into a shiny white pool.

8

It would be easy telling his mother and Joseph and the children about the North London job because it really would make very little difference to them. He could even go on living where he lived now and see them just as often. By the time Monday came, he had decided to stick to his decision and take the job on the weekly, though he still hadn't replied to the letter from Devon. A couple of days' delay wouldn't matter.

The chief sub came into his cubbyhole of an office on Monday afternoon and said he was very disappointed to have gotten John's resignation. The editor would have something to say about it when he got back from his holiday.

"I'll be gone by then," John said.

"No, you won't," said the chief sub. "You'll reconsider your decision."

"I wouldn't bank on that if I were you," John said.

He finished the diary note he was writing and caught the bus to Chingford, where he had a cup of tea and a bun in a carman's café and went on to the meeting of the Chingford Mount Residents' Association. It went on much longer than he had expected, very little real business was done, and it made John wonder how much more of this backstreet parochial stuff he could stand to cover. Whereas down in Devon, on a daily . . . But he had decided. North London it was to be.

It was nearly eight before he got to his mother's and Mary's birthday party. She had two school friends there, a nice one and a pretty one, giggly sixteen-year-olds. Mary never giggled; she was grave, quiet, sweetly affectionate. John gave her the presents and she smiled and rolled her eyes at the chocolates, but when she had unwrapped the poetry book and looked inside, she came over to him and put her arms around him and kissed him.

That made the friends giggle. One of them looked inside *Young Pegasus* and made a face, asked with more giggling if John had ever read *Forever Amber.* John nodded. It and various other works of mild (very mild) heterosexual pornography had been among the books he had made himself read a few years back in one of many attempts to reorientate his inclinations. Now, eyeing the girl who had inquired, he thought how good-looking she was, a real beauty, a Leyton Lana Turner, old for her age, appearing at least nineteen. Her beauty left him cold. He found her utterly undesirable.

The whole family was there, Stephen finishing his homework in the corner, Margaret seeming mature and grave in the presence of the younger girls, Desmond over by the wireless, listening to Phil Harris singing "The Darktown Poker Club." Joseph still sat at the table, behind the remains of Mary's birthday cake, looking quite genial for him. Mary was his favorite, the only one of them he referred to as his own child, instead of his stepdaughter or stepson.

It was Desmond who suggested they play the Game. Someone was bound to; they couldn't have had any sort of gathering without playing the Game. Desmond switched off the radio and said to the two girls, the beauty and the nice one,

"This game is called I Pass the Scissors. You have to see if you can do it right."

"Do we have to?"

The beauty could hardly keep her eyes off Desmond. They would have made a handsome couple, John thought dryly, only Desmond was no more likely to be drawn to her than he was. She pouted at him, yearning for a flirtation, but all Desmond did was say, "Yes, you have to. You'll like it."

Margaret fetched her mother's sewing scissors. They were steel, the metal worn to a deep gunmetal color, the handles bound in tape to keep fingers that constantly used them from getting sore. For years, their mother had made all the children's clothes. Mary, the birthday girl, took the scissors, opened them, and handed them to her sister.

"I pass the scissors crossed."

"I receive the scissors crossed and pass them uncrossed," said Margaret, shifting her position at the table.

"I receive the scissors uncrossed," said the beauty, "and pass them uncrossed."

"No, you don't. . . ."

At this point, Robert laid the manuscript down, got up, and walked across the room. He stood at the window with his hands on the sill and looked out into the London street, seeing nothing. When was it he had been introduced to the Game? *Where* it had been, he knew very well. At Lundy View House, of course, and Hope had been there, but not Sarah; Sarah was away at university. Not Ursula, either. Ursula had refused to play. He and his wife and his two older children, he thought. He remembered how appalled he had been. His wife had been embarrassed.

Nineteen eighty-one or eighty-two. After he had become Gerald's editor, anyway, and on their first visit. The Game, they all called it, with a capital G. Two years later, he and his wife had been forced to play it again and his wife had caught on. Presumably, Titus Romney had also been to Lundy View House and also been taught it. Robert thought it essential to find out.

The other possibility was something he dreaded to contemplate. What with the style being so like Gerald's and the family situation so much Gerald's thing . . .

Robert skipped the Game. There were pages and pages of it.

"You're not going to get it, are you?" Stephen said.

"Tell us."

"Oh, no. You'll have to try again another time."

John remembered he hadn't had anything to eat. Or, rather, his mother remembered for him and brought him Spam and scrambled eggs and tea and he had a piece of Mary's cake. The wireless was on again, someone reading a story, but Desmond couldn't stand that and started fiddling with the knobs, looking for dance music. The girls had given Mary nail polish—she would never use it—and Evening in Paris scent—she just might use that—and she had had fifteen cards. She arranged all her cards and presents on the little table by the window. It was crowded, a squeeze, because the things that had been on the table had to go somewhere else. But everything in that house was a squeeze. It didn't seem to matter.

John had a quiet chat with Joseph about the post office and the way things were changing, and a word with Desmond. He was glad Desmond wasn't going out that night, but staying home with the rest of them and maybe even going to bed when Stephen went. Of course he knew it was outrageous of him to make even silent criticisms of Desmond, which was what that was, but just the same, he couldn't help being glad when he witnessed peace and order. Then, about to leave, he told his mother he'd be in again on Wednesday, when he thought he'd have something to tell her, some news.

Everybody was agog for his news, but he didn't intend to say any more at this stage. Mothers only thought about one thing when told a son had something to tell them: that he was getting married. He laughed.

"I'm not getting married," he said.

He kissed the girls good night and he kissed

his mother. Joseph shook hands with him; he did that sometimes, gravely approving of him. The beauty and the other one had gone home; it was after half-past ten. They all crowded into the little hall to "see him off the premises," as Joseph put it, and then Joseph said, as he always did, "God bless you."

John turned back and waved. When he looked around again, they had all gone in and the door was closed. The night was chilly for July and he had to wait quite a long time for his bus.

9

Breaking the ice doesn't break it forever. It freezes over again, and the freezing seals over the cracks. John learned that on Tuesday evening. The familiarity with the place was half-gone and he was going to have to start afresh. If he had come last Thursday . . .

He went into the café and asked for a cup of tea. He sat by the window and watched the baths, seeing things he hadn't noticed before, the concrete portico, the recessed columns on either side of the front entrance, a broad crack in one of the steps. The sky above was blue, with white tumbling clouds. Seven-thirty and still as bright as at noon.

A man went up the steps, and then another. The second one was as different from the first as that friend of Mary's had been from an ordinary schoolgirl. The second one looked like the lion man at the zoo, as tall and straight and beautiful, as young. It might even have been the lion man. The sun shone on his mane of golden hair. John was afraid and excited at one and the same time.

A different middle-aged woman was selling tickets. He asked for the steam bath, and this time he didn't need directions. But there was no one ahead for him to follow. He felt almost more self-conscious than he had that first time. He took off his clothes and put them in the basket, put his cigarettes and lighter into one of his shoes and his change into the other. A man came in and looked at him, gave him a pleasant, friendly smile, and John began to feel better. He fastened the wristband with the tag around his wrist, helped himself to towels, one to be worn sarong-fashion, the other draped across his head and shoulders.

This time, he didn't dally; he went straight to the steam room. The old men sat on the lowest level. He scarcely glanced at them; he was looking for the golden man he had seen come in. It seemed darker in here today—dimmer, rather. He had a memory of a bright whiteness, but the room this time seemed more mysteriously veiled. Last week, he hadn't noticed the light fitting, but now he did and saw, too, that someone had hung a towel over it.

Someone was sitting on the fourth level, at the

far end. John couldn't see him at all clearly—he could see nothing clearly—but he saw enough to know this man was young and that he sat in a revealing pose, his knees apart, his arms resting lightly on them. If the golden man came in now, he wouldn't recognize him. Not in this mist, this soft, hot vapor. Was that what the old men relied on, hopefully, yearningly, that in the mist all cats were gray?

No one reached for him this time as he climbed the levels. The steam itself touched his chest, his shoulders, his thighs, like a hot hand, but there was no hand of flesh and bone extended. The seated young man disappeared in the steam. The light was all behind John now, ahead and above him almost impenetrable white fume.

He was at the top now, on the fifth level. As he had done that first time, he spread out his towel. Down below, he heard the door open and close again. He could see nothing and now, with one leg resting on the fourth level and the other bent at the knee, one arm across his chest and the other upraised behind his head, he lay down and closed his eyes.

The steam room was silent, hot, and still. The old men sitting down there didn't talk to one another. John thought of what it would be to him to meet someone like that lion man, to be with him, be touched by him, go all the way with him. His body was moved by his imaginings; he turned a little, twisted, relaxed again into the sensuous heat. Then he felt the presence of someone else. His eyes were closed and he felt no compulsion to open them, but he let himself sink even further into passivity. Tension seemed to trickle away from his legs, his arms, the muscles of his body, to pour out through his hanging fingertips.

Someone was there. Someone was walking along the fourth level in the hot cotton-wool whiteness, walking and slowing to stand beside him. Not to look, he sensed, beyond the first appraisal of a young delectable body, as desirable as his own. To sit down below him. Cross-legged—how did John know that? His eyes were closed as if he were asleep and dreaming. To sit down and brush John's leg with his shoulder. John could hear his breathing, slow, steady.

There was no urgency. There was all the time in the world. The head, the shoulders, leaned back against the side of his body, rested there. John did open his eyes then, turning his neck languorously, and saw the back of a dark head, the hair all wet and matted but silky-soft, beautiful shoulders like honey-colored marble. His eyes closed again. He preferred it that way now that he knew his companion was young and fine to look at.

He wanted to touch that hair, stroke it, but he was afraid. Best to accept his own passive receptiveness, wait, let the other make the running. A hand touched the calf of his leg. He held his breath. What must he do to offer himself, to make things plain?

It was as if a voice told him, but there was no voice. He reached for the towel that covered him and took it off, dropped it onto the level below. My lover, he thought, this man will be my lover. They were close now; another body would join with his. He felt its slippery-soft hardness. A mouth closed on him, warm and strong, but tender as a flower.

The heat was wonderful and terrible. Almost unbearable. John had no thoughts, his intellect was gone, he was only flesh and dream and sensation. And something he had never felt before but which he thought might be passion, a kind of painful joy that swelled and opened and unfolded and spilled happiness. He kissed, too, giving back what he had received, receiving again, exchanging liquid pleasure, while the hot fog, which was both wet as water and dry as sunshine, pressed thick and caressing on his skin.

My lover, he thought. For a moment, he was one person with his lover, his own identity was lost, and the other's, too, merged with his. Then a deep peace descended. His lover kissed his cheek, a gentle, sweet kiss. John waited a moment before opening his eyes. His lover had turned away, had his back to him and had begun to descend the levels. And now, as the ordinary usages of life began to return, John was afraid of losing him, that he would go down there into the mist and out of the door and disappear.

That must be prevented. This was someone he had to see again. A warm, passionate joy rose in him. He had never seen the man's face, but he was in love. He followed him, down through the mist, ignoring the old men, the hand that reached. John knew so much more now, was already so much more experienced. Close behind his lover now, he laid one hand on the golden marble shoulder, an intimate gesture, almost proprietorial. He followed him out through the door, out of the heat and the fog and the obscuring whiteness, and there in the next room, where the tables were and more old men and the tea lady, he lowered the towel and looked, and his lover turned to face him.

It was Desmond, his brother.

John gave a low cry of terror. He ran through the room, sliding on the slippery floor. He didn't stay to shower, but dressed, gasping, sobbing, fumbling with his clothes the way one does in dreams. He ran out of the building into the warm, still evening, the change he had taken from his shoe still jingling in his hand. Another wave of heat broke over and released another gush of sweat. For a moment, he had stopped, but now he began to run again. He ran and ran.

Joseph's voice came to him, saying, "God bless you." It rang in his ears. Memories of the past hour unreeled themselves on the screen of his mind. After that, he could never go back home, never see any of them again, not after that, the ultimate sin. Alone, he had broken the family, as if smashing with his fist a room full of glass. Outside was an empty, distant, foreign world and he was heading for it. People turned to stare at this running man, who cried as he ran, stared and turned away, embarrassed.

He had died back there in the mist. But hours were to pass, a night and half a day of agony and disbelief, before he recognized that life as he had known it was over and he must undergo a rebirth.

There will be no sleep for me tonight, thought Robert. But he went to bed and lay there with his eyes closed until the pictures which took shape in the darkness became too disturbing. At the window, watching the dawn come, he began to consider ways of telling Sarah Candless and Titus Romney what he had discovered.

García Márquez, Gabriel, *Of Love and Other Demons*
Gilman, Dorothy, *Mrs. Pollifax and the Lion Killer*
Gilman, Dorothy, *Mrs. Pollifax, Innocent Tourist*
Guest, Judith, *Errands*
Hailey, Arthur, *Detective*
Hepburn, Katharine, *Me*
Hiaasen, Carl, *Lucky You*
James, P. D., *A Certain Justice*
Koontz, Dean, *Dark Rivers of the Heart*
Koontz, Dean, *Intensity*
Koontz, Dean, *Sole Survivor*
Koontz, Dean, *Ticktock*
Krantz, Judith, *Scruples Two*
Krantz, Judith, *Spring Collection*
Landers, Ann, *Wake Up and Smell the Coffee!*
le Carré, John, *Our Game*
le Carré, John, *The Tailor of Panama*
Lindbergh, Anne Morrow, *Gift from the Sea*
Ludlum, Robert, *The Road to Omaha*
Masson, Jeffrey Moussaieff, *Dogs Never Lie About Love*
Mayle, Peter, *Anything Considered*
Mayle, Peter, *Chasing Cézanne*
McCarthy, Cormac, *The Crossing*
Meadows, Audrey with Joe Daley, *Love, Alice*
Michaels, Judith, *Acts of Love*
Morrison, Toni, *Paradise*
Mother Teresa, *A Simple Path*
Patterson, Richard North, *Eyes of a Child*
Patterson, Richard North, *The Final Judgment*
Patterson, Richard North, *Silent Witness*
Peck, M. Scott, M.D., *Denial of the Soul*
Phillips, Louis, editor, *The Random House Large Print Treasury of Best-Loved Poems*
Pope John Paul II, *Crossing the Threshold of Hope*
Pope John Paul II, *The Gospel of Life*

(continued)

Powell, Colin with Joseph E. Persico, *My American Journey*
Preston, Richard, *The Cobra Event*
Puzo, Mario, *The Last Don*
Rampersad, Arnold, *Jackie Robinson*
Rendell, Ruth, *The Keys to the Street*
Rendell, Ruth, *Road Rage*
Rice, Anne, *Servant of the Bones*
Rice, Anne, *Violin*
Rice, Anne, *Pandora*
Salamon, Julie and Jill Weber, *The Christmas Tree*
Shaara, Jeff, *Gods and Generals*
Smith, Martin Cruz, *Rose*
Snead, Sam with Fran Pirozzolo, *The Game I Love*
Truman, Margaret, *Murder on the Potomac*
Truman, Margaret, *Murder at the National Gallery*
Truman, Margaret, *Murder in the House*
Tyler, Anne, *Ladder of Years*
Tyler, Anne, *Saint Maybe*
Updike, John, *Golf Dreams*
Weil, Andrew, M.D., *Eight Weeks to Optimum Health*
Whitney, Phyllis A., *Amethyst Dreams*